Georg Wilhelm Friedrich   Hegel, Francis Plumptre Beresford
Osmaston

The Philosophy of Fine Art

Volume 4 Hegel's Aesthetik

Georg Wilhelm Friedrich Hegel, Francis Plumptre Beresford   Osmaston

The Philosophy of Fine Art
Volume 4 Hegel's Aesthetik

ISBN/EAN: 9783337364120

Printed in Europe, USA, Canada, Australia, Japan

Cover: Foto ©Andreas Hilbeck / pixelio.de

More available books at **www.hansebooks.com**

THE PHILOSOPHY OF

FINE ART

BY

G. W. F. HEGEL

TRANSLATED, WITH NOTES, BY

F. P. B. OSMASTON, B.A.

AUTHOR OF "THE ART AND GENIUS OF TINTORET," "AN ESSAY
ON THE FUTURE OF POETRY," AND OTHER WORKS

VOL IV

LONDON

G. BELL AND SONS, LTD.

1920

HEGEL

CONTENTS OF VOL. IV

excluded. Primarily what it deals with is the infinite domain of Spirit and the energies of its life

(*b*) Distinction between poetical and prosaic conception

[(*α*) Poetical anterior to the prosaic form of artistic speech. It is the original imaginative grasp of truth. Dates from first effort of man at self-expression. Endeavours to make that expression of a higher virtue than mere prose

(*β*) The kind of prose life from which poetry is separate postulates a different kind of conception and speech. The finite categories of the understanding applicable to the former. The ideal rationale of fact is aimed at by poetry. Its affinity with and distinction from pure thought

(*γ*) Difference between the relation of poetic conception to prosaic in early times and more modern, where the prosaic form of life has become stereotyped in a definite system]

(*c*) The nature of the differentiation of poetical activity in different ages and nations

[(*α*) It has no particular epoch of unique celebration. It embraces the collective Spirit of man. It is conditioned by the outlook of various nations and epochs

(*β*) Some of these have closer affinity with its essential spirit, *e.g.*, the Oriental in comparison with the Western nations, if we exclude Greece

(*γ*) Modern interest in Hellenic and certain portions of Oriental poetry]

2. The Art-product of poetry and prose

(*a*) The artistic composition of poetry generally

and insignificant fact and local conditions, actions, events, etc.

(β) The end of Art not practical as in oratory. Nor is it to edification. *Poems d'occasion*

(γ) It is an essentially infinite (self-rounded) organism. Permeated with a principle of unity. Independent of any one particular condition of Life or Nature]

3. The creative impulse of the Poet

[(a) Less under restriction in respect to his medium. The problem proposed in one respect more easy, and in another more difficult than that of the other arts. Technical control of the medium which is easier makes the demand for imaginative penetration the greater

(b) Being operative in the realm of imaginative idea itself poetry has to guard against encroaching upon the spheres of religion, philosophy, and the ordinary consciousness as such

(c) To a greater extent than in the other arts the poet has transfused the external mode of envisagement, which he creates, with the vitality of soul-life. Mohammedan poetry. The creative energy must be absolutely free from all restrictions imposed by the material handled]

II. The Expression of Poetry

1. The poetical Conception

(a) Poetical conception in its origins

[In its origin not consciously distinct from the prosaic or scientific consciousness. In general terms the poetic imagination is plastic. Illustration of difference between the concrete poetical image and the abstract concept]

11

The use of hexameter, elegiacs, and iambics in this respect

(γ) Rhythmical versification embraces the actual musical sound of syllables and words. The stem-syllable in the Greek and Latin languages. Aspects of the German language in this respect. In modern languages the element of rhythm less room for display. This in itself necessitates the alternative of rhyme as a resistant against the too exclusive assertion of ideal content]

(b) Rhyme

[(α) Rhyme a necessary feature of romantic poetry. Closer approximation to music. Reaction against the stringent character of Roman poetry. Source of rhyme in Germanic languages

(β) Difference between two systems. Rhythmical versification supreme in Hellenic poetry. Most important change effected that of the validity of the national quantity in the older system. This replaced by the intrinsic meaning of syllables and words. French and Italian poetry an extreme example of the collapse of the former system. The necessity of rhyme and its character analysed

(γ) The types of modern romantic poetry. Its alliteration, assonance, and ordinary rhyme. Scandinavian poetry. Not necessary for assonant words to come only at conclusion of line. Rhyme is the fulfilment of alliteration and assonance. Pre-eminently the form of lyric poetry. Examples]

(c) The union of rhythm and rhyme

[(α) Attempt made in modern times to return to the natural quantity of syllables. Not generally successful. Overwhelming importance in modern verse of

13

(*a*) The general World-condition of the Epos

[(α) A positive social state conjoined to primitive simplicity. Intuitive sense of right the support of moral order. Vital human association with nature and particular objects possessed. Heroic condition, *e.g.*, that of free individuality. Examples. Expresses entire horizon of national condition

(β) The mirror must be of one particular people. The Hellenic spirit in Homer. A foreign locale not necessarily prejudicial to artistic effect. The remoteness to present ideas of the "Niebelungen Lied"

(γ) Main event of poem must be a deliberately conceived purpose. It must imply collisions. The belligerent condition most pertinent. The Odyssey not only an exception. Courage the fundamental interest. Justification of such attitude]

(*b*) The individual Epic action

[(α) Must be one of individual vitality. Must appropriate form of an event, and the happening of such. Analysis. Problem of an absolute Epos. Mere biography not most complete subject-matter. "The Divine Comedy" only partially an exception

(β) Question of human personality implied. Epic character must be a totality. Achilles, the Cid, and other heroes, discussed. Circumstances as active as persons. Illustrations

(γ) The form under which the intrinsic significance of the occurrence proclaims itself, whether as ideal Necessity or disclosed spiritual forces. Destiny. What it defines. General tone of sadness in the Epic. Different modes of appearance. Poems of Ossian, and others. Loss of original freshness in Latin poetry. Virgil]

15

than positive reality

(γ) Point of departure an external occurrence either in personal experience or that of others. Element of narrative as in songs of Anacreon]

(c) The external culture condition of the Lyric.

[(α) Different from that of Epic. Not limited to one particular epoch, but exceptionally displayed in modern times. Folk-songs and the lyric poem

(β) Possesses a power of free expansion into all kinds of subject-matter, a free recognition of imaginative conception no less than artistic activity

(γ) The philosophical lyric poem. A false and a genuine style compared. Schiller's poetry]

2. Particular aspects of the Lyric

(a) The lyric poet

[(α) The poet himself supplies the principle of combination. He is the focus of unity

(β) Spontaneity of result. Sings because he cannot help it. His object himself. Self-respect. Pindar and Klopstock

(γ) Creative in dealing with personal experience. Goethe a fine example]

(b) The lyric work of art

[(α) The unity of the Lyric. Springs from memory or vivid association of poet. The formal unity of self-conscious life. Mood must be defined in its concreteness, not tend too much to generalization

(β) Nature of the progressive disclosure of content. The principle of the Lyric is assimilation. Poems limited to local description. Mainly a definition of emotional forces made vital in objects as seen by the "inward eye." Episodes permissible. Passionate intensity in its freedom 219

(γ) External form of the Lyric. Variety of metres. Varied use of caesura. Strophes which admit of much alternation, both as to length of line, and their rhythmic structure. Musical sound of words and syllables. Free use of assonance, alliteration and rhyme, especially the diversified use of last-mentioned. Association with musical accompaniment] 221

(c) Types of the genuine Lyric 225

[(α) Hymns, dithyrambs, paeans and psalms. Personal religious emotion. Greek treatment of chorus. Psalms of Old Testament 225

(β) Personal life of poet the subject-matter. Not so much the subject as the enthusiasm or personal note. Pindaric Odes. Horace. Klopstock 228

(γ) The song as such. A field of blossom ever starting anew. The Oriental and Western type. Anacreon. Protestant hymns. Sonnet, elegy, epistle, etc. Dithyrambic emotion of Schiller] 230

3. Historical evolution of the Lyric 235

(a) Oriental lyrical poetry

[Vital absorption in the object. Objective character as compared with pure romantic. Hymns of exaltation. Metaphor, image, and simile particularly favoured. Present in Chinese, Hindoo, Hebrew, Arab and Persian poetry] 236

(b) The Lyric of the Greeks and Romans

[General character that of classic individuality. Image and metaphor not so largely used. Emphasizes mainly

20

and action. Worst case where he seeks to flatter a popular prejudice. Reference to contemporary event. Aristophanes. Didactic matter only admissible in so far as it is no bar to the freedom of the entire artistic product]

2. The external Technique of a dramatic Composition (*a*) The reading or recitation of a dramatic work

[(α) True sensuous medium of drama the human voice. Modern plays often impracticable in the theatre. Contrast of Greek drama in this respect

(β) Plays written for perusal only. Theatrical reproduction a real test of dramatic vitality. Question whether dramatic works should be printed

(γ) Perusal no sufficient test of the acting possibilities of a drama. Recitation subject to the serious restriction that it is the expression of one voice only]

(*b*) The art of the Actor

[(α) Among the Greeks acting affiliated to sculpture. Ancients added music to declamation. Means of interpretation in motion of the body. The dance. Plastic character of Greek performance

(β) Speech used solely as spiritual expression in modern acting. Coalescence of actor's personality with his rôle. Facial expression. Increase particularisation in modern character. Illustrations. Increase of difficulties. Modern actor an artist]

(*c*) The theatrical art which is more independent of Poetry 289

[(α) Plays written for the display of the particular talent of actors. The Italian *commedia dell' arte*. French attitude to audience

22

Theatrical pieces exhibited for mere display of histrionic talent or psychological analysis, or as a mere social relaxation]

(b) The difference between ancient and modern Drama

[(α) No genuine Oriental dramatic art. Principle of individual freedom. Origins among Hindoos and Chinese

(β) True beginning among the Hellenes. The universal and substantive content of the end, which individuals seek to achieve. Exceptional plot and intrigue and varied display of individual character not emphasized

(γ) In modern drama it is rather the destiny of some particular character under exceptional circumstances which forms the subject-matter. Interest directed not so much to ethical vindication and destiny as to the isolation of the individual and his conditions. Crime as a motive not excluded. Formal greatness of character demanded. Variety of characterization, and maze of plot and intrigue. In tragedy further the paramount presence of a more exalted order of the world,—whether conceived as Providence or Fatality,—accepted]

(c) The concrete development of dramatic poetry and its types

[(α) Greek drama. Roman drama an attenuated reflection. Survey limited to Æschylus, Sophocles, and Aristophanes. Background of ancient tragedy the heroic condition. Analysis of modes under which ethical content of human action asserted. The unsevered consciousness of the godlike and the combating human action, presented under the form of chorus and heroic figures. Significance of chorus. Opposition between social obligation and private sense of duty. Antigone. Modern conception of guilt and innocence no place in Greek tragedy in strict sense. Final end reconciliation of forces of human action. Such a *dénouement* not merely an ethical issue. Contrast between such and the Justice of the Greek Epos. Illustrations. Antigone. Œdipus. Orestes. Conception of old classical Comedy. The laughter of the Olympian gods made present in man. Aristophanes] 312

(β) Modern dramatic art

[(i) The ends which ought to come into the process of the action as the content of the characters. Borrowed from the concrete world of religious and social life. Not however, the particular ethical forces as of individuals which assert them, *e.g.*, Christ, the saints, kings, vassals, and members of ruling families. Features of the private life accepted not within scope of ancient drama. Personal love, honour, etc. make an exclusive appeal. Faust. Wallenstein. Generally it is the inner experience of soul-life which demands satisfaction. Comparison of problem of Hamlet with that of the Choephorae.

(ii) Nature of characters and collisions. Conflict abides essentially in the character itself. Abstract characterization of French and Italian poetry, also Spanish. In contrast to this that of the English, and above all Shakespeare. Goethe and Schiller. Vacillation of character. "King Lear." **(iii) Nature of tragic issue. Justice of more abstract nature than in ancient tragedy. The issue as the effect of misfortune. "Romeo and Juliet," a kind of unhappy blessedness in misfortune. Social plays the link between tragedy and comedy. As a rule the triumph of ordinary morality celebrated. Modern comedy. Question whether folly is ridiculous only to others, or to the comic character also. The second type

---

THIRD PART

THE SYSTEM OF THE PARTICULAR ARTS

SUBSECTION III

THE ROMANTIC ARTS

(CONTINUED)

CHAPTER III

POETRY

INTRODUCTION

I

The temple of classical architecture demands a god, who resides therein. Sculpture exhibits the same in plastic beauty, and confers forms on the material it employs for this purpose, which do not in their nature remain external to what is spiritual, but are the form itself immanent in the defined content. The corporeality, however, and sensuousness, no less than the ideal universality of the

25

sculptured figure, are opposed on the one hand to subjective ideality, and in part to the particularity of the individual, in whose element the content of the religious, no less than also the worldly life, must secure reality by virtue of a novel form of art. This mode of expression, which is of subjective import, and at the same time particularized in its characterization, the art of painting itself contributes under the principle of the plastic arts. In other words it subordinates the realistic expression of form to the more ideal presentment of colour, and makes the expression of the ideality of soul the central point[1] of the presentment. The universal sphere, however, in which these arts are motived, the one in the ideal of symbolism, the other in the plastic ideal, the third in the romantic type, is the sensuous or *external* form of spirit and natural objects.

The spiritual content possesses, however, as essentially appertinent to the ideality of consciousness, a determinate existence which is for this ideality at the same time foreign to the medium itself of the external appearance and envisagement presented to it by material form. From this foreign element it is further necessary that it removes its conceptions in order to place them in a realm which, in respect to material no less than the mode of expression, is independently of an ideal or subjective character. This was the forward step which we saw *music* make, in so far as it embodied pure ideality and subjective emotion in the configurations of essentially resonant sound rather than in visible forms. It, however, passed by this very means into a further extreme, that is, an ideal mode of concentration not fully explicit, whose content in musical tones itself only found symbolic expression. For tone taken by itself is without content, and has its definition in the numerical relations, so that what is qualitative in the spiritual content no doubt generally corresponds to these quantitative relations which are expressed in essential differences, oppositions, and mediation, but in its qualitative determinacy is not entirely able to receive its impression in musical tone. If this aspect is not wholly to fail the art of music must, by reason of its onesidedness, summon to its assistance the more definite articulation of language, and requires for its more secure attachment to particularity and the characteristic expression of the content a text, without which it is unable to complete fully the ideality which is poured forth by means of musical tones.

By virtue of this expression of ideas and emotions, the abstract ideality of music receives a clearer and more secure exposition. At the same time what we have here unfolded by its means is, to a certain extent, not the point of view of idea and the artistic mode adapted to its expression, but merely the emotional life as it accompanies the same; also in part we find that here, too, music entirely divests itself of fusion with the verbal text in order to develop its own movement without restraint in the world of tone simply. For this reason the realm of idea, which is unable to remain under I such a more purely abstract mode of ideal intensity, and seeks a configuration in a world which embraces its one homogeneous and concrete reality, breaks away on its part likewise from the bond of music, and in the exclusive art of poetry discovers the adequate realization it demands.

Poetry, in other words the art of human speech, is the *third* or final step, the *totality*, which unites and embraces in a yet higher sphere, in the sphere of the very life of Spirit itself,[2] the two extremes of the plastic arts and music. For on the one hand poetry contains just as music does the principle which apprehends an ideal content in its ideality, the principle which in architecture, sculpture, and painting is lost, or at most incompletely asserted. And on the other hand it expatiates itself, under the modes of ideal conception, intuition, and feeling simply, in an objective world, which does not entirely destroy the defined forms of sculpture and painting, and is capable of unfolding all the conditions of an event, a succession or interchange of emotional states, passions, conceptions, and the exclusive course of human action with more completeness than any other art.

2. But in a still more intimate way the art of poetry constitutes a third or final term in its relation to painting and music regarded as the *romantic* arts.

(*a*) One reason of this is that its principle is that generally of an *intelligence* which has nothing further to do with gross matter as such, seeking, as is the case with architecture, to transform it through symbolism to an environment related analogically to spiritual life, or as in the case of sculpture in order to implant upon material substance the natural form congenial to such life under the spatial condition of its expression. What the end is now is to express immediately for mind the manifestations of Spirit with all its ideas of imagination and art, without setting forth their external and visible bodily presence. And a further reason consists in this, that poetry is able to grasp in the form of ideality itself and with a far greater wealth than is possible for music or painting, not merely the innermost actuality of conscious life, but also what is particular and individual in external existence, and equally able to contrast such facts in the complete diversity of their specific traits and accidental peculiarities.

(*b*) The art of poetry is, however, as totality, also again, from another point of view, essentially to be distinguished from the above-mentioned arts whose fundamental qualities it thus in a measure combines.

(*α*) In this respect, if we compare it with painting, the latter art is throughout at an advantage, where it is of importance to bring before our senses a content under the condition of its external appearance. It is true no doubt that poetry is able by various means to envisualize objects precisely in the way that for the imagination generally the principle of objectification is made real to our intuitive sense. But in so far as conceptive power, in the element of which poetry pre-eminently moves, is of a spiritual nature and implies the presence of the universality of thought, it is incapable of attaining the definition of sensuous perception. On the other hand, the varied traits which poetry brings together, in order to make the concrete form of a content visible, do not fall as with painting into one and the same totality, which is set before us wholly as a simultaneous appearance of all its details, but they break apart, inasmuch as the imagination can only give us the complexity it contains under the form of succession. This is, however, only a defect from the sensuous point of view, a defect which reason is able in its own way to rectify. That is to say, inasmuch as human speech, even in the case where it endeavours to summon before our sight a concrete object, is not concerned with the sensuous apprehension of an immediate external object, but always with the ideal relation, the mental intuition, for this reason the particular characteristics, albeit they are set before us in a series, are nevertheless fused together in the element of one essentially homogeneous spirit, which is able to qualify the effect of succession, to bring the varied array into one picture, and to secure and enjoy this picture in imaginative contemplation. Moreover, this deficiency of sensuous realization and objective definition, when we contrast poetry with painting, brings as a contrary result the possibility of an incalculable superfluity of material. For inasmuch as the poetic art in painting restricts itself to a determinate space, and even more to a distinct moment in a situation or action, for this

29

reason it is prevented from portraying an object in its entire ideal profundity no less than in the extension of its temporal development. But what is true is throughout concrete in the sense that it comprises within its embrace a unity of essential determinations. In its phenomenal appearance, however, these are not merely unfolded as a co-existent spatial phenomenon but in a temporal series as a history, whose course painting is only able to present in a relatively inadequate manner. Even in the case of every stalk, every tree, each has in this sense its history, a change, sequence, and exclusive whole of varied conditions. And this is even more true of the sphere of spirit, which can only be exhaustively portrayed as veritable spirit in phenomenal guise when it is set before our imagination as such a process.

(β) We have already seen that poetry possesses for its external medium that of tone in common with *music*. The wholly external, or, as we might say in the false sense of the expression, the objective material in the progressive series of the particular arts finally vanishes in the subjective medium of sound, which is divested of all visibility, and which suffers an ideal content only to be apprehended by a conscious state independent of sight.[3] For music, however, the configuration of musical *tone* as such is the essential end. For although the soul in the course and movement of melody and its harmonic relations presents what is ideal in objects, or its own ideal content, to the emotional life; yet the ideality thus presented is not pure ideality, but the human soul interwoven in the closest way with the musical tone as its expression, and the configuration of such musical expression which confers on music its true character. So much is this the case that music receives its independent position as an art just in proportion as the animation given by it to the emotional life is more emphasized in the world of pure music than in that of man's ordinary spiritual activity.[4] But for this very reason it is only to a relative degree capable of reproducing the variety of spiritual ideas and intuitions, the entire extension of the ideal wealth of conscious life: it remains restricted to the more abstract universality of all that it grasps as content, and the more indefinite manifestations of our emotion.

In the like degree, then, that mind (*Geist*) elaborates the more abstract universality in a concrete whole of idea, ends, actions, and events, and no less contributes to its conformation the particularizing perception, it not only forsakes the subjective life of mere emotion and builds up that life into an unfolded realm of objective reality in this case, too, within the ideal world of the imagination itself, it is compelled, by virtue of the nature of such transformation, to forsake the attempt to express the new realm thus secured solely and exclusively by means of tone relations. Precisely as the medium of sculpture is too poor to express the more ample content that it is the function of the art of painting to call into life, so too the conditions of musical tone and melodic expression are unable to realize fully the imaginative pictures of the poet. For these in part possess the ideas more accurately defined to consciousness and, in part, the form of external appearance impressed on the inner sense of perceptive reason. Spirit consequently withdraws its content from musical tone as such, and declares itself through words, which it is true do not entirely forsake the element of sound, but sink to the purely external sign of the communication. In other words, by means of this repletion with spiritual ideas, musical tone becomes the voice of articulate words; language, in its turn, is diverted from an end in itself to a means of ideal expression which has lost its independent self-subsistancy. This constitutes in fact what we have already established as the essential difference

31

between music and poetry. The content of the art of speech is the collective art of the world of ideas elaborated by the imagination, the spiritual which remains at home in its vision, which remains in this ideal realm, and, even in its movement toward an objective world, is only conscious of the same as a symbol that differs from its own conscious content. In music art reproduces the penetration of Spirit in a sensuously apparent and present form. In poetry it even forsakes the element of *musical tone* and articulation opposed to it, at least to the extent that this musical tone is no longer reclothed in fully adequate externality and the exclusive expression of that content. The ideal no doubt is expressed, but it fails to discover its real existence in the sensuous medium of tone, despite the fact that it is of a more ideal character; this it discovers exclusively in its own essential content, by virtue of which it expresses the content of mind as it is realized in the ideality of the imagination simply as such.

(c) In the *third* place, and finally, if we consider the specific character of poetry relatively to this distinction between music and painting, and we may include with it the other plastic arts, we shall find the same simply to consist in the subordination of the mode under which all poetical content is envisaged and configured by the medium of sense. In other words, when tone, as it does in the art of music, or for that matter, colour as in that of painting, no longer essentially recovers and expresses the entire content, in that case the musical treatment of the composition under its aspects of time, no less than those of harmony and melody, drops away; we have left us merely the generalized configuration of the time-measure of syllables and words, to which we may add rhythm, euphony, and the like. And further, it is to be noted that we have this, not in the sense of a genuine medium for the content, but rather as a mode of externality which is accidental, and which only receives an artistic form, because art cannot permit any mode of its external manifestation whatever to be entirely a question of accidental caprice.

(*a*) In connection with this withdrawal of the spiritual content from the sensuous medium we are at once met with the question what it is then which, under such a view, constitutes the actual externality or objectivity in poetry, that of tone being thus excluded. The answer to this is simple. It is the *ideal envisagement* and *imaginative content* itself. We have here spiritual forms substituted for sensuous, and supply a configurative material, such as we met with before in marble, bronze, colour, or musical tones. In other words, we must guard ourselves from such an inadequate statement of the facts as that ideas and imagery are nothing more or less than the *content* of poetry. This is unquestionably true in a sense, as we shall demonstrate more closely later on. Despite this, however, we are equally justified in asserting that idea, imagery, emotion, and the like are specific modes, under which every content in poetry is subsumed and manifested; and consequently, that is, owing to the fact that the sensuous aspect of the communication remains throughout a purely accidental one[5]—it is these forms which supply the real material which the poet has to elaborate artistically. No doubt the fact, the content, must in poetry, as in other arts, receive its due objectification for spirit; objectivity in this sense, however, is the exchange of what was previously an external reality for one that is ideal; one which receives an existence exclusively in conscious life itself, as something conceived or imagined exclusively by mind. Mind is here on its own ground objective to itself, and it suffers the medium of speech merely as a means, that is to say, partly as one of communication, and partly as one of immediate externality,

33

from which, as from the pure symbol merely, it is withdrawn throughout from itself into itself. For this reason, in the case of genuine poetry, it is of no consequence whether a poetical work be read in private or listened to; and for the same reason it can also, without essential depreciation of its value, be translated into other tongues, be transferred from versification into prose, and thereby transmitted in tonal relations of an entirely different character.[6]

(β) In the *second* place the question presents itself as to the *nature* of the object *for* which the ideal concept is employed in poetry. We answer that it is thus used relatively to essential truth in everything of interest to Spirit; not merely, that is, relatively to what is substantive in the same in the universality of its symbolic significance or classical differentiation, but equally to all that is at the same time specific and particular, in short, to practically everything in and with which mind is in any way interested and concerned. The art of language, consequently, both in respect to its content and the mode under which that content is made explicit, possesses a field of immeasurable compass, wholly incomparable with that of the other arts. Every content, every sort of spiritual or natural fact, event, history, deed, action, all conditions, whether ideal or external, fall within the domain and configurative powers of poetry.

(γ) Material of this most varied character is not, however, made poetical merely by reason of the fact that it is in a general way the content of idea. Ordinary consciousness is able to elaborate precisely the same content in the field of ideas, and to particularize concepts without creating any poetical result. We recognized this fact when we called the concept of mind merely the *material* or medium, which only receives a form adapted for poetry, in so far as it partakes of a novel configuration by virtue of art. In precisely the same way mere colour and tone in their immediacy are not as such the colour or tone of a painter or a musician. We may in a general way describe the distinction by stating that it is not the *idea as such*, but the *imagination* of the *artist* which creates a poetical content, under conditions, that is, in which the imagination grasps the same content in such a way that it is itself therewith associated in language, words and their more beautiful conjunction as human speech, just

35

as in the other arts we find it present in the architectonic form; the plastic of sculpture, that adapted to painting, or musical tones and harmony.

A further necessary limitation of the art's appearance is this that the content must, on the one hand, not be embraced in relations applicable to mere *thinking*, whether that of science or speculative philosophy, nor further in the form of inarticulate *emotion*, or with a clarity and self-sufficiency which appeals *exclusively* to the organs of sense;[6] neither, in another direction, must it suffer the idea to pass entirely into what we may in general terms describe as the contingency, divisions, and relativity of *finite* reality. The imagination of the poet in this respect must maintain a middle course between the abstract universality of pure thinking and the concrete corporeality of material objects, in so far as we are acquainted with the latter in the productions of the plastic arts. Furthermore such an art must generally conform to the requirements we have, in an early section of this work, insisted as essential to every art-product. In other words, the art itself must find in its content the adequate object of its appearance, must elaborate everything, which it embraces, so far as the interest appeals to the intelligence simply,[7] as an essentially independent and self-exclusive world. Only in so far as it does this is the demand of art satisfied, and the content thereof becomes, by virtue of the specific mode of *its* manifestation, an organic whole, which in its parts presents the appearance of a limited association and ideal synthesis, while at the same time, as contrasted with the world of accidental subordinations, its consistency is one of essential freedom, a whole made explicit through itself.

3. The last point to which we must in conclusion draw attention in respect to this distinction between poetry and the other arts is connected with the different mode under

which the imagination of the poet substantiates its ideas in the objective medium of its exposition. The arts hitherto considered were entirely serious in their attachment to the material of sense, a medium in which they themselves were operative, in so far as they merely bestowed on their content a form, which could be throughout accepted and elaborated by means of conglomerations of material substance, whether bronze, marble, or wood, or the media of colour and tones. [8] In a certain sense, no doubt, poetry also has to meet a condition somewhat similar. That is to say, in poetical composition we must not overlook the fact that its results have to be intelligible to mind by means of the communication of human speech. But we shall find none the less that the situation in the two cases is essentially altered.

(a) Otherwise expressed, by reason of the importance pertaining to the material aspect in the plastic arts and music, we find that, as a result of the *defined* restrictions of this material, only a *limited* number of conceptions can be fully reproduced in a particularized form of reality such as stone, colour, and tone: the content therefore and the possibilities of artistic composition are narrowed within very definable limits. It was on account of this fact that we were able to associate closely and exclusively every one of these specific arts with one particular form of artistic creation pre-eminently adapted to it. In this way the form of symbolism was appropriate to architecture, the classical to sculpture, and the romantic to painting and music. It is no doubt true that the particular arts in both directions from and toward their proper domain tended to pass over into the other forms. We took account of this fact when we found it possible to refer to a classic and romantic style of architecture, a symbolical and Christian type of sculpture, and even used the term classic in connection with painting and music. Departures such as these from the prevailing type were, however, merely experimental essays which prepared the way in subordination to a new type rather than its culminating effort; or they showed us how one art tended to pass beyond its true limits in seeking to grasp a content or a relation to its material of a type that only a further art development could adequately elaborate. Generally speaking, we have seen that architecture has least resource in the expression of its content; in sculpture there is already an increase of possibility, which is further extended to its widest range[9] by painting and music. And the reason of this is that in proportion as the ideality and particularization under all its aspects by the external medium is made more explicit the variety of the content and of the forms it receives also increases.

Poetry, on the other hand, casts itself free of all subordination to the material of sense, at least to this extent, that in the definition of external or objective expression no reason whatever remains why it should restrict itself to specific content or any limitation to its power of composition and reproduction. It is therefore exclusively united to no specific art type; rather we may define it as the *universal* art, which is capable of reclothing and expressing under every conceivable mode every content that can possibly enter into or proceed from the imagination of man. And it can do this because its material is nothing more or less than the imagination itself, which is the universal root and ground of all the particular arts and their specific types.

We have already, in another connection, when concluding our discussion of the particular artistic types, come across what was practically the same thing. What we sought for, then, in our conclusion was that art in one of its types should make itself independent of that mode of representation properly called specific, remaining thereby predominant above the entire sphere in which such a totality of particularization is reproduced. An elaboration so comprehensive is among all the particular arts by the very nature of the case only possible to poetry. Its realization is effected through the development of poetical creation in part by means of the actual reconstitution of every particular type, and partly by the liberation of the mode of conception and its content from the boundaries fixed for it in the essentially exclusive types of conception, whose character we have severally defined as symbolical, classical, and romantic.

(b) The above considerations will further serve to justify the position, which, in the course of our inquiry, regarded as the development of a philosophy, we previously assigned to the art of poetry. In other words by reason of the fact that poetry is, to a degree quite impossible to any other mode of artistic production, concerned with the universal simply as such in Art, we might appear to have some reason for insisting that it marks the commencement of an investigation in the full sense of the word philosophical, and only from such a starting point can we enter into the sphere of particularization, in which we find the series of the other arts as limited and determined by their specific sensuous medium. Looking back, however, at the result arrived at in our investigation of the particular art types we shall find that the course of philosophical evolution consisted, first, in an increased penetration of the ideal content, and, from another point of view, in the demonstration that originally Art sets forth in the search, then in the discovery of and finally with an advance beyond that content compatible with its powers. This notion of the beautiful and *Art* must enforce itself in *the arts* themselves. The starting-point of our inquiry, therefore, was architecture, in which we found merely an impulse toward the complete representation of what pertains to Spirit in a material medium. This is so much the case that it is only through sculpture that art first attains to a genuine interfusion of ideality with the medium; and further that only in the arts of painting and music do we reach the stage where, by virtue of the ideal and subjective character of their content, we find the perfected fusion effected no less under the aspect of conception than that of practical execution in the medium accepted. This process culminates most decisively in poetry, by virtue of the fact that the very nature of its objective realization can only be apprehended as an effort to draw apart from and cancel the material of sense rather than one of reproduction which does not as yet venture to clothe itself and move in the objective medium of sense-perception. In order, however, to make this liberation intelligible in philosophical terms it is of importance that we have already disposed of the question what it is from which art undertakes to liberate itself. This question stands in close relation to the fact that poetry is essentially capable of embracing the entirety of intelligible content and artistic modes of expression. We may add further that we have viewed this as the acceptance of a totality, which can only be interpreted philosophically as the abrogation of limitation in particularity. Our previous consideration of what we mean by things that are one-sided would be involved in such an exposition, the self-exclusive character of such one-sidedness being cancelled by such a totality.

It is only through the course of such an exposition that we can effectively demonstrate that poetry is the specific art in which a point is reached which marks the beginning of the disintegration of art itself, a point at which the philosophical consciousness discovers its bridge of passage to the notion of religion as such, as also to the prose of scientific thought. The boundary lines of the realm of beauty are, as we have already seen, on the one hand the prose of finite condition and our ordinary conscious life, starting from which Art makes its effort in the direction of truth, and, on the other, of the loftier spheres of religion and science, from which it passes over into a comprehension of the Absolute till more emancipate from all material association.

(*c*) Despite therefore the completeness with which the art of poetry reproduces, under a mode of objectification that is most ideal, the entire totality of Beauty, nevertheless intelligence is able to discover even here too in this final domain of art a residue of defect. We may for this purpose within our art-system directly contrast the poetic art with that of architecture. In other words architecture was still unable to subordinate the external material to the ideal content sufficiently to clothe the same in a form adequate to mind; poetry on the other hand carries the process of negating its sensuous medium so far that instead of transforming that which stands in opposition to gross spatial matter, namely tone, as architecture does with its material into a significant symbol, it rather reduces it to a mere sign of no significance. But by doing so it destroys the fusion of spiritual ideality with external existence, so thoroughly that to this extent it ceases to be compatible with the original notion of Art. In other words it comes dangerously near to bidding goodbye to the region of sense altogether, remaining wholly absorbed in that of ideality. The fair mean between these extremes of architecture and poetry is secured by sculpture, painting, and music. Every one of these arts not merely still reproduces the spiritual content completely in a medium borrowed from the objective world, but also leaves us with that which lies open to our senses, no less than our intelligence. For although painting and music, regarded as romantic arts, attach themselves to a medium already more ideal, they do none the less supply the immediacy of objective existence, which, however, in this increase of ideality, shows indications of disappearance, while again from the opposite point of view they prove themselves, through their media of colour and tone, more profuse in fulness of particularization and manifold configuration than is required from the material of sculpture.

No doubt the art of poetry in its turn also endeavours, as a set-off to this defect, to place the objective world before us with a breadth and variety which even painting, at least in a single composition, fails to secure: none the less this comprehensiveness remains throughout merely a realization confined to consciousness itself; and, if it so happens that poetry, in response to a demand for more material artistic realization, attempts to increase the impression on our senses, it is only able to do this by either borrowing these effects from music and painting, in order to secure artistic means otherwise foreign to it; or it is forced, if it seeks retain its genuine character, to employ these sister arts only under a subordinate relation of service, while the main stress is laid on the ideas of conscious life, the imagination which appeals to the imagination, with which it is above all concerned.

This will suffice for discussion of the general relation under which poetry is placed to the other arts. We shall now proceed to a closer examination of the art of poetry itself, and with a view to this propose to co-ordinate the same as follows.

We have already seen that in poetry it is the ideal concept itself from which we derive content no less than medium. By reason, however, of the fact that we already find outside Art's domain the world of idea to be the most obvious mode of conscious life, it is above everything else important to

42

distinguish the conception of *poetry* from that of *prose*. The art of poetry, however, is not complete in this ideal world of the imagination alone. It is necessary that it should clothe the same in expressive *language*. It has therefore a twofold task confronting it. On the one hand it is called upon so to arrange this world of constructed idea that it may admit of complete translation into speech: on the other it must take care not to leave this medium of language in the form appropriated by ordinary conscious life. In other words such must be treated poetically in order that the expression of art may be distinguishable in the selection of words no less than their position, and even their sound from that of ordinary prose.

Furthermore, on account of the fact that, though poetry avails itself of language as a means of expression, it secures by far the most unqualified freedom from those conditions and restrictions imposed on the other arts by virtue of the particularization of their material, it is possible for a poetical composition in a pre-eminent degree to elaborate every one of the various modes of expression, otherwise adopted unaffected by the onesidedness incidental to their application to a particular art. The subdivision of such *modes of expression* in all their variety is consequently by far the most complete in the works of poetry.

The further course of our investigation may now be epitomized as follows:

First, we have to elucidate what is in general terms *poetical,* and the *poetical composition* in particular.

Secondly, poetry will be examined as a means of *expression.*

Thirdly, we shall deal with the subdivision of the art into *Epic, Lyric,* and *Dramatic* poetry.

[1] *Mittelpunkt.* We should rather say the unifying significance of the creation.

[2] It would be perhaps better to translate *geistigen Innerlichkeit* with the words "the self-conscious life of the human reason." This is developed and explained, however, in the next paragraph.

[3] Hegel expresses this as "making the inner or ideal content perceptible to the ideal faculty," that is, *prima facie*, consciousness, or at least that sense which is nearest related to it, viz., hearing.

[4] By *statt des Geistigen* Hegel clearly contrasts pure music with music related as accompaniment to human speech in song.

[5] Lit., "one that merely plays by the way."

[6] Such a statement is obviously one which would be strongly resisted. The stress laid here on the purely ideal content as contrasted with the beauty of rhythm and modal arrangement would certainly suggest that Hegel was deficient in a sense for the musical possibilities of language I presume he does use *gebunden* in the sense of verse.

[7] Hegel's expression is *in rein theoretischen Interesse.*

[8] The medium of music is not of course strictly on all fours with the others.

[9] That is under the limits of these four arts.

I

POETICAL COMPOSITION AS DISTINGUISHED FROM THAT OF PROSE

We find it difficult to recall a single writer among all who have written on the subject of poetry who has not evaded the attempt to describe what is poetical as such, let alone a clear definition. And in fact if any one begins a discussion upon poetry, regarded as an art, without previously having investigated the nature of the content and mode of conception appropriate to Art in its most general terms, he will find it an extremely difficult matter to determine where we must look for that in which the essential character of poetry consists. To an exceptional degree is this failure to tackle this problem visible in those cases where a writer takes as his point of departure the actual execution in particular works of art, and seeks to establish, by means of this connoisseurship, some general principle which he may apply as relevant to every sort and kind of composition. In this way works of the most heterogeneous character come to rank as genuine poetry. If we once start from such assumptions, and then proceed to the inquiry by virtue of what productions of this nature can be reasonably classed together as poems we are at once confronted with the difficulty I have above adverted to. Happily our own position here is not that of these inquirers. In the first place we have by no manner of means arrived at the general notion of our subject-matter through an examination of any particular examples of its display; we have on the contrary sought to evolve the actual constitution of the same by a reference to the fundamental notion.[1] Agreeably with this it is not part of our demand that everything in ordinary parlance regarded as poetry should in our present inquiry fall into the general notion we have accepted. At least this is certainly not so in so far as the decision whether any particular work is or is not poetical is only deducible from the notion itself. Furthermore it is unnecessary now to expound more fully what we understand by the notion of poetry. To do this we should simply have to repeat again the course of our inquiry into the nature of Beauty and the Ideal as developed in general terms in the first part of this work. The intrinsic character of what is poetical stands in general agreement with the generic notion of artistic beauty and the art-product. That is to say, the imagination of the poet is not, as is the case with the plastic arts and music by reason of the nature of the *materia,* through which they are reproductive, constrained in its creative activity in many directions, and forced to accept many others of a onesided or very partial completeness; it is on the contrary merely subservient to the essential requirements and general principle of an ideal and artistic presentation.

From the many different points of view applicable to our present purpose, I will attempt to emphasize merely those of most importance, as for example, *firsts* that which relates to the distinction between the *mode of composition* employed respectively by poetry and prose; *secondly,* that which contrasts a *poetical work* as completed with one of prose; and, *finally,* I propose to add a few observations relative to the subjective faculty which creates, or, shall we say, the *poet* himself.

I. THE COMPOSITION OF POETRY AND PROSE

(*a*) In so far as the *content* appropriate to poetical composition is concerned we may, relatively speaking at any rate, exclude the external world of natural fact. It is spiritual interests rather than the sun, mountains, landscape, or the bodily human form, and the like, which are its proper subject-matter. For, although it naturally embraces the element of sensuous impression and perception, it remains none the less, even in this respect, an activity of mind. Its main object is an intuition of ideality, to which it stands as spiritual activity in closer relation and affinity than is possible for external objects, as presented in their concrete substance to the senses. The world of Nature therefore only enters into the content of poetry in so far as mind discovers therein a stimulus or a material upon which to exercise its

46

own energy; as, for example, where it is regarded as the environment of man, merely possessing essential worth in its relation to the ideality of conscious life, which moreover can put forward no claim to be itself the independent object of poetry. The object, in short, which fully corresponds to its appeal is the infinite realm of Spirit. For the medium of language, the most plastic medium possessed immediately by conscious life, and the one most competent to grasp its interests and movements in their ideal vitality, precisely as is the case with the material of the other arts, such as stone, colour, and tone, must necessarily and above all be employed to express that which it is most qualified to express. It is consequently the pre-eminent task of poetry to bring before our vision the energies of the life of Spirit, all that surges to and fro in human passion and emotion, or passes in tranquillity across the mind, that is the all-embracing realm of human idea, action, exploit, fatality, the affairs of this world and the divine Providence. It has been the most universal and cosmopolitan instructor of the human race and is so still. Instruction and learning are together the knowledge and experience of what is. Stars, animals and plants are ignorant of their law—it does not come into their experience; but man only then exists conformably to the principle of his being when he knows what he is and by what he is surrounded. He must recognize the powers by which he is driven or influenced; and it is just such a knowledge which poetry, in its original and vital[2] form, supplies.

(b) It is, however, also a content of the same character which belongs to man's *ordinary* conscious life. This too instructs him in general laws, as such at least are interpreted by the motley crowd of human life, in their distinction, coordination, and significance. The question therefore arises, as previously observed, as to the nature of the

47

distinction between the mode of conception severally adopted by prose and poetry, a similarity in the content of each being assumed as possible.

(α) Poetry is of greater antiquity than speech modelled in the artistic form of elaborate prose. It is the *original* imaginative grasp of truths a form of knowledge, which fails as yet to separate the universal from its living existence in the particular object, which does not as yet contrast law land phenomena, object and means, or relate the one to the other in subordination to the process of human reason, but comprehends the one exclusively in the other and by virtue of the other. For this reason it does not merely, under the mode of imagery, express a content already essentially apprehended in its universality; on the contrary it lingers, conformably to its unmediated notion, in the unity of concrete life itself, which has not as yet effected such a separation or such an association of mere relationship.

(αα) Under the above forms of envisualization, poetry posits all that it comprehends as an exclusive and consequently independent totality, which, despite its capacity for a rich content and an extensive range of condition, individuals, actions, events, emotions and ideas of every kind, nevertheless is forced to exhibit the same in all their wide complexity as an essentially self-determined whole, as displayed and motived by the unity, whose individual expression this or that fact in its singularity actually is. And consequently the universal or rational principle is not expressed in poetry in its abstract universality, or in the complexus which lies open to philosophical exposition or under the relation of its varied aspects apprehended by science, but on the contrary as a vital union, in its phenomenal presence, possessed with soul and self-determined throughout; and it is further expressed in such a way that the all-embracing unity, the real soul of its vitality,

48

is only suffered to be operative in mysterious guise from within outwards.

(ββ) The character of this mode of apprehending, reclothing and expressing fact is throughout one of construction. It is not the fact itself and its *contemplative*[3] existence, but reconstruction and speech which are the object of poetry. Its entrance on the scene dates from the first efforts of man at self-expression. What is expressed is simply made use of to satisfy this desire. The instant man, in the midst of his practical activities and imperative duties, seeks to summarize this effect for mind and to communicate himself to others, then we have some kind of artistic expression, some accord with what is poetical. To mention one from a host of examples, there is that distich which we read in Herodotus referring to the slain heroes of Thermopylae. As for its content it is simply the fact, the bare announcement that four thousand Peloponesians on a certain spot fought the battle with three hundred myriads. The main interest is, however, the composition of an inscription which communicates to contemporary life and posterity the historical fact, and is there exclusively to do so. In other words, the expression of this fact is poetical; it testifies to itself as a deed (εἰν ποιεῖν) which leaves the content in its simplicity, but expresses the same with a definite purpose. The language, in which the idea is embodied, is to that extent of such increased value that an attempt is made to distinguish it from ordinary speech; we have a distich in lieu of a sentence.

(γγ) For this reason, even from the point of view of language, poetry makes an effort to keep its domain singular and distinct from ordinary parlance, and to accomplish this elevates its expression to a higher virtue than that of merely articulate expression. We must, however, not only in this particular respect, but for the purposes of our present

49

inquiry generally, make an essential distinction between a primitive poetry, which arises *previous to* the creation of ordinary artificial prose, and that mode of poetical composition and speech the development of which is effected where already the conditions of our everyday life and prosaic expression exist. The first is poetical without intention, in idea no less than speech; the latter, on the contrary, is fully conscious of the sphere, from which its task is to detach itself, in order that it may establish itself on the free basis of art. It is consequently quite aware of the distinction and contrast implied in its self-creation to the world of prose.

(*β*) *Secondly*, the kind of *prose life*, from which poetry has to separate itself, postulates an entirely different nature of conception and speech.

(*αα*) In other words, looked at from one point of view, such a consciousness regards the wide expanse of reality according to that association of cause and effect, object and means, and all other categories of the mode of reflection which deals with *finite* conditions and the objective world generally, that is, the limited categories of science or the understanding. It is a feature of such thought that every particular trait should at one moment appear with a false subsistency, at another should be placed in the position of *bare* relation to something else, that as such it should be so apprehended in its relativity and dependence that no unity of a free nature whatever is possible, no unity, that is, which remains essentially throughout, and in all its branches and separate filaments, a complete and free totality, no unity, in short, where we find that the individual aspects are simply the appropriate explication and phenomenal presence of *one* content which constitutes the point of focus, the soul that unites all together, and which also finds its vital principle in this all-pervading centre of animation. Rather the type of

50

conception we above refer to as that of science goes no further than the discovery of particular laws in phenomena, and persists for this reason in the separation, or bare relation, of the particular existence with its general law, the laws themselves under this view tending to harden from each other in their isolate singularity; that their relation is, in fact, conceived exclusively under external and finite conditions.

(ββ) And, furthermore, man's *ordinary* consciousness has nothing to do with what we call the ideal principle of association, the essential core of facts, their bases, causes, ends, and so forth. It rests satisfied with the acceptance of the mere fact that something exists or happens as distinct from something else; or, in other words, with its insignificant contingency. It is no doubt true that the unity of life is not, in such a case, deliberately cancelled by any express separation; that unity, I mean, in which the intuition of the poet arrests the ideal *rationale* of the fact, its expression and determinate existence. What, however, is absent here, is just that flash of insight into this core of reason and significance, which becomes consequently for our intelligence a thing essentially vacant, possessing no further claim on our minds to a rational interest. The comprehension of a rational cosmos; and its relations is exchanged then and there for a mere flux and contiguity of indifference, which it is true may possess a large expanse of external animation, but which none the less suffers the profounder impulse of reason[4] to remain unsatisfied. True vision, no less than soul-life in its full vigour, can only obtain satisfaction, where such are made aware in phenomena, through feeling no less than contemplation, of the reality in its essence and truth which is compatible with such a world. The life which is a mere external show is defunct to our deeper sense, if all that is ideal and

51

intrinsically rich in significance fails to shine through as the very soul thereof.

(γγ) These defects, thirdly, in the conceptions of science and our ordinary conscious life *speculative thought* effaces. It stands, therefore, in one respect in affinity with the imagination of the poet. The cognizance of reason[5] is not solely, or even mainly, concerned with contingent singularity, nor does it overlook in the phenomenal world the essence of the same. It does not rest satisfied with the differentiations and external relations proper to the conceptions and deductions of the understanding; it unites them in a free totality, which in the apprehension of our finite faculty in part fails to preserve its self-consistency, and in part is posited in a relation that possesses no synthetic unity. Pure thought, however, can have but one result, namely thoughts. It evaporates the mode of reality in that of the pure notion. And although it grasps and comprehends actual things in their essential separation and their actual existence, it does also nevertheless translate this particularity into the ideal element of the universal, in which alone thought is at home with itself. Consequently there arises, in contrast to the world of phenomena, a world that is new in this sense, that though the truth of the Real is present, it is not displayed in *reality* itself as the power itself which gives it form and the veritable soul thereof. Thinking is simply a reconciliation of truth with reality in *Thought*. The creations and reconstruction, however, of the poet is a reconciliation under the mode of phenomenal reality itself, albeit such a *real appearance* is merely ideally conceived.

(γ) We have, therefore, two distinct spheres of consciousness, that of poetry and prose. In former times, in which there is neither present a deliberate outlook on the world elaborated, in respect to its religious belief and its general knowledge, under the co-ordinated form of scientific ideas and cognition, nor an actual world of human condition regulated conformably to such a standard, poetry is confronted with a lighter task. Prose is not in such a case opposed to it as an essentially independent field of ideal and external existence, which it has first to overcome. Its problem is for the most part simply limited to deepening all that is significant or transparent in the forms of ordinary consciousness. If, on the contrary, the prose of life has already appropriated within its mode of vision the entire content of conscious life, setting its seal on all and every part of it, the art of poetry is forced to undertake the task of melting all down again and re-coining the same anew. In every direction it finds itself involved in difficulties by the unresponsive nature of prosaic existence. It has, in short, not only to wrest itself from the adherence of ordinary consciousness to all that is indifferent and contingent, and to raise the scientific apprehension of the cosmos of fact to the level of reason's profounder penetration, or to translate speculative thought into terms of the imagination, giving a body to the same in the sphere of intelligence itself; it has further to convert in many ways the *mode of expression* common to the ordinary consciousness into that appropriate to poetry; and, despite of all deliberate intention enforced by such a contrast and such a process, to make it appear as though all such purpose was absent, preserving the original freedom essential to all art.

(*c*) We have now summarized in its most general terms that in which the content of poetry consists. We have further distinguished the form of poetry from that of prose. In conclusion, it is of importance to draw attention to the particularization which the art of poetry, to a degree unattained by the other arts, whose development is not nearly so rich in results, admits of. We find, no doubt,

53

architecture illustrated in the arts of very varied peoples, and continuous through many centuries. But of sculpture, at least, it is true that it reaches its culminating point in the ancient world of Greece and Rome, just as painting and music have done more recently in Christendom. The art of poetry celebrates its epochs of brilliancy and bloom among all nations and in all ages almost that present any real artistic activity at all. It embraces the collective Spirit of mankind, and it is differentiated through every kind of variation.

(a) Furthermore, inasmuch as poetry does not accept the universal in scientific abstraction from its object, but seeks to represent what is rational under the mode of individuality,[6] the specific traits of national character are essential to its growth; the content and the particular mode of its presentation are in fact conditioned by the nature of these and the general outlook in each case. We find it consequently adapting itself to every variety of form and peculiarity. It matters not what the poetry may be, whether Oriental, Italian, Spanish, English, Roman, Hellenic, or German, each and all differ totally in their spirit, emotional impulse, general outlook and expression.

A similar distinctive variety asserts itself in particular epochs as they are favourable to the art of poetry or the reverse. The results secured, for example, by our German poetry were impossible in the Middle Ages, or the times of the thirty years' war. The particular motives, which in our own day excite the greatest interest, are inseparable from the entire evolution of contemporary life. And in the same way every age has its own wider or more restricted, more exalted and liberal, or more depressed phase of emotional life, in short its specific outlook on the world, which it is the express aim of poetry to bring home to the artistic consciousness in the most intelligible and complete manner,

54

inasmuch as language is the one medium capable of expressing the human spirit wherever and in whatever form it may be manifested.

(β) Among these national characteristics, or views and opinions peculiar to particular epochs, some have closer affinity with the poetic impulse than others. The Oriental consciousness is, for example, in general more poetic than the Western mind, if we exclude Greece. In the East the principle predominant is always that of coherence, solidity, unity, substance. An outlook of this nature is intrinsically most penetrative, even though it may fail to reach the freedom of the Ideal. Our Western point of view, especially that of modern life, is based on the endless breaking up and division of its boundless material into fragments, in virtue of which process, the extreme emphasis laid here on particular facts, what is merely finite becomes substantive for the imagination, and despite of this must be once more subsumed under the converse action of relativity. For the Oriental nothing persists as really substantive, but everything appears as contingent, discovering its supreme focus, stability and final justification in the One, the Absolute, to which it is referred.

(γ) By means of this diversity of national traits and the evolutionary process of the centuries we find that what is shared by all mankind alike, no less than all that claims to be artistic, is drawn as a common element within the reach of other nations and epochs, intelligible and enjoyable to the same. It is in this twofold connection that of late years to an exceptional degree Hellenic poetry has roused the admiration and imitation of most diverse nationalities. And this is so because in the content of it no less than in the artistic form it receives the simply human is disclosed with most beauty. The literature of India itself, however, despite all the difficulties attendant on an outlook and artistic expression so alien to our own, is not wholly outside our sympathy; and the boast is no empty one that in our modern era pre-eminently a keen sense for all that art and the human spirit embraces in every direction has begun to unfold itself.

Were we in our present investigation of this impulse toward individualization, pursued so persistently by poetry, under the aspects we have already described, to restrict the same to a *general* treatment of the art of poetry, such a generalization, however established, could not fail to be abstract and devoid of content. It is therefore of first importance, if our object be to consider poetry of a really genuine type, that we include in our survey the forms of the creative spirit as presented in their national form, the unique product of one age; and further we must not overlook the individuality which creates, the soul of the poet. Such, then, are the main points of view to which I would draw attention by way of a general introduction to poetical creation and conception.

2. THE ART-PRODUCT OF POETRY AND PROSE

Poetry is not, however, exhausted by the imaginative idea alone: it must necessarily proceed to make itself articulate and complete in the *poetical work of art.*

Such an object of study opens a large field of investigation. We may conveniently arrange and classify the course of our discussion as follows:

First, we shall endeavour to point out what is of most importance relatively to the *poetical composition generally.*

Secondly, we shall distinguish it from the principal types of *prose composition*, in so far as the same are compatible with artistic treatment.

We shall then, *finally* be in a position to deduce with some completeness the notion of the *free art-product*.

(*a*) In respect to the poetical work of art under its generic aspect all that is necessary is once more to enforce our previous contention that it must, no less than any other production of an unfettered imagination, receive the form and independence of an organic whole. This demand can only receive satisfaction as follows:

(*α*) In the *first* place that which constitutes a homogeneous content, whether it be a definite object of action and event, or a specific emotion and passion, must before everything else possess intrinsic unity.

(*αα*) All else must be posited under relation to this bond of unity, and thereby combine to form a freehand concrete coherence of all parts. This is only possible under the condition, that the content selected is not conceived as abstract *universal*, but as the action and emotion of men, as the object and passion which are actually present in the mind, soul, and volition of definite individuals, arising as such from the distinctive basis of an individual nature in each case.

(*ββ*) The universal, which is to receive representation, and the individuals, in whose character events and actions the manifestation of poetry is asserted must not consequently fall into fragments, or be so related that the individuals are merely of service as an abstract universal; both aspects must combine in vital coalescence. In the Iliad, for example, the contest of Greeks and Trojans, and the victory of the former is inseparably bound up with the wrath of Achilles, which for this reason becomes the common focus welding all together. No doubt we also find poetical works in which the fundamental content is partly more abstract in its generalization, and also partly is executed in a way that expresses a universal of more significance. Dante's great epic

57

poem is an illustration, which not only embraces the world divine throughout, but displays individuals of the most varied character in their relation to the punishments of hell, purgatory and the blessedness of Paradise. But even here we find no entirely abstract separation, of the two points of view, no mere relation of service between the particular objects. For in the Christian world the focus of conscious life is not conceived as nothing more than an accident of Godhead, but as essential and infinite cause or end itself, so that here the universal purpose, that is the divine justice in condemnation and salvation can verily appear as immanent fact, the eternal interest and being of the individual himself. In this divine world the individual is throughout of pre-eminent importance. In that of the State he can of course be sacrificed in order to save the universal, that is the State. In his relation to God, however, and in the kingdom of God he is essentially and exclusively the end.

($\gamma\gamma$) We must, however, *thirdly*, conceive the universal, which supplies the content of human emotion and action as self-subsistent, intrinsically complete where it is, and constituting as such in itself a definitive and exclusive world. When, for instance, in our contemporary life mention is made of any officer, official, general, professor, and so forth, and we try to imagine what kind of action such a man or personality is likely to attempt or carry out under his own particular conditions of environment, we place before ourselves simply a content of interest and activity, which in part is not itself a rounded and self-substantive whole, but one which stands in infinitely manifold external connections, relations and conditions, in part also, if we regard it as abstract totality, one which can receive the form of a universal concept in its separation from the individuality of the, in other respects, entire personality, as for instance that of personal obligation. Conversely we

58

may have no doubt a content of sterling character, making, that is to say, an essentially independent whole, which, despite of this, and without further development and advance, is complete in one sentence. It is really impossible to say whether a content of this nature belongs more properly to poetry or prose. The grand affirmation of the old Testament, "God said Let their be Light and there was Light," is at once in its penetration, no less than the precision of its embrace,[7] as much essentially sublime poetry as it is ordinary prose. Of a similar nature is the command, "I am the Lord thy God, thou shalt have no other gods but me"; or that, "Honour thy father and thy mother." The golden epigrams of a Pythagoras and the wise sayings of Solomon are of the same type. Phrases, so rich in content as the above, have their origin in a world where the distinction between poetry and prose is as yet absent. We can, however, hardly affirm of such that they are a poetical work of art, even though many such phrases may be combined together. The independence and rounding off of a genuine poetical work must be assumed at the same time to be of the nature of a process, and a differentiation of parts: we assume it therefore to be a unity, the true character of which is only made explicit by emphatic insistence upon its diversity. This process, absolutely essential in the plastic arts, regarded at least according to the requirements of their form, is also more generally of the greatest moment in a poetical composition.

(β) This introduces us, then, to a *second* feature of the work of art, namely, the organic differentiation of its several parts, essential to it not merely that it may be presented as an organic unity, but that the elaboration of all it implies may be rendered complete.

(αα) The most obvious reason of this necessity is referable to the fact that Art in general tends instinctively to particularization. The effect of the scientific faculty is that what is particular and singular fails to receive its complete vindication. And this is so not merely because the understanding apprehends the manifold, as such theoretic faculty, starting from its principles of generalization, causing the particular fact thereby to evaporate in its abstract deductions and categories; but also because it makes this manifold subserve ends of purely practical import. Severe adherence to that purely relative value, which strictly belongs to the nature of the process, appears to the understanding as useless and tedious. To the conception and composition of poetry on the contrary every part, every phase in the result must remain of essential interest and vital. It dallies therefore with delight in detail, depicts the same with enthusiasm, and treats every part as an independent whole. However great, therefore, in addition the content may be of a poetical work in its central interest, the organic completeness is equally asserted in subordinate detail, precisely as in the human organism every member, every finger is rounded with exquisite delicacy in its unified completeness, and as a rule, we find in Nature that every particular existence is enclosed within a perfect world of its own. The advance of poetry is therefore more slow than that compatible with the judgments and conclusions of the understanding, where we find that, whether regarded theoretically as science or with reference to practical conduct and action, the main stress is on the final result, this rather than on the path by which it is reached. As for the degree in which poetry approaches realization in its tenderness for such detail we have already pointed out that it is not its vocation to describe with excessive diffuseness what is exterior in the form of its sensuous appearance. If it therefore undertakes extensive descriptions without making them reflect at the same time the claims and interests of soul-life it becomes heavy and tedious. Above all it must take care not to enter into deliberate rivalry with the actual detail, in its exact completeness, presented by natural fact itself. Even painting in this respect should aim at circumspection and restriction. We have therefore here and in the case of poetry a twofold point of view to consider. On the one hand we must remember that the impression is on our mental vision; and on the other the art can only place before the mind the object, which in Nature we can survey and comprehend in a single glance in a series of separate traits. For this reason it is important that poetry does not carry its elaboration of detail so far, that the vision of the whole in its entirety becomes inevitably disturbed, confused, or lost. It is obvious therefore that difficulties of an exceptional nature have to be overcome when the attempt is made to place an action or event of varied nature before our vision, and where in actual life such happen in a single moment of time, and in close connection with such immediacy, for all it can do is to present the same in a continuous series. As respects this difficulty, no less than the general way in which poetry, as already described, approaches the detail of Nature, we find the demand of the several generic types of the art differs very considerably. Epic poetry, for instance, attaches itself to the particularity of the external world with an emphasis totally different from that of dramatic poetry, with its rapidity of forward movement, or from that of lyrical poetry with its exclusive insistence on the ideally significant.

($\beta\beta$) It is through an elaboration of this kind that the several parts of a composition secure *subsistency*. No doubt this appears to stand in direct contradiction to the unity which we established as a primary condition: as a matter of fact the opposition is merely apparent. This independence should not, that is to say, assert itself in such a way that the several parts are placed in absolute separation from each other: it must on the contrary only be carried so far that the several aspects and members of the whole are clearly seen on their own account to be asserted in the vital form peculiar to each, and to stand on their own free basis of independence. If, on the contrary, this individualized life is absent from the several parts, the composition becomes, precisely as Art generally can only invest the universal with determinate existence under the form of actual particularity, cold and defunct.

($\gamma\gamma$) Despite of this self-subsistency, however, these several parts must remain likewise in conjunction to the extent that the *one* fundamental motive or purpose, made explicit and manifest in and through them, must declare itself as the unity which pervades the whole, and in which the parts coalesce and to which they return. This is the condition of art, and pre-eminently so of poetry, where it falls short of its noblest reach, upon which it most readily is wrecked, and the work of art declines from the realm of a free imagination into that of mere prose. To put it in another way, the connexion into which the parts fall must not merely be one of final *cause and effect*. For in the relation of teleology the end is the universal as essentially presupposed and willed, which it is true succeeds in making the several aspects tally with the process, yet employs them none the less as means and to this extent robs them of all really free stability and thereby of every sort of vitality. In such a case the parts merely fall under a relation of purpose to one end, which is asserted imperiously to the disadvantage of all else, and which accepts the same in abstraction as subservient and subordinate to itself. The freedom and beauty of art contradict flatly this servile relation of the abstract faculty of science.

(γ) On these grounds the unity, asserted in the several parts of the composition, must be of another character. The definition of this may be stated under two aspects of conception, as follows.

(*αα*) In the *first* place, the vital presence we have already referred to as peculiar to every part separately must be maintained. If we direct our attention, however, to that which in fact justifies the introduction of any detail whatever into the composition, we find the point of departure to be *one* fundamental idea which the same as a whole is undertaken to manifest or interpret. Consequently everything defined and particular must announce that as the source of its own specific appearance. In other words, the content of a poetical work must not be itself intrinsically abstract, but concrete, one that by reason of its own wealth conducts us to a rich unravelment of its varied aspects. And when this variety, even assuming that in its realization it falls to every appearance into plain contradictions, yet is as a matter of fact rooted in the essentially unified content we have adverted to, in that case we may affirm that by necessity the content itself, in a form agreeable to its notion and being, comprises what is fundamentally an exclusive and harmonious totality of particular characteristics, which it possesses as its own, and in the continuous expatiation of which what it is in its real significance is in truth rendered explicit. It is only *these* several parts, which originally belong to the content, and which consequently should be carried into the composition under the mode of actual and essentially sound and vital existence. In this respect, therefore, despite all appearance the display of particular characteristics present of opposition to others, they are throughout combined in a union of mysterious accord, rooted in its own nature.

(*ββ*) *Secondly,* since the composition is presented under the form of *natural* phenomena, the unity must, in order to preserve the vital appearance of such reality, only be the *ideal* bond, which to all appearance without intention holds together the parts and includes them in an organic whole. It is just this animating union of organic life which alone is able to bring into being true poetry as contrasted with the expressed intention of plain prose. That is to say whenever particularity exclusively appears as means to a definite end, it does not possess and cannot conceivably possess an independent and unique vitality of its own; what it does testify to, on the contrary, is that it exists for the sake of something else, that is the end proposed. Purpose of this type declares its sovereignty over the objective facts through which it is fulfilled. An artistic composition should, however, confer upon all that is particular within it, all in the expatiation of which it displays continuously the central and fundamental content selected, the appearance of an unfettered stability. This is absolutely necessary, because what we here comprise under the term particularity is just that content itself under the mode of the reality which corresponds with it. We may therefore recall to our minds the analogous task of speculative thought, which in the same way has on the one side to develop the particular to the point of self-subsistency or freedom from that which is at first an indefinite universality; and likewise, too, it is called on to demonstrate how within this totality of what is particular, in which that and that only is divulged which essentially reposes in the universal, the unity is on this very account once more asserted, and indeed then and only then is truly concrete unity, established through its own differences and their mediation. Speculative philosophy is thus, in the same way, through the method of dialectic above adverted to, responsible for works which resemble in this respect those of poetry, containing, that is, by virtue of the content, an essential identity of self-seclusiveness and a revelation of differentiated material in accord with it. We must, however, despite this similarity between these two activities, and apart from the obvious difference between the evolution of pure thinking and creative art, draw attention to a further essential distinction. The deduction of philosophy no doubt vindicates the necessity and actuality of particularity, but none the less, in virtue of the dialectic process in which this aspect of reality is asserted, it is expressly demonstrated of this particularity and all of it, that it for the first time discovers its truth and its stability in the concrete unity.[8] Poetry, on the contrary, does not proceed to any such express demonstration. The concordant unity must no doubt be completely vindicated in every one of its creations, and be operative there in all their manifold detail as the soul and vital core of the whole; but this presence remains for Art an ideal bond which is implied rather than expressly posited, precisely as the soul is immediately made vital in all the bodily members, without robbing the same of the appearance of an independent existence. We have the same truth illustrated by colour and tone. Yellow, blue, green and red are different colours which admit of the most absolute contrast; but none the less, on account of the fact that as colour they all essentially belong to one totality, they maintain a harmony throughout; and it is not, moreover, necessary that this union as such should be expressly declared in them. In a similar way the dominant, the third and the fifth remain independent as tones, and yet for all that give us the harmony of the trichord; or, rather, we should put it that they only produce this harmony so long as each tone is permitted to assert its own essentially free and characteristic sound.

(γγ) In connection with this organic unity and articulate synthesis of a poetical composition we have further to consider essential *features of distinction* which are due to the particular *artistic form* appropriate to the composition under review, no less than the particular *type* of poetry in which we discover the specific character of its working out. Poetry, for example, of symbolic art is unable, owing to the more abstract and indefinite traits which constitute its essential and significant content, to attain to a fully organic fusion in the degree of transparency possible to the works of the classical art-form. In symbolism generally, as we have already established in the first part of this enquiry, the conjunction of general significance and the actual phenomenon, in association with which Art embodies its content, is of a less coherent character: as a result of this we find that what is particular in one direction preserves a greater consistency; in another, as in the case of the Sublime, only so far asserts this quality in order, through the negation thus implied, to render more intelligible the *one* supreme power and substance, or merely to advance the process to a condition of mysterious association of particular, but at the same time heterogeneous no less than related traits and aspects of natural and spiritual facts. Conversely, in the romantic type, wherein the ideality of truth reveals itself in essential privacy to soul-life only, we find a wider field for the display of the detail of rational reality in its self-subsistency; in this latter case the conjunction of all parts and their union must necessarily be present, but the nature of their elaboration can neither be so clear or secure as in the products of classical art.

In a similar way the Epic gives us a more extensive picture of the external world; it even lingers by the way in episodical events and deeds, whereby the unity of the whole, owing to this increased isolation of the parts, appears to suffer diminution. The drama, in contrast to this, requires a more strenuous conjunction, albeit, even in the drama, we find that romantic poetry permits the introduction of a type of variety in the nature of episode and an elaborate analysis of characteristic traits in its presentation of soul-life no less than that of external fact. Lyric poetry, as it changes conformably to the fluctuation of its types, adapts itself to a mode of presentment of the greatest variety: at one time it is bare narration; at another the exclusive expression of emotion or contemplation; at another it restricts its vision, in more tranquil advance, to the central unity which combines; at another it shifts hither and thither in unrestrained passion through a range of ideas and emotions apparently destitute of any unity at all.

This, then, must suffice us on the general question of a poetical composition.

(b) In order now, — this is our *second* main head in the present discussion, — to examine more closely the distinction which obtains between the organic poem as above considered and the prose composition, we propose to direct attention to those specific types of *prose* which, despite their obvious limitations, do none the less come into closest affinity with art. Such are, without question, the arts of history and oratory.

(a) As regards history, there can be no doubt that we find ample opportunity here for *one* aspect of genuine artistic activity.

(aa) The evolution of human life in religion and civil society, the events and destinies of the most famous individuals and peoples, who have given emphasis to life in either field by their activity, all this presupposes great ends in the compilation of such a work, or the complete failure of what it implies. The historical relation of subjects and a content such as these admits of real distinction, thoroughness and interest: and however much our historian must endeavour to reproduce actual historical fact, it is none the less incumbent upon him to bring before our imaginative vision this motley content of events and characters, to create anew and make vivid the same to our intelligence with his own genius.[9] In the creation of such a memorial he must, moreover, not rest satisfied with the bare letter of particular fact; he must bring this material into a co-ordinated and constructive whole; he must collectively conceive and embrace single traits, occurrences and actions under the unifying concept; with the result that on the one hand we have flashed before us a clear picture of nationality, epoch of time, external condition and the spiritual greatness or weakness of the individuals concerned in the very life and characterization which belonged to them; and on the other that the bond of association, in which the various parts of our picture stand to the ideal historical significance of a people or an event, is asserted from such without exception. It is in this sense that we, even in our own day, speak of the art of Herodotus, Thucydides, Xenophon, Tacitus, and a few others, and cannot cease to admire their narratives as classical products of the art of human language.

(ββ) It is nevertheless true that even these fine examples of historical composition do not belong to free Art. We may add that we should have no poetry even though we were to assume with such works the external form of poetry, the measure or rhyme of verse and so forth. It is not exclusively the manner in which history is written, but the nature of its *content*, which makes it prose. Let us look at this rather more closely.

Genuine history, both in respect to aim and performance, only begins at the point where the heroic age, which in its origination it is the part of poetry and art to vindicate, ceases, for the reason that we have here the moment when the distinct outlines and prose of life, in its actual conditions, no less than the way they are conceived and represented, come into being. Herodotus does not for instance describe the Greek expedition to Troy, but the Persian wars, and takes pains, in a variety of ways, with

68

tedious research and careful reflection, to base the narrative proposed on genuine knowledge. The Hindoos, indeed we may say the Orientals generally, with almost the single exception of the Chinese, do not possess this instinct of prose sufficiently to produce a genuine history. They invariably digress either into an interpretation and reconstruction of facts of a purely religious character, or such as are fantastic inventions. The element of prose then native to the historical age of any folk may be briefly described as follows.

In the *first* place, in order that we may have history we must presuppose a common life, whether we consider the same on its religious side, or that of a polity, with its law, institutions, and the like, established on their own account, and possessing originally or in their subsequent modification a validity as laws or conditions of general application.

It is out of such a common life, *secondly*, that we mark the birth of definite activities for the preservation or change of the same, which may be of universal import, and in fact constitute the end or motive of their continuance, and to complete and carry into effect which we have to presuppose individuals fitted for such a task. These individuals are great and eminent in so far as they show themselves, through their effective personality, in co-operation with the common end, which underlies the ideal notion of the conditions which confront them: they are little when they fail to rise in stature to the demand thus made on their energy: they are depraved when, instead of facing as combatants of the practical needs of the times,[10] they are content merely to give free rein to an individual force which is, with its implied caprice, foreign to all such common ends. Where, however, any of such conditions obtain we do not have either a genuine content or a condition of the world such as we established in the first part of our inquiry as essential to the art of poetry. Even in the case of personal greatness the substantive aim of its devotion is to a large or less extent something given, presupposed, and enforced upon it, and to that extent the unity of individuality is excluded, wherein the universal, that is the entire personality should be selfidentical, an end exclusively for itself, an independent whole in short. For however much these individuals discover their aims in their own resources, it is for all that not the freedom or lack of it in their souls and intelligence, in other words the vital manifestation of their personality, but the accomplished end, and its result as operative upon the actual world already there, and essentially independent of such individuality, which constitutes the object of history. And, moreover, from a further point of view we find manifested in the historical condition the play of contingency, that breach between what is implicitly substantive and the relativity of particular events and occurrences, no less than of the specific subjectivity of characters displayed in their personal passions, opinions and fortunes, which in this prosaic mode of life present far more eccentricity and variation than do the wonders of poetry, which through all diversity must remain constant to what is valid in all times and places.

And *finally*, in respect to the actual execution of affairs within the cognisance of history we find here again the introduction of a prosaic element, if we contrast it with the impulse of genuine poetry, partly in the division asserted by personal idiosyncracy from a consciousness of laws, principles, maxims and so forth, which is thereby necessarily absorbed in the universal condition or fact; and in part also the realization of the ends proposed involve much preparation and arrangement, the means to effect which extend far, and embrace many necessary or subservient relations, which have to be readjusted and adapted, in order to carry out the course proposed, with intelligence, prudence and prosaic circumspection. The work in short cannot be undertaken offhand, but only to a large extent after extensive introduction. The result of this is that the particular acts of execution, which, it is here assumed, come into effect for the *one* main purpose, are often either wholly contingent in respect to their content, and remain without ideal union, or are asserted under the form of a practical utility regulated by a mind dominated by the aims proposed; in other words, they do not proceed unmediated from the core of free and independent life itself.[11]

($\gamma\gamma$) The historian then has no right to expunge these prosaic characteristics of his content, or to convert them into others more *poetical;* his narrative must embrace what lies actually before him and in the shape he finds it without amplification,[12] or at least poetical transformation. However much, therefore, it may become a part of his labours to make the ideal significance and spirit of an epoch, a people, or the particular event depicted, the ideal focus and bond which holds all together in one coherent whole, he is not entitled to make either the conditions presented him, the characters or events, wholly subordinate to such a purpose, though he may doubtless remove from his survey what is wholly contingent and without serious significance; he must, in short, permit them to appear in all their objective contingency, dependence and mysterious caprice. No doubt in biography the full animation of personality and an independent unity is conceivably possible, because in such a work the individual, no less than all which proceeds from him and is operative in moulding such a figure, is throughout the focus of the composition. A historical character is, however, exclusively one of two opposed extremes. For although we deduce a unity of subject from the same, none the less from another point of view various events and transactions obtrude, which in part are without any essential ideal connection, and in part come into contact with such individuality without any free co-operation on the part of the same, and to this extent involve the same within the contingency of such an external condition. So, for example, Alexander is without question a personality, pre-eminent above all others of his epoch, and one which, in virtue of its unique forces, falling as they do in accord with contemporary world conditions, becomes engaged in the Persian invasion. The continent of Asia none the less, which Alexander vanquishes, is in the capricious variety of its nationalities a whole united by no necessary bond.[13] Historical events pass before him as the bare panorama of purely objective phenomena. And, finally, if the historian adds to his survey his private reflections as a philosopher, attempting thereby to grasp the absolute grounds for such events, rising to the sphere of that divine being, before which all that is contingent vanishes and a loftier mode of necessity is unveiled, he is none the less debarred, in reference to the actual conformation of events, from that exclusive right of poetry, namely, to accept this substantive resolution as the fact of most importance. To poetry alone is the liberty permitted to dispose without restriction of the material submitted in such a way that it becomes, even regarded on the side of external condition, conformable with ideal truth.

(*β*) *Secondly, oratory* appears to have a closer affinity with the freedom of art.

(*αα*) For although the orator avails himself of the opportunity for and content of his effort out of actual life and definite circumstances and opinions, all that he utters remains none the less, in the *first* place, subject to his free choice. His personal aims and views are immanent therein, in virtue of which he can make the same a complete and living expression of his personality. And, *secondly*, the development of the subject of his oration and the mode of delivery depends entirely on himself, so that the impression he makes is as though we received in his speech a wholly independent expression of mind. And, *finally*, it is his vocation not merely to address himself to the trained or ordinary intelligence of his hearers, but to work upon their entire humanity, their emotions, no less than their judgment. The substance of what he has to say and in which he strives to awake interest, is not merely the abstract aspect of it, nor is it this aspect of his main purpose, in the

73

fulfilment of which he invites co-operation, but rather for the most part also a definite and very real thing. For this reason the substance of the orator's address, while embracing what is essentially substantive in its character, ought equally to grasp his general principle under the form of its specific manifestation, and render the same intelligible to conscious life in the full concrete sense of the term. The orator then must not merely satisfy our understanding with the cogency of his deductions and conclusions, but has it in his power to address the soul itself, to rouse human passion and carry it captive, to absorb the whole attention, and by such means, through all the avenues of spirit, to ravish and convince his audience.

(ββ) Despite, however, such considerations, looked at rightly we find that it is just in the arts of oratory that this apparent freedom is almost wholly subordinate to the rule of practical *utility*. In other words what confers upon public speaking its unique motive force is not implied in the particular purpose, to promote which the speech is made; we must refer it to the general principle, the laws, rules, axioms which the particular case suggests, and which are already essentially present in this form of universality, partly, as actual laws of the State, partly too as ethical, juristic or religious maxims, emotions, dogmas, and so forth. The particular circumstance and end, which we find here as the point of departure, and this universal are in every respect separate from each other, and this separation is the relation maintained throughout. No doubt the orator intends to make these two aspects unite: what, however, in poetry, in so far as poetry is really present, attests as already from the first accomplished, is present in oratory merely as the personal aim of the orator, the fulfilment of which lies outside the speech itself altogether.

The only alternative we have left us is a process of

subsumation, whereby the phenomenon, the actual and defined thing, here the concrete case or end, is not unravelled in immediate unity with the universal as such, and freely from its own substance, but only receives validity by virtue of its dependence upon general principles and in its relation to legislative acts, morality, customs, and the like, which on their own account possess independent stability. It is not the spontaneous life of the fact in its concrete manifestation, but the prosaic division between notion and reality, a mere relation of both to each other and a mere demand for their union, which constitutes the fundamental type under consideration.

Such a process of thought is frequently adopted by the religious teacher. For him religious doctrines, in their widest connotation, and the principles of morality or of philosophy, political or otherwise, which follow in their train, are in fact precisely the object whereto he can refer cases of every conceivable variety; and they are this for the reason that these doctrines have to be accepted, believed and recognized by the religious consciousness as essentially and in their own worth the substance of all particular appearance. No doubt the preacher may at the same time appeal to our heart, may suffer the divine laws to unveil from the depth of soul-life as their source, and face to face with his audience may refer them to such a source. But it is not in their absolutely individual guise that he must necessarily present and assert them; on the contrary, he must bring effective universality to consciousness under precisely this form of commands, promises and maxims of faith. The oratory of courts of law is even a better illustration. Here we find in addition the twofold point of view, that while on the one hand all turns most obviously on the particular case, yet conversely the subsumation of this case to general considerations and laws is equally a necessity. As regards the *first* aspect, we may remark that the element of prose is already implied in the enforced investigation of the actual facts and the collocation and able reconstruction of all singular circumstances and accidents; a process such as this at once opens our eyes to the poverty involved in this investigation of the truth of such a legal case, no less than the tedious ingenuity engaged in its display, if we contrast it at least with the free creations of poetry. We have in fact to carry our analysis of the concrete facts to a yet further point. Such must not merely be traced in a series that does justice to all features, but every one of such features, no less than the whole case, have to be referred back to the statute accepted from the first as of independent validity. At the same time, even in this prosaic affair, we still have considerable scope for an impression on the heart and emotions. For it is possible so to present the rightness or wrongness of the case under discussion to the imagination that we are no longer bound to acquiesce in the bare knowledge of the facts and a general conviction; on the contrary, the case in its entirety is capable of becoming, by virtue of the style adopted in its exposition, so marked with the characteristics of personality to everyone who hears it, that no one can fail to discover there a personal interest as of something which concerns himself.

Secondly, in the oratorical art, artistic delivery and elaboration is not that which constitutes the ultimate and highest interest of the speaker; he possesses in addition and beyond his art an ulterior aim, that the entire form and working out of his discourse should rather be used exclusively as the most effective means to promote an interest which is outside. From this point of view the audience too have to be influenced not on their own independent account, but the effort is rather to excite emotion and conviction exclusively as a means toward the attainment of the purpose, the fulfilment whereof the orator has proposed from the first. The mode of presentation, therefore, ceases to be an end for itself even to the listener; its claim becomes exclusively that of a means to some particular conviction, or an incentive to definite conclusions or activities.

For these reasons from this point of view also the art loses its freedom of form; it becomes a means to a purpose, to a further demand,[14] which, this is a *third* point, in relation to the *consequence,* is not satisfied in the actual speech itself and its artistic handling. The composition of poetry on the contrary has no other object than the manifestation and enjoyment of beauty. End and accomplishment reposes here immediately and essentially in the independent work, which for that reason is complete; artistic activity is no means to an essentially ulterior result, but an end which at once is rounded in itself by virtue of its own execution. In oratory art receives merely a position of service to something collateral; the genuine end is therefore not as such consonant with art, but of a practical character, that is to say, instruction, edification, judgment of legal matters or political affairs, and therewith a reference to some matter which has first to happen, or to a decision not yet carried out, but which, however, are in neither case terminated or completed through the resultant effect of the art in question, but can only be so in various ways after a contact with quite other activities. A speech in fact may often conclude with a dissonance, which the hearer has first to resolve as judge, and only then is able to act agreeably with such a verdict. Just as, for example, the oratory of the pulpit starts from the point of the unconverted soul, and in the result makes the hearer pass judgment over his own self and his soul's condition. In such a case religious conversion is the object of the preacher; but whether such a conversion follows as a result of all the edification and excellence of his eloquent exhortations, and thus the end proposed is carried out, is a point of view which the sermon itself cannot deal with; it must be perforce relegated to subsequent conditions.

(γγ) In all these directions the notion of eloquence will fall rather under the main principle of utility than maintain itself within the free and organized whole of the poetical art-product. In short the orator must necessarily and above all make it his mark to subordinate the whole, no less than the parts, to that purpose in his mind, from which his effort proceeds, a process in which the self-consistent independence of his exposition disappears, and in lieu of which we must assume a relation of service to a definite end that ceases to be of artistic significance. And above all, inasmuch as the object in view is one of practical influence upon human life, he must keep throughout before his mind the nature of the place in which he speaks, the degree of education, the receptive powers, and, in short, the general atmosphere of his audience, that he may not fall short of the practical success desired through an inability to meet the local conditions of the moment, and the idiosyncrasies of his audience. By reason of this very attachment to external conditions it is impossible that either the entirety of his address or its parts can any longer originate in a free artistic activity;[15] it will constantly tend in its detailed elaboration to appropriate utilitarian points of association, and be dominated by conceptions of cause and effect, and other categories more proper to science.

(c) And, *thirdly*, we may, as flowing from the above distinction between what is really poetical and the creations of the historian and the orator, establish the following points pertinent to the poetical composition itself.

(α) We found that in history the element of prose consisted

above all in this that however much the content thereof could be ideally substantive and possessed of a downright penetrative power, the actual form of the same was, however, invariably accompanied with many conditions of relative validity, massed together with much that was contingent, and finally often referable to caprice simply as its ground, aspects of immediate objective fact which the historian was not entitled to translate into the terms of a reality of profounder grasp.

(αα) The effort of such a transfiguration is in fact a fundamental *desideratum* of the poetical art when it, so far as its material is concerned, steps into the arena of history. It is its business in short in such a case to discover the mere ideal core and significance of an event, action, or a national type, a famous historical personality, and as decisively to brush aside aspects of contingency, everything in fact purely incidental or indifferent, which plays round such types or individuals, and stands to them in a purely relative connection. It has then to establish, in the place of the circumstances and traits it rejects, others which reveal the ideal essence of the facts in their clarity, to the intent that in this transfigured presence such shall so discover concrete truth in its fulness that the reason, which has hitherto lain concealed, though implied in them, shall now for the first time assert itself as evolved and declared in complete realization. By this means alone poetry is able in the proposed work to make its content coalesce in the secure unity of a centre, able as such to round and unfold itself in a whole. And this is possible because it not only is operative as a more effective bond between the parts, but also because, without compromising the unity of the whole, all its varied particularity is suffered to assert its claim to an independent impression.

(ββ) Poetry may in this respect make a yet further advance,

when, it accepts as its main content, in lieu of the material and significance of the historical fact, some fundamental idea, some human collision in general associated with it in a close or more remote affinity, and employs the historical *factum* and personages, everything local in short, merely in the guise or garment of individualization. The difficulty to be encountered here is twofold: either the historically ascertained data, when appropriated by the composition, may fall out of line with the fundamental idea; or, conversely, it may be that the poet in some measure retains these data, but also too in essential features moulds them conformably to his purposes, and by doing this work fails to harmonize the element of stability with that of original design which were both essential to our conception of the poetical product. To dispel such an opposition and to reassert the accordant note able to do this is a difficult matter; it is none the less necessary, for objective reality has itself too an unquestionable title to what is essential in the character of its appearance.

(γγ) We may extend the reach of poetry yet further and we shall still find that the demand to be met is the same. In other words, all that the art of poetry represents in external local condition, characterization, actions, passions, situations, conflicts, events, and human destiny, all this material is borrowed, far more so in fact than is generally credited, from the facts of life itself. This being so, poetry here too is on the historical arena; and, consequently, its deviations or variations of such data must, in this field also, find their point of departure in the rational core of the facts in question and the demand of the art to discover for this ideal essence a form that exhibits it with greatest adequacy and life. And this must not be sought for in the poverty of a superficial knowledge, an inability to penetrate what is really vital in fact, or in the moods of caprice and with the

80

craving after the quaint or perverse ingenuities of a spurious originality.

(β) And further, as already stated, oratory is allied to prose on account of the practical end which is thereby proposed, and, to carry out which, it is forced to admit to the full the claims of utility.

(αα) In this respect poetry must take care to detach itself from any end of this kind outside Art's domain, and the claim of artistic enjoyment simply; that it may not fall into the sphere of prose. For if any purpose of this sort is made to appear of essential importance, as part of the entire conception and presentation, the composition at once descends from that loftier region, in whose free atmosphere it floats on its own account and on no other, and is drawn into that of relation merely. As a result of this we have either a breach made between the fundamental aim of art and the ends of ulterior intendments; or art is used as a means simply, contradicts its substantive notion, and becomes the menial of utility. The edifying effusions of many church hymns are of this character. Particular ideas are simply admitted on religious grounds, and receive a style of composition which is alien to the beauty of poetry. And, speaking generally, poetry, simply as poetry, has no right to edify in a *religious* sense, or at least *exclusively* in this sense. If it does so we are carried into a region, which no doubt possesses relationship with both poetry and art, but is for all that distinct from it. We may say the same of teaching generally, ethical instruction, political treatises, or writings of all kinds written for our momentary recreation and enjoyment. All these are objects, to whose attainment the art of poetry is, or can be more than any other, contributory. But such contributions must not enter into the purpose, if the spirit of the work is to assert itself freely in its own character. In the poetical effort it is only what is really poetic, eliminated from all that is foreign to this quality, which must remain paramount as the end proposed and accomplished. And in fact such ulterior aims as the above can be carried out far more appropriately by quite other means.

(*ββ*) The art of poetry, however, from the converse point of view, should strive to assert no absolute and isolated position; it ought, as a part of life itself, to enter freely into life. Already in the first part of this inquiry we found how many points of contact there were between art and ordinary existence, whose content and phenomenal appearance are repeated in its content and form. In poetry this vital relation to actual existence and its specific circumstances, private or public events, appears with most obvious variety in the so-called *poems d'occasion*. With a broader interpretation of the expression we may define as such most poetic compositions; in the more narrow and correct meaning of the term, however, we should restrict it to those productions whose origin is traceable to a single event of present time, which it is the express aim of the poet to emphasize, adorn, and celebrate. In this weaving together of the actual threads of life, however, poetry tends once more to decline to a position of dependence; it is therefore by no means unusual for writers on aesthetic to attach a purely subordinate value to poetry of this class in general, although as to a part of it, notably in the case of the lyric, we find here the most famous compositions.

(*γγ*) The question consequently arises by virtue of what poetry may be enabled to still maintain its independence even in the conflict above described. The answer is simple. It must regard and assert the occasional facts it borrows from life not as its essential aim, while it is itself merely accepted as a means. Rather the reverse process is the right one, which absorbs the material of such reality within its own substance, and informs and elaborates the same conformably to the claims of an unfettered imagination. In other words poetry has nothing to do with the accidental or incidental fact as such. This material supplies the external opportunity, that is the stimulus which prompts the poet to draw upon his own profounder penetration and more transparent mode of presentment: by this means he creates from his own resources, as something newborn, that which, without such mediation, would have, in the plain and blunt particular case, wholly failed to impress us with the free spirit he communicates.

(γ) In conclusion then we may affirm that every genuine work of poetry is an essentially infinite organism.[16] In content rich, it unfolds this content under a mode of appearance which is adapted to it. It is permeated with a principle of unity, but not one referable to the form of utility, which subordinates the particular to itself in an abstract relation, but rather one that absorbs the same in the singularity relevant to one identical and entirely vital self-consistency, in which the whole, without any visible intention, is sphered within one rounded and essentially self-enclosed completeness. It is indeed replete with the *materia* of the visible world, but is not on that account placed, either in relation to its content or determinate existence, under a condition of dependence to any one circle of life. Rather it freely creates out of its own plenitude, striving to clothe the ideal notion of its material in its genuine manifestation as truth, and to bring the world of external fact into reconciled accord with its own most ideal substance.

3. THE CREATIVE IMPULSE OF THE POET[17]

I have already discussed at considerable length, in the first part of this work, the talent and genius, the enthusiasm and originality of the artist. I will consequently merely touch upon one or two points in the present reference to the art of poetry which appear of importance, if we contrast this activity as effective here with that operative in the plastic arts and music.

(a) The architect, sculptor, painter and musician have to deal with an entirely concrete and sensuous material, in and through which each has to elaborate his creations. The limitations of this material condition the specific form that the type of the conception no less than the mode of artistic execution assume. The more fixed and predetermined the general lines of his definition are upon which the artist has to concentrate himself, the more specialized becomes the talent required for the assertion of the same in any one and no other mode of presentment; and we may add in the powers of technical execution which accompany it. The talents adapted to the poetic art, regarding the same from the point of view of an ideal envisagement in a specific *materia*, is subordinated in a less degree to such conditions; it is consequently more open to universal practice, and in this respect more independent. The need here at least is merely that of a gift for imaginative creation. Its limitation is confined merely to this, namely, that for the reason that this art is expressed in language, it has to guard itself on the one hand from deliberate rivalry with external objects in their sensuous completeness, in the form, that is, where we find the plastic artist apprehends his subject-matter in its external configuration: and, from a further point of view, it is unable to rest in the unspoken ideality, the emotional tones of which constitute the realm of music. In these respects the problem proposed to the poet, if we contrast him with artists in other arts, is at once more *facile* and more *difficult* It is more easy, because, although the poet, in the poetical elaboration of speech, must possess a trained

84

talent, he is spared the relatively more manifold task of triumph over technical difficulties necessary in the other arts. It is more difficult because, just in proportion as poetry is less able to complete the objective envisagement, it is compelled to seek some compensation for this loss on the side of sense in the genuine core of Art's own ideality, in the depth of imagination and a really artistic mode of conception.

(*b*) For this reason the poet is, in the *second* place, constrained to penetrate into all the wealth of the spiritual content, and to lay bare to the vision of mind what is concealed in its depths. For however much in the other arts, too, the ideal must shine forth through its corporeal manifestation, and does so in life itself shine forth, yet the medium of speech remains that most open to intelligence, and the means most adequate to its revelation. It is the one medium able to grasp and declare everything whatever that flows through or is present in consciousness, whether regarded in its ascent or profundity. In consequence of this the poet finds himself confronted with difficulties which the other arts are not called upon to overcome or satisfy to the like degree. In other words, for the very reason that poetry is actually operative in the world of idea or imagination itself, and is not concerned with fashioning for its images an objective existence independent of such ideality, it is placed in an element or sphere in which the religious, scientific and everyday consciousness are active; it must therefore take care to make no excursion into the domain or mode of conception proper to any of these, or to get mixed up with them. No doubt in the case of every art we find points of contact with other arts. Artistic creation of every kind proceeds from *one* mind or spirit, which comprehends in itself all spheres of self-conscious life. But with the other arts the distinction of conception in each case is in its mode complete, for the reason that this, in its ideal creation, persists throughout in permanent relation to the execution of its images in a definite sensuous material, and consequently is absolutely distinct, no less from the forms of the religious consciousness, than it is from the thinking of science and the intelligence of ordinary life. Poetry, on the contrary, avails itself, in its manner of objective communication, of the very means adopted in these spheres of mental activity, that is to say, human speech; it finds itself, consequently, otherwise placed than are the plastic arts and music, which occupy a different field of conception and expression.

(c) *Thirdly*, we have the final demand made upon the poet for the most profound and manifold transfusion of the subject-matter of his creations with the animating soul of life, because it is his art which is capable of absorbing most profoundly the entire fulness of the spiritual content. The plastic artist, in a similar way, must apply himself to a transfusion of ideal expression in the *external form* of architectonic, plastic and the forms peculiar to painting. The musician must likewise rivet his attention on the *inner soul* concentrated in emotion and passion and their outpouring in melodic expression. In both cases the artist must be steeped in the most ideal intention and substance of his content. But the sphere of the poet's creative activity extends yet further, for the reason that he has not merely to elaborate an ideal world of soul-life and the self-conscious mind. He has, in addition, to discover for this ideal realm an external mode of envisagement fitted thereto, a mode by virtue of which that ideal totality shines through in more irresistible perfection than is possible in the case of other arts. It is incumbent upon him to know human existence, both as soul-life and objective life, to receive into his inmost being the full breadth of the world and its shows, and to have felt through it there, penetrated, enlarged, deepened and revealed to himself all it implies. Only after that, and in order that he may find it in his power to create, as from his own spiritual experience outwards, a free whole, —ay, even in the case where he restricts his effort to a comparatively narrow and particular range, —he must have liberated himself from all embarrassment with his subject-matter, whether of a *technical*[18] character or otherwise, able in short to survey the ideal and external aspects thereof with the same free glance. From the point of view of *instinctive* creative vigour[19] we may in this respect pre-eminently praise the Mahomedan poets of the East. The starting-point in such compositions is a freedom which, even in the moment of passion, remains aloof from such passion, and in all the variety of its interests retains exclusively throughout the *one* substance as its veritable core, in contrast to which everything else appears small and transitory, and nothing of finality is left either to passion or lust. This is a philosophical outlook, a relation of spirit to the facts of the world, which comes more readily to age than youth. For in old age no doubt the interests of life are still present; but they are not there with the urgency of youthful passion, but rather in the guise of shadows, and to this extent are more readily conformable to ideal relations such as Art demands. In opposition to the ordinary view that youth with its warmth and vigour is the fairest season for poetic creation, we may rather, at least from this point of view, maintain just the opposite, that the ripest season belongs to the autumn of old age, provided that it is able to preserve its energies of outlook and emotion. It is only to a blind old man, Homer, that we ascribe those miraculous poems which have come down to us under that name. And we may also affirm of our Goethe that only in old age, after he had fully succeeded in liberating his genius from all restricting

87

limitations of sense, that he gave us his most exalted creations.[20]

———

[1] That is, the essential notion (*Begriff*) of Art generally.

[2] *Substantiellen*, *i.e.*, the form that most corresponds to its essence.

[3] *Theoretisch.* Hegel doubtless has the Greek word in his mind. It is a *Bildung* for the mind rather than with a view to action. It assumes contemplation rather than volition.

[4] It is not quite clear whether Hegel means by *Bedürfniss* the need of spiritual life, or the profounder demand of reality. It might stand for either.

[5] That is, the *Vernünft*.

[6] *Das individualisirte Vernünftige*, *i.e.*, reason as realized in concrete personality.

[7] *In seiner Gediegenheit und schlagenden Fassung. Gediegenheit* here thorough grasp. *Schlagenden* may possibly mean arresting character of the conception rather than definite, precise.

[8] That is, the notion.

[9] By *aus dem Geiste* it is quite possible that there is no reference to individual genius. In that case the translation would be "in terms of human intelligence," *i.e.*, from the resources of human reason.

[10] This seems to be the meaning of *die Sache der Zeit*.

[11] Lit., "They do not come forth from self-substantive and immediately free vitality (Lebendigkeit)." *Lebendigkeit* is here the ideal and creative force or bond of soul-life as above described.

[12] The German word would imply here an interpretation of symbolic or at least ideal significance.

[13] This I presume is the general meaning of the sentence: *Asien aber, das er besiegt, ist in der vielfachen Willkühr seiner Einzelnen Völkerschaften nur ein zufälliges Ganzes.*

[14] *Ein Sollen.*

[15] It is possible that too much stress is laid on this line of difference. The fundamental difference between oratory and poetry is that of form. At least it can hardly be denied that the power of the orator to meet the demands of local conditions is a vital feature of his art, that in this respect a Demosthenes is greater than Burke. It is surely a mistake to assume that such limitations in themselves or necessarily are an obstacle to creative genius. It is rather the sign of supreme oratorical power that it can mould them and command them in conjunction with its more majestic spirit. In this lies an essential part of the art itself, just as a sculptor or a painter, such as Tintoret in the S. Rocco Scuola, dominates the defects of local condition.

[16] Infinite, that is, not in the temporal sense, but as a complete and self-realized whole.

[17] Hegel calls it "the poetising subjectivity"; that is, the personal activity essential to poetic composition.

[18] *Practischen.*

[19] This appears to be the meaning of *des Naturells.*

[20] This is perhaps less true of Goethe than it is of either Milton or Shakespeare. It is possible that Hegel thought more highly of the second part of "Faust" as art than do the majority of modern critics. But the truth is there, if subject to a good deal of qualification in respect to certain aspects of poetry. As Meredith says:

"Verily now is our season of seed,
Now in our Autumn."

And Meredith was not one to do less than justice to the superb Dream of imaginative youth.

II

THE EXPRESSION OF POETRY

The field of vision which first will occupy our attention, but the boundless expanse of which we can only traverse with a few general observations, is that which concerns the poetic generally, the content no less than the mode of conception and organic association adapted to the poetic work of art. This background will help to emphasize the *second* aspect of our subject, which is *poetic expression* more strictly, the idea in the ideal objectivity of the word appropriated by it as symbol of the image, and the melodious vehicle of its speech.

We may infer the nature of the relation between poetic expression generally and the mode of presentment proper to the other arts from our previous examination of the characteristics of the poetic art. Language and the sounds of words are neither a symbol of spiritual conceptions, nor an adequate mode of projecting ideality under the condition of spatial objectivity in the sense applicable to the corporeal forms of sculpture and painting, nor yet an intonation in musical sound of the entire soul. They are an abstract *sign* simply. As the vehicle of the poetic image or conception, however, it is necessary that this side also, in theory no less than deliberate elaboration, appear as distinct from the kind of expression appropriate to prose.

We may for this purpose emphasize with more detail three main points of distinction.

Our *first* point is this, that although poetic expression is throughout exclusively embodied in articulate words, and apparently as such is simply related to human speech, yet in so far as the words themselves are merely abstract signs representative of *ideas,* the true source of poetic speech is not to be discovered in the selection of particular words, and in the manner they are associated in sentences and elaborated phrases, nor in harmonious rhythm, rhyme and so forth, but in the type of *conception* employed. We have, in short, to look for our point of departure for the constructive use of expression in the choice of the idea or image, find our first and foremost question will be what kind of conception will give us an expression suitable to poetry. *Secondly*, however, it remains the fact that the imaginative idea essentially pertinent to poetry is exclusively made objective in *language*. We have consequently to investigate the expression of speech according to its purely verbal aspect, in the light of which poetic words are distinguishable from those of prose, poetic phrases from those of our ordinary life and prosaic thought, abstracting in the first instance the mere sound of them to our sense of hearing.

Finally, we have to recognize the fact that poetry is a mode of articulate speech, the sounding word, which in its temporal duration no less than its actual sound, must receive a definite configuration, one that implies the presence of time-measure, rhythm, melodious sound and rhyme.

I. THE POETIC CONCEPT OR IDEA

What in the plastic arts the sensuous visible *form* expressed by means of stone and colour is, or what in the realm of music animating strains of harmony and melody are, this— we must repeatedly insist on the fact—can only be, in respect to poetic expression—the idea or image itself. The force of the poet's creation centres consequently, in the fact that the art moulds a content in an ideal medium, and without bringing before us the actual forms of external Nature and the progressions of musical sound; by doing so, therefore, it translates the objective presence accepted by the other arts into an ideal form, which Spirit or intelligence expresses for the imagination under the mode which is and must remain that of our conscious life.

A distinction of this very character was already insisted on when we had occasion previously to establish a distinction

91

between the earliest type, of poetry and its later modes of reconstruction from the data of prose.

(*a*) Imaginative poetry in its *origin* is not as yet a consciously distinct form from those extremes of ordinary conscious life, one of which brings everything to vision under the mode of immediate and therewith contingent singularity, without grasping the ideal essence implied therein, and the manifestation of the same; while the other, in one direction, differentiates concrete existence into its various characteristics, making use of abstract generalization, and in another avails itself of the scientific faculty as the correlating and connecting focus of such abstractions. The idea is only poetical in so far as it holds these extremes in unviolable mediation, and thereby is able to maintain a position of genuine stability midway between the vision of ordinary consciousness and that of abstract thought.

In general terms we may define the poetic imagination as *plastic*[1] in so far as it brings before our vision concrete reality rather than the abstract generalization, and in the place of contingent existence an appearance of such a kind that we recognize what is substantive immediately in it by virtue of its embodiment itself and its individuality, and as inseparable from it, and by virtue of this are able to grasp the concrete conception-of the fact in question no less than its determinate existence as one and the same vital whole reposing in the ideal medium of the imagination. In this respect we find a fundamental distinction between that whereof the plastic or constructive idea is the source and all that is otherwise made vivid to us through other means of expression. The same truth will appear to us, if we analyse what we mean, by mere reading. We understand what the letters mean, which are indicative points for articulate utterance, by the mere act of sight, and without being further obliged to listen to their sound. Only the illiterate reader will find it necessary to speak aloud the separate words that he may understand their sense. But in the case of poetry just what seems to be here the mark of stupidity is an indication of beauty and excellence. Poetry is not satisfied with an abstract effort of apprehension, nor does it bring objects before us as we find them in the form of reflection and in the unimaginative generalization of our memory. It helps us to approach the essential notion in its positive existence, the generic as clothed in its specific individuality. In the view of ordinary common sense I understand by language, both in its impression on my hearing or sight, the meaning in its immediacy, in other words, without receiving its image before the mind. The phrases, for instance, "the sun," or "in the morning," possess each of them no doubt a distinct sense; but neither the Dawn or the Sun are themselves made present to our vision. When, however, the poet says: "When now the dawning Eos soared heavenwards with rosy fingers," here without question we have the concrete fact brought home to us. The poetical expression adds, however, yet more, for it associates with the object recognized a vision of the same, or we should rather say the purely abstract relation of knowledge vanishes, and the real definition takes its place. In the same way take the phrase, "Alexander conquered the Persian empire." Here, no doubt, so far as content is concerned, we have a concrete conception; the many-sided definition of it, however, expressed here in the word "victory," is concentrated in a featureless and pure abstraction, which fails to image before us anything of the appearance and reality of the exploit accomplished by Alexander. This truth applies to every kind of similar expression. We recognize the bare fact; but it remains pale and dun, and from the point of view of individual existence undetermined and abstract. The poetic conception consequently embraces the fulness of the objective phenomenon as it essentially exists, and is able to

93

elaborate the same united with the essential ideality of the fact in a creative totality.

What follows as a primary result of this is that it is of interest to the imagination to *linger* near the external characteristics of the fact, to the extent at least that it seeks to express the same in its positive reality, deems this as essentially worthy of contemplation and insists on this very attitude.

Poetry is consequently in its manner of expression *descriptive* Description is, however, not the right word for it. We are, in fact, accustomed to accept as descriptive, and in contrast to the abstract definition, in which a content is otherwise brought home to our intelligence, much that the poet passes by, so that from the point of view of ordinary speech poetic composition can only appear as a roundabout way and a useless superfluity. The poet must, however, manage to bring his imagination to bear upon the explication of the actual phenomenon he is attempting to depict with a vital interest.[2] In this way, for instance, Homer adds a descriptive epithet to every hero. So Achilles is the swift-footed, the Achaeans bright-greaved, Hector as of the glancing helm, Agamemnon the lord of peoples, and so forth. The name is no doubt descriptive of a personality, but the name alone brings nothing further to our vision. To have some distinct idea of this we require further attributes. We have in fact similar epithets attached by Homer to other objects, which are essential to our vision of the epic, such as sea, ships, sword and others, epithets which seize and place before us an essential quality of the particular object, depicting it more precisely, and which enable us to apprehend the fact in its concrete appearance.

Secondly, we must distinguish such reconstruction of actual facts from definition *wholly imagined*. This offers a further point of view for discussion. The real image merely places before us the fact in the reality it possesses. The expression of the poet's imagination, on the contrary, does not restrict itself to the object in its immediate appearance; it proceeds to depict something over and above this, by means of which the significance of the former picture is made clear to our mind. Metaphors, illustrations, similes become in this way an essential feature of poetic creation. We have thereby a kind of veil attached to the content, which concerns us, and which, by its difference from it, serves in part as an embellishment, and in part as a further unfolding of it, though it necessarily fails to be complete, for the reason that it only applies to a specific aspect of this content. The passage in which Homer compares Ajax, on his refusing to fly, to an obstinate ass is an illustration. To a pre-eminent degree oriental poetry possesses this splendour and wealth in pictorial comparisons. There are two main reasons of this. First, its symbolic point of view makes such a search for aspects of affinity inevitable, and in the universality of its centres of significance it offers a large field of concrete phenomena capable of comparison; secondly, on account of the sublimity of its predominant outlook there is a tendency to apply the entire variety of all that is most brilliant and glorious in its motley show to the embellishment of the One Supreme, which is held before the mind as the sole One to be exalted. This object of the imagination, moreover, is not to be apprehended as merely the work of fanciful caprice or comparison, possessing as such nothing in it essentially actual and present. On the contrary the transmutation of all particular existence into further existence in this central idea grasped and clothed by the imagination is rather to be understood as equivalent to the assertion that there is nothing else essentially present, nothing that otherwise can put forward a claim to substantive reality. The belief in the world as we apprehend it with the vision of ordinary common sense is converted into a belief in the imagination, for which the only world that verily exists is that which the poetic consciousness has created. Conversely we have the romantic imagination, which is ready enough to express itself in metaphor, because in its vision what is external is for the essentially secluded life of the soul only accepted as something incidental, something that is unable adequately to express its own reality. To reclothe this consequently unreal externality with profound emotion, with all the fulness of detail envisioned, or with the play of humour upon the conjunction of such opposites is an impulse, which constrains and charms romantic poetry to ever novel discoveries. The object of importance here is not so much to make the fact clear and distinct to the vision; on the contrary the metaphorical employment of these outlying phenomena is itself the aim proposed. The emotion of the poet concentrates itself as the centre, which the environment enriches with its wealth; it absorbs this as part of itself, adapts it with genius and wit to its adornment, steeps it in its own life, and finds in this movement to and fro, this elaboration and self-reflection of its creation its own source of delight.

(b) *Secondly*, we have the contrast present between the poetic mode of conception and that of *prose*. The thing of importance in the latter case is not that which is imaged, but the significance as such which constitutes the content. It is on account of the latter that the idea or image becomes a mere means to bring the content before the mind. The composition of prose is therefore neither compelled to place the more detailed reality of its objects before our vision, nor to summon before us, as is the case with the metaphorical mode of expression previously described, another idea which carries us beyond the immediate object to be expressed. No doubt it is also necessary in prose to indicate in firm and distinct outlines the positive appearance of objects; but this is so not on account of their figurative character,[3] but to meet a specific and practical purpose. Generally speaking we may therefore affirm *accuracy* to be from one point of view the ruling principle of prose composition, and from another a *clear definition* and intelligibility of statement. In contrast to this the language of metaphor and imagery is in general and relatively less clear and more inaccurate. For in that mode of direct expression, such as we have presented by our first form of the poetic conception, the fact in its simplicity is carried away from our immediate apprehension of it as a mere object into the actual world of concrete fact, and we have to recognize it as a part of this, while in that second and more oblique form some phenomenon of affinity merely and one even aloof from the essential significance of our subject is made present to us. We do not, therefore, wonder that prosaic commentators of our poets have no easy task when they seek to separate, by means of their scientific analyses, the image from the significance, to extract their abstract content from the vital form, and thereby expound poetic modes of composition to the prosaic mind.

In poetry this accuracy, this rigour in unfolding the content as we find it in its simplicity, is not alone the essential principle. On the contrary, though prose is forced to confine its ideas on parallel lines of almost mathematical precision with the nature of its content, poetry introduces us to a different sphere altogether, that is, the *visible appearance* of the content itself, or other natural phenomena related to it. For it is just this objective reality which in poetry ought to appear, and while unquestionably from one point of view revealing that content, yet at the same time from another it has to liberate itself from the purely abstract content, it being essentially an object of the art to direct attention to its actual existence in the visible world, and to arouse the interest of mind in the forms of life itself.

(c) If these three essential requirements of poetry are conditioned by an age, in which the accuracy of the prosaic mind is become the ordinary type of conscious life, the art, so far as its figurative characteristics are concerned, is placed in a more difficult position. That is to say, in such an epoch the type of penetration exercised by conscious life is generally a separation of emotion and the ordinary outlook from scientific thought, which either converts the ideal and external material of feeling and perception into a stimulus of knowledge and volition simply, or into a plastic medium subservient to observation and action. In such a sphere poetry calls for energies of more definite purpose in order that it may free itself from the abstraction of the prevailing mental attitude and enter into the world of concrete life. Where, however, such a goal is realized, not only do we find that this breach between thinking, which makes for generalization, and perception and feeling, which grasp the particular, vanishes, but these last-mentioned modes of conscious life are, together with their subject-matter and content, at the same time freed from their exclusive relation of service; and the process culminates in a victorious reconciliation of such modes with what is essential universality. Inasmuch, however, as both the modes of poetic and prosaic thought and general outlook are united in one and the same conscious life, we find in it indications of trouble and derangement, even possibly an actual conflict between the two, one which, as the poetry of our times testifies, only genius of the highest order is able successfully to deal with. Added to this there are other collateral hindrances, which I only propose to define now, and that briefly, in their relation to the figurative aspect already discussed. In other words, if the prosaic intelligence takes

98

the place of that creative imagination which previously obtained, then and in that case the rejuvenescence of the poetic faculty, both in all that is associated with the positive expression of facts and what is metaphorical, readily offers the semblance of artificiality, which even where it falls short of actual purpose, is only with great difficulty reconciled with that directness of immediate truth which is demanded. Much in fact which was still fresh in former times, through repeated usage, and the habits thus originated, has itself become gradually a custom and a part of prosaic life. Moreover, where poetry strives after novelties in its composition, we often find that, despite of itself, in its figurative expressions and descriptions, even where it escapes the charge of exaggeration and an excess of such material, it none the less leaves an impression of artificiality, over nicety, a straining after what is piquant and select, work incompatible with a simple and healthy outlook and state of feeling. Such work tends to regard objects in an artificial light and reckons on mere effect. Consequently it will not permit their natural lighting and colour. Defects of this nature are still more obvious in cases where, as a rule, the metaphorical type of imaginative composition is exchanged[4] for the more direct, and our poet is driven to outbid the forces of prose; and, in order to assert an originality, plunges into the subtleties of or the fishing for effects which have still some appearance of freshness.

2. VERBAL EXPRESSION

Inasmuch as the poetic imagination is distinct in its operation from that of all other artists in virtue of the fact that it necessarily clothes its images in words, and communicates the same through human *speech*, it becomes imperative that throughout this process it should endeavour to co-ordinate all its ideas, in the form which with most completeness will disclose them, through the means articulate speech thus places at its disposal. And, in short, we may affirm that the poetic content only assumes the form of poetry in its restricted sense after it has been actually embodied and rounded off in the vehicle of words.

This literary aspect of the art of poetry would readily supply us with a boundless field of discursive observation and logical argument, which I must, however, pass over in order that I may reserve space for more weighty problems which lie before us. I merely propose, therefore, to touch very briefly on a few fundamental points.

(*a*) Human art should in all its associations place us on a ground quite other than that we confront in ordinary life, or indeed in our religious consciousness, active life, or the speculations of philosophy. This is possible on the side of literary or verbal expression only in so far as another mode of speech is adopted than that obtaining in those other spheres. Art has therefore not only, from one point of view, to avoid that in its instrument of expression which will fail to rise above the trivialities of ordinary speech and ordinary prose, but it must, furthermore, avoid falling into the tone and manner of religious edification and philosophical research. Above all it must keep aloof from the precise analyses and *methods* of the scientific faculty, the categories of pure thinking as we find these illustrated in the logical forms of judgment and deduction. These at once remove art from the imaginative realm to another region altogether. But in all these respects it still remains a difficult matter to determine the lines of boundary on which we may actually affirm that poetry ends and prose begins. And in fact we may admit absolute precision and confidence of statement to be impossible from the nature of the case.

(*b*) If we pass now to a discussion of the particular *means* which poetic-speech can appropriate as instrumental to its task the following points appear to me pregnant and suggestive.

(α) *First*, we find particular *words* and exclamations[5] that are obviously peculiar to poetry, whether they be used to ennoble it, or to introduce the vulgarity and excess of comedy. We find a similar novelty in the specific collocation of various words or turns of expression. In such a field poetry is no doubt entitled on the one hand to borrow from an obsolete nomenclature, obsolete at least in everyday speech, and on the other to declare itself as pre-eminently an innovator, moulding novel modes of speech. Such a field, provided only the vital genius of the language is preserved, supplies material for astonishing boldness of invention.

(β) *Secondly*, we have the problem of verbal order. It is here that we meet with those so-called figures of speech, in so far as, we should add, the same have reference to verbal embodiment as such. The use of these, however, easily degenerates into rhetoric and declamation in the bad sense of these terms; the vitality of individual character is destroyed where we find that such forms substitute a fixed and artificial mode of expression for the genuine impulse of feeling or passion, and thereby offer the very opposite to the personal, laconic and broken utterance required, the utterance whose emotional depth is incapable of saying much, and for this reason, in romantic poetry especially, is of great effect as a presentment of suppressed[6] states of soul. But generally speaking we may admit that the relative order of words is an instrument of the external form of poetry of quite extraordinary resource.

(γ) *Thirdly*, we have still to draw attention to the construction of *periods*,[7] which essentially embrace all the other aspects of composition and which, by means of either their simple or more involved course, their restless

101

dislocations and distortions, or their quick onward motion, their acceleration and their flood contribute so materially to the reflection of such soul experience. And, in short, it is essential that the external presentment in speech should mirror and assume a character similar to the ideality of such experience in all its variety.

(c) In the *application* of the means of speech above considered it will be useful to distinguish once more the several stages of poetic thought to which they correspond and to which we drew attention when we considered the nature of poetic conception or composition.

(α) Poetic diction can, in the first instance, appear with real vitality among a people and at an epoch when the general speech is not as yet perfected, but in fact only by virtue of its poetry receives its real development. At such a time the utterance of the poet, as generally expressive of soul-life, is from the first a real novelty, which stirs admiration on its own account by revealing in its speech what remained previously unveiled. This new creation appears as the marvel of a gift and personal power. The weight of custom has not as yet fallen upon it. It enables that which is buried in the depths of the human heart for the first time to freely unfold itself before the amazement of men. Under such conditions it is the native force of the expression, the creation of the fact of speech, not so much the varied and craftful elaboration of the same, which is the main point. Diction here remains exceedingly simple. In such early times it is indeed impossible that we should have either much fluency of idea or any varied versatility of expression. The subject-matter of such poetry is depicted with an artless directness, which has not yet attained the delicate nuances, transitions, mediatory matter and other advantages of a later artistic culture. In such an age the poet is in fact the first person to give an utterance to the national voice, to express ideas in speech, and thereby to encourage the imagination itself. Speech is, if we may so express it, not yet inseparable from ordinary life, and poetry can still freely, with an effect of freshness, avail itself of all that in later times, as the speech of common life, gradually is severed from art. In this respect, for example, Homer's type of expression is to the modern man barely distinguishable from ordinary speech. For every idea we have the direct word[8]; metaphorical expressions are comparatively rare; and although the poem is composed with a close attention to detail, the speech itself remains very simple indeed. In a similar way Dante was able to create for his own nation a vital form of poetic expression, and asserted in this, as in other respects, the dauntless energy of his creative genius.

(β) When, however—this is a *further* point—the circle of ideas enlarges with the appearance of methodical modes of thought the ways in which idea is associated with idea increase, and in this very process the ability to use it increases also, and the expression of speech is elaborated in all the fluency of which it is capable. When this is so the position of poetry on the side of verbal expression is wholly changed. In other words, we have now a nation possessing the fully developed prose speech of everyday life, and poetic expression must now, in order to retain its interest, swerve aside from ordinary parlance, and receive a resurrection under the re-moulding energy of genius.[9] In our daily life the contingency of the moment is the motive of speech. In the creation of a work of art, however, we must have deliberate circumspection[10] in the place of instantaneous feeling; even the spirit of enthusiasm must be judiciously restrained. The creation of genius should be permitted to unfold itself from the artistic repose,[11] and become informed under the prevailing temper of an intelligence[12] that surveys the whole with clarity. In former times this

103

spirit of concentration and tranquillity is to be inferred from the fact and utterance of poetry itself. In a more recent age, on the contrary, the nature of the composition and execution has itself to enforce the distinction which obtains between the expression of poetry and prose. In this respect poems which belong to epochs in which we find already an elaborated prose diction differ essentially from those of times and peoples in which the art originates.

The executive talent of a poet can be carried so far in this direction that the elaboration of formal expression becomes the main thing, and the aim is less directed to ideal truth than to formal construction, a polished elegance and mere effect of the composition under its literary aspect. We have then a situation, in which, as already observed, rhetoric and declamation are elaborated in a manner destructive to the ideal vitality of the poetic spirit. The formative intelligence asserts itself under the principle of *purposiveness*, and a selfconsciously regulated art disturbs that more genuine effect, which ought to present the appearance of ingenuous openness and simplicity. Entire nations have, with the rarest exceptions, failed to produce any type of poetic creation other than this rhetorical one. The Latin language, even in Cicero, still preserves a genuine ring of naïveté and naturalness. With the Latin poets, however, such as Virgil, Horace and the rest, we already feel that Art is to a real extent nothing but artifice, elaboration of effect on its own account. We recognize a prosaic content, which is merely set off with an external embellishment. We find a poet who, in the absence of original genius, endeavours to discover, in the sphere of literary versatility and rhetoric effects, some compensation for that which in genuine power and effect of creation and composition he fails to possess. France too, in the so-called classical period of its literature, has produced poetry very similar, a poetical style to which didactic poems and satires are singularly appropriate. Rhetorical figures of speech in all their variety are here in their rightful place. The exposition remains for all that, as a whole, prosaic; and the literary expression is at its best rich in image and embellishment, much in the style of Herder's or Schiller's diction. These last-mentioned writers, however, availed themselves of this style of literary expression mainly in the interests of prose composition; and by the weightiness of their reflections and the happy use of such a style knew how to win both a critical assent and a hearty approval. The Spanish poets also are not wholly free from the ostentation inseparable from the too self-conscious diction of art. And, as a general rule, Southern nations, such as the Spaniards and the Italians, and previously to them the Mohammedan Arabs and Persians, are conspicuous for a wealth and tedious prolixity of image and simile. With the ancients, more especially in the case of Homer, the flow of expression is characterized by smoothness and tranquillity. With the nations above mentioned, on the contrary, we have a vision of life gushing forth[13] in a flood which, even where the emotions are in other respects at rest, is ever intent upon expatiation, and owing to this expressly volitional effort of the will is dominated by an intelligence which at one time is visible in abrupt parentheses, at another in subtle generalization, at another in the playful conjunction of its sallies of wit and humour.

(γ) Genuine poetic expression in short is as far removed from all rhetorical declamation as above described as it is from all ostentation and witty conceits of diction, in so far at least as such defects do injury to the ideal truth of Nature, and the claims of the content are forgotten in the verbal form and expression of the composition. It is, however, possible, despite of this, that the author's free enjoyment in his work declare itself with real beauty. In a

105

word that aspect of the composition we define as formal diction ought not to be treated on its own and independent account alone, or as an aspect of first and even exclusive importance. And, generally speaking, in this analysis of the composition of poetry under its formative aspect, we repeat that what is the product of careful thought must not lose the appearance of genuine spontaneity: everything should impress us as though it had of itself blossomed from the ideal germ or heart of the subject-matter.

3. VERSIFICATION

Our *third* and final aspect of poetic expression is necessitated by the fact that the imagination of the poet does not merely invest ideas in words, but does so in the form of the uttered speech; and by doing so he consequently enters the domain wherein our senses are made aware of the actual sounds and music of speech. We are thus introduced to versification. Versified prose may give us verses, but that is not necessarily poetry. We have a parallel case in the merely poetic expression of a composition in other respects prosaic with its result of poetic prose simply. Yet for all that metre or rhyme is an essential demand of poetry, bringing, as it were, a perfume of its own to the senses; nay, it is even more essential than a richly imaginative and so-called beautiful diction.

And in truth the artistic elaboration of this sensuous medium[14] unfolds to us—it is the very demand of the art itself—another realm, another field, which we only really enter after having left behind us the prose of ordinary life, whether viewed as action or as literary composition. The poet is thereby compelled to move in a literary atmosphere outside the boundary of everyday speech, and to shape his compositions with an exclusive regard to the rules and requirements of Art. It is therefore only a superficial theory which would banish all versification on the ground that it contradicts natural expression. It is true that Lessing, in his hostility to the false pathos of the French Alexandrine metre, attempted, more particularly in tragedy, to introduce a form of prose speech as most appropriate. Both Schiller and Goethe have, in the more stormy works of their youth, and under the natural impulse of compositions carrying a greater surfeit of content, adopted the same principle. But Lessing himself, in his Nathan, finally returns once more to the iambic. And in the same way with his Don Carlos Schiller deserted the old path. Goethe too was so little satisfied with the earlier prosaic treatment of his Iphigeneia and Tasso, that he transferred them to art's more proper domain, remoulding them both from the point of view of expression and prosody in that purer form, wherein these compositions continue and will continue to excite our admiration.

No doubt the artificiality of the verse measure or the recurrent echoes of rhyme has the appearance of an unyielding[15] bond between spiritual ideas and the sensuous medium, more rigorous indeed than colour in painting. External objects and the human form are coloured in Nature, and the colourless is an arbitrary abstraction. The idea, on the contrary, in association with the sounds of human speech, which are employed in the wholly capricious symbols of their utterance, possess only a distant or no ideal thread of connection at all. This being so, the exacting demand of the prosodical rules will very readily appear as a fetter to the imagination, in virtue of which it is no longer possible for the poet to communicate his ideas in the precise form in which they float upon his phantasy. The inference is natural that although the stream of rhythm and the music of rhyme exercises upon us as an unquestionable fascination, it is nevertheless not unfrequently and too much so the demand of this very charm to our senses that the finest poetic feeling and idea should be sacrificed. But the objection for all that will not hold water. In other words it is not true that versification is simply an obstruction to spontaneous movement. A genuine artistic talent throughout moves in its sensuous material as in its native element, which so far from being oppressive or a hindrance acts as a stimulus and a support. And in fact we find that all really great poets move with freedom and confidence in the measure, rhythm or rhyme they have created; and it is only when they are translated that our artistic sense is frequently pained or shocked at the attempt to retrace their rhythm and melody. Moreover it is part of the liberality of the art that the very circumstances of the restraint, involving much change, concentration or expansion of the ideas expressed, should suggest to our poet new thoughts, incidents and creations, which, apart from such difficulties, had never crossed his mind. But in truth quite apart from this relative advantage this sensuous and determinate form of being—in the case of poetry the melodious chain of words—is once for all essential to art. It is absolutely necessary that the result should not remain in the formless and undefined stream that we have in the immediate contingency of ordinary conversation. It must appear in the vital design and elaboration of art. And although this form no doubt in the music of poetry may sound too as a purely external instrument, it has nevertheless to be treated as an end on its own account, and as such as an essentially harmonious self-defined whole. This attention, which is due to the medium of sense, contributes, as in Art universally, and in the interest of seriousness,[16] yet another point of view where we find this very austerity vanishes; both poet and listener feel it no more. They are lifted into a region of exhilarating charm and grace.

In painting and sculpture the artist is given the form in its material and spatial limitations for the portrayal and colouring of human limbs, rocks, trees, clouds and flowers. In architecture also the requirements and objects of the buildings proposed dictate more or less the defined shape given to walls, towers and roofs. In the same-way music already possesses stable definition in the fundamental laws of harmony. In the art of poetry, however, the sound of language to our aural sense is, in the first instance, unbridled;[17] the poet has consequently to regulate such absence of rule within objective limits, and to outline a more stable conture, a more definite framework of sound for his conceptions, their structure and their objective beauty.

Just as in musical declamation the rhythm and melody should accept and adapt itself to the nature of the content, versification is also a kind of music, which, at its own distance, is capable of essentially re-echoing the mysterious, but none the less definite, course and character of the ideas. Agreeably with this the verse-measure ought to reflect the general tone and, as it were, the spiritual perfume of an entire poem, and it is by no means a question of no consequence whether the external form is one of iambics, trochaics, stanzas, alcaics or any other metre.

In the heads of discussion we propose to follow of most importance are *two* systems, whose distinction from each other we shall endeavour to explain. The *first* is *rhythmical* versification, which depends upon the actual length or shortness of the verbal syllables, whether we regard such in the association of varied figures of speech, or under the relation of their time-movement.

The *second* is that which is responsible for *tonal quality* as such, not merely in the case of isolated letters, consonants or vowels, but also in that of entire syllables and words, the configuration of which is in part regulated by the laws of the uniform repetition of identical or similar sounds, and in part by those of symmetrical change. It is to this system that we refer the alliteration, assonance and rhyme.

Both systems stand in intimate connection with the prosody of speech. This is so whether such systems are rather based throughout on the actual length or shortness of syllables, or on the accent which the mind requires,[18] as attached to the obvious importance of such syllables.

And, *finally*, we have also to *unite* together this general rhythmical movement with the music of the independent formal structure as rhyme.[19] And in this effort, inasmuch as the repeated echo of the rhyme strikes the ear with a marked emphasis, which asserts itself predominantly over the purely temporal condition of duration and advance, the rhythmical aspect will, in such a conjunction, tend to fall back, and arrest our attention with less force.

(*a*) *Rhythmical Versification.*

In discussing the rhythmical system which is without rhyme the following points are of the most importance:

First, we have the firm and fast time-measure of syllables in their plain distinction of *long* and *shorty* as well as their manifold association with definite conditions and metres of poetry.

Secondly, we have the animation of rhythm in accent, caesura and opposition between the verse accent and that of separate words.

Thirdly, there is the aspect of *euphonious sounds* which, within this movement, is forthcoming from the sound of the words, without any further concentration in rhyme.

(*a*) For that rhythmical movement which the *time duration* and the movement itself makes of first importance rather than the melodic sound as such and singled in its isolated effect, (*αα*) we find our starting point in the *natural* length and shortness of syllables to the obvious distinctions of which the sound of the actual words, the expression of their letters, in consonants and vowels, contribute the essential basis.

Pre-eminently long by nature are the diphthongs ai, oi, ae, and the rest, for the reason that essentially—whatever our modern schoolmaster may say to the contrary—they are themselves a twofold, concrete tone, which combines, much as green does among the colours. The long-sounding

111

vowels are equally so. As a third principle, which obtains already in Sanscrit, no less than the Greek and Latin languages, we have associated with them peculiar conditions of position. In other words, if two or more consonants are placed between two vowels the relation constitutes what is unquestionably a difficult transition in speech. The organ of articulate utterance requires a longer period to pass over the consonants; this necessitates a pause which, despite of the presence of the short vowel, makes the syllable sound in its rhythm long, though it is not actually lengthened. If I speak the words for example—*mentem nec secus*—the movement from the one vowel to the other in *mentem* and *nec* is neither as simple or easy as in *secus*. More modern languages do not retain this last distinction with such stringency, but rather give effect, in the matter of long and short accent, to other criteria. But for all that syllables which are treated as short, despite of the position referred to, at least will not unfrequently create a harsh impression, because they obstruct the quicker movement our ear demands.

In contradistinction to the long quantity we have in diphthongs, long vowels and length created by position, we have the vowels which are by nature *short*, that is, those which are short, or which are not placed in words, where one of them and another immediately following are separated by two or more consonants.

(ββ) For the reason, then, that words, partly on their own account, as of several syllables, include a number of long and short beats, and in part, although of one syllable, are nevertheless associated with other words, we have thereby to start with a definite, but accidental interchange of various syllables and words without any stable measure. To regulate this accidental relation is just the function of poetry, precisely as it was that of music to define with accuracy the

112

unregulated duration of particular tones by means of the unity of time-measure. Poetry therefore establishes specific combinations of long and short syllables as the law, by virtue of which, under the aspect of *time-duration,* it has to arrange the series of syllables. What we therefore get in the first instance are the different successions of time. The simplest is the mutual relation of pure equality, as, for example, we find it in the dactyl and anapaest, in which the two short syllables may coalesce according to definite rule in two long syllables (the spondee). Secondly, a long syllable may be placed next one short; in that case we have a profounder distinction of derivation, though under its simplest form. Such are the iambus and the trochee. We find a more complicated combination, when a short syllable is interposed between two long ones, or one short precedes two long, as in the cretic and bacchius.

(γγ) Such *isolated* time-relations would, however, open the door to unregulated contingency if they were permitted to follow one another anyhow in their motley differences. In fact the entire aim of such regulation would vanish under such conditions, in other words the regulated series of long and short syllables. From another point of view we should wholly fail to secure a definite beginning, conclusion, and central position, so that the caprice which here once again asserted itself would entirely contradict that which we previously established, when considering musical time-measure and beat, as to the relation in which the percipient ego stood to the duration of tones. In other words, the ego requires a combination on its own account,[20] a return out of the continuous forward movement in time; and only seizes on the same in virtue of definite unities of time and their, as such, emphasized commencement,[21] regulated in their entire series and terminations. This is the reason why, in the *third* place, poetry also sets out the particular time-

113

relations in a series of *verse-lines*,[22] which in respect to the type and number of their feet, no less than in that of their commencement, progress, and conclusion, are subject to rule. The iambic trimeter, for instance, consists of six iambic feet, of which any two constitute an iambic dipody. The hexameter consists of six dactyls, which again, in certain positions, may coalesce in spondees.

Moreover, as it is no objection to such lines of verse-writing that they are repeated over and over again in the same or practically under the same mode, we find in respect to the entire series, on the one hand, a lack of definition so far as the one final conclusion is concerned, and on the other a monotony, which creates perceptibly a sense of deficiency in the ideal aspect of their manifold composition. In order to mitigate such defects poetry makes a final advance in its creation of the strophe and its varied organization, more particularly with a view to lyric expression. As an illustration we have the elegiac measure of the Greeks; there is also the alcaic and sapphic strophe, not to mention the modes of lyric art elaborated by Pindar and the famous Greek dramatists in their choric effusions or interludes.

However much, in their relation to time-measure, music and poetry partake of similar conditions, we ought not, therefore, to fail to draw attention to their dissimilarity. The most important feature of this is that of the *beat*. The question whether there is any real repetition measurable in time-beats of identical length in the metre of the ancients has been the subject of strenuous controversy. Generally speaking I think it may be affirmed that poetry, which uses language in its words as a mere means of communication, is unable, in respect to the time-length of its utterances, to subordinate the same to an absolutely fixed measure of its movement in the abstract form that is present in the time-beat of music. In music tone is simply sound, without pause

114

as such, and it essentially requires a stability such as we find in the time-beat. Human speech does not require such security, for one reason because it already possesses something fixed and substantive in the idea, and for another because it is not thus wholly committed to the objective medium of sound or resonance; rather this very ideality of conscious life is the medium in which it consists as art. For this reason poetry in fact discovers the more substantive means of defining its arrest, continuance, pause or delay immediately in the ideas and emotions which it clearly enunciates in language. Music, too, in its recitatives, marks the beginning of a similar process of separation from the immutable equality of the time-beat. It follows from this that, if poetical metre were wholly subjugate to the regularity of the time-beat, the distinction between music and poetry, in this sphere at least, would vanish altogether, and the element of time would receive a more predominant significance than is compatible with the essential characteristics of poetry. Supported by such a conclusion we may therefore insist that, though a *time-measure* is of imperative value in poetry, there is no such necessity for the abstract *time-beat*; meaning and signification[23] of the actual words must here remain the relatively speaking more controlling force. If we examine in this respect more closely the particular verse-measures of the ancients the hexameter will no doubt appear most nearly attached to a forward movement compatible with the stringency of the time-beat. The elder Voss in fact assumed this, though, as a matter of fact, such an assumption is already excluded by the catalexis of the last foot. When in addition to this Voss proceeded to place the time-measure of the alcaic and sapphic strophes on a similar basis of abstract equality, we can only regard such a theory as a wilful caprice which does violence to the poetry. The contention throughout is apparently due to the habit of treating our German iambic in identical lengths of

115

syllable measure and time-measure. As a matter of fact the beauty of the iambic trimeter of the ancients consisted above all in this, that it was not composed of six iambic feet of identical lengths of time; but quite the contrary in order that, in the first position of every dipody, spondees, or, in their resolution, also dactyls and anapaests were permissible; and, by reason of this, the monotonous repetition of the same time-measure, and thereby all that is consistent with the time-beat, vanishes. We may add that the possibility of change is yet more obvious in lyric strophes, so that if we wish to establish such a thesis at all it must be on the *à priori* principle, that the time-beat is essentially necessary. As a deduction from the plain facts we see nothing of the kind.

(*β*). With the introduction of the *accent* and the *caesura* we have for the first time the animation of the time-measure; we may parallel with this that rhythm in music, which we have discussed as the time-beat.

(*αα*) In short in poetry also every definite time relation has, in the first instance, its particular accent; in other words, regularly defined intervals are asserted, which attract others and only in this way are rounded off in a whole. Owing to this fact much play is given to the *manifold possibilities* of the value of syllables. On the one hand generally long syllables appear emphasized in their contrast to short, so that now, if the ictus falls upon them, their significance is doubled as against the shorter, and in fact stand out themselves as distinct from long syllables not thus accented. On the other hand, however, it may also happen that shorter syllables receive the ictus or accent, so that a similar emphasis is created to the one described in the converse case.

Above all, as already observed, the beginning and termination of the particular feet ought not with abstract precision to be identical with the beginning and conclusion

116

of single words. For, in the *first* place, the reach forward[24] of the essentially exclusive word over the termination of the foot of the line affects the connection of the otherwise disparate rhythms. *Secondly*, when the verse accent falls on the final sound of a word carried forward as above described, we get on account of this in addition a distinct interval of time, the conclusion of a word having already come to a pause in something else, so that it is in fact this pause, which, in virtue of the accent united with it, is expressly made perceptible as a segment of time in the otherwise unbroken current. Caesuras of this sort are inevitable with every kind of verse. For although the distinct accent already confers on particular feet a more intimate and essential distinction, and thereby a certain variety, this sort of animation, especially in the case of verses, in which the same feet repeat each other without a break, as, for example, in our iambic, remain for all that in a measure entirely abstract and monotonous, and furthermore allow the particular feet to fall apart without a common bond. It is this gray monotony which the caesura checks, introducing a connection and more genuine animation within what was otherwise, with its undifferentiated regularity, the halting flow of verse, a life which, by virtue of the various positions in which the caesura may assert itself, is itself as manifold as is possible agreeably with the condition that its regulated definition is held free from any approach to lawless caprice.

A *third* accent is furthermore attached to the verse accent and caesura, which the words in other respects and independently possess, apart from their metrical employment. By this means the mode and degree in which the particular syllables are emphasized or the reverse increases in its variety. This verbal accent may, on the one hand, no doubt appear in conjunction with the accent of the verse and the caesura; and, if this is the case, the strength of the accents respectively is increased. But from another point of view it may stand independently of them on syllables which do not receive any further emphasis, and which we may say, in so far as they moreover require an accentuation to bring out their particular significance as verbal syllables, assert an effect counter to the verse rhythm, an effect which confers on the whole a novel and unique vitality.

To appreciate the beauty of rhythm in all the above aspects is for our modern ears a very difficult matter, because in modern languages the elements which combine to produce. this kind of metrical effect are no longer in some measure present in the sharp and secure insistence they possessed for the ancient world; rather we have other means substituted for them, in order to satisfy other demands of artistic taste.

(ββ) But over and above all this, paramount over all valid claims of syllables and words within their metrical position, there is, secondly, the worth of that significance we gather from the line or verse as *poetical idea*. It is in relation to this, which the language implies, that its other metrical effects are either emphasized or, comparatively speaking, are restrained as void of significance; and it is by this means alone that the finest perfume of spiritual vitality is instilled through the poetry. But notwithstanding this fact, such poetical effect is not to be carried so far that it directly contradicts in this respect the rules of metrical rhythm.

(γγ) Moreover, a *definite* type of *content* corresponds with the entire character of a particular verse measure, particularly from the point of view of rhythmical movement, and above all that particular kind implied in the movement of our feelings. Thus, for example, the hexameter, in the tranquil wave of its forward stream, is particularly adapted to the even flow of epic narration. Where, however, it is more in the nature of the strophe in its association with the pentameter and its symmetrically consistent caesura, it is, in its none the less generally simple regularity, fitted to express elegiac emotion. The iambic again moves forward with rapidity, and as such is peculiarly suitable to dramatic dialogue. The anapaest indicates the clear-slipping march of joyful exultation. Other characteristics may readily be associated with other modes of verse-measure.

(γ) *Thirdly*, this province of rhythmical versification is not confined to the mere configuration and vivication of time-intervals; it embraces the actual musical sound of syllables and words. In respect to such sound, however, the classic languages, in which rhythm is retained, as above described, as an essential feature, offer a real contrast to other more recent ones more conspicuously adapted to rhyme.

(αα) In the Greek and Latin languages, for example, the stem syllable is modified, by virtue of its modes of inflexion, through an abundance of variously toned syllables, which of course possess an independent meaning, but only as a modification of such syllable; this consequently, it is true, asserts its force as the substantive significance of that variously expanded sound, but it does not, so far as its sound is concerned, stand forth as such in pre-eminent and unique ascendancy. When we hear, for example, the word *amaverunt*, three syllables are attached to the word, and the accent is already substantially differentiated throughout the number and extension of these syllables in direct relation to the stem syllable, even assuming no naturally long ones had been included, by which means the *fundamental significance* and the emphasis of *accent* are *separated* from each other. In such a case consequently, and in so far as the accentuation is not identical with the *main* syllable, but falls on another, which merely expresses an *incidental* significance, the ear can from this basis at once listen to the sound of the different

119

syllables and follow their movement, retaining, as it does, perfect liberty to attend to that prosody peculiar to the word or phrase, and finding itself then invited to incorporate within its rhythm these naturally long and short syllables.

(ββ) The case of our modern German language is wholly different. That which in the Greek and Latin languages is expressed, as above described, by means of the prefix and suffix, and other modifications, is in more modern languages for the most part resolved in verbs of the stem syllable; the result of this is that the inflexion syllables that have been in the former case unfolded in one and the same word, with collateral meanings of a varied character, are now split up and isolated in separate words. As illustrations of this we have the constant employment of many subsidiary words denoting time, the independent indication of the optative by means of distinct verbs, the separation of pronouns, and other examples. By such means, on the one hand, the word—which in the previous case adduced was expanded in all the variety of tone which attached to its many syllables, under which every accent of the root, that is the root idea, was cancelled—persists as a simple totality concentrated in itself, without appearing as a series of tones, which being, as they are, mere modifications, do not, by virtue of their specific *sense*, assert an influence with such a strength that the ear is unable to attend to their independent tonal quality and its temporal movement. And, on the other hand, on account of this concentration the main significance is moreover of such a force that it attracts the fall of the accent upon itself exclusively; and just because the emphasis is thus fastened upon the fundamental sense this very coalescence does not suffer the quantity of the other syllables, whether long or short ones, to appear; they are simply overwhelmed. The roots of the majority of words are unquestionably as a general rule short, compact,[25] of

120

one or two syllables. If thus, as is for instance pre-eminently the case with our mother tongue, these root-stems appropriate almost invariably the accent to themselves, such an accent is to an overwhelming degree one of the sense, *significance'*, not a definition, however, in which the medium —that is, the utterance as sound—would be free, or could assert the relation of the length, shortness, or accentuation of syllables independently of the intelligible content of the words. Consequently a rhythmical configuration of time-movement and emphasis liberated from the stem syllable and its meaning can here no longer be maintained. We have merely left us, in contradistinction to the former hearing of the ample sound and duration of such long and short beats in their varied juxtaposition, a general impression of sound, [26] which is apprehended. entirely aloof from the accented fundamental syllable with its weight of significance. And, indeed, apart from this, as we have seen, the ramification of the stem into syllables as modified into particular words is also an independent process. Such words receive thereby an independent worth, and, while preserving their own significance, they make us at the same time hear the identical coalescence of meaning and accent, which we have observed in the case of the stem or root word around which they are ranged. We are therefore forced to restrict our attention to the sense of every word; and, instead of being occupied with the natural length and shortness of syllables and their sensuous[27] accentuation, are only able to hear the accent asserted by the main and substantive meaning.

($\gamma\gamma$) In such modern languages the element of rhythm has little room for its display, or at least the soul has little freedom left to expatiate within it, because, as observed, time and the equable stream of syllabic sound as emitted from its movement is superseded[28] by a more ideal relation—that is to say, by the sense and meaning of the words, and thereby the force of the more independent configuration of rhythm is suppressed. We may in this connection compare the principle of rhythmical versification with the plastic arts. We find in both that the ideal significance is not as yet asserted in its independence, nor does the former expressly define the length and accent of syllables, but rather the meaning of the words is wholly blended with the sensuous medium of the inherent time duration and sound, with a result that does complete justice to the claim of such externality, wholly absorbed in the ideal form and movement of the same. If, however, such a principle is renounced, and yet despite of this, but in accordance with the necessary demand of art, the sensuous medium is permitted to retain a certain force of resistance as against the exclusive assertion of ideal content, [29] in order to this end to divert the ear's attention,—in the case that is, where what we may call the plastic moment of that more ancient mode of syllabic quantity, as it is on its own account, and the tonal quality inseparable from the general rhythm rather than independently asserted—when this, as I say, has been destroyed, then we have no other means[30] at hand save the express and artistically configurated sound of articulate speech simply, and retained as such in its isolation. And this leads us to our second main type of versification—in other words, *rhyme*.

(b) Rhyme

From an objective standpoint it is possible to seek to explain the need of a novel treatment of language from the deterioration into which the classical languages fell through their contact with foreign relations. Such a development, however, lies in the nature of the facts themselves. The earliest example of conformity with the ideality of its content attempted by poetry is to be traced in the length and shortness of syllables in independence from their significance, for the mutual relations of which, caesurae and so forth, art elaborates its rules, rules which it is true generally coincide with the character of the content in its broad outlines, but which none the less, in matters of individual detail, do not suffer either the length or shortness of a syllable, nor its accent, to depend exclusively on the intelligible significance making such a formal aspect subordinate, to the point of entire detachment, to the same. [31] The more ideal, however, and spiritual the represented idea becomes, the more it tends to detach itself from this objective aspect, which increasingly fails to present such ideality in plastic guise, and finally reaches a point of self-concentration in which the, so to speak, corporeal element of speech is in a measure wholly wiped away, and for the rest merely asserts that wherein the intelligible significance is reposed as necessary to its communication; all else is only admitted, by way of by-play, as insignificant. Now romantic art, in respect to the entire type of its conception and presentation, effects a similar passage over to this concentrated synthesis of ideality, when it sets out in search for the material which corresponds to this subjective content in audible sound.[32] Following these lines romantic poetry also, inasmuch as it generally lays most stress on the ideal tones[33] of feeling, becomes absorbed in its preoccupation[34] with the distinct and independent ring and tones of letters, syllables, and words; perfecting such a process to its final satisfaction, as it learns, either in their association with ideality, or in their connection with the architectonically intelligible penetration[35] of such music, to separate such syllabic and other verbal sounds or to relate or interlace them one with another. From this point of view we may affirm that it is not simply by way of accident that rhyme is elaborated in romantic poetry. It is a necessary feature of it. The requirement of soul-life, to discover itself again, is thereby more fully asserted, and finds a real source of satisfaction in the identity of the rhyme, which declares an indifference[36] to the unyielding laws of the time-measure, and, by virtue of its recurrence of similar sounds, gives exclusive effect to an effort which conducts the conscious self back to itself. It is by this means that versification is made to approach more closely the musical art as such, that is, the vivid tones of soul-life itself, and is, from this point of view, liberated from the, relatively speaking, gross material of human speech, in other words from what we have referred to as the natural measure of quantity.

With regard to points of special interest in this subject, I will confine myself to the following general observations:

First, upon the origin of rhyme.

Secondly, upon a few more definite features by which we may distinguish the sphere of rhyme from that of rhythm in verse.

Thirdly, upon the types under which we may classify rhyme generally.

(α) We have already seen that rhyme belongs in its form to the art of romantic poetry, which requires such a more pronounced emphasis of its configurated syllabic sound posited thus on its own account. And it is thus effected to the extent that the ideal activity of volition[37] discovers its own presence by this means in the objective medium of tone. Where such a need is asserted we have a mode of speech in part meeting absolutely the conditions of form I outlined above when discussing the necessity of rhyme; and in addition it makes use of the old forms of language at hand, the Latin for example, which, though of other constitution and mainly applicable to rhythmical versification, it employs agreeably to the character of the new principle, or reconstructs the same so far into a new language that the element of rhythm disappears, and rhyme becomes, as in the Italian and French languages, the matter of all importance.

($\alpha\alpha$) In this respect we find throughout Christendom that rhyme is introduced into Latin versification at a very early date with much insistence, although, as observed, it rested on other principles. These principles, however, are rather adapted from the Greek language; and, so far from testifying to the fact that they originated from the Latin speech itself, rather prove, under the modified character they possess, a tendency which itself approaches the romantic type. In other words, the poetry of Rome, on the one hand and in its earliest days, discovered its source not in the natural length and shortness of syllables, but rather measured the value of syllables relatively to their accent; and in consequence of this it was only through a more accurate knowledge and imitation of Greek poetry that the prosodical principle of this was received and followed. And, moreover, the Romans rendered more obdurate the flexible, joyous sensuousness of Greek metres, more particularly by their use of more insistent pauses at the caesura, as we find such not only in the hexameter, but also in the alcaic and sapphic metres, hardening the effect thus to a structure of more stringent outline and more severe regularity. And indeed, apart from this, even in the full bloom of Latin literature, and from their poets of finest culture, we have already plenty of rhymes. Thus from Horace, in his *Ars poetica* (verses 99-100), we get the following:

> Non satis est, pulchra esse poemata: dulcia *sunto*,
> Et quocunque volent, animum auditoris *agunto*.

Though the poet was probably quite unconscious of the fact, it is none the less a strange coincidence that, in the very passage in which Horace enforces the obligation that poems should be *dulcia*, we discover a rhyme. Similar rhymes occur in Ovid with still more frequency. Even assuming such to be accidental, the fact remains that they appear to have been not offensive to Roman ears, and might consequently be permitted, although as isolated exceptions, to slip into the composition. Yet the profounder significance of romantic rhyme is absent from such playful exceptions. The former does not assert the recurrent sound merely as sound, but the ideal content or meaning implied in it. And it is precisely this which constitutes the fundamental difference between modern rhyme and the very ancient rhyme of the Hindoos.

As for the classical languages, it was after the invasion of barbarism, and on account of the destruction of accentuation and the assertion of that uniquely personal note of emotion referable to Christianity, that the rhythmical system of verse passed into that of rhyme. Thus, in his hymn to the Holy Spirit, Ambrosius entirely regulates the versification according to the accent of the meaning expressed, and breaks into rhyme. The first work of St. Augustine against the Donatists is in the same way a rhymed song; and also the so-called Leonine versicles, as expressly rhymed hexameters and pentameters, are easily distinguishable from the accidental exceptions of rhyme previously noticed. These and other examples like them mark the point of departure of rhyme from the more ancient rhythmical system.

(ββ) Certain writers have no doubt attempted to trace the origin of the new principle of versification in *Arabian* literature. The artistic education, however, of the famous poets of the East is of later date than the appearance of rhyme in western Christendom; and any Mohammedan art of a more early time exercised no real influence on the West. We should, however, add that we find from the first in Arabian poetry essential affinities with the romantic principle, in which the knights of Europe, at the time of the crusades, very readily made themselves at home; and consequently it is not difficult to understand how, in the affinity of spiritual tendencies[38] which they shared, and in which the poetry of Eastern Mohammedanism no less than Western Christianity finds its source, though removed in the world from each other, we meet for the first time and on its own independent footing a novel type of verse writing.

(γγ) A *third* source, to which again, independently of either the influence of the classic languages or the Arabic, we may trace the origins of rhyme and all that it implies, are the *Germanic* languages, as we find them in their earliest Scandinavian development. As illustration of this we have the songs of the ancient Edda, which, though only in more recent times, collected and edited, unquestionably date from a former age. In these, as we shall see later on, it is not, it is true, the genuine rhyme-sound which is elaborated in its perfection, but rather an effective emphasis upon particular sounds of language, and a regularity defined by rule, with a definite repetition of both aspects.

(β) Yet more important than the question of origin is the characteristic *difference* between the new system and the old. I have already adverted to the fundamental feature of importance here; it only remains to establish it more narrowly.

Rhythmical versification attained its most beautiful and richest development in the field of Hellenic poetry, in which we may discover the most eminent features of the type wherever it obtains. Briefly they are as follows:

First, the sound, as such, of letters, syllables, or words does not here constitute its material, but rather the syllabic sound in its *temporal duration*, so that attention must neither exclusively be directed to particular syllables or words, nor

127

to the purely qualitative similarity or identity of their sound. On the contrary, the sound still remains in inseparable union with the static time-measure of its specific duration; and in the forward movement of both the ear has to follow the value of every separate syllable no less than the principle which obtains in the rhythmical progression of all equally together. *Secondly*, the measure of long and short syllables, no less than that of rhythmical rise and fall, and varied animation derived from more deliberate caesurae and moments of pause, depends upon the *natural* element of the language, without permitting any introduction of that type of accentuation, by virtue of which the actual *meaning* of the word leaves its impress on a syllable or a word. The versification asserts itself in its collocation of feet, its verse accent, its caesurae, and so forth in this respect as fully independent as the language itself, which also, outside the domain of poetry, already accepts accentuation from the natural quantity of syllables and their relations of juxtaposition, and not from the significance of the root-syllable. On this account, *thirdly*, we have as the vital emphasis of certain syllables, first, the verse accent and rhythm, and, secondly, all other accentuation, both of which aspects, in their twofold contribution to the varied character of the whole, pass in and out of one another without any mutual derangement or suppression; and in like manner respectively they satisfy the claim of the poetical imagination in fully admitting the expressiveness due, by virtue of the nature of their position and movement, to words which, in respect to their intelligible meaning, are of a greater importance than others.

(αα) The first alteration, then, effected by rhymed verse in the previous system is this indisputable validity of *natural quantity*,[39] If, therefore, any time-measure at all is permitted to remain, it is compelled to seek for a basis for such quantitative pause or acceleration, which it refuses any longer to find in the natural quantity, of syllables, in some other province. And this, as we have seen, can be no other than the intrinsic meaning of syllables and words. It is this *significance* which in the final instance determines the quantitative measure of syllables, so long as such is still regarded as essential at all, and by doing so transfers the criterium from the purely objective medium[40] and its natural structure to the ideal subject-matter.

(ββ) A further result follows from this of yet more importance. As I have already pointed out, this collocation of the emphasis on the significant stem-syllable dissipates that other independent diffusion of it in manifold forms of inflexion, which our rhythmical system is not yet forced to treat as negligible, in contrast to the stem, because it deduces neither the natural quantity of syllables nor the accent which it asserts from the intelligible significance. In the case, however, where such an explication,[41] with its co-ordination in verse-feet according to the quantity of syllables in their natural stability, falls away the entire system therewith necessarily collapses, which reposes on the time-measure and its laws. Of this type, for example, is French and Italian poetry, the metre and rhythm of which are absolutely non-existent as understood by the ancients. The entire question is here merely one of a definite number of syllables.

(γγ) For such a loss there is only one possible compensation —that of *rhyme*. In other words, if—this is one aspect—it is no longer time-duration which receives objective expression, by means of which the sound of syllables flows on freely in the even movement that intrinsically belongs to them; if, furthermore, the intelligible significance dominates over the stem-syllables, and coalesces with the same without further organic expatiation into a determinate unity, we have no sensuous medium, such as is able to maintain itself independently of the time-measure, no less than this accentuation of the stem-syllables, finally left to us other than just this syllabic sound.

Such a sound, however, if it is to secure an independent attention, must, in the *first* place, be of a far more insistent kind than the interchange of different tones, such as we met with in the older verse metres; and its assertion must be of a far more overwhelming character than the stress of syllables can lay claim to in ordinary speech. What we now require has not only to compensate us for the loss of the articulate time-measure, but it further undertakes to reassert the sensuous medium in its opposition to that unqualified predominance of the accentuated significance. For when once the conceptive content has essentially attained the ideality and penetration of mind,[42] for which the sensuous aspect of speech is of no importance, the verbal sound must enforce itself still more positively and coarsely as distinct from this ideality in order to arrest our attention at all. In contrast, therefore, to the gentle movements of rhythmical euphony, rhyme is a crude expedient,[43] which requires an ear by no means either so trained or sensitive as that presupposed by Greek verse. *Secondly,* though it is true that rhyme does not here assert itself so much as distinct from the meaning of the stem-syllables simply as it does from the entire ideal content, yet it does at the same time so far assist the natural verbal sound as to win for it a relatively secure stability. But this object can only be attained if the sound[44] of particular words affirms itself in exclusive distinction from the resonance of other words, and thus secures an independent existence, by virtue of which *isolation* it satisfies the claims of the formative aspect of the verbal medium in forceful beats of sound. Rhyme is therefore, at least in its contrast to the evenly transfused movement of rhythmic

130

euphony, a detached exhibition of exclusive tonal expression. *Thirdly,* we found that it was the ideality of the conscious self which, by virtue of its effort of ideal synthesis, came into its own, and discovered its personal satisfaction in such recurrences of sound. If, then, the means used in the older type of versification, with its copious variety of structure, disappear, there only remains, if we look at poetry, under the aspect of its *medium,* to support this principle of self-recovery, the more formal repetition of wholly identical or similar sounds, whereby again we are able to unite under an intelligible scheme[45] the assertion and relation of closely associated meanings in the rhyme-sounds of expressive words. The metre of rhythmical verse we may regard as a variously articulate interrelation of manifold syllabic quantities. Rhyme, on the contrary, is from one point of view more material;[46] yet, on the other hand, is itself more abstractly placed within this medium. In other words, it is the mere recollection of mind and the ear of the recurrence of identical or related sounds and significations — a recurrence in which the poet is conscious of his own activity, recognizes, and is pleased to recognize, himself therein as both agent and participant.

(γ) Finally, on the question of the particular *types* under which we may classify this more modern system of romantic poetry, I only propose to advert briefly to what appears to me of most importance in respect to alliteration, assonance, and ordinary rhyme.

(αα) The first, or at least the most thorough, example of *alliteration* is that we find elaborated in the earliest Scandinavian poetry, where it supplies the fundamental basis, whereas assonance and the terminal rhyme, albeit these two aspects play a by no means unimportant part, are, however, only present in certain particular kinds of such poetry. The principle of alliterative rhyme, letter rhyme, is

131

rhyme in its most incomplete form, because it does not require the recurrence of the entire syllable, but only that of one identical letter, and primarily the initial letter only. Owing to the weakness of this type of recurrent sound it is, in the first place, therefore necessary that only such words should be used in its service, which already independently possess an express accent on their first syllable; and, secondly, these words must not be remote from one another, if the identity of their commencement is to make a real impression on the ear. For the rest, alliterative letters may be a vowel, no less than a double or single consonant; but it is primarily consonants which are of most importance in the scheme. Based on such conditions, we find in Icelandic poetry[47] the fundamental rule that all alliterative rhymes require accentuated[48] syllables, whose initial letters must not in the same lines occur in other substantives which have the accent on the first syllable; and, along with this, of the three words, the initial letters of which constitute the rhyme, two must be found in the first line, and the third, which supplies the dominant alliteration, must be placed at the commencement of the second line. We may add further that, in virtue of the abstract character of this identical sound of initial letters, words are generally made alliterative proportionally to the importance of their signification. We find, therefore, that here, too, the relation of accented sound to the meaning of words is not entirely absent. I cannot, however, pursue this subject into more detail.

(ββ) Secondly, *assonance* has nothing to do with initial letters, but makes a nearer approach to rhyme in so far as it is a recurrence in identical sound of the same letters in the middle or at the termination of different words. It is not necessary, of course, that these assonant words should in all cases come at the conclusion of a line; they may fall into other places. Mainly, however, it is the concluding syllables of lines which come into this mutual relation of assonance, as contrasted with alliteration which is effective rather at the line's commencement. In its richest elaboration we may associate this assonance of language with the Romance nations, more especially the Spanish, whose full-toned language is peculiarly adapted to this recurrence of the same vowels. As a rule, no doubt assonance is here restricted to vowels. But the language further permits of other variety of assonance, not only that of vowels, but also that of identical consonants and consonants in association with one vowel.

(γγ) That which, as above described, alliteration and assonance are only able to establish with incompleteness is abundantly fulfilled by *rhyme*. In it, and expressly to the exclusion of initial letters, we have asserted the wholly equable sound of entire verb stems,[49] which are, by virtue of this equability, brought into an express relation with their tonal utterance. We have no mere question now of the number of the syllables. Words of one syllable, no less than others of two or more, may be rhymed. By this means we not only get the masculine rhyme, which is restricted to words of one syllable, but also the feminine rhyme, which embraces words of two syllables, as also the so-called gliding rhyme, which reaches to three or even more syllables. It is in particular the languages of Northern Europe which incline to the first type, Southern languages to the second, such as the Italian and Spanish. The German and French languages would appear to lie between these two extremes. Rhymes of more than three syllables are rarely to be met with in any language.

The position of the rhyme is at the conclusion of the lines, in which the rhyming word, although there is certainly no reason that it should ever concentrate in itself the ideal expressiveness of the significance, nevertheless does attract attention to itself so far as the verbal sound is concerned;

and, furthermore, it makes the different verses or stanzas follow one another either in accordance with the principle of a wholly abstract recurrence of the same rhyme, or by uniting, separating, and mutually relating them in a more elaborate mode of regulated change, and variously symmetrical interweaving of different rhymes with correspondent relations, sometimes more near, at others more remote, of every degree of complexity. In such a process the particular rhymes will at one point stare us in the face at once, or they will appear to have a game of hide-and seek; so that in this way our ear, as it listens, will at one time receive instant satisfaction, at another it will only find it after considerable delay, wherein the expectation will, as it were, be coquetted with, deceived, and kept on the stretch, until the assured end from point to point of artistically arranged recurrence is reached, and with it the hearer's approval.

Among the various types of the poetic art it is pre-eminently *lyric* poetry, which, by virtue of its ideality and personal quality of expression, most readily avails itself of rhyme, and thereby converts language itself into a music of emotion and melodic symmetry, a symmetry not merely of time-measure and rhythmical movement, but of the kind of resonance which finds a responsive echo in the inner life itself. To promote this, therefore, the art elaborates in its use of rhyme a more simple or complex system of strophes, every one of which is part of one organic whole. Examples of such an interplay of melodic sound, whether steeped in emotion or rich in ingenuity, are the sonnet, canzonet, triolet, and madrigal. Epic poetry, on the contrary, so long as it does not mingle lyrical subject-matter with its more native character, preserves a more equable advance in its construction, which does not easily adapt itself to the strophe. We have an obvious illustration of this in the triplet stanzas of Dante's

"Divine Comedy," as contrasted with the lyrical canzonets and sonnets of the same poet. However, I must not permit myself to go further into detail.

(*c*) Now that we have in the above investigation separated rhythmical versification from rhyme, and *contrasted* the same, we may now proceed, *thirdly*, to ask ourselves whether a *combination* of the two is not also intelligible, and, indeed, actually employed. The existence of certain more recent languages will render exceptional and important aid to the solution; in other words, we cannot deny to these either a partial reassertion of our former rhythmical system, or, in certain respects, an association of the same with rhyme. We will, for example, confine our attention to our mother tongue, and, in reference to the first-mentioned aspect, it will be sufficient to recall Klopstock, who would have as little of rhyme as possible; who not merely in epic, but also in lyrical poetry, set himself to imitate the ancients with the greatest enthusiasm and persistency. Voss and others have followed in his steps, ever striving to enforce with increased strictness principles upon which to base this rhythmical treatment of our language. Goethe, on the contrary, never felt quite himself in his classical syllabic measures. He asks himself, not without reason:

> Stehn uns diese weiten Falten
> Zu Gesichte, wie den Alten?[50]

(*a*) I will in this connection merely reiterate what I already have observed upon the distinction which exists between ancient and more modern languages. Rhythmical versification is based upon the *natural* quantity of syllables, possessing therein an essentially stable criterion, which the ideal expression can neither limit, alter, or weaken. Such a natural measure is, however, abhorrent to more recent languages; in these it is only the *verbal* accent of the ideal

135

significance, which makes one syllable long in its contrast to others, which are defective in such significance. Such a principle of accentuation, however, does not supply any audible compensation for the absence of the natural quantity, or rather it adds to the actual uncertainty of such a measure. For the more strongly emphasized significance of a word can at the same time make another short, despite the fact that, taken by itself, it possesses a verbal accent, so that the criterion accepted is wholly one of mutual relation. *Du liebst*, can, for instance, according to the stress of the emphasis which is thrown, according to the sense intended, either on both words, or one or the other, be a spondee, iambus or trochee. No doubt the attempt has been made, even in our own tongue, to return to the *natural* quantity of syllables, and to create rules with this intent; but in the presence of the overwhelming importance that the intelligible significance and the accent it asserts has secured such a reference to theory is quite impracticable. And in truth this agrees with the state of the facts. If the natural measure is really to constitute the essential basis, the language ought not as yet to have become such an instrument of soul expression as it is of necessity in our own times. Once allow, however, that it has already in its course of development thus secured such a mastery of the intelligible purport over the sensuous or native material, and it follows that the fundamental test for the value of syllables is not to be deduced from the objective quantity itself, but rather from that whereof words are themselves indicative as means. The emotional impulse of a free intelligence refuses to allow the temporal activity of language, as such, to establish itself in the independent form of its native and objective reality.

(β) Such a conclusion, however, does not necessarily imply that we are forced to oust altogether from our German language the rhymeless rhythmical treatment of the syllabic measure; it merely in essential respects points to this, that it is not possible, conformably with the character of the structure of our modern speech, to retain the plastic consistency of the metrical medium as it was secured by the ancient world. We must consequently seek for and elaborate some further element in poetical composition by way of compensation, which on its own independent account is of a more ideal[51] character than the stable natural quantity of syllables. Such an element is the accent of the verse, no less than the caesura, which as now constituted, instead of moving independently of the verbal accent, coalesce with the same, and thereby receive a more significant, albeit a more abstract assertion, in virtue of the fact that the variety of that previous threefold accentuation, which we discovered in the rhythmical type of classical poetry, on account of this very coalescence necessarily disappears. It, however, equally follows as a result that we only retain the power with conspicuous success to imitate the rhythmic movement of such poetry where its impression on our ear is most emphatic. We no longer possess, that is to say, the stable quantitative basis for its more subtle distinctions and manifold connections, and the more crude mode of accentuation, which we do possess in its place, to emphasize our measure, is intrinsically no sufficient substitute.

(γ) To state, then, finally, what this actual *association* of the rhythmical mode of verse with rhyme is, we may go so far as to affirm that it is the absorption, although to a limited extent, by the more modern form of versification of the more ancient one.

($\alpha\alpha$) The predominant distinction of the natural syllabic quantity by means of the verbal accent is in fact not an entirely satisfactory principle of the *mere medium*. It does not arrest the ear's attention, even on the side of sense simply, so

137

far as to make it appear, absolutely and everywhere unnecessary, where the ideal aspect of the poetical content is paramount, to summon the complementary assistance of the sound and response of syllables and words.

($\beta\beta$) It is, however, at the same time necessary in the interest of metre that an equally strong contrasting force should be set up to that of the rhyme sound. In so far, however, as it is *not* the distinction of syllables in their natural quantity and *its variety*, which has to be co-ordinated and made predominant, we have, in respect, to this temporal relation, no other expedient left but the *identical repetition* of the same time-measure; in this the element of accented *beat* will tend to assert itself in a far more emphatic degree, than is compatible with the rhythmical system. As an illustration we have our German rhymed iambics and trochaics, in the recitation of which far more beat stress is admitted than is proper to the scansion of the unrhymed iambics of the ancients, although the caesura pause is capable of bringing into emphatic relief isolated words whose accent is mainly referable to their meaning, and is capable of further making all that remains dependent upon them a resisting effect to the abstract equality of the verse, and by so doing introduces a varied animation. And as in such a particular case, so we may assert generally, the time-beat cannot be of actual service in poetry with the force that is required of it in most musical compositions.

($\gamma\gamma$) Although, however, we may affirm it as a general rule that rhyme should be associated merely with such verse metres, which, by virtue of their simple changes of the syllabic quantity and their continuous recurrence of similar verse feet, do not on their own independent account give sufficiently effective modality to the element of sensuous medium in modern languages which admit at all of rhythmical treatment, yet the application of rhyme to the more profuse syllabic metres imitated from classical models, as, for instance, to borrow one example only, the alcaic and sapphic strophe, will not merely appear superfluous, but even an unresolved contradiction. Both systems repose on opposed principles, and the attempt to unite them in the way suggested, can only involve us in a like opposition, which can produce nothing but a contradiction we are unable to mediate, and which is therefore untenable. It follows, therefore, that we ought only to make use of rhyme in cases where the principle of the older versification merely makes itself effective in more remote implication, and through a transitional process essentially deducible from the system of rhyme.

The above, then, are the points which we have sought to establish as, in a broad sense, of most vital concern to poetical expression in its contradistinction from prose.

[1] *Bildlich,* here not so much creative as simply plastic or constructive.

[2] *Vorliebe.* His interest must be already centred in it.

[3] *Bildlichkeit, i.e.* their claims as images of something else.

[4] *Vertauscht.* I have translated "exchanged," but Hegel may mean "mistaken for."

[5] It is not very clear what Hegel means by the word *Bezeichnungen.* "Turns of expression," which first occurred to me, appears to be covered by *Flexionsformen* lower down.

[6] *Gedrungenen.* The idea is suppression into a compact mass—a cloud unable to burst save in occasional flashes.

[7] I presume Hegel refers here to the synthetic arrangement of genuine paragraphs rather than phrases, composition generally.

[8] *Das eigentliche Wort.* The word, that is, which expresses the fact in its immediacy.

[9] More literally, "being remoulded with the life and wealth of Spirit."

[10] *Besonnenheit, i.e.,* real thought-fullness.

[11] *Der künstlerischen Ruhe.* The personal predilection of Hegel for classic art here once more asserts itself.

[12] The German word is *Sinnen,* but I think, though the emotional sense is partly implied, the main emphasis is on a presiding mind—or rather a wide-visioned genius.

[13] *Eine sprudelnde Anschauung.* A view of things that bubbles forth like a fountain.

[14] That is, the medium of literary form.

[15] *Ein hartes Band.* The idea is not so much difficult as unyielding, unmalleable.

[16] *Zum Ernste des Inhalts.* That is, the earnestness of a product of mind as such. Hegel seems to contrast with this the spontaneity of an art which, as inspired by genius, comes to us with the freshness of Nature herself, take Shakespeare's songs for example.

[17] *Ungebunden.* That is, it is contingent.

140

[18] Hegel calls this the *Verstandesaccent,* and speaks of this importance (*Bedeutsamkeit*) as a product of the syllables.

[19] I presume the words *das für sich gestaltete Klingen* refer to rhyme.

[20] *Eine Sammlung in sich,* that is, an independent collection or aggregate.

[21] *Anheben* may possibly mean appearance in the defined series generally.

[22] By *Versen* Hegel means rather lines than a number of them.

[23] The dative appears to be a misprint. The passage should be read *der* and *die,* instead of *dem* and *der.*

[24] I am not quite sure what Hegel refers to in what he describes as *das Hinübergreifen des Wortes.* I presume he means what are known as weak endings to a line.

[25] *Gedrungen.* I suppose this is the meaning. The entire passage is a difficult one to follow.

[26] *Ein allgemeines Hören.*

[27] That is, the accent of the syllables as a mere medium of uttered speech.

[28] Lit., has its flank turned, *überflügelt.*

[29] *Die blosse Vergeistigung.*

[30] No other means to divert the ears attention. The sentence is rather involved, and I have not seen my way to simplify it.

[31] *Abstract unterworfen.* Hegel apparently means abstract as detached from the natural medium of language—becoming thereby the abstract symbol of idea exclusively.

[32] As in musical art.

[33] *Seelen-tonen, i.e.,* the wave and flow of the emotional life itself.

[34] *In das Spielen.* Hegel repeats his use of the expression above, *beiher Spielen,* lit., the playing with not as a toy but as something serious.

[35] I suppose this is the meaning here of *Sharfsinn,* but "subtlety" may be included.

[36] Indifferent, that is, as asserting the creative freedom of the

poet, he can select his own rhymes as he wills. Hegel, however, seems rather to miss the essential spontaneity of really good blank verse.

[37] So I translate *die innere Subjectivität*, but it may refer perhaps to the entire creative personality.

[38] That is, I presume, their relation to romantic art.

[39] That is, the primary feature changed is that of the validity of natural quantity.

[40] *Dem Äusseren Daseyn*. That is, of language.

[41] *Entfaltung*. Such an explication of rhythmical euphony as the previous system discloses.

[42] *Geistes*. All that pertains to conscious life.

[43] Lit., a blunt or coarse sound, *ein plumpes Klingen*.

[44] *Tonen* implies sound no less than accent. I have rendered it in various ways.

[45] *Von Seiten des Geistes*. Perhaps rather "as aspects of the poet's intelligence"—that is, with reference to the self-assertion above explained.

[46] More nearly related to the natural medium of language.

[47] *Die Verslehre der Isländer v. Rask, verd. von Mohnike*, Berlin, 1830, pp. 14-17.

[48] *Betonte*, see above note on *Tonen*.

[49] *Stämme*, the stem of verbs, rather than the root of substantives, which would be more correctly *stammwort*.

[50] "Do we moderns face broad reaches such as these, as did the ancients?" *Falten*, folds, expatiation of subject-matter. I presume, though I do not recall the context, that the allusion is mainly to elegiacs.

[51] *I.e.*, more related to active intelligence.

III

THE SEVERAL GENERIC TYPES OF POETRY

The two fundamental aspects, according to which we have hitherto examined the poetical art were, in the first instance, that of poetical significance or content *in the broadest sense,* the nature of the outlook of a poetical composition and the creative activity of the poet; secondly, poetical *expression,* not merely respectively to the ideas which have to be embodied in *words,* but also to the modes under which they are expressed and the character of *versification.*

I. What we, above all, in these respects endeavoured to enforce consisted in this, that poetry has to embrace the ideality of conscious life as its content; yet, in its artistic elaboration of the same, it cannot rest satisfied with the objective form of direct perception as other plastic arts; nor can it accept as its form the emotional ideality which alone reverberates through our soul-life, nor yet that of thinking and the relations of reflective thought. It has to maintain a mediate position between the extremes of immediate objectivity and the inner life of feeling and thought. This intermediate sphere of conception overlaps both sides. From thought it borrows the aspect of ideal *universality,* which binds together the immediate particularity of the senses in more definitive simplicity; while, on the other hand, its mode of envisagement shares with plastic art the haphazard[1] juxtaposition of objects in space. The poetic imagination, moreover, is essentially distinct from thinking in that it permits, under the mode of sensuous apprehension from which it starts, particular ideas to remain in an unrelated series or contiguity; pure thinking, on the other hand, demands and promotes the reciprocal dependence of determinate concepts on each other, an interstructure of relations, consequential or conclusive judgments, and so forth. When, therefore, the *poetical* imagination in its art-products renders necessary an ideal unity of all particularity, such integration may easily meet with obstruction by virtue

143

of the above-mentioned diffuseness[2] which the nature of its content forbids it wholly to eschew; and it is just this which puts it in the power of poetry to embody and present a content in organic and vital inter-connection of successive aspects and divisions, yet impressed at the same time with the apparent independence of these. And by this means it is possible for poetry to extend the selected content at one time rather in the direction of abstract thought, at another rather under the condition of the phenomenal world, and consequently to include within its survey the most sublime thoughts of speculative philosophy, no less than the external objects of Nature, always provided that the former are not put forward in the logical forms of ratiocination and scientific deduction, or the latter as void of all vital or other significance. The function, in short, of poetry is to present a complete world, whose ideal or essential content must be spread before us under the external guise of human actions, events, and other manifestations of soul;life, with all the wealth and directness compatible with such art.

2. This explication, however, does not receive its sensuous embodiment in stone, wood, or colour, but exclusively in language, whose versification, accentuation, and the rest are in fact the trappings[3] of speech, by means of which the ideal content secures an external form. If we ask ourselves now, to put the thing somewhat crudely, where we are to look for the *material* consistency of this mode of expression, we must reply that language is not essentially on all fours with a work[4] of plastic art, independent, that is, of the artistic creator, but it is the *life of our humanity itself* the individual speaker alone who is the vehicle of the sensuous presence and actuality of a poetical work. The compositions of poetry must be recited, sung, acted, reproduced, in short, by living people, just as the compositions of music are so reproduced. We are no doubt accustomed to read epic and

lyric poetry, and only to hear drama recited and to see the same accompanied by gesture. Poetry, however, is essentially and according to its notion, *sonorous expression*, and we may, in particular, not dispense with this, if a complete exposition of the art is our aim, for the reason that it is the aspect and the only aspect, under which it comes into genuine contact with objective existence. The printed or written letter is, no doubt, also in a sense objectively present, but it is merely as the indifferent symbol of sounds and words. We no doubt have in a previous passage regarded words as the purely external means which give us the signification of ideas. We must not, however, overlook the fact that poetry, at any rate, so informs the temporal element and sound of these signs, as to ennoble them in a medium suffused with the ideal vitality of that, whereof, in their abstractness, they are the symbols. The printing press merely makes visible to our eyes this form of animation under a mode which, taken by itself, is essentially indifferent and no longer coalescent with the ideal content; it consigns it, in its altered form of visibility, to the element of time-duration and the sound of ordinary speech,[5] instead of giving us in fact the accented word and its determinate time-duration. When we, therefore, content ourselves with mere reading we do so partly owing to the ease with which we can thus picture to ourselves what is real as actually uttered in speech, partly because of the undeniable fact that poetry alone among the arts, in aspects of fundamental importance, is already completely at home in the life of spirit, and neither the impression of it on our sense of sight or hearing give us the root of the matter. Yet for all that, precisely by virtue of this ideality, poetry, as art, ought not wholly to divest itself of this aspect of objective expression, if at least it is anxious to avoid an incompleteness similar to that in which, for instance, the mere outlined drawing attempts to reproduce the picture of famous colourists.

145

3. As an artistically organic whole referred no longer to a specific type of exclusive execution on account of the onesided character of its medium, the art of poetry accepts in a general way for its determinate form various types of art-production, and it is consequently necessary to borrow the *criteria* of our *classification* of such *poetical types* or species from the *general* notion of artistic production.[6]

(*A*) In this respect it is, *first,* and from one point of view, the form of objective reality, wherein poetry reproduces the evolved content of conscious life in the ideal image, and therewithal essentially repeats the principle of plastic art, which makes the immediate object of fact visible. These plastic figures of the imagination poetry furthermore unveils as determined in the activities of human and divine beings, so that every thing, which takes place, issues in part from ethically self-subsistent human or divine forces, and in part also, by virtue of obstructive agencies, meets with a reaction, and thus, in its external form of manifestation, becomes an *event,* in which the facts in question disclose themselves in free independence, and the poet retires into the background. To grasp such events in a consequential whole is the task of *Epic* poetry, inasmuch as its aim is just to declare poetically, and in the form of the actual facts, either an essentially complete action, or the personalities, from which the same proceeds in its substantive worth or its eventful complexity amid the medley of external accidence. And by so doing it represents the *objective* fact itself in its objectivity.

And, moreover, the minstrel does not recite this positive world before conscious sense and feeling in a way that would seem to announce it as his personal phantasy, and his own heart's passion; rather this reciter or rhapsodist recites it by heart, in a mechanical sort of way, and in a metre which, while it repeats something of this monotony

146

with its uniformity of structure, rolls onward in a tranquil and steady stream. What, in short, the minstrel narrates must appear as a part of real life, which, in respect to content no less than presentation, stands in absolute independence aloof from himself, the narrator; he is throughout, in relation that is to the facts of his tale no less than the manner in which he unfolds them, not permitted wholly to identify his own personality with their substance.

(B) In direct contrast to epic poetry we have our *second* type, that namely of *lyrical* poetry. Its content is that within ourselves, the ideal world, the contemplative or emotional life of soul, which instead of following up actions, remains at home with itself in its own ideal realm, and, consequently, is able to accept *self-expression* as its unique and indeed final end. Here we have, therefore, no substantive totality, self-evolved as external fact or event, but the express outlook, emotion and observation of the individual's self-introspective life shares in what is substantive and actual therein as its own, as its passion, mood or reflection; we have here the birth of its own loins. Such a fulfilment and ideal process is not adequately realized in a mechanical delivery such as we saw was conceded as appropriate to epic poetry. On the contrary the singer must give utterance to the ideas and views of lyrical art as though they were the expression of his own soul, his own emotions. And inasmuch as it is this *innermost world*, which the delivery has to animate, the expression of it will above all lean to the musical features of poetical reproduction; whether permitted as an embellishment or a necessity we shall here meet with the varied modulation of the voice, either in recitation or song, and the accompaniment of musical instruments.

(C) Our *third* and final mode of poetical composition unites the two previous ones in a new totality. In this we not only discover an *objective* exposition, but also can trace its source in the ideal life of particular people; what is objective here is therefore portrayed as appertinent to the conscious life of individuals.[7] To put the case conversely, the conscious life of individuals is on the one hand unfolded as it passes over into actual life experience, and on the other as involved in the fatality of events, which brings about passion in causal and necessary connection with the individual's own action. We have here, therefore, as in Epic poetry, an action expanded to our view in its conflicts and issues; spiritual forces come to expression and battle; the element of contingency is everywhere involved, and human activity is either brought into contact with the energy of an omnipotent destiny, or a directive and world-ruling Providence. Human action, however, does not here only pass before our vision in the objective form of its actual occurrence, as an event of the Past resuscitated by the narrative alone; on the contrary, it is made to appear as actually realized in the particular volition, morality or immorality of the specific characters depicted, which thereby become central in the principle of *lyric* poetry. Add to this, however, that such individuals are not merely disclosed in their inner experience as such; they also declare themselves in the execution of passion directed to ends; whereby they offer a criterion—in the way that epic poetry asserts what is substantive in its positive reality[8] for the evaluation of those passions and the aims which are directed to the objective conditions and rational laws of the concrete world; and it is, moreover, by this very test of the worth and conditions, under which such individuals continue in their resolve to abide, that their destiny is discovered by implication. This objective presence, which proceeds from the personality itself, no less than this personal experience, [9] which is reproduced in its active realization and all that

148

declares its worth in the world, is Spirit in its own living totality; it is this which, as *action*, supplies both form and content to *dramatic poetry*.

Moreover, inasmuch as this concrete whole is itself no less essentially conscious life than it is, under the aspect of its external realization, also a self-manifestation, quite apart from all question of local or other artistic means of realization, we are bound, in respect to this representation of actual facts, to meet the claim of genuine poetry that we should have the *entire personality* of the individual envisaged; only as such the living man himself is actually that which is expressed. For though, on the one hand, in the drama, as in lyric poetry, a character ought to express the content of its own soul-life as a veritable possession, yet, from another point of view, it asserts itself, when, in its entire personality it is confronted with other personalities, as effective in its practical existence, and comes thereby into active contact with the world around it, by means of which it attaches itself immediately to an active disposition,[10] which, quite as truly as articulate speech, is an expression of the soul-life, and requires its artistic treatment. Already we find in lyrical poetry some close approach to the apportionment of various emotions among different individual speakers, and the distribution of its subject-matter in acts or scenes.

In the drama, then, subjective emotion passes on likewise to the expression of action; and, by so doing, renders necessary the manifestation to our senses of the play of gesture which concentrates the universality of language in a closer relation with the expression of personality,[11] and by means of position, demeanour, gesticulation and other ways is individualized and completed. If, however, this aspect of deportment is carried forward by artistic means to a degree of expression, that it can dispense with speech, we have the art of pantomime, which resolves the rhythmical movement of poetry in a harmonious and picturesque motion of limbs, and in this, so to speak, plastic music of bodily position and movement gives animated life in the dance to the tranquil and cold figures of sculpture, that it may essentially unite by such means music and the plastic art.

<hr>

[1] *Gleichgültige*, that is, the impressions of sense are received from without, from a manifold indifferent to ourselves.

[2] *Losheit.* A word coined by Hegel to denote this relation of poetry to external objects in their independence.

[3] *Die Gebehrden*, lit., gestures, in which sense it is used in a subsequent passage.

[4] We should rather have expected "the material of plastic art." The contrast is rather between the nature of the medium in each case than the finished product. So far as the latter is concerned the musical composition is as dependent, even more dependent for its presentment on human activity as poetical composition.

[5] *Des Klingens unseres Gewohnheit.* It is not quite clear what the meaning is here. The meaning may be as in the interpretation above. But it is rather difficult to see how, so far as mere print goes, we can be conscious of actual sound at all, unless it is intended here to include at least the act of reading; an alternative interpretation would be the "habitual verbal accent," but we should in that case have rather expected the substantive *Nachdrucks* for *Klingens.*

[6] Hegel means of course that as that notion stands midway between the objectivity of sense-perception and the concept of thought, so too this classification will be based on the attitude of the art either to the personal life, or the objects of sense, as the one aspect is more strongly represented or the other.

[7] *Dem Subject.* That is, I understand, the individual subject generally, not merely the conscious life of the poet or the singer.

[8] *In seiner Gediegenheit, i.e.*, as concrete.

[9] *Dies Subjektive.* The realization of self in the world is part of

that world regarded as a rational and self-conscious process, Spirit.

[10] *Sich die Gebehrde anschliesst, i.e.* a practical attitude to the world, involving gesture and other actions.

[11] Hegel's expression is "the personality of expression," *i.e.,* the personal aspect of expression.

A. EPIC POETRY

The Epos, word, saga, states simply what the fact is which is translated into the word. It acquires an essentially self-consistent content in order to express the fact *that it is* and how it is. What we have here brought before consciousness is the object regarded as object in its relations and circumstances, in their full compass and development, the object, in short, in its determinate existence.

We propose to treat our subject-matter as follows:

First, we shall attempt to describe the *general* character of what is Epical:

Secondly, we shall proceed to some *particular* features, which in respect to the real Epos are of exceptional importance:

Thirdly, we shall enumerate by name certain *specific* methods of treatment, which have been actually in use in particular epic compositions within the historical elaboration of the type.

1. THE GENERAL CHARACTERISTICS OF THE EPIC TYPE

(*a*) The most simple, but nevertheless in its abstract concentration, still one-sided and incomplete mode of epic exposition consists in the assertion of that which is essentially fundamental and necessary among the facts of the concrete world and the wealth of mutable phenomena, and in the expression of such on their own account, as focussed in epic phraseology.

(α) We may begin our consideration of the type with the *epigram* i, in so far as it really remains an epigram, that is an inscription on columns, effects, monuments, gifts and so forth, and at the same time points with an ideal finger to something else, and by doing so explains through words, inscribed on an object, somewhat otherwise plastic, local, something present outside the words expressed. In such an example the epigram states simply what a definite fact is. The individual does not as yet express his concrete self; he attaches a concise interpretation to the object, the locality, which he has immediate perception of and which claims his interested attention, an interpretation which goes to the heart of the fact in question.

(β) A yet further advance may be discovered in the case where the twofold aspect of the object in its external reality and the fact of inscription disappears, in so far, that is, as poetry, without any actual representation on the object, expresses its idea of the fact. To this class belong the gnomes of the ancients, ethical sayings, which concentrate in concise language that which is more forceable than material objects, more permanent and universal than the monument of some definite action, more perdurable than votive offerings, columns, and temples. Such are duties in human existence, the wisdom of life, the vision of that which constitutes in action and knowledge the firm foundations and stable bonds for human kind. The epic character of such modes of conception consists in this, that such maxims do not declare themselves as exclusively personal emotion and reflection, and also, in the matter of their impression, are quite as little directed with the object even of affecting our emotions, but rather with the purpose to emphasize what is of sterling

152

validity, whether as the object of human obligation or the sense of honour and propriety. The ancient Greek elegiacs have in some measure this epic tone. We have still extant a few verses of Solon of this kind, though the transition here into a hortatory tone and style is easily made. Such include exhortations or warnings with reference to the common social life, its laws and morality. We may also mention the gold sayings, which tradition ascribes to Pythagoras. Yet all such are of a hybrid nature, and referable to this, that though in general we may associate with them the tone of our distinct type, yet, owing to the incompleteness of the object, it is not fully realized, but rather there is a distinct tendency to involve with it that of another poetical type, in the present case the lyrical.

(γ) Such dicta may, however, *thirdly*, as already suggested, by being divested of this fragmentary and self-exclusive isolation, go to form a larger whole, be rounded off, that is, in a totality, which is altogether of the *Epic* type; we have here neither a purely lyrical frame of mind nor a dramatic action, but a specific and veritable sphere of the living world whose essential nature, as emphasized in its general characteristics, no less than as situated to particular aspects, points of view, occurrences or obligations, supplies us with an integrating unity and a genuine focal centre. In complete agreement with this type of epical content, which displays what is of permanent and universal import along with, as a rule, a distinct ethical purpose of admonishment, instruction or exhortation to an, in all essentials, ethically stable life, compositions of this kind receive a *didactic* flavour. Nevertheless, by reason of the novelty of their wise sayings, the freshness of their general outlook and the ingenuousness of their observation we must keep them quite distinct from more recent didactic poetry. They wholly justify, inasmuch as they give the necessary play to matter entirely descriptive, the conclusion that these two aspects taken together, instruction and description, are directly deduced as the substantive summary of facts which have been throughout experienced. As an obvious illustration I will merely mention the "Works and Days" of Hesiod, the teaching and descriptive power of which, in its primitive style and as a poetical composition, exercises a fascination upon us wholly different from the pleasure we experience in the colder elegance, the scientific or systematic conclusions of Virgil's poems on agriculture.

(*b*) The above described modes of epigram, gnome, and didactive poem accept their *specific* provinces of Nature or human life as their subject-matter, while endeavouring to fix attention in concise language, with more or less limitation of survey, on that which is of permanent worth and essential truth in this or that object, condition, or activity; and even under the still more restricted condition which the art of poetry imposes on such a task the practical result upon human effort is still maintained. There is, however, a further or *second* type of such compositions, which is, on the one hand, profounder in its penetration, and, on the other, lays less stress on instruction and reform. Such are the cosmogonies and theogonies, no less than those most ancient works of philosophy, which are still unable entirely to liberate themselves from the poetical form.

(*a*) In this way the exposition of the Eleatic philosophy in the poems of Xenophanes and Parmenides still remains poetic in form; and this is exceptionally so in the introduction prefaced by the latter to his work. The content is here the One, which, in its contrast to the Becoming or the already Become, all particular phenomena in short, is eternal and imperishable. No particularity is permitted to bring content to the human spirit, which strives after truth, and, in the first instance, is cognizant of the same in its

154

most abstract unity and concreteness. Expatiating in the greatness of this object, and wrestling with the might of the same, the impulse of soul inclines instinctively to the lyrical expression, although the entire explication of the truths into which the writer's thought here penetrates carries on its face a wholly practical and thereby epic character.

(β) It is, *secondly*, the *becoming* of objective things, in particular natural objects, the press and conflict of activities operative in Nature, which supplies the matter of the cosmogonies, and impels the poetic imagination to disclose in the still more concrete and opulent mode of actions and events real eventuality. And the way this faculty does this is by clothing the forces of Nature in relatively more or less personified or figurative images placed in distinct stages, and through the symbolical form of human events and actions. Such a type of epic content and exposition pre-eminently belongs to Oriental Nature-religions; and above all among them the poetry of India is to an excessive degree prolific in the invention and portrayal of such modes of conception, frequently of an unbridled and extravagant type, concerning the origin of the world and the powers that are active therein.

(γ) We find, *thirdly*, similar characteristics in theogonies. Such occupy their true position mainly in so far as, on the one hand, the many particular gods are not suffered exclusively to possess the life of Nature as the more essential content of their power and creation, nor, conversely, is it one god that creates the world out of thought and spirit, and who, in the jealous mood of monotheism, will tolerate no other gods beside himself. This fair mean is alone exemplified in the religious outlook of the Greeks. It discovers an imperishable subject-matter for theogony-building in the forceful emancipation of the family of Zeus from the lawlessness of primitive natural forces, no less than

155

in the conflict waged against them. It is a process and a strife which we may indeed affirm gives us the historical origins of the immortal gods of poetry itself. The famous example of such an epic mode of conception we possess in the theogony known to us under the name of Hesiod. In this composition the entire course of event is throughout wedded to the form of human occurrences; it becomes less and less symbolical just to the extent that the gods, who are summoned to a spiritual dominion, are themselves liberated through an intelligent and ethical individuality adequate to their essential nature, and consequently are rightfully claimed and depicted as acting like human beings. What is, however, still absent from this type of Epic composition is, in the first place, a genuinely complete *result*[1] as poetry. The acts and events, which are within the scope of the survey of such poems, are no doubt an essentially necessary succession of occurrence, but they are not an individual action which issues as from a centre, wherein it discovers its unity and independence. From a further point of view the content of such poetry does not, and in virtue of its character cannot, present to us an essentially *complete whole*. It does, and for the above reason must, exclude the real activities of mankind, which are indispensable as the truly concrete material for the active display of the Divine forces. Epic poetry, therefore, is bound to free itself from such defects, if it is to receive its most perfect expression.

(*c*) This actually does take place in that sphere which we may designate the true *Epopœa*.

In the types hitherto discussed, which as a rule are wholly passed over, what we call the epic tone is unmistakably present, but the content is not as yet poetical in the concrete sense. Particular ethical maxims and philosophemata still persist as part of the material. What is, however, poetical in the full sense is concrete ideality in individual guise; and the epos, inasmuch as it makes what actually exists its object, accepts as such the happening of a definite action, which, in the full compass of its circumstances and relations must be brought with clarity to our vision as an event enriched by its further association with the organically complete world of a nation and an age. It follows from this that the collective world-outlook and objective presence of a national spirit, displayed as an actual event in the form of its self-manifestation, constitutes, and nothing short of this does so, the content and form of the true epic poem. As one aspect of such a totality we have the religious consciousness in every degree of profundity attained by the human spirit; it furthermore embraces the particular concrete life, whether political or domestic, not excluding all the detail of external existence, and the means by which human necessities are satisfied. All such material the epos makes of vital account as a growth in close contact with individuals; and for this reason, that for poetry the universal and substantive is only realized in the living presence of spirit life.

Such a comprehensive world, together with the human characterization it embraces, must then pass before us as real in a tranquil stream, without any undue haste, either as positive history or dramatic action, towards its aim and conclusion. We must thereby be permitted to linger round isolated facts, to penetrate into the different pictures of its movement and to enjoy them in all their detail. And by this means the entire panorama receives in its objective mode of realization the form of an external series of events, the basis and limitations of which must be implied in the essential ideality of the particular epic content, and of which the positive assertion is alone absent. If, consequently, the epic poem is, in its links of connection, more diffuse, and, by virtue of the relatively greater independence of portions of it, inclined to suffer from lack of coherency, we must not allow ourselves the impression that it could ever have been actually sung throughout in this manner. Rather it is an imperative in its case, as in that of any other artistic production, that it should be finished off in an essentially organic whole, which, however, moves forward in apparent tranquillity, in order that the particular fact and the images of actual life it contains may engage our interest.

(*a*) Such a primitive whole is the epic composition, whether known as the saga, the book, or the bible of a people. We may add every great and important nation can claim to have such primitive books, in which we find a mirror of the original spirit of a folk. To this extent these memorials are nothing less than the real foundations of the national consciousness; and it would be of profound interest to make a collection of such epic bibles. Such a series of Epopees, however much they fell short of artistic compositions in the modern sense, would at least present to us a gallery of the genius of nations. At the same time it is doubtless the fact that it is not every national bible which can claim the poetic form of the epopœa; nor do all nations which have embodied their most sacred memorials, whether in relation to religion or secular life, in the form of comprehensive compositions of the epic type, possess religious books. The Old Testament, for example, contains no doubt much epic narrative and genuine history, no less than incidental poetic compositions; but despite of this the whole is not a work of art. In a similar way the New Testament, as also the Koran, are mainly limited to a religious subject-matter, starting from which the life of the world at large is to some extent and in later times a consequence. Conversely, though the Hellenes have a poetic bible in the poems of Homer, they are without ancient religious books in the sense the Hindoos and the Parsees possess such. Where, however, we meet with the primitive epopoea, we must essentially distinguish between primitive poetic books and the more recent classic compositions of a nation, which do not any longer offer us a mirror of the national spirit in all its compass but do no more than reflect it partially and in particular directions. The dramatic poetry of the Hindoos, for example, or the tragedies of Sophocles present no such exhaustive picture as we find in the Ramajana and the Maha-Bharata, or the Iliad and the Odyssey.

(β) And insomuch as in the genuine Epos the naïve national consciousness is expressed for the first time in poetic guise, the real epic poem will appear for the most part in that midway stage in which, though no doubt a people is aroused from its stupidity, and its life is to that extent essentially strengthened to the point of reproducing its own world and of feeling itself at home therein, yet, for all that, everything which at a later stage becomes fixed religious dogma or civic law and ethical rule, still remains in the fluency of life as mere opinion, inseparable from the individual as such. And along with this volition and feeling are not as yet held distinct from one another.

($\alpha\alpha$) It is only after the separation of the individual's personal self from the concrete national whole, with its conditions, modes of opinion, exploits and destiny; it is only, further, after the division in man himself between his emotion and volition, that the lyric and dramatic types of poetry in turn replace the epic type and attain their richest development. This consummation is only reached in the later life-experience of a people, in which the general lines laid down by men for the due regulation of their affairs are no longer inseparable from the sentiments and opinions of the nation as a whole, but already have secured an independent structure as a co-ordinated system of jurisprudence and law, as a prosaic disposition of positive facts, as a political constitution, as a body of ethical or other

159

precepts; and being so, individuals are now confronted with material obligations rather as a necessary force external to themselves than one which their own inner life asserts, and which it compels them to substantiate as its fulfilment. As opposed to such an already actual and independent system, the individual life will seek in part to find expression in an equally independent world and growth of personal vision, reflection and emotion, which are not carried further into the sphere of action, and will further give *lyrical* utterance to its selfabsorption, its pre-occupation with the content of such a soul-experience. And, in part also, it will make its active passion of main importance, and will seek to assert itself independently in action, in so far as it is able to divest external conditions, the event and its concomitants of any claim to truly epic self-subsistency. It is just this increase to the strength and stability of individual character and aims in their relation to action which opens the way to *dramatic* poetry. To return, however, to the epic, we repeat that it is the above-mentioned unity of feeling and action which it demands, that unity between the self-fulfilled object of the personal life and the external accident and event; a unity which, as observed, is only present without blemish as it first appears in the earliest periods of the national life or the national poetry.

(ββ) At the same time, we must not yield ourselves, therefore, to the impression that a people in its heroical time simply as such, and as the home of its epos, there and then was in possession of art, or could necessarily depict its life in the mirror of poetry. As a matter of fact, an essentially poetical nationality in its actual world-presence is one thing; the art of poetry regarded as the imaginative consciousness of poetical material, and the artistic presentment of such a world is quite another. The felt want to express oneself *as idea* in terms of the latter, the trained knowledge of art, are

160

later acquisitions than the life and spirit itself, which discovers itself in all simplicity at home in its unreservedly poetical existence. Homer and the poems under his name are centuries later than the Trojan war, which is to myself quite as much an historical fact as the personality of Homer. In the same way we may affirm of Ossian, always assuming that the poems ascribed to him are really his, that he celebrates an heroic past, the sunset splendour of which inspires him to recall and reclothe the same in poetical form.

(γγ) Despite, however, such a separation, some intimate bond of association must exist between the poet and his subject-matter. The poet must still stand on even terms with the conditions, the general point of vision, the beliefs which he depicts. All he should find it necessary to do is to attach to these the poetic consciousness and the art capable of portraying them; in other respects they are still essential factors in his own life. If such an affinity as that above described is absent in our poet's epic creation, his poem must infallibly contain disparate and irreconcilable features. For both these aspects—namely, the content, the epic world, which it is the intention to portray, and the world of the poet's conscious life and imagination, which is in other respects independent of the above—are of spiritual derivation; they each of them possess intrinsically a definite principle, in which particular traits of characterization are involved. If, then, the personal life of the artist is essentially of a different order to that by virtue of which the historical and national life depicted came into actual being, we must necessarily become conscious of a cleft in the artistic result which will disturb and injure its effect. We shall have, in short, scenes placed before us of a previous condition of history, combined with modes of thought, opinions, and views more pertinent to other periods; and, in consequence of this, the configuration of primitive beliefs will, in its contact with the more developed reflection of a later time, lose the warmth of conviction, become, in short, a mere superstition, an empty embellishment of the mere poetical instrumentation, from which all the vitality of its actual life has vanished.

(γ) And this brings us to the general question what position the poet himself of genuine epic poetry really ought to take up.

(αα) Now, however much the Epos ought also to be positive in the sense that it is the objective presentment of a world based upon its own foundations, and realized in virtue of its own necessary laws, a world, moreover, with which the personal outlook of the poet must remain in a connection that enables him to identify himself wholly with it; yet it is equally true that his artistic product, which reproduces this world, is throughout the *free creation* of himself. In this connection we shall do well to recall that fine expression of Herodotus: "Homer and Hesiod have created the gods of the Hellenic race." And, in truth, this free and audacious spirit of creation, which Herodotus attaches to the abovementioned poets, already is some testimony to the fact that although the Epopœa belongs to the early age of a nation, it is not its function to depict the most primitive condition of all. In other words, every nation possesses in its earliest origins more or less an alien culture of some kind, is confronted with a religious cult of foreign importation to which it submits, or which it regards as sacrosanct. And, indeed, we find that the minstrelsy, the superstition, the barbarous elements in human life, no less than the most exalted have their source just in this, that instead of being entirely at home with themselves, they are experienced as something aloof from themselves, that is not the natural product of their own national and individual consciousness. In this way, for example, the Hindoos must certainly, long

162

before the date of their great Epopees, have experienced many an important revolution of religious beliefs and secular condition. The Greeks no less, as previously remarked, had to transform much material of an Egyptian, Phrygian, and Asiatic descent. The Romans, in their turn, were confronted with much of a Greek origin; and the barbarians, in the period of national invasion, with Christian or Roman antecedents, and so on. Not until the poet is able with a free hand to cast from him such a yoke, is able to take stock of what he really possesses, is conscious of his own worth, and we are thereby released from all perturbed state of mental vision, will the dawn break of a genuine epic creation. In contrast to such an outlook we have the age and the society modified by a cult abstract in its origin, with its elaborate dogmas, established political and moral maxims, all of which take us away from the concrete life at home with itself. The world of the truly epic poet maintains its opposition to such conditions. Not merely in respect to universal forces, passions, and aims which are operative in the soul-life of individuals, but also in such a poet's attitude to all external facts, be his creation never so independent, he is entirely as one in his own province. In just this way Homer is at home in all that he sings to us of his world, and where we are conscious of such intimacy in another we are infected with a like feeling, for we are here face to face with truth, with that spirit which lives in its world, and discovers therein its true being; and it does us good to feel this, inasmuch as the poet is himself present therein heart and soul. Such a world may, indeed, belong to a less advanced stage of evolution and culture than our own; but at least it does remain faithful to that of a poetry and beauty which is open to all, so that we essentially recognize and understand here everything which our higher life, our humanity in its fundamental demands, whether it be the honour, the opinions, the emotions, the

163

exhortation, or the exploits of each and every hero; and we are able to enjoy such characters, in all the detail of their portraiture, as themselves united to such a life and the richness of its actual presence.

($\beta\beta$) But on account of the emphasis upon the objective independence of this whole, it is a further necessary contrast that the poet fall into the background and become lost in his *subject*. What is to appear is the creation, not the poet; and yet withal, that which the poem expresses belongs to him. He has imagined all in his mind's eye; he has implanted there his soul, his genius. All this, however, is not expressly asserted. So we find, for instance, that at one time a Calchas will give the outline of events; at another, a Nestor. Yet, for all that, such interpretative matter is the gift of the poet himself. Nay, actual changes in the soul-life of his heroes he explains in objective fashion as an entrance of gods upon the scene, as in the case where Athene appears before Achilles in his rage, counselling self-restraint. And inasmuch as the Epos does not disclose the soul-life of the creator, save indirectly, but the positive facts of external life, the subjective aspect of his creations must completely fall into the background, no less than the creator himself vanish behind the world he unfolds to our vision. From this point of view a great epic style makes the work appear to be itself its own minstrel. It seems to pass before us self-begotten, a work of independent birth.

($\gamma\gamma$) Moreover, the epic poem, if a true work of art, is the exclusive creation of *one* artist. However much an epic may express the affairs of the entire nation, it remains the fact that it is the individual who is the poet, not the nation as a whole. The spirit of an age, of a people, is no doubt the essential operative cause; but realization is only secured in the work of art as conceived by the constructive genius of a *particular* poet, who brings before our vision and reproduces

164

this universal spirit and its content as his own experience and his own product. Poetical composition is a real spiritual birth, and spirit or intelligence only exist as this or that actual and individual conscious and self-conscious life. When we have already an artistic creation in a particular style,[2] we have no doubt something to start from; and others are then able to copy with more or less success something like it, just as we have to listen nowadays to some scores of poems written in the Goethesque manner. To continue to sing many compositions in the same kind of key, however, will never create the unified creation, which is throughout the work of *one* inspiring genius. This is a point of real importance not only in our attitude to the Homeric poems, but also the Niebelungen Lied. For the last-mentioned work we are unable to determine an author with any historical certainty; and as for the Iliad and Odyssey, the opinion of some critics is notorious that the Homer of tradition—that is, the sole author of these books—never existed at all. They are the production in different parts of various authors, parts which have finally been patched together in the two larger works we possess. With regard to such a theory the question of most importance is whether either or both of these extant works constitute an independent organic whole in the epic sense, or, as is the view fashionable nowadays, they possess no inevitable beginning or conclusion, but rather might be continued on present lines for ever. We may, of course, admit that the unity of the Homeric poems is, as part of their essential form, less compact than that we associate with the terse concentration of a dramatic work. Inasmuch as every separate portion may be and may appear as relatively independent, they give free play to many interpolations and abrupt transitions; but, despite of this, they do unquestionably constitute throughout a true, ideally organic, and epic totality. Such a whole can only be the composition of *one* author. This notion of a conglomerate without essential unity, of a mere patching together of various rhapsodies composed in a similar strain, is a wild sort of idea opposed to all artistic canons. Of course, if such a view merely amounts to this, that the poet, in his bare individuality, vanishes in his creation, it is the highest form of praise. This is merely a statement that we are unable to recognize any positive traces of wholly personal opinions and feeling. So much is certainly true of the Homeric poems. What we have before us, and we have only this, is the positive fact, the objective outlook of a people. But the song of a people requires a voice, a voice which can sing forth the contents of heart and soul, as harvested from the national granary; and an essentially self-integrated work of art calls for yet more than this from the *unique* genius of its creator.

2. PARTICULAR CHARACTERISTICS OF THE GENUINE EPOS

We have previously in our consideration of the general character of epic poetry briefly drawn attention to certain incomplete types, which, although of an epical strain, are not epopees in their completeness. They, in short, neither represent a national condition, nor a concrete event, within the boundaries of such a sphere. It is these latter features, which were then excluded, which offer us for the first time a content wholly equal to the perfected Epos, whose fundamental traits and conditions are thus stated.

Having recalled these points it becomes necessary now to investigate more closely what it is we require by way of completing our notion of the epic work of art. We are, however, on the threshold of this enquiry confronted with the difficulty that we have little or nothing to say on features of specific interest, if we confine our attention to generalities; Ave must rivet our attention on historical evidence, and those varied epic and national compositions,

166

works which on account of the extraordinary diversity of the times and peoples to which they refer do not make us very hopeful of securing either a definite or a congruous result. We find, however, some compensation in the fact, that from among all the many epic bibles of the past we can place our finger on one at least, in which we have the clearest evidence of all which it is possible to establish as the true and fundamental character of the genuine epos. Such are the Homeric poems. These, then, above all, will be the source from which I shall borrow the characteristics, which, in my view, essentially determine the nature of such poetry, whether from the point of view of fact or theory. We propose to summarize our enquiry under the following heads:

First, we have to deal with the question, of what structure *the general* world condition ought to be, on the basis of which the epic event is permitted to receive an adequate reproduction.

Secondly, we shall investigate the quality of this specific type of historical event itself.

Lastly, we shall direct attention to the form in which these two aspects of our subject-matter coalesce and are completed in the unity of a single work of art, that is, in the epic poem.

(*a*) *The General World-condition of the Epic Poem*

We have already, when Ave started on this subject, seen that it is not a single isolated action which is accomplished in the true epic event; the subject of the narrative is not, in short, a wholly accidental occurrence, but an action which is dovetailed into the entire complexus of a particular age and national circumstances, which in consequence can only be placed before us with success as a constituent part of an extensive world, demanding as it does the reflection of such a world in its entirety. In respect to the actual poetical content of this background I shall be brief, inasmuch as I have already indicated the fundamental points of interest when, in the first part of this work, I discussed the general world-condition which the ideal action presupposed. In the present context therefore I shall restrict myself to the question what is of most importance to the Epos simply.

(a) That which is most adapted, as the all-embracing condition of human society, to form the background of the Epos consists in this, that it already possesses for particular individuals the form of a positive condition actually present, and yet continues with them in closest association with the simplicity of primitive life. For if the heroes who are placed as the crowning fact of all, are first to found a collective condition the determination of what is or ought to come into existence falls into the more personal sphere of character to a greater extent than is compatible with the nature of the Epos, and therewith all appearance of the same as objective reality is impossible.

(aa) The relations of ethical life, the aggregate of the family, of the people regarded as a complete nation, not merely with a view to war, but also in their peaceful security, must have become a positive fact in their evolution; yet along with this their organization cannot as yet have assumed the settled form of co-ordinate regulations, obligations, and laws independent in their validity of the direct personal and private activities of individuals, and possessive of the power to maintain themselves against such particular wills. Rather it is the *intuitive sense* of right and fairness, the moral habit, the temperament, the personality, which supply the support, as they are the source, of such a social order; we have, in short, no theoretic intelligence in its precipitated form of prosaic reality able to establish and secure such a resistance to the heart, the opinions and passions of individuals. We may dismiss the thought that a community with a fully organized constitution and an elaborate system of law, judicial courts, government officials and police, would supply the environment of a really epic action.[3] The conditions of positive morality must, no doubt, be present in the general will and conduct, but the instruments of its realization can only be the action and personality of individuals, and a determinate mode of its existence, of universal application and independent stability, is necessarily absent. We find, in short, in the Epos no doubt the substantive reciprocity of objective life and action, but we find no less a freedom in this world of life and action, which has all the appearance of originating exclusively from the isolated volition of individuals.

($\beta\beta$) The same considerations apply to the relation of the individual to the *natural* environment, from which he borrows the means to *satisfy* his wants, no less than discovers the best way to do so. In this respect, too, I would refer the reader back to what I have observed at greater length, when discussing the external definition of the Ideal.

What mankind requires in its external life, house and farm, tent, settle, bed, sword, lance, the ship, in which he crosses the sea, the chariot, which bears him into battle, his soup, his roast of meat, and drink—not one of these things need perforce become to him a lifeless instrument; he ought still to communicate to the same something of his entire life and substance, his essential self, and thereby leave the stamp of his own human individuality, by his active association on that which is otherwise wholly external. Our present life with its machinery and factory-made products, no less than the kind of way we seek to satisfy generally the needs of our external life, is in this respect quite as much as that of our political organization, wholly unfit to form the background which the Epos in its primitive guise demands. For just as the scientific faculty with its generalizations, its imperious conclusions, delivered independently of all personal views, can never have asserted its claim under the world-condition of the poetic type we are considering, so, too, we may assume that man did not yet appear divested of his vital connection with Nature, and the fresh and vigorous comradeship, whether as friends or opponents, which is therein implied.

($\gamma\gamma$) Such is the world-condition which, in a previous passage, and in contrast to the idyllic, I have called the *heroic*. We find it depicted in Homer with the noblest poetry, and with all the wealth of entirely human characterization. We have no more here, whether in domestic or public life, a barbarous state of things, than we have the wholly conventional prose of a regulated family and political organization; what we do find is that primitive mean of poetry much as I have already described it. A fundamental feature in such a condition is unquestionably the free individuality of all the principal personages. In the Iliad, for example, Agamemnon is, no doubt, a king of kings—all other chieftains are subject to his sceptre—but his superiority is no merely formal mutual relation of command and submission of the lord, that is, to his vassals. On the contrary, much circumspection is required of him; he must be shrewd enough to know where he ought to give way, for each particular chieftain is independent even as himself; they are not merely governors or generals summoned by him. They have assembled around him of their own free will, or are induced to follow his lead in a variety of ways. He must take counsel with them; and if they disagree with his judgment they are at liberty, as Achilles did, to remain aloof from the battle. It is this freedom of acceptance, no less than this free right to assert disapproval, which secures the absolute independence of such individuality, and attaches its poetical atmosphere to every situation. We find much the same thing in the poetry of Ossian, as also in the relation of the Cid to the princes, whom this poetical hero of romantic and national chivalry serves as vassal. In Ariosto and Tasso this free relation is still unimpaired; and indeed in Ariosto the individual heroes set forth in practically unqualified independence on their own path of adventure. And the mass of the folk stand in much the same relation to their leaders as that of the separate chieftains to Agamemnon. These too follow voluntarily. There is still no paramount legal obligation by which they are constrained. Honour, reverence, humility in the presence of men more mighty than themselves, ever able to enforce that might, the imposing presence of the heroic character in short and all it

171

implies, such are the essential grounds of their obedience. The order of domestic life is maintained in a similar way. It is not enforced as an accepted rule of service, but as dependent on personal inclination or ethical habit. All is made to appear as though it had grown up spontaneously. Homer, for example, tells us of the Greeks, when narrating one of their battles with the Trojans, that they had lost many valiant fighters, but not so many as the Trojans; and the reason given is that they were always mindful to ward off from one another the extreme of necessity. In other words, they assisted each other. And if we, in our own days, had occasion to define the difference between a well-disciplined and an uncivilized army we could not express it more directly than by laying stress on this very coherence and spirit of cameraderie, this unity enforced by all in a felt association, which distinguished the former. Barbarians are simply human mobs, in which no individual can rely on his neighbour. What, however, in our modern example, being as it is the final result of a stringent and tedious military discipline, rather appears as the exercise and command of an established regime, in Homer's case is still an ethical habit asserted of its own accord, springing from the vital strength of the individual in his private capacity.

We may explain in a similar way Homer's great variety in his descriptions of Nature and external condition. In the prose romances of our own day we do not find much stress laid on the natural aspects of things. Homer, on the contrary, gives us every detail in his portrayal of a staff, sceptre, bedstead, armour, clothing, doorpost; he does not even omit to mention the hinges on which the door turns. Such things appear to us wholly outside our attention and insignificant; or rather we may say that it is the tendency of our education to affect an extremely severe superiority to a whole number of objects, matters, and expressions, and we deliberately classify in their claim to our notice such things as various kinds of dress, furniture, implements, and so on. Add to this the fact that in our day all the means supplied or prepared for the satisfaction of our wants are so split up into every kind of machinery product from work-shop and factory, we come to regard the medley of supply as something beneath us, neither deserving enumeration or respectful attention. The heroic existence is, on the contrary, confronted with a primitive simplicity of objects and inventions; it readily lingers on their description. All these possessions are, in short, regarded as of one standard of value, as chattels or instruments in which man still discovers evidence of his craftsmanship, his positive wealth and interest whereof he may be justly proud. His entire life is not abstracted from such material things, nor exclusively occupied with a purely intellectual sphere. To slaughter oxen and prepare their flesh for the table, to pour out wine and things of that sort are part of the heroic life, carried out with purpose and delight; with us a meal, if it is not to be a very commonplace affair, must not merely carry with it something of the culinary art, but is incomplete without really good conversation. Homer's detailed descriptions in these matters must not therefore be looked upon as a purely poetical embellishment of things of little moment; such a copious attention is nothing more or less than the actual spirit of the men and circumstances depicted. We find just the same prolixity of speech on external things in the case of our own peasants; and for that matter do not the dandies of our own day dilate without limit upon their stables, horses, top-boots, spurs, pants, and the like. In contrast to a life of profounder intellectual interest such things will doubtless appear somewhat jejune.

Such a world ought not merely to embrace the *limited* universality of the particular event, which occurs on the *definite* background presupposed; it must coalesce in its expansion with the *entire horizon* of the national vision. We have a supremely fine example of this in the Odyssey, which not only brings us into contact with the domestic life of the Greek chieftains, their servants and subordinates, but also unfolds the richest variety with its tales of the many opinions of foreign peoples, the hazards of sea-life, the dwellings of distant lands, and so forth. But in the Iliad also, though the nature of its subject restricts to some extent the horizon of our vision, and not unnaturally on its battle-fields has comparatively little to tell us of more tranquil scenes, Homer, at least, has on the shield of Achilles managed in a wonderful way to give us a view of the entire compass of terrestrial existence, no less than human life, in marriages, judicial affairs, agriculture, the might of armies, the private wars of cities, and much else. And these descriptions we 'shall do well not to regard as a wholly incidental feature of the poem. In contrast to such a treatment the poems we identify with the name of Ossian introduce us to a world that is too limited and indefinite. It has for this very reason rather a lyrical character; and as for Dante we may say that his angels and devils inhabit no truly positive world open to our detailed approach; it exists solely as instrumental to the final fruition or due punishment of mankind. And above all in the Nibelungenlied the absence is complete of any definite realization of a visible world or environment, so that the narrative tends in this respect to assume the strain or tone of the mere balladsinger. The narrative is, no doubt, diffusive enough; but it is all much as if some journeyman had picked it up first as gossip, and then retailed it as such afterwards. We are not brought to close quarters with the facts, but are merely made aware of the impotence and tedious effort of the poet. This wearisome expanse of poetical debility becomes of course even more pronounced in the

Book of Heroes, until finally the whole business is handed over to the true poetical journeyman, in other words, the Master singers.

(β) Furthermore, for the reason that the Epos has to embody in art a specific world, in all its separate characteristics carefully defined, one, in short, for this reason itself essentially individual, the mirror of such a world must be that of a one *particular* people.

(αα) In this respect all truly primitive Epopees present to our view a national spirit in the ethical structure of its family life, its public dispositions in times of peace or war, its wants, arts, usages, and interests—in a word, a picture of the relative type and stage of the national consciousness. What the epic poem reveres more than anything else, observes most narrowly, that which, as previously noted, it expatiates upon, is the power to let our inward eye see as in a mirror the individual genius of nations. We have presented us, as the result of such a gallery, the world-history itself, and what is more, we have it in its beautiful, free, and emphasized vitality, manifestation, and deed. From no source, either so impregnate with life or simplicity, can we, for example, better understand the Hellenic spirit and Greek history, or at least grasp the principle of that content, which this people embodied, and which it brought with it when it first set forth to engage in the conflict of its wholly authentic history, than from this of the poet Homer.

(ββ) Now the national substance in its realization is of a *twofold* nature. First, we have an entirely *positive* world of specialized usage or custom peculiar to the nation in question, a definite period of history, a definite environment, whether geographical in its streams, hills and forests, or in its climatic situation. Secondly, we have that ideal *substance* of its spiritual life, whether in the religious sphere, the family or the community generally. If thus an Epos of the primitive type is, under the conditions already indicated, to be and remain a permanently effective bible, the nation's Book, in that case that which is positive in the reality of the Past can only claim such a continuously vital interest in so far as the characteristic features accepted are placed in an ideal connection with the actually substantive aspects and tendencies of the national life. Otherwise what claims to be of positive value will be entirely contingent and a matter of indifference. Native geographical conditions, for instance, enter into the conception of nationality. But if they do not confer on a folk its specific character, the addition of other natural environment, provided that does not contradict national character, is not in certain cases prejudicial to the effect, but may even prove attractive to the imagination. No doubt the sensitive experience of youth is interwoven with the immediate presence of its native hills and streams; but where the deeper bonds of the entire spiritual outlook are absent, such an association assumes a more or less external character. And, apart from this, where we have, as in the Iliad, a warlike expedition, it is impossible to preserve the *locale* of the fatherland. In such a case the scenery of a foreign land in itself fascinates and attracts. The enduring vitality of an Epos is, however, more seriously impaired, where, in the course of centuries, the spiritual consciousness and life has so entirely changed that the links between the more recent Past and the original point of departure already adverted to are completely severed. This is actually the case with the poet Klopstock in another province of poetry, where he attempts to establish a national religion, and, in order to do so, gives us his Hermann and Thusnelda. We may affirm the same kind of defect of the Nibelungenlied. The Burgundians, the revenge of Chriemhilda, the exploits of Siegfried, the entire social condition, the fated downfall of an entire race and many like facts—all this is no longer vitally held together with the domestic, civil, and judicial life, the institutions and constitutions of the present day. The biography of Jesus Christ, with its Jerusalem, Bethlehem, and Roman jurisdiction, even the Trojan war itself, come home to ourselves far more nearly than the events of the Niebelungen; the latter are for present consciousness a state of things wholly gone for ever, swept away once and for all with a besom. To attempt to compose of such something of national significance, to say nothing of a national bible, betokens the extreme limit of folly and superficiality. In times when it was rashly[4] assumed that the flame of youthful enthusiasm had flashed up anew, such a conceit was taken as a proof of the sere leaf of an age once more become childlike in the approach of death; and it refreshed itself with a past that was dead, and deemed it possible to associate others with a similar refreshment and renewed presence.

($\gamma\gamma$) If, however, a national Epos is to secure in addition the permanent interest of foreign nations the world which it depicts must not merely be of a *particular* nationality, but of a type that is, in this specific folk, its heroism and exploits, equally impressed with the stamp of our common humanity. In the poems of Homer, for example, the superb directness with which he deals with matters of divine or ethical import, the nobility of the characters and of everything living therein embraced, the pictorial quality of their presentment to the reader, all this insures an undying truth for succeeding ages. In this respect we find a remarkable contrast in the creation of different peoples. We cannot deny, for instance, that the Ramajana reflects with the essential directness of life the national spirit of the Hindoos, more particularly from the religious point of view; but the character of the entire Hindoo race is so overpoweringly of a unique type, that the essential features of our common humanity are unable to assert themselves through the veil of this national idiosyncracy. A remarkable contrast to this is the way in which the entire Christian world, from the earliest times, has found itself at home in those epic passages of Old Testament narrative, above all in the pictures of the patriarchal state, and able to repicture for itself to the life the events portrayed over and over again with the greatest enjoyment. The testimony of Goethe is unequivocal. Here was the *one* focal centre, he assures us, on which, in his young days, amid much that he learned of a miscellaneous and unconnected character, his intellect no less than feeling concentrated itself. Even in later life he still remarks upon them that "after all our wanderings through the East we always returned in the end to these writings as the most invigorating spring of waters: here and there they might be troubled; not unfrequently they hid themselves in the earth; but it was only to rise up again pure and fresh as ever."

(γ) *Finally*, the general condition of a particular people must not in this tranquil universality of its individual character wholly oust what is more directly the object of the Epos, in other words, be described with no reference to that. It ought only to appear as the *foundation*, upon which an event throughout its entire process is transacted, one which is in contact with all aspects of the national life, and one which illustrates the same as it proceeds. Such an eventuality must not be a purely external incident; it must imply a deliberately conceived purpose executed by equally deliberate effort. If, however, these two aspects, namely, the general condition and the particular action, do not coalesce, then the event in question must seek its justification in the particular circumstances, the causal conditions which dominate its movement. That is practically to say the world of Epos which is reproduced must be conceived under a specific situation which is so concrete that the definite

178

objects which it is the function of the epic narrative to realize, are necessarily made explicit by it. We have already, when discussing the ideal action,[5] pointed out on general lines that this realization presupposes situations and circumstances which bring about collisions, actions that do injury and consequently necessary reactions. The particular situation, therefore, in which the epic world-condition of a nation is made actual to us, must of itself be essentially one implying such *collisions*. In this respect, therefore, epic poetry enters the field already occupied by dramatic poetry; and we may find it convenient at once to determine in what respects the collisions of these two types of poetry differ.

(αα) Under the broadest review of this question we may say that the conflict of the *belligerent* condition is that which supplies the Epos with its most pertinent situation. In war it is obviously the entire nation which is set in activity, and which, as a whole placed under similar conditions, is moved and stimulated in a novel way, in so far at least as it possesses any claim, as such a whole, to participate in it. We may admit that the above conclusion stands in apparent contradiction not merely with Homer's Odyssey, but also the subject-matter of many poems that are epic in an otherwise intelligible sense. It finds, however, ample corroboration in the majority of the most famous Epopees. Moreover, the collision of operations in the events of which the Odyssey informs us, derives part of its source from the Trojan war; and even under the aspect of domestic life in Ithaca, no less than that of the home-returning Odysseus, although the narrative is no actual account of conflicts between Greeks and Trojans, yet it deals with facts which are the immediate consequence of that war. Nay, it is itself war under a new aspect, for many chieftains are forced to reconquer their homes, which after their ten years' absence they find under wholly altered conditions. We have

179

practically but one example of the religious Epos, Dante's "Divine Comedy." Even here, too, the fundamental collision is deducible from that original Fall of the evil angels from heaven, which brings in its train and within the sphere of human experience the ever active external and ideal conflict between the Divine Father and the conduct of men, whether hostile or well-pleasing to Him, a conflict eternally perpetuated in condemnation, purification, and blessedness, or in other words, hell, purgatory, and paradise. Also, too, in the Messias it is the former war against the Son of God which supplies the focal centre. At the same time the most vital and truly pertinent examples are those which actually describe the belligerent state. We have already drawn attention to such in the Ramajana, and, most instructive of all, in the Iliad; further examples are the famous poems of Ossian, Tasso, Ariosto, and Camoens. In war *courage* is and remains the fundamental interest; and warlike courage is a state of the soul and an activity, which is neither so suitable for lyrical expression nor for dramatic action, but is pre-eminently adapted to the descriptive power of the Epos. In dramatic poetry it is rather the ideal strength or weakness of spiritual life, the ethically justified or reprehensible pathos which is the main thing: in the Epos, on the contrary, it is rather the native characteristics of a personality. For this reason, where it is national exploits which are undertaken, bravery is in its right place; it is in fact not an ethical state, [6] in which the will is determined through its own initiative as an intelligent consciousness and volition. It rather depends on natural temperament, unites in direct equilibrium, as by fusion, with the sphere of self-conscious life, and, in order to bring into effect practical ends, which can be more fitly expressed in epic description than under the conceptions of lyrical emotion and reflection. And these conclusions with regard to bravery in war apply with equal force to the exploits of war and their consequences. The

180

activities of personal volition and the accidents of the external event supply the two scales of the balance. The bare event, with its wholly material obstructions, is excluded from the drama, inasmuch as here what is exclusively external is not permitted to retain an independent right, but is causally related to the aim and ideal purposes of individuals, so that as to all contingent matter, if by any chance it appears to arise and to determine the result, we are none the less compelled to look for the real operative cause and justification thereof in the spiritual nature of human character and its objects, no less than in that of its collisions and their necessary resolution.

($\beta\beta$) A basis of the epic action such as this of active hostilities is obviously the source of a very varied subject-matter. We may have placed before the imagination a host of interesting actions and events, in which bravery in action supplies the leading rôle, and the claim of external forces, whether asserted in circumstance or incident, is maintained unimpaired. At the same time we must not overlook a respect in which the possibilities of epic narration is essentially restricted. It is only wars waged between one foreign nation and another which partake of a truly epic character. In contrast to this conflicts between dynasties, civil wars and social revolution, are more suited to dramatic exposition. And in fact Aristotle long ago[7] advises the tragic poet to select subject-matter which is concerned with the conflicts of brother against brother. Of this type is the war of the Seven against Thebes. It is Thebes' own son who storms the city; and its defender is the actual brother of the aggressor. Hostility of this type is something more than that of a mere foe; its significance is bound up with the individuality of the opposed brothers. We have similar examples with every kind of variety in Shakespeare's historical tragedies. In these, almost without exception,

181

agreement between particular individuals is what might be legitimately looked for, and it is only the private motives of individual passion and a personality absorbed in its own aims and satisfaction which bring about collisions and wars. As an example of an action of this kind treated in the epic manner, and therefore defectively, I will mention the "Pharsalia" of Lucan. However indisputably important the conflicting aims in this poem may appear to be, yet for all that the opposing parties are here too closely related on the common ground of one fatherland: their conflict, consequently, instead of being a war between two national entities, is nothing more than a strife of parties, either of which, by the very fact that it splits asunder the substantive national unity, points in one direction, namely, that of tragic guilt and demoralization. Held to this the objective facts are not placed before us in their clearness and simplicity, but are inweaved with one another in a confused manner. The same objections are equally pertinent to Voltaire's Henriad. In contrast to this the hostility of *foreign* nations is something substantive. Every nation constitutes a totality essentially distinct from and in opposition to that of another. When these come into conflict we do not feel that any positive ethical connection is shattered, nothing at least of essential value to either is violated,[8] no necessary whole broken into fragments. Rather it is a conflict waged in order to maintain such a totality unimpaired and to justify its claim to be so. Hostility therefore of this type is suited in every way to the essential character of epic poetry.

(γγ) Not every war, however, waged under ordinary conditions between two hostile nations is necessarily on that account of an epic character. We must have a further condition satisfied, namely, the justification on broad historical grounds for the bellicose attitude thus adopted. Only when we have this do we obtain a picture of an enterprise at once novel and more exalted, which does not present the appearance of something apart from universal history, the purely capricious subjugation of one state by another, but is absolutely and essentially rooted in a profounder principle of necessity, however much at the same time the more superficial and obvious motive of the undertaking may assume from one point of view the aspect of deliberate wrong,[9] and from the other that of a private revenge. We have something analogous to such a situation in the Ramajana. But the supreme example is that of the Iliad, where the Greeks invade an Asiatic people, and in doing so fight out as it were the preludic conflict of a tremendous opposition, the wars of which practically constitute the turning point of Greek history as we see it on the stage of universal history. Of the same type is the struggle of the Cid against the Moors, or in Tasso and Ariosto the battles of the Christians against the Saracens, or in Camoens the strife of the Portuguese against the Indians. And indeed we may assert that in all the greatest Epopees we find nations which differ from each other in moral customs, religion, and language, in a word, in all that concerns their spiritual and external life, brought into collision; and we are ready to contemplate such without any revulsion on account of the triumph we find asserted there of a nobler principle of world-evolution over a less exalted, a victory assured by a bravery that is simply annihilating. If any one should, in this sense, and in emulation of past Epopees, which have sought to depict the triumph of the West over the East, of the European principle of moderation, of the individually articulate and truly organic type of beauty over Asiatic splendour, over the magnificence of a patriarchal unity, which does not attempt to secure such organic completeness, or is at least merely held together by abstract and superficial conjunctions, if such, I say, should aspire to write the Epopee of the future, he will be necessarily restricted to the portrayal of the victory of some future and intensely vital rationality of the American nation over the prison-house of the spirit which for ever pursues its monotonous task of self-adjustment and particularization.[10] In the Europe of our day every nation finds itself conditioned[11] by its neighbour, and cannot venture on its own account to wage any war with another European nation. If we lift our eyes beyond Europe, there can be only one direction, America.

(b) The Individual Epic Action

It is on such an essentially limited foundation then of conflict between entire nationalities that the epic event is realized, the leading characteristics of which we have now to determine. We may summarize the form we propose our investigation should take as follows:

Firsts what actually takes place consists essentially in this that the object of the epic action ought necessarily to be of *individual vitality* and definition, however much it may rest on a basis of the most general extension.

Secondly, for the reason that it is only of individuals that we can predicate actions we have the problem to solve of the general nature of the epic *character* or personality.

Thirdly, in the epic eventuality the form of objectivity is not exclusively that of external appearance: it consists quite as much in the significance of all that is itself intrinsically necessary to and substantive in the exposition. We have consequently to determine the form in which this intrinsic significance of the occurrence proclaims itself as effective, either in part as the ideal necessity which is therein concealed, or as the disclosed direction[12] of eternal and providential forces.

(a) We have postulated as a necessary background of this

184

epic world an enterprise of national significance, in which the entire compass of a national spirit can express itself in the bloom and freshness of its heroic condition. From this fundamental substratum in its simplicity we now further assume the apparition of a *particular* end, in the realization of which all other aspects of the national character, whether in belief or action, can be represented to our vision. The original postulate is in fact bound up in the closest way with such an all-embracing actuality.

($\alpha\alpha$) This purposed object, which is infused with the vital principle of individuality on the lines of which, regarded in its particularized content, the entire process moves forward, must further, as already ascertained, appropriate to itself in the Epos the form of an *event*. It will be therefore above all important to recall at once the specific character of the mode, under which human volition and action generally combine in what we designate as the event. Now, in the *first* place, action and adventure are the outcome of conscious life, the content of which is not only ideally expressed in emotions, reflections, and thoughts, but also quite as much in a practical way. We may regard such realization from two distinct points of view. *First*, we have the ideal substance of the end presupposed and purposed, the general character of which the individual must recognize, will, calculate and accept. *Secondly*, there is the external reality of the spiritual or human and the natural environment, within which he is only able to act, and the accidental features of which at one time obstruct and at another assist his path; so that either in the one case he is carried forward by virtue of this favour to a successful issue, or, if in the other he is not prepared wholly to give way to such opposition, he finds it necessary to overcome them with his individual energy. If now the world covered by this volitional power is conceived as the indivisible unity of these two aspects, with the result that the right of assertion by both is equally asserted, in that case what is most pertinent to conscious life likewise enters into the formal structure of the event, the form, that is, which confers on all human action the *configuration of events*, in so far as the conscious or subjective will, with its purposes, motives of passion, principles and aims, can no longer appear the fact of most importance. Or, in other words, in human *action* everything is referred back to human personality, personal obligation, opinion and intention. In the case of the *event*, on the contrary, the external constitution of things is permitted to assert its inviolable claim. Here it is objective reality itself, which constitutes either the form assumed by the whole, or from another point of view a fundamental part of the content. In agreement with such a view I have already stated that it is the function of epic poetry to demonstrate the *happening* of an action, and thereby not only to establish the external disposition of the execution of ends, but also to meet as readily the claims of external condition, natural occurrences, and all else of a contingent character, which, in action taken simply as such, the ideal element of conscious life claims exclusively as its province.

(ββ) With regard to the *particular* end, the carrying out of which the Epos unfolds under the mode of the event, it follows from our previous conclusions that it must be no mere mental *abstraction*, but on the contrary of wholly *concrete* definition. At the same time, inasmuch as it is realized within the substantive actuality of the national unity, such a process must exclude the notion of merely capricious activity. The political state as such—the fatherland, let us say—or the history of a State and country, are essentially something universal, which, regarded in the light of such universality, does not appear under the mode of a subjectively individual existence, or, in other words, in

186

inseparable and exclusive coalition with one definite living individual. For this reason the history of a country, the development of its political life, its constitution and destiny may also no doubt be narrated as event; if, however, the facts thus described are not placed before us as the concrete deed, the conscious aim, the passion, the suffering and accomplishment of particular heroes, whose individuality supplies the form and content of the realization in all its parts, the event merely assumes the rigid form of its independent forward movement in the prosaic history of a people or an empire. In this respect no doubt the most exalted action of Spirit would be the history of the world itself. We can conceive it possible that our poet might in this sense undertake to elaborate in what we may call the absolute Epos this universal achievement on the battlefield of the universal spirit, whose hero would be the spirit of man, the *humanus*, who is drawn up and exalted from the clouded levels[13] of conscious existence into the clearer region of universal history. But in virtue of the very fact of its universality a subject-matter of this kind would so be quite unfitted for artistic treatment. It would not adapt itself sufficiently to individualization. For on the one hand we fail altogether to find in such a subject a clearly fixed background and world-condition, not merely in relation to external *locale*, but also in that of morality and custom. In other words, the only basis for all we could possibly presuppose would be the universal World-Spirit or intelligence, whom we are unable to bring visibly before us as a particular condition, and who is possessed of the entire Earth as his local environment. And in like manner too the one end fulfilled in such an Epos could only be the end proposed by the World-Spirit himself,[14] who can only be apprehended and explicitly disclosed in his true significance through the processes of thought. If he is, however, to be represented in the form of poetry, or, at least, if the whole is

187

to receive its proper meaning and coalescence from such a source, it is necessary that his presence should be expressed as that which acts independently from its own resources. This could only be possible for poetry, in so far as the ideal Taskmaster of history, the eternal and absolute Idea, which is realized in humanity, either was envisioned as a directive, active, perfecting individual person, or was merely made effective under the concealing veil of an ever-operative Necessity. In the first case, however, the infinity of such a content must shatter the necessarily limited artistic vessel of determinate individuality, or, as the only way of avoiding such a defect, must assume the inadequate form of a dispassionate allegory of general reflections over the destination of the human race and its education, over the final purpose of mankind, its moral consummation, or over whatever result the end of this World-history might establish. In the alternative case it is the genius of the various peoples which has in each example to be presented (in the heroic figure) in the conflicting existence of whom history expands and moves forward in progressive evolution. If, however, the genius of nations is really to appear in poetical form this can be carried out in only one way, namely, by placing before us the actual world-historical figures as operative through their deeds. We should, however, then merely have a series of particular characters, which emerged and again disappeared in a wholly external succession, the objects of which lacked individual unity and connection; and this would be so for the reason that the controlling World-Spirit, under our conception of it, as the ideal essence and destiny, could not, in the case supposed, be set forth as itself an active individual and the culminating agent in the process. And if, further, anyone was desirous of appropriating the spirits of different nationalities in their universality, and of displaying them as agents in such a substantive form, we should still only have a similar series, the individuals whereof, apart from the fact that they would merely possess an appearance of positive existence similar to Hindoo incarnations, would, in the fictitious form of the imagination they received pale into nothingness when contrasted with the truth of the World-Spirit as realized in actual history.

(γγ) We may consequently lay it down as a general principle that the particular epic event is only able to secure a vital form in poetry when it is united in the closest state of fusion with *one* individual. Precisely as it is *one* poet who thinks out and executes the whole, so too *one* individual must crown the edifice, with whom the event is associated and in connection with whose single identity it is continued and completed.

We must point out, however, that here too we are limited by essential conditions. For just as in our previous discussion it was the world-history, so too now, from the converse point of view, it is possible that the biographical treatment in a poetic composition of a definite life-history may appear to supply the most complete and adequate subject-matter of the Epos. This, however, is not the case. No doubt in biography the individual is one and the same throughout; but the events, through which the life-development proceeds, may entirely fall apart, and only retain the subject of the same in a wholly formal and accidental bond of relation. If, on the other hand, the Epos is essentially homogeneous, the event also, in the form of which the content of the poem is disclosed, must itself possess intrinsic unity. Both aspects, in short, the unity of the individual and that of the objective event, as it is evolved, must coalesce and be united. In the life and exploits of the Cid it is unquestionably true that on the field of the Fatherland it is only one great personality which without intermission remains true to himself, and in his development, chivalry and end constitutes the interest. His deeds pass before him, much as if he were the sculptured god; and finally all is gone and vanished for us, no less than for himself.[15] But the poems of the Cid are also as rhymed chronicles no genuine example of the Epos; and, in their later form of romances, they are, as their specific type necessitates, merely isolated situations split off from this national hero's life, which do not necessarily coalesce in the unity of a particular event.

The finest examples, however, of the observance of the above rule are to be met with in the Iliad and Odyssey, where Achilles and Odysseus are respectively the prominent figures. The Ramajana, too, resembles these poems in this respect. Dante's "Divine Comedy" is an illustration, but in quite a unique way. In other words, it is the Epic poet himself with whose single personality, in his wanderings through hell, purgatory, and paradise, all and everything is so associated that he is able to recount the picture of his imagination as a personal experience, and is consequently entitled to interweave with the general substance of his composition his private emotions and reflections to a larger extent than is possible for other epic poets.

(β) However much then, speaking generally, epic poetry informs us of actual fact and its occurrence, and thereby makes the objective world its content and form, yet on the other hand, inasmuch as what happens is an *action,* which passes in successive views before us, it is rather, and for this reason, to *individuals,* and their deed and suffering that the main emphasis is attached. For it is only individuals, be they gods or men, who can veritably act; and just in proportion as they are interwoven in the vividness of life with such a panorama, to that extent they are entitled to attract the main interest to the fulness of their exposition. From this point of view epic poetry stands on level terms with lyric no less than dramatic poetry. It is therefore of some importance that we attempt to define more closely what the *specific* features are which distinguish the portrayal of personality in the epic composition.

(*αα*) Now, first, what is essential to the objective aspect of an epic character—I am speaking mainly of the leading personages—is that they should be themselves essentially a *totality* of such traits, in other words complete men, and thereby display in themselves all aspects of emotional life, or to put it better, should represent in a typical way, national opinion and its active pursuits. In this respect I have already in the first part drawn attention to the heroic characters of Homer; and, in particular, to the variety of genuinely human and truly national qualities which Achilles unites in himself so vitally, the hero of the Odyssey supplying an admirable companion picture. The Cid is similarly presented us with much variety of characterization and situation, as son, hero, lover, husband, father, householder, and in his relations to king, friends, and foes. Other Epopees of the Middle Ages are a great contrast, far more abstract in their type of personification, particularly so where their heroes merely champion the cause of chivalry as such, and are removed from the sphere of the true and actual life of the nation.

It is then the fundamental characteristic of the exposition of epic personality that it should unfold itself as such a totality in the most diverse scenes and situations. The characters of tragedy and comedy may no doubt also possess a similar wealth of ideality; for the reason, however, that in their case the sharp contrast between a pathos that is never other than one-sided and a passion opposed to it is within very definable limits and ends the thing of most importance, such a varied character is in part, where it is not entirely superfluous, at least more in the nature of a prodigality

191

which is incidental, and in part is also, as a rule, overpowered by the *one* passion, its motives and ethical considerations, and thus forced by the type of presentation into the background. In the whole of the epic composition, on the contrary, all aspects assert an equal right to assert themselves, and expand with freedom and breadth. That they should do so is indeed fundamental to the principle of epic composition; and from a further point of view the personality here, in virtue of the entire world-condition he presupposes, possesses a right to be, and to make all that valid wherein his existence is realized, and for the good reason that he lives in an age to which precisely this *objective* being, this immediate individuality is appropriate. It is, of course, for instance, quite possible for us, with regard to the wrath of Achilles, to point out, as moral reflection may suggest, the injury and loss which that wrath entailed, and therefrom to conclude that the superiority and greatness of Achilles is very appreciably removed from any approach to ideal perfection, whether as hero or man, having no power apparently on a single occasion to moderate his anger or exercise self-restraint. But for all that we do wrong in blaming Achilles. And this is not because we may overlook the wrath in virtue of his other great qualities. Achilles is, in other words, simply nothing more or less than this portrait. So far as Epic poetry is concerned, that is the end of the matter. The same observations apply to his ambition and his love of glory. The main justification of these great characters is the energy of their achievement; they carry, in fact, a universal principle in their particularity. Conversely, ordinary morality tends to depreciate its native personality, and hold in reserve the resources of its life-force, and discovers its essential being in this attitude. What an astonishing self-esteem, for instance, an Alexander asserted over his friends and the life of I know not how many thousands. Self-revenge, even traits of brutality, testify to an energy of the same type in heroic times; and even in this respect Achilles, in his rôle of epic hero, has little to learn.

($\beta\beta$) And it is just on account of this fact that such preeminent figures are complete individuals, who have in resplendent degree all that concentrated in them which otherwise is diffused and separate in the national character, and thereby are throughout great, free, and humanly beautiful characters that they are rightly set in the chief place; and we find that the event of most significance is inviolably linked with such individuality. The nation is, as it were, focussed as a single living soul in them, and as such they fight out its main enterprise, and suffer the hazards of its resulting experience. In this respect Gottfried von Bouillon, in Tasso's "Jerusalem Liberated," is no such overpowering figure as Achilles, this typical youthful bloom and perfection of the entire Grecian host; nor is he even an Odysseus, although he is selected as the wisest, bravest, and most just of leaders to command the entire army. The Achæans are unable to win a victory if Achilles stands aloof from the contest; it is he alone who, by means of his triumph over Hector, carries victory into Troy itself; and in the return home of Odysseus we find a mirror of the return of all the Greeks from Troy, only with the difference that it is just in that which it is his destiny to endure we have placed exhaustively before our vision the entire compass of the sufferings, life experience, and conditions which are implied in the whole subject-matter. The characters of the drama, on the other hand, are not so represented as in themselves the absolute crowning point of all the rest, which becomes objective in and through them. They rather are set forth independently and for themselves in their purpose, which they accept as the outcome of their character, or as the result of definite principles which have grown up in conjunction with their more isolate personality.

(γγ) There is a *third* distinguishing feature in epic characterization due to the fact that the Epos does not portray an action simply as action, but an event. In drama the matter of importance is that the individual manifests himself as operative for his specific purpose, and is expressly represented in such activity and its consequences. This undeviating consideration for the realization of a distinct purpose is absent in the Epic. No doubt in this case, too, heroes have desires and aims, but the main thing here is all that they may happen to experience while fulfilling it, not the nature of their conduct in the carrying it out. The circumstances are just as active as themselves, frequently more active. The return to Ithaca, for example, is the actual project of Odysseus. The Odyssey, however, does not merely display this character in the active execution of his predetermined end, but expands its account into all the variety of occurrence which he happens to experience in his wanderings, what he suffers, what obstructions meet him in the way, what dangers he has to overcome, and all, in fact, that moves him. And this varied experience is not, as would be necessary in the drama, a direct result of his action, but is in great measure rather incidental to his journey, in the main even independent of the concurrent action of the hero. After his adventures with the Lotophagi, Polyphemus, and the Laestrygones, the godlike Circe detains him for a full year. Further, after he has visited the lower world and suffered shipwreck, he dallies with Calypso, until he falls into home-sickness, wearies of the damsel, and stares with tearful eyes over the solitary sea. Thereupon it is Calypso herself who finally provides him with the means wherewith he builds his boat, who provides him with food, wine and raiment, and takes her right anxious and kindly farewell of him. Finally, after his sojourn among the Phæacians, he is carried in sleep—he knows not how—to the shores of his island. To carry out a purposed end in this sort of way

194

would not be possible for dramatic poetry. Again, in the Iliad, the wrath of Achilles, which, along with all else that results from this compelling force, constitutes the specific object of the narrative, is throughout not an end, but rather an emotional state. When Achilles is insulted he rages. In this condition, so far from doing anything truly dramatic, he withdraws apart, does nothing with Patroclus by the ships on the seashore, sullenly angry that he is not honoured by the lord of the folk. Then follow the consequences of his retirement, and only at last, when his friend has been slain by Hector, do we find Achilles once more plunge into the conflict. In another way, again, is the end prescribed to Æneas, which he has to carry out, where Virgil recounts all the events as the result of which its realization is in such varied ways postponed.

(γ) We have just one further important feature to mention in respect to the form of the event in the Epos. I have already observed that in the drama the conscious will, and that which the same demands and wills, is essentially the determining factor, and constitutes the permanent foundation of the entire presentation. All that is carried out appears throughout as posited already by the personal character and its aims; and the main interest above all turns upon the justification or its absence of what is done within the situations presupposed and the conflicts they bring about. If consequently it so happens also that in the drama the external conditions are themselves active, they nevertheless only retain their validity by virtue of that which conscious feeling and volition makes of them, and the ways and means under which character reacts upon them. In the Epos, however, the circumstances and external accidents are effective on level terms with the personal will itself. All that man accomplishes passes before us precisely as any other event of the world outside him, so that the

195

human exploit is in this case likewise and equally conditioned, and must be shown to be carried forward by the development of such an environment. The individual, in short, in epic poetry does not merely act freely of himself and independently. He is placed in the midst of an assemblage of facts, whose end and actuality in its wide correlation with an essentially unified world of conscious life or objective existence supplies the irremovable foundation of the life of each separate individual. This typical system is, in fact, predominant in the Epos through all its content, whether in that of passion, determined result, or general achievement. It is true that at first sight we might expect that, on account of an equal cogency being accorded to external condition in its independent eventualities, we should find indisputable opportunity given for every shade of contingency. And yet we have seen that it is the function of the Epos to present what is truly objective—what is, in short, essentially substantive existence. The solution of this contradiction is to be found in this, that the principle of *necessity* is involved in the events, whether taken in detail or generally.

(αα) In this connection we may affirm of the Epos—not, however, as is generally assumed of the drama—that *Destiny* is a predominant force. No doubt the dramatic character by the kind of end accepted, which he endeavours to carry out despite all obstruction under the circumstances given and recognized, makes of *himself* his Destiny; but in the Epos, on the contrary, it is *made for him*, and this force of circumstances, which stamp their particular form on the deed, apportions to each individual his lot, determines the result of his actions—is, in short, the genuine control of Destiny. What happens is appertinent to itself. It is so, and only thus; it is the fiat of necessity. In lyric poetry we are conscious of emotion, reflection, the personal interest, and yearning. The drama converts the ideal claim of human action into an objective presence. The presentation of epic poetry, on the other hand, moves, as it were, within the element itself of essentially necessary existence. Therefore, the individual has no choice but to follow this particular substantive condition; and, in its process of being, to adapt himself to it or not, and then to suffer as he is able and is forced to suffer. Destiny, in short, defines what is and inevitably must be, and in the result success, misadventure, life, and death are plastic precisely in the sense that individuals are plastic. What does actually unfold before us is a condition of universal expanse, in which the actions and destinies of mankind appear as something isolated and evanescent. This fatality is the great justice, and is not tragic in the dramatic sense of the term, in which the individual appears judged as a *personality*, but in the epic sense in which judgment is passed on man in all that concerns him. [16] The tragic Nemesis consists in this, that the greatness of his concerns is too great for the individual concerned. Consequently a certain tone of sadness[17] prevails over the whole. What is most glorious is seen very early to pass away. In the fulness of his life Achilles mourns over his death; and at the conclusion of the Odyssey we view him and Agamemnon as spirits that have passed away as shades, with the consciousness that they are shades. Troy, too, falls; old Priam is slain hard by the altar of the home; women and maidens become slaves. Æneas, in obedience to the divine command, departs to found a new kingdom in Latium, and the victorious heroes only return after manifold suffering to the happiness or bitterness that awaits them at home.

(ββ) This necessity of events may, however, be represented in very different ways.

The most obvious and least elaborate is the bare exhibition of such events without any further explanation of the poet of a necessary element existing in the particular occurrences and their general consequence by his addition of a controlling world of gods disclosed in the decision, interference, and co-operation of eternal powers. In such a case we must, however, have the feeling brought home from the entire atmosphere of the exposition, that in the recounted events and great life-destinies of single individuals and entire families or races, we are not merely confronted with what is mutable and contingent in human existence, but with destinies which have an essential foundation, whose necessity remains, however, the obscure operation of a power which is not placed before us poetically as such a power in its divine controlling energy to the point of defined individualization and in its explicit activity. The Niebelungenlied retains this general tone strongly, albeit it does not ascribe the direction of the blood-stained final result of all committed deed either to Christian Providence or the pagan world of gods. For in regard to Christendom, we merely hear of churchgoing and mass. We have, indeed, the remark of the bishop of Spejevs to the beautiful Ute, when the heroes withdraw into king Etzel's country: "Please God, He will keep them there!" We have also no doubt dreams of warning, the prophecy of the Danube maidens to Hagen, and other examples of a similar kind, but no really conclusive witness to the control and interference of gods. This leaves an impression on this poetry as of a something unriddled, unyielding, a mournfulness that is at the same time objective, and consequently wholly epic in its tone. It is a great contrast to the poems of Ossian, in which in the same way no gods appear, yet in which, on the other hand, we find lamentation over the death and downfall of the entire heroic stock presented under the form of the private sorrow of the dismayed minstrel, and as the yearning of a woe-begone recollection.

Essentially distinct from the above type of conception is the complete interlacement of all human destiny and natural event with the resolution, volition and action of a many-sided world of gods such as we find in the great Hindoo Epopees, and in Homer, Virgil, and others. I have already expressly drawn attention to the varied poetic interpretation which the poet himself supplies of events, which are apparently accidental, through his assumption of the co-operation and apparition of gods, and attempted to enforce the same by particular examples from the Iliad and the Odyssey. Here we may observe that the condition of most importance to the poetry in question is that in this reciprocal action of gods and men the relative independence of both aspects is maintained, so that neither the gods fall into lifeless abstractions, nor the human individuals become purely subservient vassals. How such a danger is to be avoided I have already discussed at length in a previous passage. The Hindoo Epos is in this respect unable to force its way fully to the truly ideal relation between gods and mankind; on such a stage of imaginative symbolism the human aspect still remains aloof in its free and beautiful actuality, and the activity of individuals in part appears as the incarnation of gods, and in part, as something of more incidental merit, vanishes, or is depicted under the guise of ascetic exaltation to the condition and power of gods. Conversely the variously personified powers, passions, genii, angels, and so forth, that we meet with in Christendom possess for the most part too little individual independence, and consequently tend only to affect us in a cold and abstract sort of way. The case is much the same in Mohammedanism. Through the deification of Nature and the world of mankind, through the conception of a prosaic co-ordination of reality, it is hardly possible to avoid the danger, more particularly where we enter a region of fairyland, wherein a miraculous interpretation is given to that which is essentially contingent and indifferent in external circumstances, which are themselves only present as a simple occasion for human action and as the ordeal of individual character, without possessing therewith an ideal consistency and foundation. By reason of this no doubt the infinitely extensible connection of cause and effect is broken, and the many sections in this prosaic concatenation of circumstances, which cannot be throughout made clearly distinct, are brought all of a sudden into one union. If, however, such a result is secured without the principle of necessity and ideal reasonableness, such a mode of elucidation, as, for example, frequently in "The Thousand and one Nights," appears as little more than the sport of an imagination, which endeavours to unfold as causality possible and actual, by means of such inventions, what is otherwise incredible.

The fairest mean, on the other hand, in this respect is that retained by Greek poetry, inasmuch as it is able to bestow both on gods and men a reciprocally indestructible power and freedom of independent individuality. And such is harmonious with its fundamental standpoint.

($\beta\beta$) There is, however, particularly in the epic conception of it, a point of view relative to the collective world of gods, which I have already referred to above in another connection. This is the contrast which the *primitive* Epopee presents to the *artificial* composition of later times. This difference is very pronounced if we compare Homer and Virgil. The level of education, from which the Homeric poems originated, still continues in a fair harmony with the poetic subject-matter. With Virgil, on the contrary, we are reminded by every single hexameter that the general outlook of the poet is totally different from the world, which it is his endeavour to depict; and the gods more particularly have lost the freshness of their original vitality. Instead of being living persons in their own selves, actual witnesses to us of their existence, they have rather the appearance of being mere creations of the poet and external instruments, which it is neither possible for the poet or his audience to take quite seriously, although there is an open pretence made that they have been taken thus seriously. Throughout the whole of the Virgilian Epic we feel ourselves in the atmosphere of ordinary life; the old tradition, the saga, the fairyland of poetry enters with prosaic distinctness into the frame of our common-sense faculties. What we have in the Æneid is very much what we find in the Roman history of Livy, where ancient kings and consuls make speeches, precisely as an orator made his speech in the Agora of Rome, or the school of the rhetoricians in the days of Livy himself. And, on the other hand, in what is really retained from tradition, as an example of primitive speech, such as the fable of Menenius Agrippa[18] about the functions of the belly, we find a contrast which is almost repulsive. In Homer, however, the gods are wafted in a magical light between poetry and reality: they are not permitted to approach the imagination so nearly, that the apparition of them confronts us with all the detail of ordinary life; nor are they left so undefined, that they lose all appearance of vital reality as we look at them. All that they do is readily explained by the soul-life and activities of men; and that which supports our faith in them is the substance and content upon which they essentially repose. From this point of view the poet, too, is thoroughly in earnest with his creations, though he treats with irony their form and external reality. In agreement with this it appears that the ancients themselves believed in this external form merely as works of art, which receive their confirmation and significance as a gift of the poet. This light-hearted and human freshness of presentment, in virtue of which the gods appear human and natural, is one of the pre-eminent qualities of the Homeric poems. The divine figures of Virgil float before our vision as so many invented wonders, as members of an artificial system. Virgil has not wholly escaped the charge of mere travesty, despite his earnestness; nay, this earnest mien of his is rather the cause of it, and Blumauer's Mercury with his boots and spurs and riding-whip is not without its justification. There is no necessity for any one else to make the Homeric gods ridiculous. His own picture of them makes them quite ridiculous enough. Nay, in his own story the gods themselves have their laugh over the lame Hephestus, and over the cunning net in which Mars lies in company with Venus, to say nothing of the box on the ear that Venus gets, and the howl of Mars as he collapses. By means of these touches of natural lustiness and gaiety the poet at once liberates us from the external form which he set up, and enforces all the more emphatically our common human nature, which he values, and which suffers, however, the necessary and substantive power involved therein, and the faith in the same, to remain. But one or two more examples of similar detail. The tragic episode of Dido is so entirely to the modern colour, that it was able to inspire a Tasso with emulation, nay, even in part to a literal translation. Even nowadays the French are moved to something like ecstasy over it. And yet how totally different in their human naïveté, simplicity and truth are the Homeric narratives of Circe and Calypso. The contrast is the same in Homer's account of the descent of Odysseus into Hades. This obscure and twilight like retreat of the shades is shown us through a dusky cloud, in an intermingling of imagination and reality, which takes hold of us with astonishing force. Homer does not suffer his hero to descend into any Underworld ready to hand. Odysseus himself digs a pit, and pours therein the blood of a ram he has killed; he summons the shades, which are then under constraint to circle round him, and bids some of them drink

202

fresh blood that they may address him, and give him news, and drives away others with the sword as they throng round him in their thirst for life. Everything that happens here is bound up with the life of the hero, whose general demeanour is the reverse of the humble attitude of Æneas and Dante. In Virgil's account Æneas descends in the ordinary way; and the flight of steps, Cerberus, Tantalus, and all the rest leaves us with the impression of a definitely organized family establishment, quite to the pattern of an orthodox compendium of mythology.

With yet more force will this artificial *compôte* of the poet appear as such rather than a work that springs naturally from the subject where we are already cognisant of the substance of the tale that is told us in its fresh and primitive form, or as actual history. Examples of this are Milton's "Paradise Lost," the "Noachid" of Bodmer, Klopstock's "Messias," Voltaire's "Henriade," and others. In all these poems we cannot fail to detect a real cleft between the content and the reflection of the poet which modifies his description of the events, characters and circumstances. In Milton's case, for example, we find emotions and observations obviously the growth of an imagination and ethical ideas inseparable from his own age. In the same way with Klopstock we have God the Father, the history of Jesus Christ, patriarchs and angels combined with our German education of the eighteenth century, and the ideas of Wölffian metaphysic. This twofold aspect asserts itself in every line. No doubt in these cases the content itself offers many difficulties. For God the Father, the heaven of the angels, and the angelic host are far less adapted to the individualization of a free imagination than are the Homeric gods, which, in a manner similar to the in part fantastic creations in Ariosto, in their external mode of appearance, and so far as they do not epitomize[19] human action, but rather independently confront each other as individuals, do of themselves suggest the gibe over such a presentment.[20] Moreover Klopstock, so far as a religious outlook is concerned, introduces us to a world devoid of foundation, which he crowds with the brilliant effects of a rather exhausting imagination, and compels us to take everything as seriously as he means it himself. This is particularly unfortunate in the case of his angels and devils. Such creations only really have substance and can be brought home to us in their individuality in so far as the material of their actions, as with the Homeric gods, is rooted in the spiritual experience of humanity, or in a reality already known to us, as in cases where they claim importance as being the guardian spirits or angels of men or cities, but who, apart from such a concrete significance, assert what is just so much the more merely the vacancy of imagination in proportion as a serious actuality is ascribed to them. Abbadona, for instance, the repentant devil,[21] possesses neither a truly allegorical meaning—for in the abstract notion of devil there can be no inconsistency of guilt which can be converted into virtue—nor is such a figure one that is essentially and truly concrete. If Abbadona were a man, a conversion to God would no doubt be reasonable; but where we have evil regarded as something independently substantive, which is not an individual human evil, such a conversion is merely a triviality of sentimental emotion. It is in fact a distinguishing characteristic of Klopstock's invention that it creates such unreal personages, conditions and events, which have nothing in common with the actual world and its poetical content. And he fares no better in the machinery of his judicial condemnation of riotous living in high places, least of all in the contrast he presents to Dante, who condemns the famous personalities of his time to hell with a power of detailed realization of another type altogether. Equally destitute of real content as poetry is the

204

joy of the resurrection among the assembled spirits of Adam, Noah, Shem, Japhet, and the rest, as depicted by Klopstock, who, in the 11th canto of the Messias, at the command of Gabriel, once more revisit their graves. Reason and rational ground are alike absent here. The souls have lived in the Divine Presence; they now behold the Earth, but they enter into no renewed relation with it. We may presume that they could not do better than appear to men; but of this there is not a single example. No doubt we find here beautiful emotions, endearing situations; and above all the moment in which the soul is once more united to a body is depicted in a way that arrests us; but the *content* remains none the less an invention that possesses no real claim to credibility. In contrast to such abstract ideas the blood-drinking of the phantoms in Homer, their reanimation in memory and speech, possess for us infinitely more the truth and realization of ideal poetry. And though from the point of view of imaginative resource these pictures of Klopstock are decorative enough, what is most essential in them is throughout the lyrical rhetoric of angels, who appear merely as instruments of service, or of patriarchs and other Biblical figures whose speeches and harangues have little in harmony with their historical characters as we have received the same from tradition. Mars, Apollo, War, Knowledge, and so forth—powers of this kind are neither in respect to their content wholly inventions, as the angels are, nor are they simply historical persons borrowed from historical sources, as are the patriarchs; they are on the contrary permanent forces, whose *form* and mode of appearance is alone the *poet's creation*. In the "Messias," however, admitting its excellence in certain directions—its purity of feeling, the brilliancy of its phantasy—yet it cannot be denied that by reason of the very type of such a phantasy we have here very, very much indeed that is hollow, without definite substance, and utilized simply as machinery for something else, all of which, combined with the absence of continuity in the content and its mode of conception, has even already covered the entire poem with oblivion. Things only live and remain green, which, essentially vital in themselves, unfold to us original life and activity in their pristine mould. For this reason we must hold fast to the primitive Epopees, and keep aloof, not only from modes of conception which are antagonistic to the actual presence which is vindicated in such, but also and above all from false aesthetic theory and predilection, at least if we are really anxious to enjoy and study the original world-outlook of nations, that great and spiritual[22] natural history. We have every reason to congratulate recent times, and our German nation in particular, that it is now on the road to the attainment of this object; that it has, in short, broken through the former obtuseness, of ordinary methods of thinking, and by its liberation of the mind from restricted views made it more receptive to ideas of the world which it is imperative that we as individuals enter into, and which alone are able to restore to us, to the full extent of their claim, the resurrected spirits of nations, whose ideal significance and deed thus appear struck into life in these their own Epopees.

(c) *The Epos as Unified Totality*

Hitherto, in considering the necessary qualifications of a genuine Epos, we have on the one hand discussed the *general* world-environment and from a further point of view the nature of the particularized event transacted on such a background by *individuals* either acting under the direction of gods or subject to destiny. These two fundamental aspects have yet further to coalesce in one and the same epic totality. In respect to this I will merely confine the reader's attention to the following points of interest:

In the *first* place we propose to consider the *collective aggregate of objects*, a satisfactory exposition of which is necessary to disclose the connection between the particular action and the substantive ground referred to.

Secondly, we have to examine the nature of the difference which obtains between the epic mode of *disclosure* and that of lyric or dramatic poetry.

Thirdly we have to deal with the *unity* in which an epic composition is rounded off despite all its breadth of extension.

(*a*) The content of the Epos, as already observed, is the entirety of a world in which an individual action is eventuated. In such a world the greatest variety of objects appear necessarily appertinent to the general views, deeds, and conditions of such a world.

(*αα*) Lyrical poetry is, no doubt, involved in definite situations, within which the subject of the lyric is permitted to import a great variety of content into its emotion and reflection. In this type of poetry, however, it is throughout the form of conscious life itself which characterizes such content; and for this reason excludes the outlook on the objective world in all its breadth of extension. Conversely the dramatic composition presents us characters and the carrying out of the action itself with all the animated appearance of life, so that here, too, the portrayal of local accessories, the external form of the active personages and all that happens, in the nature of the case tends to disappear. As a rule, what we have to express is the soul-motive and purpose rather than its extensive relations with the surrounding world of objects, or a description of individuals in their positive appearance as part of them. In the Epos, however, quite apart from the national actuality in the widest sense, upon which the action is based, we must find room for the ideal or soul aspect no less than the external or world aspect. We have in this type, therefore, under review and in coalescence the entire totality of all that we may reckon as comprised in the poetic presentation of our human existence. In this content we must not merely include on the one side the natural environment in the sense of this or that specific locality in which the action takes place, but also the more universal objective outlook such as I have already pointed out is a feature we find illustrated in the Odyssey, enabling us to understand how the Greeks in the times of Homer regarded the shape of the Earth, the configuration of the seas, and similar geographical facts. At the same time these natural aspects are not the object of most importance in the poem; they are merely the foundation; there is, in short, the further and more essential aspect of the composition unfolded in the existence, activities, and co-operation of the entire world of divinities; and between these two extremes we have humanity simply as such in its collective relation to domestic, public, peaceful, and warlike situations, ethical habit, customs, characters and events. And, moreover, throughout we have to assume in both directions, whether that is from the point of view of the individual event, or the general condition, the all-embracing national and other actual complexus.

Finally, if we consider the nature of this intelligible content it is not merely an external *événement* that is presented us, but in conjunction with such we must have, too, placed before us the ideal world of emotion, the aims and purposes of mind, all that may contribute to justify or condemn a deliberate line of conduct. In short, the real subject-matter of lyric and dramatic poetry is not wholly excluded, although in the epic type these aspects merely are valid as subordinate features; they do not, as in the former cases, constitute the essential form of the exposition, nor do they deprive the Epos of its distinctive character. We may consequently affirm that the distinctive note of the Epic is absent, when lyric expression determines both tone and colour, as is the case, for example, in Ossian, or when passages are emphasized in which the execution of the poet is made as consummate as possible, as is to some extent the case with Tasso, and to a still more marked degree characteristic of Milton and Klopstock. Emotions and reflections ought rather, no less than the portrayal of objective fact, to be transmitted as something done, already spoken and thought, and not interrupt the tranquil course of the Epic narrative. The incoherent exclamation of emotion, the direct outcry of the soul mainly intent with its utterance upon self-revelation, is out of place in such poetry. It will for the same reason and as strongly abstain from an imitation of the animation of dramatic dialogue, in which individuals carry on a conversation as though face to face with each other, where the aspect of most importance throughout is the contrast presented by different types of character in their interchange of speech as they strive to convince, command, impose upon, or passionately unravel their motives to one another.

(ββ) And, *secondly*, the Epos has not merely to bring before our vision the manifold content above described in its actually independent and subsistent objective form, but also the form in which it essentially becomes the Epos is, as I have more than once already described it, an *individual* event. If this essentially limited action is to remain united with all other material introduced, this additional accretion of fact, must throughout be brought into definite relation with the course of the individual event, that is to say, it must not fall outside it as independent. We could not find a more perfect illustration of this interweaving of all threads than that of the Odyssey. The domestic arrangements of the Greeks, for instance, no less than the ideas we get of foreign and barbarous folk and countries, or of the realm of the shades, and much else, are so closely interwoven with the personal wanderings of the home-returning Odysseus and the fortunes of Telemachus on his journey after his father, that not one of these aspects of the tale is held in a loose and independent position apart from the main event, or, as with the chorus of tragedy, which does not usually enter into the action and merely deals with generalized reflections, is able to relapse inactive into retrospection, but co-operates in the actual progress of the event. In a similar manner Nature also and the world of gods for the first time receives, not so much on their own account as in their relation to the particular events, which it is the function of the godlike to direct, an individual representation and one of rich vitality. Only when such a condition is fulfilled, or, in other words, when the narrative throughout informs us of the progressive movement of the event, which the poet has selected as the unifying material of his composition, can it never appear as a mere portrayal of independent objects. On the other hand, the particular event for its part should not be involved in and absorb the substantive national basis and totality upon which it moves forward to such a degree, that these are themselves divested of all independent existence, and fall by necessity into a relation simply of service. In this respect the expedition of Alexander against the East would not supply satisfactory subject-matter for the true Epopee. An heroic exploit of this kind not merely in respect to the original resolve, but also to its manner of execution, depends so entirely on this *one* single individual, his personality and character is so exclusively that which supports it, that we lose altogether the independent existence and self-assertion of the national basis, the host and its leaders, which we have shown to be a necessary condition. Alexander's army is his people, wholly bound up with him and his command: it follows him rather in the relation of vassalage than that of free will. In contrast to this the true vitality of the epic consists in this, that both these fundamental aspects, the particular action with its individual agents and the general world-condition, while no doubt continuing under a mediated relation, yet in this relation of reciprocity no less preserve their necessary independence and thereby enforce themselves as one existing whole, at the same time securing and possessing an independent entity.

($\gamma\gamma$) In a previous passage we laid it down generally that in order to have an individual action the substantive basis of epic poetry must offer the opportunity of collisions, and furthermore observed, that the general foundation must not appear as wholly independent but under the form of a specific event; we may now add that it is in this individual *événement* that we must seek the point of *departure* for the entire epic poem. This is pre-eminently of importance for the situations connected with its commencement. Here, too, we may take the Iliad and Odyssey for models. In the first the Trojan war is placed before us as the general background of contemporary life, but only so far as it comprises the particular events connected with the wrath of Achilles. And for this reason the poem commences without any possible

211

confusion with situations which excite the passion of the principal hero against Agamemnon. In the Odyssey there are two classes of subject-matter which determine the content of its opening, that is to say, the wanderings of Odysseus and the domestic complications at Ithaca. Homer brings them together by giving us briefly information concerning Odysseus on his home-journey to the effect that he is detained by Calypso, and then at once passes to the sorrows of Penelope and the voyage of Telemachus. We are, consequently, able to review at one glance what obstacle stands in way of the return, and what is consequently rendered necessary for those left behind at home.

(β) The advance, then, of the epic poem from a commencement such as this is totally different from that of lyric or dramatic poetry.

($\alpha\alpha$) In the first place we should draw attention to the possibilities of *extension* within the range of the Epos. These are quite as much due to the form as they are to the content. We have already seen what a variety of objects may be comprised in the world of the Epic as fully elaborated, not merely in its ideal capacities, motives, and aim, but also in respect to its objective situation and environment. Inasmuch as all these aspects assume an objective form, an appearance of reality, each one of them takes to itself a form of essentially independent ideality and externality, in which the epic poet, either in his exposition or description, is permitted freely to linger, and to disclose in its positive appearance. The lyric, on the contrary, concentrates all that it lays hold of within the ideal realm of the emotions, or refines it away in the generalized vision of reflection. In the objective world it is the immediate complex in juxtaposition, or the varied wealth of manifold characteristics, which is presented us. In this respect we find that in no other type of poetry is the claim to introduce episodical matter, even to the point of to all appearance absolute independence, more indisputable than in the Epos. The delight, however, in actual fact for its own sake and in its natural form must, as already observed, not be carried so far as to import into the poem circumstances and facts which have no real connection with the important action. Such episodes must assert themselves as effective in the advance of such action, whether as events which are obstructive to its course, or assistant in their mediation. Yet, despite of this, the particular portions of the epic poem will be somewhat loosely bound together. This is a necessary result of the mode of its objectivity. For in what is objective mediation persists as the ideal essence; what in contrast to this confronts the external aspect is the independent existence of particular aspects. This defect in the direction of a stringent unity and the emphasized relation of specific portions of the epic poem, which, according to its primitive form, possesses moreover a primitive period of origination, has this result, that it lends itself more readily than lyric or dramatic compositions to subsequent additions and continuations; and, further, it is enabled to appropriate under its more recent and embracing whole even examples of the saga which have already received artistic expression of a definite, if not so exalted character.

(ββ)*Secondly*, if we look at the way in which epic poetry may be justified in its *motivisation* of the progress and course of events, we shall find that it ought not either exclusively to take the ground of what happens from the individual mood, nor yet from what is purely personal character. In other words, it should not encroach upon what is the proper sphere of the lyric and drama; it must, in this respect too, adhere to the form of objectivity which constitutes the fundamental epic type. We have, in fact, seen more than once previously that external conditions were of no less importance, for an exposition that takes the form of

213

narrative, than states of soul which revealed character. In the Epos character and the necessary rational condition coalesce completely on terms of equality, and the epic character may therefore give way to external conditions, without impairing his poetic individuality, may be, in short, in his action, the result of relations in such a way that these appear as the predominant factor rather than the exclusively effective character as we find it in the drama. We find in the Odyssey that the progress of events is almost entirely motived in this way. We find the same thing in the adventures of Ariosto and other Epopees, where the material of the song is borrowed from the the Middle Ages. The divine command, too, which induces Æneas to found Rome, no less than the varied episodes which extend its embrace over a wide field, would involve a type of motivisation wholly uncongenial to the drama. A further illustration of this is Tasso's "Jerusalem Delivered," in which, quite apart from the brave antagonism of the Saracens, many a natural event is opposed to the object of the Christian host. Such examples might be indefinitely multiplied from almost all the more famous Epopees. And, indeed, it is precisely material of this kind, in which an exposition of this type is possible and necessary, that the epic poet ought to select.

The same thing is effected where it is bound to appear as the result of the actual decision of individuals. Here, too, we have neither to assert nor to express that which the character in the dramatic sense of the term—that is, according to his aim and the individual passion which uniquely animates him—makes of the circumstances and relations, in order to maintain his personality against this external resistance no less than against other individuals. Rather the epic character excludes this action viewed simply in reference to its personal character, just as it excludes the tumult of purely subjective states and feelings. Instead of this it cleaves fast, on the one hand, to the circumstances and their reality; and on the other that, whereby its movement is effected, must necessarily render explicit all that is essentially valid, universal, and ethical. In Homer, as in no other writer, we shall find inexhaustible material for pertinent thought on this head. The lament of Hecuba over Hector, for instance, or of Achilles over the death of Patroclus—episodes which, so far as content is concerned, would lend themselves admirably to lyric treatment—are in Homer held throughout within the epic temper. And to quite as little extent do we find this poet handle in dramatic style situations which would primarily adapt themselves to dramatic exposition, such as the conflict between Agamemnon and Achilles in the council of the chiefs, or the parting of Hector and Andromache. Only to glance at the last-mentioned scene, this belongs unquestionably to one of the finest conceivable efforts of epic poetry. Even in Schiller's dialogue between Amalia and Carl in "The Robbers," where the same subject ought to be treated in the lyric vein throughout, we distinctly hear an epic reverberation from the Iliad. How consummately epic in its effect, however, is Homer's description in the sixth book of the Iliad of the way in which Hector vainly seeks for Andromache at home, then at last meets her on the way to the Scæan gate, how she hurries toward him, and when close to him, as he looks with a peaceful smile on his little boy lying on the arm of his nurse, exclaims: "Amazing man, thy courage will destroy thee, and thou compassionest neither thy infant boy nor me, hapless wight, who will soon be widowed of thee. Ay, for soon the Achaeans will slay thee, storming against thee together. And if I lose thee it were better for myself to pass beneath the earth. No other comfort is left for me, but only sorrow, if thou art stricken by fate! Neither have I my father any more, nor yet my lady mother." After which she narrates at length all the story about her father and the death of her seven brothers, all of whom Achilles had slain, also the captivity, ransom, and decease of her mother. Then at length she turns with earnest plea to Hector, who is henceforward to her father and mother, brothers, and spouse in the bloom of life, and implores him to remain on the walls, and not to make his son an orphan and his wife a widow. Hector replies in much the same spirit: "All this is also a care to me, wife; but I fear too much the Trojans, if I avoid the battle here, like a coward; the eddy, too, of the moment worries me not, who am wont to be ever dauntless, and to fight in the foremost ranks of the Trojans, protecting the high fame of my father and mine own. Ay, well indeed I wot, both in mind and soul, that the day will come in which sacred Troy shall fall, as also Priam and the folk of the king cunning with the spear. But I sorrow not so much for the Trojans, nor yet for Hecuba herself and Priam, nor the brothers of my flesh, who shall fall beneath the foe, as for thee, when some bronze-greaved Achæan shall bear thee away, robbing thee of thy day of freedom, and thou shalt spin from the flax of another in Argos, or wearily draw water, loth indeed, but the might of necessity will be upon thee; and I doubt not there will be someone who will say, as he sees thee weeping: 'See yonder Hector's wife, the bravest of all who fought among the Trojans when the fight was over Ilium.' Thus perchance shall someone speak; and woe will come upon thee, that thou hast no longer such a husband, to fend thee from such serfdom. As for myself, may the earth cover me, or ever I hear thy bitter cry and thy carrying off." All that Hector says here is full of feeling, pathetic enough, yet not merely expressed in a lyrical or dramatic manner, but in the epic vein, inasmuch as the picture which he outlines of suffering, and which brings pain to himself, in the first place depicts circumstantially objective conditions as such, and in the second place because

216

all that affects and moves him does not appear as personal volition, or individual resolve, but rather as a necessity which is not at the same time his own aim and will. Of much the same epic effect are the pleas with which the vanquished plead, as they may on various grounds, for their life with their victors; for a movement of the soul, which proceeds merely from circumstances, and only attempts to affect us through the causative effect of objective relations and situations, is not dramatic, although modern tragedians from time to time also make use of such a type of effect. The scene, for example, in Schiller's "Maid of Orleans," on the battle-field between the English knight Montgomery and Joan,[23] is, as others have already justly observed, rather epic than dramatic. In the moment of danger all courage forsakes the knight; yet, for all that, when pressed by the fierce Talbot, who punishes cowardice with death, and the Maid, who conquers even the bravest, he is unable to have recourse to flight, and exclaims:

> O, wär ich nimmer über Meer hieher geschifft,
> Ich unglücksel'ger! Eitler Wahn bethörte mich,
> Wohlfeilen Ruhm zu suchen in dem Frankenkrieg,
> Und jetzo führt mich das verderbliche Geschick
> In diese blut'ge Mordschlacht. Wär ich weit von hier
> Daheim noch an der Savern' bluhendem Gestad
> Im sichern Vaterhause, we die Mutter mir.
> In Gram zurückblieb und die zarte süsse Braut.[24]

Expressions such as these are unmanly, and make the figure of this knight neither fit for the genuine Epos nor the tragic drama, are in fact rather suggestive of comedy. And when Joan, after exclaiming,

> Du bist des Todes! Eine britt'sche Mutter zeugte dich!
> [25]

advances towards him, he throws away sword and shield

and pleads at her feet for his life. The reasons he gives at length in order to arouse her sympathy: his defencelessness; the wealth of his father, who would ransom him with gold; the gentleness of the sex to which Joan belongs as maid; the love of his sweet bride, who waits for his return home in tears; the grief of the parents whom he has left at home; the grievous fate of death unwept for in a foreign land—all these motives are themselves, in one aspect of them, essentially objective conditions, effective and of value as such, and on the other hand, the tranquil exposition of them is itself in the epic vein. In the same way the poet motives the condition, that Joan must hearken to him, through the external circumstance of the defencelessness of the pleader, although from the dramatic point of view she ought without delay and at the bare sight to have slain him, being as she was the relentless foe of all Englishmen, and in fact expresses such destructive hatred with every resource of rhetoric, justifying her action by the statement that she is bound with most fearful vow to the spirit-world.

> Mit dem Schwert zu tödten alles Lebende, das ihr
> Der Schlachten Gott verhängnissvoll entgegenschickt.
> [26]

If the point of importance to the maid were merely that Montgomery ought not to die defenceless, he possessed apparently an excellent means in his grasp of retaining his life; in other words he had merely to refuse to take up his weapons. This view is supported by the fact that Joan has already listened to him so long. Yet when she demands that he should fight for his life with her, of mortal flesh like himself, he again takes up his sword and falls by her hand. Such a *development* of the scene had been more in keeping with the drama had it dispensed with all this varied epic exposition.

($\gamma\gamma$) In general, then, we may characterize the type in which we have the poetic passage of epic events set before us in the following way, namely, that the epic presentation does not merely linger over the picture of objective reality and ideal conditions, but over and above this provides *obstacles* to a final solution. This not only applies to its relation to the wide field of external condition, to which the more immediate vision enforces us, but also in respect to the culminating movement of the action, more especially in its contrast to dramatic poetry. For this reason above all it diverts us from the execution of the fundamental purpose, the connected course of whose evolved conflict a dramatic poet ought never to lose sight of, into much digressive matter; and, moreover, by this means avails itself of the opportunity, to bring before our vision the complex unity of a world of circumstances, which otherwise could not have been expressed in speech. We have an illustration of such an obstacle in the beginning of the Iliad. Homer here at once tells us about the fatal sickness, which Apollo had spread throughout the Greek camp, and connects with it the strife between Achilles and Agamemnon. This wrath is the second impediment. Even more obviously in the Odyssey is every adventure that Odysseus has to pass through, a delay to his home return. More particularly, however, the distinct episode serves to interrupt the unimpaired progression of the story, and is to a great extent an obstacle to this. Such, for instance, is the shipwreck of Æneas, his love for Dido, the appearance of Armida in Tasso, and we may add as a rule the many independent love affairs of particular heroes in the romantic Epos, which, in the poetry of Ariosto, accumulate and interlace with such profusion, that the conflict between Christian and Saracen is thereby entirely hidden. In the "Divine Comedy" of Dante we do not find such definite examples of obstruction to the plot or narrative. In this case we must associate the slow advance of the Epic denouement partly with the generally pausing manner of the description, and in part with the many little episodical histories and conversations with particular characters, whether damned or otherwise, about whom the poet permits himself more detailed information.

In this connection it is above all things necessary that impediments of this description, which interfere with the flow of narrative to its final end, should not be presented as though they were merely means directed to objects of an objective character. For inasmuch as already the general condition, on the basis of which the movement of the epic world is carried forward, is only truly poetical where it appears as a self-constructed growth, so too its entire course, either in virtue of circumstances or the inherent destiny, must also appear self-originated without our being able to detect thereby the personal views of the poet; and this is all the more so because, in the form of its objectivity —not merely under its aspects of phenomenal reality, but also in respect to the substantive character of its content—it claims for the whole no less than its divisible content that it is a positive growth, spontaneous in its origin and independent. If, however, a directive world of gods is its apex, controlling the course of events, it is even more necessary that the poet himself should possess a lively and vivid faith in them, because in that case it is generally through the instrumentality of these that obstructions such as we have referred to are asserted; consequently where these divine forces are treated merely as some lifeless mechanism, it is inevitable that everything for which they are responsible must equally become so in a poetic composition which is artificial even in intention.

(γ) Having thus briefly adverted to the totality of objects, which the Epos is able to unfold by interweaving a particular event with a universal national world-condition, and, further, having discussed the manner in which the course of events is developed, we have now, *thirdly*, and in conclusion, to examine the problem as to the nature of the *unity* and *rounding off* of an epic composition.

(αα) This is a point all the more important for the reason that in our own day people are ready to take up the view that we may end an Epic as we like, or continue it just as capriciously. Although this is the opinion of men of talent and learning—it is in fact the contention of F. N. Wolff—it remains none the less a crude and illiterate view. It in fact amounts to nothing less than excluding from the finest ethic compositions any genuine character of artistic composition. For it is only in virtue of the fact that an Epos depicts an essentially exclusive, and thereby, for the firs time independent world, that it is at all a work of fine art in contrast to what is, in part, the diffuse, and, in part, the finite, series of independent sections, causes, effects, and other modes of self-causative reality. One can, of course, so far admit that for the genuine and primitive Epos the wholly aesthetic review of the design and organization of the parts, of the position and completion of the episodes, of the kind of similes employed, and so forth, this is not the point of most importance, inasmuch as here, more than in lyrical poetry of a later date, and its artificial elaboration of the drama, the general world-outlook, the faith in divine beings, and, in a word, what is most essential in such national Bibles, must be expressed as the aspect of most weight. Nevertheless, these great national books, such as are the Ramajana, the Iliad, and the Odyssey, and even the "Song of the Nibelings," ought not to lose that quality which alone, in respect to both their beauty and their art, can endow them with the worth and freedom of artistic works, the quality, that is, whereby they bring before our vision a complete sphere of action. What we have simply to do, therefore, is to discover the appropriate form of this exclusive unity.

(ββ) The term Unity, if employed in this general sense, has become a very commonplace one even for tragedy, one capable of much misuse. For every event, in its causes and effects, creates an infinite chain, which, in the direction of the past no less than the future, and in a way that is in both directions incalculable, leads to a further series of particular circumstances and actions, it being impossible to determine all that may form part of the circumstances and detail in other respects, or the mode of their coalescence. If we merely confine our attention to this series, no doubt an Epos may be extended backwards and forwards indefinitely; and, over and above this such always offers opportunity for digression. But it is just such a series as this which makes the composition prosaic. To adduce an example the Greek cyclic poets have celebrated the entire cyclus of the Trojan war, and in doing so continue at the point where Homer stops, with a beginning, too, from the egg of Leda. But it is precisely on account of this that they degenerate into prose, if we contrast them with Homer's compositions. Just as little —I have already drawn attention to this—can an individual as such surrender the central focus of his unity, inasmuch as it is from this that the most varied events issue, and are able to effect a union in the same, though they may be entirely without connection regarded simply as events. We have consequently to seek for another type of unity. In this respect we must briefly determine the distinction between a mere *event*, and a *definite action*, which accepts the form of event in the epic narrative. We may define a mere event as the external aspect and realization of every human action, without involving with it the execution of a particular end; or, in general terms, we may call it every external modification in the form and appearance of what actually exists. When anyone is struck by lightning, that is a mere event, an external occurrence. More is implied in the sack of a hostile city; we have here the fulfilment of a predeterminate purpose. An essentially distinct object of this kind, such as the liberation of the Holy Land from the yoke of the Saracens and heathen, or better still the satisfaction of a specific impulse, such as the wrath of Achilles, must, under the mode of the epic eventuality, constitute the synthetic unity of the Epopaea; and by this I mean that the poetic narrative must restrict itself to that which is uniquely the effect of this conceived purpose or specific impulse, and in this co-operation be rounded off in an essentially exclusive unity. Action and execution of this type is, however, only possible to human agency; so that, as the culminating point of our composition, we must have in progressive conjunction with purpose and impulse a *human personality.* Furthermore, if the action and satisfaction of the entire heroic character, from which both purpose and impulse proceed, are merely the result of wholly definite situations and motives, which are dissipated as we look back in an extensive complexity of relation, and if, further, the execution of the purpose, as we look forward, carries with it a variety of result, then in that case on the one hand no doubt a large number of presuppositions will be involved with such a specific action, and on the other hand we shall have many effects of reaction, which, however, will not be placed in any more intimate poetic connection with just this determinate character of the end under exposition. In this sense, for instance, the wrath of Achilles has as little connection with the rape of Helen or the judgment of Paris, although the one fact is presupposed in the other, as it has with the actual sack of Troy. When, therefore, it is contended that the Iliad neither possesses a necessary beginning, nor an appropriate conclusion, such a verdict is due to an inability to see distinctly that it is the wrath of Achilles which is the main subject of the Iliad, and which

223

consequently should supply the focus-point of unity. If, on the contrary, we form a stable conception of the heroic figure of Achilles, and assume that this, as asserted in the wrath aroused in him by Agamemnon, is the connecting thread of the whole, we shall be unable to conceive either a beginning or termination of greater beauty. It is, as I have already pointed out, the direct motive of this anger, which forms the poem's commencement; the consequences of the same are comprised in all that follows. Against this critics have attempted to enforce the view that in such a case the last cantos are irrelevant, and might just as well be omitted. Such an opinion, if we look at the poem itself, is untenable. For just as the dallying of Achilles himself by the ships and his abstinence from the conflict are purely the result of his indignant wrath, and are in this inactivity bound up closely with the almost immediate success of the Trojans over the Grecian host, no less than with the fight and death of Patroclus, so, too, the lament and revenge of the noble Achilles and his victory over Hector is closely linked with this fall of his brave friend. If in the previous opinion it is implied that death is the end of everything, and after that we may as well pack and be off, such a view merely indicates extreme crudity of imaginative conception. With the idea of death it is merely *Nature* that is brought to a standstill; man is not so, nor yet are the obligations of his *ethical life* and *habit*,[27] with their claim of honourable recognition for the fallen hero. In this sense the sports that form part of the funeral rites of Patroclus, the heartrending pleas of Priam, the reconciliation of Achilles, who returns the father the corpse of his son, in order that in this case, too, honour to the dead may not be absent, each and all are connected with the previous events, and contribute to the supreme and satisfying beauty of the narrative's conclusion.

(γγ) Inasmuch, however, as we have attempted above to

make a specifically individual action, which issues in accordance with a deliberate purpose or heroic impulses, conform to the type of an epic whole in which focal points are ascertainable that bind it together and round off its completeness, the view is at least possible that we have made the *unity* of the Epos too nearly identical with that of the *drama*. For in the drama also it is *one* particular line of action issuing from self-conceived purpose and character with its conflict which constitutes the focal centre. In order, therefore, not to involve these two types of poetry, the epos, that is, and the drama, in confusion, though the confusion merely appear to be such, I will yet again draw the reader's attention emphatically to my previous explanation of the distinction between human action and event. And quite apart from this the epic interest is not simply confined to those characters, objects, and situations which have their ground in the particular action as such, whose progress is the subject of the epic narrative, but this action possesses the further stimulus to its opposed factors and their resolution, and in fact is directed throughout its course and exclusively within a *national* and *collective whole*, or substantive content, which claims on its own account to assert a variety of characters, conditions, and events. In this respect the final consummation of the Epos does not merely consist in the particular content of the predominant action selected, but quite as much in the entire synthesis of the *general world-survey* whose objective reality it undertakes to depict; in fact, the epic unity is only then fully complete when the particular action, from one point of view no doubt, in its independent character, but also from another, regarded in its progression as the essentially rounded world within the sphere of which it moves, is placed before us as one indissoluble totality; and both of these spheres, or aspects of one sphere, repose together in the mediating fulness and unimpaired unity of very life.

Such, then, are the most essential characteristics we find it possible, within the limits accepted, to draw attention to in respect to the genuine Epos.

It is, however, possible to apply the same form of objectivity to other subject-matter, whose content does not carry with it the true significance of genuine objectivity. It is very possible that a theorist in Art will feel embarrassment when, with such modes of speech before him, he is asked to make a classification adapted to all poems without distinction; and we must not forget that under the generic term of poem these hybrid forms have also to be reckoned. In any really just classification, however, we ought only to include that which only conforms with a definition of the generic notion.[28] All that is, on the contrary, incomplete in content or form, or both, precisely for the reason that it is not as it ought to be, is only subsumed defectively under the notion, or in other words under the definition, which gives us the thing as it ought to be, and in truth actually is. I only propose, therefore, in conclusion and by way of supplement, to add a few observations upon such subordinate and collateral branches of the true epic composition.

To this class of poetry above all the *idyll* belongs in the modern sense of that term, viz., that in which poetry stands aloof from the profounder interests of spiritual and ethical life, and depicts mankind in its innocence. Innocent life in this sense amounts to little more than an ignorance of everything except eating and drinking. We may add that what we eat and drink here is extremely simple, it is goat's milk merely, or sheep's milk, or at the most cow's milk, roots, acorns, vegetables, and cheese made from milk. I should say that bread is no longer in the truly idyllic sphere; we must, however, allow to it flesh-eating; for it is hardly possible that our idyllic shepherds and shepherdesses

226

could have wished to sacrifice their herds exclusively to the gods. Their occupation will consist in looking the whole day long after their beloved herds with their faithful hound, in providing their food and drink, and along with this giving vent, with as much sentimental feeling as possible, to every kind of mood which does not disturb this condition of repose and contentment. In a word, they are satisfied with their peculiar piety and gentleness, piping away on their reed or oat-pipes, warbling to each other, and above all making love with the greatest tenderness and innocence.

The Greeks, on the contrary, possessed in their plastic representations a more jubilant world, with its attendants of Bacchus, Satyrs and Fauns, who, in their harmless service of a god, stimulated animal life and human joviality with a vivacity and truth totally different from the above pretentious innocence, piety, and emptiness. We may also recognize the same essentially animated outlook on the world as illustrated in lively pictures of national condition, in the Greek Bucolic poets such as Theocritus; this is so whether our poet lingers over actual situations of the life of fisher-folk, or shepherds, or extends the mode in which he expresses this, or similar spheres of life, to a yet wider circle, either depicting such states in an epic form, or treating them in lyric form and that of the objective drama. Virgil already sings to us with less warmth in his Eclogues. Most tedious of all, however, is Gessner, so tedious that I suppose no one reads him nowadays. We can only wonder that the French ever had so much taste for him that they even ranked him highest among German poets. Their morbid sensibility on the one hand, which evades the tumult and changes of life, while yearning also for some kind of movement, and on the other the absence of all true interest in such poetry, so that the otherwise disturbing influences of our culture were not represented—both of these factors, no doubt, contributed to this preference.

We may reckon as a further class of this hybrid type of Epic those poems which are half description and half lyrics, a favourite type with the English, and one which for the most part accepts for its subject-matter Nature, the Seasons, and similar subjects. We may also associate with this type the various *didactic* poems concerned with physical science, astronomy, medicine, chess, fishing, and hunting—in short, the art which loves to elaborate in a poetic form what is really the content of prose, an art which has been cultivated with much talent in later Greek poetry, and after that by the Romans, and, in our time, pre-eminently by the French. Such poetry, despite its general epic temper, will very readily pass over into the lyric treatment.

The *romances* and *ballads*, which we find both in the Middle Ages and modern times, are no doubt poetry of a kind, though it is impossible to define accurately their type; so far as their content is concerned they are in part epic. If we look at the form of their composition, however, they are for the most part lyrical, so that we have perforce to reckon them from different points of view to different types.

The *romantic* novel, that Epopaea of *modern society*, opens a different field altogether. In this we possess, on the one hand, in all its completeness and variety, an epic prodigality of interests, conditions, characters, and living relations, the extensive background in fact of an entire world. We have also the epic exposition of events. What fails us here is the *primitive* world-condition as poetically conceived, which is the source of the genuine Epos. The romance or novel in the modern sense pre-supposes a basis of reality already organized in its *prosaic form*, upon which it then attempts, in its own sphere, so far as this is possible from such a general point of view, both in its treatment of the vital character of events and the life of individuals and their destiny, to make good once more the banished claims of poetical vision. For this reason one of the most common collisions in the novel, and one most suitable to it, is the conflict between the poetry of the heart and the prose of external conditions antagonistic to it, including with such the contingency such imply. This is a conflict which may be resolved on the lines of tragedy or comedy, or finds its settlement in the twofold conclusion, first, that the characters which in the first instance contend with the ordinary course of life are taught to recognize in it what is the genuine heart of things, becoming thereby reconciled to their conditions and ready to cooperate with them; and, secondly, that they learn how to brush away the purely prosaic aspect of all that they do and accomplish, and thereby replace the prose which they have found there with a reality allied and congenial to beauty and art. In so far as the form of the exposition is concerned, the genuine romance pre-supposes, precisely as the Epos does, the synthesized purvey of the world and life as one whole, the manifold contents of which are manifested within the reach of the individual event which supplies the focal centre of the entire complexus. In his attitude to detail, however, the poet must here permit himself a freer play both of conception and execution, and all the more so because he is here less able to avoid the prose of actual life in his descriptions, though this freedom should not make him any more inclined to dwell exclusively in such an atmosphere of prose and ordinary occurrence.

3. THE HISTORICAL DEVELOPMENT OF EPIC POETRY

In looking back upon the course of our previous consideration of the other arts, we find that we reviewed the different stages of the art of *building* throughout in their historical development as successively in symbolic, classic, and romantic architecture. In the case of sculpture, on the contrary, we accepted the Greek type, by virtue of its complete identity with the notion of this *classic* art, as the real focal centre, from which we proceeded to develop the specific characteristics of importance, so that here we did not find it necessary to extend so far as in the previous case the range of our historical survey. This contrast is further illustrated in our treatment of the *romantic* art-character of painting, which, however,[29] not merely in respect to the fundamental notion of its content, but also in that of the mode of its presentation, embraces an equally wide and important range of development in different nations and through different schools, so that in this case it was necessary to make our reference to history more extensive and varied. The nature of the art of music invited us to historical comparisons of the same kind. Inasmuch, however, as I have neither obtained access to the foreign literature dealing with the history of this art, nor can claim personally to possess the adequate knowledge, I have been forced to restrict myself to the mere outlines of what is required incidentally. With regard to our immediate subject, that is, *epic* poetry, the course of our enquiry will be very much that followed in the case of sculpture. In other words, though the mode of exposition branches off in several direct or collateral divisions, and embraces many historical periods and peoples, yet we have already recognized in the Epos of Greek literature the genuine type of it in its consummate form and most artistic mode of realization. And the reason of this is that in general the Epos possesses the closest affinity with the plastic of sculpture and its objective presence; and, not merely in respect to its substantive content, but equally so in the form of its presentation as that of phenomenal reality. It is therefore by no means simply an accident that we find epic poetry, no less than the art of sculpture, assert itself pre-eminently among the

230

Greeks in its original and unsurpassed perfection. Stages of development, no doubt, are to be met with on either side of this culminating point, stages which are neither intrinsically subordinate or insignificant, but are necessary conditions of the art's growth, inasmuch as all nations are essentially within the sphere of poetic creation, and it is above all the Epos which brings before us the heart and core of the national life. And for this reason, the historical development of the Epic is of greater importance than was the case with sculpture.

We may then classify the entire compass of epic poetry, or, to express ourselves more accurately, of the Epopaea, in three fundamental stages; and these, speaking generally, constitute the course of the art's evolution.

Firsts we have the Oriental Epos, which makes the symbolic type its focal centre.

Secondly, there is the classical Epos of the Greeks, with its imitation in Roman authors.

Finally, we have the abundant and many-sided unfolding of epic-romantic poetry among Christian peoples; which, however, in the first instance appears in Teutonic paganism; and again, from another point of view, that is quite apart from what we may style the chivalrous poetry of the Middle Ages, we find the old classic world active in another province of life as instrumental to the purification of literary taste or style, or still more directly utilized as a model, until finally the modern romance replaces the Epos altogether.

We may now proceed to some review of single epic compositions: in this it will only be possible to emphasize what is of most importance; and, generally speaking, I can only pretend to give a rapid outline of this field in the space at my disposal.

231

(*a*) In the case of Oriental peoples the art of poetry is, as we have already observed, generally of a more primitive type, inasmuch as it remains more closely related to what we may style the essential[30] mode of envisagement, and the diffusion of the individual consciousness in the sublime Unity of the *One*. And because of this, as a further aspect, and relatively to the specific divisions of poetic composition, it is unable to work out individual personality in the self-subsistency of determinate characterization, with its aims and collisions, an elaboration which is of first importance in the composition of genuine dramatic poetry. The most essential result therefore we meet with here is limited—if we exclude from attention an endearing, sweet-scented, and delicate type of lyric, or one that uplifts itself to the one unutterable God—to poems, which are to be counted of the epic mould. Nevertheless it is only among the Hindoos and the Persians that we come across the genuine Epopaea; but here at least we do meet it in colossal proportions.

(*a*) The Chinese, on the contrary, possess no national Epos. The prosaic basis of their imaginative vision, which even to the earliest origins of history offers the jejune form of a prosaically organized historical reality, opposes from the first to this the most noble type of epic composition an insuperable obstruction. The religious conceptions of this people, little adapted as they are to artistic configuration, contribute to the same result. We find, however, at a later date and as some compensation, for their elaboration is most profuse, little narratives, and romances spun out to great length, which astound us by the vividness in which situations are realized, the accuracy with which private and public relations are depicted, the variety, fine breeding, or rather I should say frequently the fascinating tenderness they display, more particularly in their female characters, and in short by the art in every respect which succeeds in making works so consummate.

(β) A world of great contrast to the above presents itself in the Hindoo Epopaea. We find already in the most primitive compositions, if we may form an opinion from the little made known to the general public up to the present time from the Veda, most fruitful germs for a mythology fitted to epic exposition; and these, associated with the heroic exploits of men many centuries before Christ—for chronological accuracy is still impossible—are elaborated into genuine Epopaea, works, however, which are still composed in part from the wholly religious point of view, and in part from that of unfettered poetry and art. Pre-eminently do the two most famous of these poems, namely the Ramajana and the Maha-Bharata, place before us the entire world-outlook of the Hindoo race in all its splendour and glory, its confusion, fantastical absurdity and dissolution, and withal, from the reverse point of view, in the exuberant loveliness and the here and there fine traits of heart and emotion, which characterize the profuse vegetation of its spiritual growth. Mythical exploits of men are expanded into the actions of incarnate gods, whose deed hovers vaguely between the divine and human nature, and the determinate outlines of personality and exploit are dissolved in an infinitude of extension. The substantive bases of the whole are of a type such as our Western world-outlook, assuming that it does not choose to surrender the higher claims of freedom and morality, is neither able to find itself truly at home in or to sympathize with. The unity of the particular parts is of an extremely unstable kind; and layers upon layers of episodical matter, consisting of tales of the gods, narratives of ascetic penances, and the powers they create, tediously long expositions of philosophical doctrines and systems, so entirely impair the collective unity that we are forced to regard many of them as later

233

accretions. But, however this may be, the spirit from which these stupendous poems have originated bears constant witness to an imagination, which is not only anterior to all prosaic culture, but as a rule is wholly incompatible with the faculty of ordinary common sense, and is capable in fact of endowing the fundamental tendencies of this national consciousness, in its essentially unique and collective conception of the universe, with an original artistic form. The later Epics, on the contrary, which are called *Puranas*, in the more restricted sense of the term, that is, poems of the Past, appear rather to be compiled in the prosaic and dull style similar to that adopted by post-Homeric cyclic poets, and pursue their downward course at great length from the creation of the gods and the universe to the genealogies of human heroes and princes. Finally the epic care of the old myths dissolves into vapour and artificial elegance of a purely external poetic form and diction, while on the one hand the phantasy, which exhausted itself in a dreamy wonderland, becomes the wisdom of fables whose most important function is to instruct us in morality and worldly wisdom.

(γ) We may compare side by side in a *third* division of epic Oriental poetry that respectively belonging to Hebrews, Arabs, and Persians.

(αα) The sublimity of the Jewish imagination no doubt in its conception of the Creation, in the histories of the Patriarchs, the wandering in the wilderness, *the* conquest of Canaan, and in the further historical course of national event, full as such a vision is of sterling content and natural truth, possesses many elements of primitive epic poetry; the religious interest is here, however, so predominant, that, instead of being genuine Epopaea, they merely approximate either to religious myths in the guise of poetry, or to religious narratives which are wholly didactic.

($\beta\beta$) The Arabs have always possessed a poetic nature, and from very early days we find genuine poets among them. Even their heroic songs of lyric narrative, styled the moallakat, which in part originate in the century immediately previous to Mahomet, depict either with a few bold and detached strokes and vehement ostentation, or at other times with more tranquil self-possession, or a melting softness, the original conditions of the still pagan Arabs. Here we find the honour of the clan, the passion of revenge, the rights of hospitality, love, delight in adventure, benevolence, sorrow, and yearning, in undiminished strength, and in traits which remind us of the romantic character of Spanish chivalry. Here, too, we meet with in the East for the first time a real poetry, without fantastic elements, or prose, without mythology, without gods, demons, fairies, genii, and everything else of the kind common to the East, but rather with solid and self-sufficient characters and, however unique and marvellous in the play of its images and similes, yet for all that humanly real and self-contained. We have the vision of a similar pagan world also set before us by a later age in the collected poems of Hamasa, as also in the not yet edited "Divans of the Hudsilites." After the extensive and successful conquests of the Mohammedan Arabs this primitive heroic character gradually disappears; and, in the course of the centuries, the province of Epic poetry is replaced in part by the instructive fable and the witty proverb, in part by the fairy-like narratives, of which the "Thousand and One Nights" is an example, or in those tales of adventures which Rückert, through a translation which reproduces for us the equally witty and artistically elaborate Macamen of the Hariri in their metre, rhymes, and articulate meaning, has unveiled in a manner deserving thoughtful attention.

($\gamma\gamma$) In some contrast to this the efflorescence of Persian poetry falls in the period of that reconstructed culture effected by the change of language and nationality under the influence of Mohammedanism. We, however, come across, in the very first opening of this lonely springtime, an epic poem which, at least in its material, takes us back to the remotest Past of ancient Persian saga and myth, and carries forward its narrative through the heroic age right down to the last days of the Sussanides. This comprehensive work is the Shahnameh of Firdusi, the son of the gardener of Tus, a work the origins of which are traceable to the Bastanameh. [31] We are, however, unable to call even this poem a genuine Epopaea, because it does not make any specific and individual line of action its focal centre. On account of the lapse of centuries we lose our hold of the costume appropriate to an age or a locality, and in particular the most ancient mythical figures and gloomy intricate traditions hover in a world of the phantasy, among the indefinite outlines of which we are often at a loss to know whether we are face to face with persons or entire clans; and then again we are often suddenly confronted with really historical characters. As a Mohammedan the poet was no doubt able to handle his subject-matter more freely; but it is just in this type of freedom that we fail to meet with the stability in definite characterization, as it was present in the design of the primitive heroic songs; and, on account of the great gulf which separates him from that long-buried world of saga, the freshness and breath of its immediate life vanish, though absolutely necessary to the national Epos.

In its further course the epic art of the Persians expands into Love-epopees of excessive softness and sweetness, as an author of which Risami is pre-eminently distinguished. It further makes use of its rich stores of life-experience in the interest of the teacher. In this sphere the far-travelled Saadi was master. Finally, it plunges into that pantheistic

236

Mysticism, which Dschelaleddin Rumi recommends and teaches in tales and legendary narrative.

I must, I fear, restrict myself to the above sketch.

(b) In the poetry of *Greece* and *Rome* we find ourselves for the first time in the genuine sphere of epic art.

(α) Among these above all are included of course the *Homeric* poems, which we have already noted as the culminating point of all.

(αα) Either of these poems, despite all that may be advanced to the contrary, is essentially self-complete, so definite and sensitive to its construction as a whole, that in my own opinion the very view which regards the present form of both as merely that in which they were sung and handed down to posterity by rhapsodists, simply amounts to little more than the just eulogy of such works in virtue of the fact that they are, with regard to the entire atmosphere of their content, national and realistic, and even in their particular parts are so consummately finished, that all and each of them may be taken as a whole in itself. Whereas in the East what is substantive[32] and universal in the poet's survey still impairs the individuality of character, and its aims and exploits by its symbolism or deliberate instruction, and thereby injures the definite articulation and unity of the whole. Here for the first time in these poems[33]we find a world beautifully suspended as it were between the general life-conditions of morality in family, state and religious belief, and the individuality of distinctive character, and in this fair balance between the claims of spirit and Nature, intentional action and objective event, between a national basis of enterprise and particular aims and deeds, even though individual heroes appear as the predominant feature in their free and animated movement, yet this too is so mediated by the distinctiveness of the aims proposed and the

237

severe presence of destiny, that the entire exposition can only remain even for ourselves the *ne plus ultra* of all attainment that we can either enjoy or admire in epic composition. For we find no difficulty here in recognizing the real significance of even the gods who withstand or assist these primitive masculine heroes in their bravery, their straightforward and noble actions: nor can we fail to return the merry smiles of an art which depicts them as we see them here in all the *naïveté* of their very human, if also godlike impersonations.

(*ββ*) The *cyclic* poets of an age subsequent to the Homeric poems depart more and more from this genuine type of epic poetry. On the one hand the tendency here is to break up the completeness of the national world-survey into its petty provinces and aspects; and from another point of view, instead of retaining a firm grasp of the poetic unity and distinctive character of an individual action, to insist more exclusively on the completeness of events as an historical series, or on the unity of the personality, and by so doing to assimilate epic poetry with the already emphasized historical impulse of the logographers in their historical compilations.

(*γγ*) Finally Epic poetry of a still later date after the time of Alexander either turns aside to the more limited province of bucolic poetry, or introduces more learning and artifice than is compatible with the truly poetic Epopaea being at last wholly didactic, a type which increasingly suffers to escape every vestige of the primitive freshness, simplicity and animation.

(*β*) This characteristic, with which the Epos of the Greeks terminates, is from the first predominant among the *Romans*. An epic Bible, such as are the Homeric poems, we shall therefore seek for here in vain, however much critics have attempted, even quite recently, to resolve the most ancient

238

Roman history into national Epopaea. On the other hand, even from the earliest times, along with genuine epic art, of which our finest extant example here is the Æneid, the historical Epos and the didactic poem supplies us with a proof that it is the Romans who are mainly responsible for the elaboration of that province of poetry which is already half prose; just as also it was in their hands that the *satire* received its most perfect form, being also that most congenial to their character.

(*c*) For this reason epic poetry could only be infused with a fresh breath and spirit through a change in its outlook on the world and in its religious belief, and through the actions and destinies of new nationalities. This is what we have in the case of the *Germans*, not only as we see them in their primitive paganism, but also after their conversion to Christianity. It may be further illustrated by the Romance nations and all the more strongly, in proportion as their subdivision into groups is more complete, and the principle of the Christian view of life and reality is unfolded in all its various phases. Yet it is precisely this many-sided expansion and subdivision which oppose to a brief survey great difficulties. I will consequently only draw attention to and emphasize fundamental tendencies.

(*a*) In our *first* group we may reckon the residue of genuine poetry, which later nationalities have still retained from an age previous to Christianity, for the most part by means of oral tradition, and consequently not wholly unimpaired.

We may include above all among these the poems which are usually ascribed to *Ossian*. Although English critics of repute, such as Johnson and Shaw, have been blind enough to publish them as the sole composition of Macpherson, it is none the less wholly impossible that a poet of our own time could create from his own resources alone such ancient social conditions and events; consequently we must presuppose here previous poems as the foundation of such a work, although too in their entire atmosphere, and the mode of conception and feeling expressed in them, many changes more in accord with our modern life may have been introduced in the course of so many centuries. It is true their actual date is not established; they may, however, very well have retained a vital form in the mouth of the folk for one thousand or even fifteen hundred years. Taking them as a whole their form appears to be predominantly lyric. Ossian is here presented as the old minstrel and hero, who has lost his sight, and suffers in a retrospect of lament, the days of glory to rise before him. Yet although his songs originate in woe and mourning they nevertheless are in themselves fundamentally epic; for even these lamentations refer to what has been, and depict this world which has now just vanished, with its heroes, its love-adventurers, its exploits, its expeditions aver sea and land, its chance of arms, its destiny and its downfall, in just the same epic and realistic way—although broken here and there with lyrics—as we find in Homer the heroes Achilles, Odysseus, or Diomede, talking of their exploits, expeditions, and mischances. Yet the development of spiritual emotion, and indeed of the entire national existence, despite the fact that here heart and sentiment have a more exacting rôle to play, is not carried so far as in Homer's case. Most of all we miss the assured plastic form of his characterization and the daylight clarity of his presentment. We are, in short, so far as *locale* is concerned, exiled in the tempestuous mists of the North, with its gloomy sky and heavy clouds, upon which the spirits ride or appear to heroes, raimented in their form. We may add that it is only quite recently that other Gaelic minstrels of olden time have been discovered, rather connected, so Wallis informs us, with England than Scotland or Ireland, minstrelsy having been for a long time continuous in that country, which already must have possessed a considerable literature.

In these poems we have among other things reference to emigrations to America. Mention is also made of Caesar; but the reason here given for his invasion is a private passion for some king's daughter, whom he saw in Gaul and followed to England. As a striking characteristic of their form triads are worthy of attention, which combine in three organic parts three events of similar character, though dating from different periods of time.

Finally, and more famous than these poems, are on the one hand the heroic songs of the more ancient Edda, and on the other the myths with which for the first time in this cycle of song along with the narrative of human destinies we also come across various histories concerning the origin, exploits, and downfall of the gods. I must, however, confess I have been unable to acquire a taste for the empty exuberance of these origins of a natural philosophy of symbolism, which, however, are further attached to the appearance of particular human form and physiognomy, such as Thor with his hammer, the Werewolf, the wild mead-carousals, and in a word, the savagery and troubled confusion of such a mythology. We must admit, of course, that all that intimately concerns this folk of the North lies nearer to ourselves than, say, the poetry of the Persians and Mohammedanism; but to press upon the educated man among us such an admission to the point that it has still at this time of day a claim upon his sympathy, and indeed ought to pass for us as something national—such an assumption, though often ventured, means not merely to overrate conceptions, which are to a great extent misshapen and barbarous, but also to wholly misunderstand the significance and spirit of our own times.

(β) If we, *secondly*, cast a glance over the poetry of the

241

Christian Middle Ages, what we ought in the first instance and above all to consider are those works which have, without more direct and penetrating influence of the old literature and culture, sprung up from the fresh spirit of the Middle Ages and consolidated Catholicism. Here we find the most multifold elements ready to supply the material and stimulus of epic poetry.

(αα) We may in the *first* place draw retention to that truly epic subject-matter which comprises in its content interests, exploits, and characters of the period mentioned of a wholly *national* character. Among these the Cid is pre-eminently worthy of our notice. The significance of this blossom of national heroism in the Middle Ages to the Spanish, this is set before us in epic guise in the poem Cid, and then at a later date with more attractive excellence in a succession of narrative romances, which Herder first brought to the notice of Germany. We have here a string of pearls, every single picture entirely complete in itself, and yet all so admirably in tune with each other that they make a consistent whole; though throughout composed in the spirit of chivalry, yet at the same time Spanish and national; eminently rich in the content of their varied interests, whether these concern love, marriage, honour, or the mastery of kings in wars waged between Christians and Moors. All this material is voiced in so epic and plastic a style, we have set before us the pertinent fact so simply in the purity of its exalted content, and withal with such a wealth of the noblest pictures of human life displayed in a panorama of the most glorious exploit, and all this bound together in a wreath so fair and fascinating, that we moderns may compare it with the most beautiful creations of the ancient world.[34]

As a matter of fact it is as impossible to compare the Nibelungenlied, as it is the Iliad and Odyssey, with this

242

world of romance, which, however dissevered in fragments it maybe, is none the less epic in its fundamental type. For although in the former precious and truly German work we have no lack of a national and substantive content, in respect to family, matrimonial affection, duty of vassalage, loyalty of service, heroism, and, in a word, genuine marrow and substance, yet the entire collision, despite all its epic breadth of vision, is rather one of a dramatic type, than truly epic, and the exposition, with all its detail, neither tends towards the individualization of its abundance, nor to a presentment that is wholly lifelike; and from a further point of view it is frequently squandered in pure harshness, savagery and ferocity, so that the characters, although we find them compactly braced and robust in action, yet in their abstract ruggedness rather resemble coarse images of wood, than are comparable to the humanely evolved, genial individuality of the Homeric heroes and women.

($\beta\beta$) A second fundamental source of such literature is to be traced in the religious poems of the Middle Ages, which take as their subject the life of Christ, or those of the Madonna, the Apostles, the saints and martyrs and the Last Judgment. The most essentially complete and rich composition, however, the genuine art-Epic of Catholic Christianity in the Middle Ages, the greatest subject-matter and the greatest poem is in this sphere Dante's Divine Comedy. It is true that we cannot call even this severely, rather I should systematically organized poem, an Epopaea in the ordinary sense of the term. For we have not here one progressive action, individual and exclusive, on the broad basis of the entire poem: what, however, we do get in a conspicuous degree in this Epos is the most secure articulation and consummate finish. Instead of a particular event it has for its subject-matter the eternal event, the absolute end, the Divine Love in its imperishable eventuality, and in its unalterable circles' of relation to the object. Possessing further Hell, Purgatory, and Paradise for its locality, it plunges the living world of human action and suffering or, more closely, that of individual acts and destinies in this changeless existence. Everything single and particular in human interests and aims here vanishes before the absolute greatness of the purpose and end of all things; at the same time, however, what is otherwise most perishable and evanescent in the living world receives here a completely epic form objectively based on its own innermost life, and adjudged in its worth and unworth by the supreme notion of all, that is God. For as individuals were in their life and suffering, their opinions and accomplishment on Earth, so are they here set before us for ever consolidated, as it were, into images of bronze. It is in this way that the poem embraces the totality of the most objective life, that is, the eternal condition of Hell, of Purification, and of Paradise; and it is on these indestructible foundations that the characters of the actual world move in their particular personalities, or rather they *have* already moved, and are henceforward rendered moveless, together with their action and being, in the everlasting righteousness, and are themselves eternal. The Homeric heroes indeed endure in *our* memories through the song of the Muse. These characters assert their condition on their own account, and in the cause of their own individuality: they do not so much exist in our imagination; they are *themselves* essentially eternal. The perpetuation through the Mnemosyne of the poet has here the objective force of the very judgments of God, in whose Name the most dauntless spirit of his time has damned or beatified the entire present and past.

The exposition also must perforce follow the above character of an object, which is received rather than given. It can only be a wandering through a world that is for ever determined; which, although it is discovered, organized, and peopled with the freedom of the imagination wherewith Hesiod and Homer created their gods, nevertheless undertakes to give us a picture and a report of what has actually happened, an account full of energetic movement, yet plastic in the rigidity of its pains; rich in the flashes of its horror, yet mitigated pitifully in Hell through Dante's own sympathy; more gracious in purgatory, but none the less fully and completely elaborated; and, finally, translucent as light in Paradise, and for ever without materia form in the eternal ether of thought.

The ancient world no doubt peers into this world of the Catholic poet, but only as the guiding star and companion of human wisdom and culture; for, where it is a question of doctrine and dogma, it is the scholasticism of Christian theology and love which speaks.

($\gamma\gamma$) A *third* fundamental subject-matter, which arrests the interest of the poetry of the Middle Ages, is that of *chivalry*. This interest is not merely limited to its worldly and romantic association with love-adventure and tilting matches, but is occupied with religious objects in virtue of the mysticism of Christian knighthood. The actions and events of such compositions have no relation to national interests; they are matters effected by individuals, which only concern the personal agent as such; they are generally similar to what I have described in my previous reference to romantic chivalry. Individuals are consequently placed in a position of complete freedom and independence. A novel form of heroism is thereby created within a social environment that is not as yet stereotyped to the prosaic mode and temper; a heroism, however, which, on account of interests which in part are due to religious phantasy, and in part—that is from the worldly point of view—are wholly personal and imaginary, eschews that substantive Real, upon the basis of which the Greek heroes are united, or as units contend, are victorious or are vanquished. Despite all the varied epic compositions, which such a course as the above occasions, the adventurous character of the situations, conflicts and plots rather tends, on the one hand, in the direction of a treatment usually met with in romances, where the various examples of adventure are loosely interwoven in no more stringent bond of unity, and on the other to that which, while sharing the general features of such works, is not evolved on the background of a consistently organized civic order and a truly prosaic condition of general life. Moreover the imagination is not content with the mere invention of knightly characters and adventures outside the pale of the ordinary world of things; it furthermore associates the exploits of the same with important legendary centres of interest, pre-eminent historical personages, decisive conflicts of the age, and receives by doing so, if we view its broader lines, at least a foundation such as we found indispensable to epic creation. Such a basis, however, we shall find is as a rule commingled with fantastic elements, and is unable to secure the clarity of objective vision in its elaboration, which above all distinguishes the Homeric Epos. Add to this the fact that on account of the very similar treatment accorded to the same subject-matter by Frenchmen, Englishmen, Germans, and to some extent even Spaniards, we fail to find here relatively at least, and if we contrast it with that of the Hindoo, Persian, Greek, and Celt, the essentially national temper, which in the last-mentioned cases constitutes in its security the epic core of the content and its execution. I must, however, excuse myself here from entering further into the detail of this aspect, either by way of illustration or critical judgment.

It will be sufficient if I merely draw attention to the larger circle, within which the most important of these Epopaea of knight-errantry are to be met with if we estimate them relatively to their subject-matter.

As a *leading* figure in this respect we have first Charles the Great with his peers in the conflict fought against Saracens and pagans. In this Frankish circle of legend feudal chivalry forms a background of prime importance, and branches off into poems of every description, whose most significant material is concerned with the exploits of one of the twelve heroes, such as Roland or Doolin, of Maintz and others. More particularly in France during the reign of Philip Augustus many of such Epopees were composed. We have a *further* garland of legend with an English source, one which aims at reproducing the exploits of King Arthur and the Round Table. Legendary tale, the chivalry of Normans and Englishmen, service to woman, the fealty of the vassal, are all here involved together in melancholy or fantastic combination with Christian mysticism. The search for the Holy Grail, that chalice containing the sacred blood of Christ, is, indeed, one main object of all knightly exploit, and every description of fantastic adventure originates in this source, until, finally, the entire company takes flight to Abyssinia. The above two subjects of legendary story are worked out with most completeness in Northern France, England, and Germany. And as a last illustration we have a *third* circle of chivalrous poetry, composed with yet more caprice and less substantive content, which ever tends to emphasize knightly heroism to an excess with ideas of fairyland and fable; this rather points to Portugal or Spain as its original nursery. In this the family of the Amadi are accepted as principal heroes.

The great allegorical poems, so much beloved mainly in Northern France in the thirteenth century, are more nearly prose compositions in their abstract type. I will only mention one example of these, that is, the famous *Roman de la Rose*. We may compare or rather contrast such with the many anecdotes and still lengthier narratives, the so-called *fabliaux* and *contes*, which rather borrow their subject-matter from contemporary life, tales of knights, priests, citizens, and above all *amours*, lawful and the reverse, retailed to us sometimes in the comic vein, at others in the tragic, now in prose, and again in verse. Such was the type of writing which the clear intellect and trained culture of a Boccaccio carried to its perfection.

There is a final class of such compositions, which, turning to the ancients—with a casual knowledge of the Epic of Homer and Virgil, or ancient legend, celebrates also, in precisely the manner of the Epopaea of chivalry, the exploits of Trojan heroes, the foundation of Rome by Æneas, the conquests of Alexander, and other like subjects.

And this will conclude what I have to say upon the Epic poetry of the Middle Ages.

(γ) In a *third* principal group of which I have still to speak, the rich and pregnant study of *ancient* literature marks a point of departure for the purer artistic taste of a new culture, in whose learning, assimilation, and blending of diverse elements, however, we frequently miss that primitive creative power, which we admire in the Hindoos, Arabs, as also in Homer and writers of the Middle Ages. In the many-sided development in which, dating from this age of the re-awakened sciences and their influence on national literatures, the actual conditions of mankind undergo a reform in religion, political condition, morals, and social relations, epic poetry also seizes hold of the most varied content, as also the most manifold forms, the historical course of which I can only direct attention to in its most essential characteristics.

(αα) *First,* we may remark that it is still the *Middle Ages,* which now, as previously, supplies the material for the Epos, although the same is conceived and presented in a new spirit, namely, one permeated with the culture of classic literature> We find here pre-eminently two directions in which the art of epic poetry displays itself.

On the one side the awakening consciousness of the age shows a necessary tendency to treat as ridiculous all that is capricious in the adventurous feats of the Middle Ages, all that is fantastic and exaggerated in chivalry, all that is merely formal in the independence and personal isolation of the heroes, and which is now contained within a social reality embracing more abundance of national conditions and interest; a consciousness which further brings this entire world before our vision in the light of comedy, which does this, however much what is really genuine within it is also asserted, with seriousness and delight. As the culminating points of this genial conception of the entire world of chivalry I have already pointed to Ariosto and Cervantes. I will therefore in the present passage merely draw attention to the brilliant facility, the charm and wit, the loveliness and intense ingenuousness, with which Ariosto, whose poem still hovers among the poetic aims of the Middle Ages, merely in a more veiled and humorous fashion makes what is fantastic vanish away by means of the incredibility of his nonsense, while the profounder romance of Cervantes already assumes knight-errantry to be a Past behind it; which, consequently, can only enter into the real prose and presence of life as vanity in its isolation and fantastic folly; yet at the same time it gives equal prominence to its great and noble aspects in their contrast to what is awkward, stupid, devoid of reason and order in this very prosaic reality, making the defects of the same live

250

before our eyes.

Among writers who have contributed to a *second* phase in this type of epic development I will merely mention the representative name of Tasso. In his "Jerusalem Delivered" this poet, in contrast to the poetry of Ariosto, selects for his central theme, without any admixture of the humorist's temper whatever, the great and common aims of Christian chivalry, the recovery of the Holy Sepulchre, the victorious pilgrimage of the Crusades, and, after the model of Homer and Virgil, creates an Epos with enthusiasm and study, which may even be compared with the great prototypes abovementioned. And no doubt we do discover in this work, quite apart from a genuine, and, in part, too, national and religious interest, a type of unity, development, and elaboration of the whole such as we have previously fixed as a primary condition. We may add to this a fascinating music in the verse, which makes the same still harmonious to living speech. What, however, is pre-eminently wanting in this poem is just that kind of primitive origin which is alone able to create the real Bible of an entire nation. In other words, instead of having, as in Homer's case, a work which, as true Epos, expresses once for all in language, and with direct simplicity, that which the nation is through its actions, the epic in question rather appears simply a poem, that is, a poetically constructed event. We are mainly pleased and satisfied with it in virtue of the artistic effect of its beautiful speech and form, whether we consider its more lyrical aspects, or its epic descriptions. Consequently, however much Tasso may have taken Homer for his model in the collective arrangement of his material, in the entire spirit of the conception and presentation it is rather and in chief the influence of Virgil that we actually discover in the work, and of course do so not to the poem's advantage.

Finally, among the great Epopaea, which are constructed

upon the basis of a classic culture, we must include the "Lysiad" of Camoens. In the subject-matter of this entirely national composition, which celebrates the bold sea-faring of the Portuguese, we are already beyond the true Middle Ages, and have interests unfolded, which inaugurate a new era. But here, too, despite the glow of its patriotism, despite the life-like character of the descriptive matter, based for the most part upon the author's own experience, we are still conscious of a real barrier between the subject that is national and an artistic culture which is partly borrowed from the ancients and in part from the Italians, and which impairs its impression as a truly original epic.

($\beta\beta$) The essentially new manifestations in the religious belief and actual composition of modern life originate in the principle of the Reformation. The whole tendency of this general change of outlook is, indeed, rather favourable to lyric and dramatic, than epic poetry. But we do find nevertheless, even in the latter sphere, an autumnal blossoming of the religious Epopaea, of which the pre-eminent examples are Milton's "Paradise Lost" and Klopstock's "Messias." In breadth of culture, gained through study of the ancients, and the correct elegance of his language, Milton is no doubt an admirable master of his age. In the profundity of his content, in energy, original invention and execution, and, above all, in the epic objectivity of his presentment, however, he is in every respect inferior to Dante. For not only does the conflict and the catastrophe of "Paradise Lost" take a direction which is contrary to its dramatic character; but, as I have above incidentally observed, it is, in a unique way, supported by a lyrical impulse and ethical or didactic predilections, which lie far enough away from the subject in its original form.[35] I have already, in discussing Klopstock, referred to a similar cleft between the material and the form, which a particular

252

age gives to it in its epic reflection. In the case of Klopstock, moreover, an endeavour is throughout apparent through a rhetoric, which is little more than the caricature of the Sublime, to infuse the reader with that recognition of the worth and solemnity of his subject, which the poet has himself experienced. From a somewhat different point of view we arrive at very much the same conclusion in the case of Voltaire's "Henriade." At any rate here too the poetry is an artificial production, and all the more so, inasmuch as the material, as already observed, is not adapted to the truly primitive Epos.

($\gamma\gamma$) If we try to discover really epic compositions in our own day we shall find ourselves in an atmosphere totally different from that of the genuine Epopaea. The general condition of the world to-day has assumed a form, which, in its prosaic character, is diametrically opposed to everything which we found indispensable to the genuine Epos, while the revolutions, which have been imposed upon the actual social conditions of states and nations, are still too strongly riveted in our memory as actual experiences that they should be able to receive an epic type of art. Epic poetry has consequently taken refuge from the great national events in the narrow circle of the domestic life of individuals in the country and in the small town, striving to find here the material adapted to epic composition. In this way, more particularly among us Germans, the Epic has become idyllic, after the genuine Idyll, of the sweet sentimentality and wishy-washy type, died out.

As an example lying close to hand of an idyllic Epos I will merely mention the "Luise" of Voss, as also and above all Goethe's masterpiece, "Herman and Dorothea." In the latter work we have no doubt our attention directed to the background of the greatest world-event of our age, with which the circumstances of the innkeeper and his family, of the pastor and the apothecary, are directly associated. And inasmuch as the little country town is not placed before us in its political relations we at once remark a gap in the narrative which is not explained or mediated by any connecting link. Yet it is precisely through this omission of the intermediate link that the whole keeps its unique character. For with the stroke of a master Goethe has removed the revolution into the background, despite the fact that he has known how to make the most happy use of it in the enlargement of his poem. He only interweaves such circumstances with the action as, in their simple humanity, connect themselves absolutely without constraint with domestic and civic conditions. The main point, therefore, is that Goethe in this work has succeeded in detaching from the reality of our modern life traits, descriptions, conditions, and developments, and depicting the same, which in their province once more make that alive which contributes to the imperishable charm of those primitive human conditions of the Odyssey and the patriarchal picture of the Old Testament.

In respect to other spheres of our present national and social life I would observe in conclusion that in the field of epic poetry there are practically unlimited opportunities for the *romance*, the *narrative*, and the *novel*. I am, however, unable, even in the most general outline, to follow the history of these in the breadth of their development from their first appearance until the present time.

━

[1] *Die echt poetische Abrundung.* Not, however, merely literary finish, but complete ideal totality.

[2] *Einem bestimmten Tone.* Perhaps more truly "a particular strain or atmosphere." But both aspects are suggested.

[3] There is a misprint here *eine recht* for *einer echt,* and also I should prefer eight lines lower down *die* for *das* agreeing with

Freiheit rather than *Leben.*

[4] This sentence is obviously ironical, but the sense intended is not very clear. The words *die sic* are clearly a misprint for *die sick,* and I presume *kindisch* is not used in its more common depreciatory sense of childish. I am, however, not very confident of my translation. *War es ein Zeichen* would apparently refer back to the general intention of the previous sentence, *i.e.,* the attempt of Klopstock and others to make a national book.

[5] See vol. I, pp. 240-289, and particularly pp. 270-289.

[6] *Eine Sittlichkeit.*

[7] Poet., c. 14.

[8] That is to say, that the whole remains intact in its opposition. The question of international ethics is not directly considered, though reference is here made to historical evolution in its widest sense.

[9] Wrong that is inflicted on a state which is, as a whole, innocent.

[10] I presume the reference is mainly to the United States. Hegel's sentence is *so möchten diese nur den Sieg dereinstiger Americanischer lebendiger Vernünftigkeit über die Einkerkerung in ein ins Unendliche fortgehendes Messen und Particularisiren darzustellen haben.* It may be doubted, perhaps, whether he would have expressed himself with equal confidence in our own day. At least the position of the German States of his own time no doubt was strongly present in his mind.

[11] *Von einem anderen beschränkt.* Curtailed, I imagine, as a spontaneous and free power.

[12] That is acting in subservience to eternal forces, not directing those forces. Hegel conceives the event as supplying the lines of direction through which the forces are effective.

[13] *Aus der Dumpfheit des Bewusstseyns.* Out of the confusions of consciousness.

[14] I have adopted the masculine gender in accordance with the text, though of course it does not imply personality in the ordinary sense.

[15] I suppose the meaning is that it is a purely objective

panorama.

[16] *Seiner Sache,* Somewhat vague and difficult to translate. It means more than his affair or business.

[17] *Trauer.* Mournfulness or gloom is perhaps better.

[18] Liv., ii, c. 32.

[19] Lit., so far as they do not emphasize essential phases in (*Momente*).

[20] I presume the allusion is to the way, already illustrated, the Homeric gods do not take themselves seriously.

[21] Messias, Canto II, w, 627-850.

[22] It is possible Hegel means by *geistige* intelligible.

[23] Act II, sc. 6.

[24] "O, that I had never shipped hither over the sea, unhappy that I am! Vain was the fancy which befooled me to seek an empty fame in France; and now a fatal destiny carries me to this bloody field of death. O that I were far from here housed at home on the banks of the blue Severn, where the mother remained behind and the gentle sweet bride mourning for me."

[25] "To Death thou art decreed! A British matron it was that conceived thee!"

[26] "With vow to slay at everything alive with the sword that the fateful god of battles confronts her with."

[27] *Sitte und Settlichkeit.*

[28] That is of the Epos.

[29] The course of painting is similar to that of sculpture in virtue of the fact that it is wholly of one type, viz., romantic, but it differs from it in being less objective and requiring more historical illustration.

[30] *Substantiellen, i.e.,* an outlook which concentrates attention on the one Divine substance, the essence beneath the phenomenal.

[31] I presume this is another Persian composition, but it may be a cult of some kind.

[32] Substantive as contrasted with phenomenal.

[33] That is the Iliad and Odyssey.

[34] What Hegel means to say by this and the following paragraph is by no means clear. He first seems to state as a fact that a rivalry may be asserted, or at least has been asserted by others, between the Spanish romances and the finest Greek and Latin epic literature, and then immediately afterwards denies the fact so far as the Iliad and Odyssey is concerned. The confusion and indeed uncertainty seems to be due to the fact that while explaining the disadvantage in which the German work is placed as compared with the Spanish romances, he merely contrasts the Homeric poems with the former. What he apparently means us to infer is that the latter are as superior as the German work is, at least as an Epos, inferior. The words "we moderns" are apparently ironical. In any case the entire passage is, I think, clearly one which needed revision, and it is possible that the two paragraphs have been tacked together by Hegel's editors from different connections.

[35] As we find it, presumably, in Genesis.

(B.) LYRIC POETRY

The poetic imagination does not, as the plastic arts do, present the objects of its creation before our vision in an objective shape, but only envisages them to the inward vision and emotions. No doubt from the first, relatively to certain aspects of this universal type of composition, it is the *personal* quality of ideal creation and construction which pre-eminently asserts itself in the presented work, and as such is to be contrasted with plastic construction. But when epic poetry offers to our contemplation its object either in its substantive universality, or under a mode comparable with that of sculptor and painter—in other words, in its living presence—in that case, at least where the art is most consummate, the individual mind and soul of the creator involved in the creation disappears before the objective

257

result created. The above personal or subjective aspect of mind can only completely be discarded in so far as, in the first place, the entire world of objects and relations are essentially absorbed by it and then permitted to stand forth freely from the veiled presence of the individual consciousness, and, further, in so far as the self-centred soul unbars its doors, opens wide its ears and eyes, extends the purely unenlightened feeling to vision and idea, and attaches to this wealth of hidden content word and speech as the vehicle of its intimate self-expression. And just in proportion as this kind of communication persists in shutting itself away from the objective manifestation of epic art, to that extent, and precisely for that reason, the subjective type of poetry is bound to find its own forms, in a province of its own, wholly independent of the Epos. In other words, the human spirit descends from the objectivity of the object into its own private domain; it peers into its particular conscious life; it endeavours to satisfy the desire to reproduce the presence and reality of *that*, as displayed in soul, in the experience of heart and reflected idea, and in doing so to unfold the content and activity of the personal life rather than the actual presence of the external fact. But, again, inasmuch as this expression, if it is not simply to remain the chance expression of mere individuality[1] in its immediate feeling and conception, must assert itself in speech as the reflection of an inner life that is *poetic*, all that is thus envisaged of feeling or otherwise—and however much, too, it may be a part of the poet's unique personality, and be presented by him as such—must nevertheless possess a universal validity, in other words, it must essentially include feelings and reflections for which the art of poetry is able to discover the vital and adequate means of expression. And although, apart from this, pain and desire, as conceived, described, and expressed in speech, may lighten the heart, and poetic ebullition is unquestionably

258

permissible for such a purpose, yet its function is not restricted to such domestic service. Rather it has a nobler vocation, which is not so much to liberate the human spirit from emotion, but in the medium of the same. The blind tumult of passion surges on in a union with the entire soul-life unenlightened, unawakened to the grasp of mind. In such a state the soul cannot assert itself in idea and expression. It is the function of poetry no doubt to free the heart from such a prison house, in so far as it presents that life as an object to it. But it does more than this mere translation of content from the immediacy of emotional experience; it creates therefrom an object which is purified from all mere contingency of the passing mood; an object in which the soul-life in this deliverance returns once more to itself freely and with self-conscious satisfaction, and remains there at home. Conversely, however, this primary objectivisation ought not to be carried to the point of a reflection that actually discloses the individual activity of the soul-life and its passions as it is carried forward in practical impulse and *action*; in other words, in the self-return of the individual upon himself in veritable deed. For the most pertinent reality of our inner life is still itself an inward something, and consequently this passage from itself can only give us the *sense* of deliverance from the immediate concentration of heart in its blind and formless presence, which now unbars itself in self-expression, and in doing so grasps and expresses what was previously merely felt in the form of a self-conscious vision and ideas. And with these remarks I think we have determined in their essential features both the sphere and function of lyric poetry as contrasted with the epic and dramatic types.

As regards the more detailed examination and classification of our new subject-matter, we cannot do better than follow the course previously adopted in our examination of epic poetry.

First, we have to discuss the *general* character of lyric composition.

Secondly, we shall consider the *particular* characteristics which make the lyric work of art and the types of the same worthy of attention in their more direct relation to the lyric poet.

Thirdly, we shall conclude the survey with a few remarks upon the *historical* development of this class of poetic work.

Generally I may remark that this survey will be extremely restricted, and for two reasons—first, because I am compelled to reserve the necessary space for the discussion of the dramatic field; secondly, because I must limit myself exclusively to general considerations, inasmuch as the detail embraced by it possesses far more incalculable resources of manifold complexity than in the case of the Epos, and could only be treated in greater fulness and completeness if viewed historically, which is not within the aim of the present work.

1. GENERAL CHARACTER OF THE LYRIC.

In the stimulus of epic poetry is the desire to hear the thing or matter which is unfolded on its own account, and independently of the poet,[2] as an objective and essentially exclusive totality. In the lyric, on the contrary, it is the converse need which finds its satisfaction in self-expression and the coming to a knowledge of the soul in this expression of itself. With regard to the nature of this effusion,[3] we may enumerate its most important constituents as follows:

First, there is the *content* in which soul-life is aware of itself and reflects itself in idea.

Secondly, there is the *form*, in virtue of which the expression of this content becomes lyric poetry.

Thirdly, there is the stage of conscious life and culture from which the person thus lyrically viewed discloses his feelings and ideas.

(*a*) The content of the lyric work of art cannot comprise the development of an objective action in its possibilities of expansion into all the breadth and wealth of a world. It is the single person, and along with him the isolated fact of situation and objects, no less than the mode and manner in which the soul is made aware of itself in such content, with its private judgments, its joy, its wonder, its pain, and its feeling, which it presents to our vision. Through this principle of division and particularity, as present in the Lyric, the content may be of the greatest variety, associated with every tendency of national life. There is, however, this essential distinction, that whereas the Epos combines in one and the same work the spirit of a people in all its breadth, and in its actual deed and fashion, the more definite content of lyrical poetry limits itself to one particular aspect, or at least is unable successfully to attain to the explicit completeness and exposition which the Epos ought at least to possess. The entire wealth of lyrical poetry in a nation may, therefore, no doubt embrace the collective exuberance of national interest, idea, and purpose; but it is not the single lyrical poem that can do this.

The Lyric is not called upon to produce Bibles such as we have discovered in Epic poetry. It does, however, enjoy the advantage of being able to touch upon every conceivable aspect of national development; whereas the true Epos is limited to distinct epochs of a primitive age, and its success in our more recent times of prosaic culture is very jejune.

(*α*) Within this field of particularization we have, to start with, the *universal* as such—the supreme height and depth of human belief, imagination, and knowledge—the essential content of religion, art, ay, even of scientific thought, in so far as the same is adaptable to the form of imagination and creation, and can enter the sphere of emotions. Consequently general opinions, what is of permanent substance in a view of the world, the profounder grasp of far-reaching social conditions are all not excluded from the Lyric; and a considerable part of the material I have referred to[4] when discussing the more incomplete types of the Epic falls rightly, and with pertinency into the sphere now under review.

(*β*) And along with such essentially universal topics we have associated the aspect of *particularity*, which can be so interwoven with what is thus substantive that any specific situation, feeling, or idea is thereby seized in its profounder significance and expressed in a way wholly accordant thereto. This is, for example, almost always the case in Schiller's lyrical work, as also in his ballads; in this connection I will merely recall the superb description of the Eumenides chorus in the Cranes of Ibicus, which is neither dramatic nor epic, but lyrical. From a further point of view we may have this combination so asserted that a variety of particular traits, moods, occurrences are introduced by way of testimony to comprehensive views and maxims, interlaced in vital coalescence by virtue of the general principle. This style of writing is frequently employed in the elegy and epistle, and generally in reflections upon life of a comprehensive character.

(*γ*) In conclusion, inasmuch as in lyrical composition what is self-expressed is the *individual person*, a content, which is extremely slight, will primarily suffice for this purpose. It is, in other words, the soul itself, subjective life simply, which is the true content. The emphasis is therefore throughout upon the animation of feeling, rather than upon the more immediate object. The most fleeting moods of the moment, the overjoyment of the heart, the swiftly passing gleams or clouds of careless merriment and jest, sorrow, melancholy, and complaint, in a word, all and every phase of emotion are here seized in their momentary movement or isolated occurrence, and rendered permanent in their expression. What we find here in the domain of poetry may be paralleled with what I previously referred to when describing *genre* paintings. The content, the subject-matter, is here the wholly contingent, and what is over and above this important is exclusively the character of the individual conception and mode of presentment, the charm of which in the Lyric will either consist in the aroma of exquisite feeling, or in the novelty of arresting points of view, and the genial suggestion of literary phrases and turns which surprise.

(*b*) In the *second* place we may observe in general with respect to the *form*, wherein the Lyric is composed, that here too it is the individual person, in the intimacy of his ideas or emotion that constitutes the focal centre. The growth of the whole is rooted in the heart and temperament; it starts, to be more precise, from a particular mood and situation of the poet. By virtue of this fact the content and conjunction of the particular aspects of its growth are not inferred from it objectively as a substantively independent content, or from its external manifestation as some really self-exclusive event, but are borrowed from the individual subject as such. But for this reason it is essential that the individual in question should himself appear poetical, rich in fancy and feeling, or imposing and profound in his views and reflections, and above all should be essentially independent, the possessor of a unique ideal world, from which the servility and caprice of a prosaic nature is excluded.

The lyric poem, then, retains a mode of unity wholly

different from that of the Epos, in other words, the mysterious intimacy of the mood or reflection, which expatiates upon itself, mirrors itself in the objective world, describes itself, or concerns itself as it wills with any other matter, always, however, retaining the right in the pursuit of such an interest to begin and break off very much as it pleases. Horace, for instance, very frequently comes to a stop at the very point, where, in the commonplace view of its literary treatment, we might suppose he had only just started with his subject. In other words, what he describes is simply his feelings, commands or arrangements for a banquet, say, without giving us further information as to how it went off. In the same way we have every conceivable mode of progression and combination supplied by the nature of the mood, the actual condition of the individual soul-life, the degree of passion, its excitement or rapid transition of conflicting emotion, or the tranquillity of the heart or the mind in some long-drawn process of contemplation. As a rule, in respect to all such subject-matter, we are able to determine very little that is fixed, owing to the repeated changes in the ever varied facets of the soul. I will therefore restrict myself to a few salient points of distinction.

(α) Just as we met with several specific kinds of epic poetry which showed a tendency to adopt a lyric vein of expression, so, too, the Lyric may accept as its subject-matter and its form an occurrence, which, so far as content and external appearance are concerned, are epic, and to this extent it will approximate to the latter type. Heroic songs, romances, and ballads belong to such a class. The form of the whole is in such examples narrative, inasmuch as it is the progressive advance of a situation or event, as among other instances, a particular direction in the fate of a nation, which is communicated. And yet at the same time the fundamental temper is wholly lyric, inasmuch as the main object is not to give us a description and representation of the actual fact apart from all relation to the narrator, but rather to disclose his personal attitude to it in the way he conceives and feels it, whether with delight or complaint, whether as a stimulus to good or depressed spirits, the mood in short that rings throughout it. And similarly the nature of the impression which the poet endeavours to produce thereby is entirely that of the province of the lyric. In other words, what the poet seeks to effect in his audience is precisely that state of emotion, which the recounted event has produced in himself, and which he therefore has attached to his composition. He expresses his dejection, mourning, merriment, his fire of patriotism, and so forth, in an appropriate occurrence in such a way that it is not this fact so much which contributes, as it were, the focus, but rather the state of his emotional life we find reflected therein. And for this reason he, above all emphasizes those traits, and depicts the same with feeling, which are in accord with his own personal impulses; and in the degree of vivacity with which these are expressed by them the same feelings are likely to be excited in his audience. And thus, though the content may be epic, the treatment is lyrical.

($\alpha\alpha$) To come yet more directly to detail there is, first, the example of the *epigram*, in such a case where it is not merely an inscription which states concisely the bald nature of some fact, but further associates with this an emotional state; where, in short, the content, regarded as the bare statement of external fact, is merged in a condition of the soul. In other words, the writer here ceases to surrender himself wholly to the object: rather he makes his own personality expressive in it; he records his desires with regard to it; he attaches to it his own sportive fancies, his acute or unexpected suggestions and associations. The

Greek Anthology contains many such witty epigrams which have lost the epic manner. In more recent times we find similar examples in the piquante couplets of the French, abundantly illustrated in their Vaudevilles. We Germans have much the same thing in our didactic distiches, Xenien, and the like. Even tomb inscriptions frequently approximate to this lyrical character in virtue of the strong emotions expressed.

($\beta\beta$) In much the same way the Lyric accepts a wider range in descriptive narrative. I will merely mention, as a composition of this class, the *romance*. It is the most obvious and simple form of it, in so far that is as it isolates the different scenes of an event, and then depicts rapidly and with the full force of their most important characteristics each on its own account, in descriptions marked throughout by sympathetic feeling. Such a consistent and well-defined grasp of the characteristic features of a situation, together with an emphatic assertion of the writer's absolute sympathy with his subject, is above all nobly represented in Spanish literature and makes such romances strikingly impressive. A peculiar clarity of atmosphere surrounds these lyrical representations which rather identifies them with the clear-cut definition of objective vision, than with the ideal world of the imagination.

($\gamma\gamma$) The class of the *ballad*, in contrast to the above, includes for the most part, if in less degree than the truly epic poem, the completeness of an independent event, whose reflection, of course, it merely embodies in the most conspicuous of its phases, while it seeks at the same time to give full, if concentrated and ideal emphasis, to the depth of the sentiment with which it is throughout interwoven, and therein the plaint, dejection, joy, and so forth, of the soul. English literature above all contains many such poetic compositions in the early and more primitive epoch of its history; and, generally, popular poetry delights in the narration of such histories and collisions, usually unfortunate, with a true and emotional emphasis calculated to make both heart and voice thrill and falter with anguish. But in more recent times also among ourselves Bürger and, most famous of all, Goethe and Schiller, have composed masterpieces in this field; Bürger in virtue of his sombre tone of naïveté; Goethe through the impeccable clarity of his emotional, no less than imaginative vision, which forms the lyrical thread throughout; and Schiller, on account of his superb emotional emphasis on the fundamental thought which he seeks, in a wholly lyrical manner, to express under the form of an event, in order thereby to affect the hearts of his readers with a similar lyric movement of feeling and contemplation.

(β) The purely *personal* element of lyric poetry is rightly emphasized in those cases, when the fact of a given situation is taken by the poet as an effective means of expressing his *own* individuality therein. Such is the case in the so-called poems *of occasion.* So far back as the poems of Callinus and Tyrtaeus we find elegies of battle based on conditions regarded as real, which are made the stimulus of a personal enthusiasm, albeit the poet's own individuality, his purely private affections and feelings, are as yet not so much in evidence. The Pindaric Odes also bring to light in their panegyrics of particular contests, victors, and circumstances, a vein or impulse that is more private; and yet more in some of the odes of Horace we mark a definitely personal motive, or rather expressed thought to the effect, "I will as myself a man of culture and fame, write a poem on this subject." But the best illustration of all we have in our own Goethe, whose partiality for such a style was due to the fact that he discovered a poem in every incident of his life.

($\alpha\alpha$) If, however, the lyric work of art is to be divested of all *dependence* of external occasion and purpose, that may be implied in it, and to be composed as a self-subsistent whole on its own account, it is obviously essential that the poet also only make use of such external stimulus as an opportunity to express *himself*, his mood, delight, sorrow, or modes of thought and reflection generally. The condition of most importance to such an intimate mode of personal expression consists in the poet's ability to absorb the real content absolutely, converting it thereby into his own possession. The true lyric poet lives a life of introspection, he grasps relations in the light of his poetic individuality; and, however in varied fashion his inner life may be blended with the world around him, in its conditions and destiny, what he presents to us exclusively in such material is the unique and independent animation of his own emotions and observations. When, to take our former example, Pindar was invited to celebrate a victor of the Hellenic games, or undertakes this uninvited, he made himself so entirely master of his subject-matter, that his composition no longer so much appears a poem *on* the victor as an effusion of song created from his own resources.

($\beta\beta$) If we consider more closely the manner of presentment of such a poem *d'occasion*, we shall, no doubt, be ready to admit that the same can to a real extent borrow its more defined material and character, no less than its conceived organization as an artistic work, from the actual features of the occurrence or individual which constitute its content. It is, in fact, precisely from this content that the emotional movement of the poet proceeds. As the most illuminating, though an extreme example, I will merely mention Schiller's "Song of the Bell," which makes out of the varied stages of bell-foundry the significant and arresting moments in the composition of the entire poem, and only subject to this introduces the emotional element relevant thereto, as also the various observations upon human life and the description of its conditions. In a somewhat different manner, too, Pindar makes use of the place of birth of the victor, the exploits of the family to which he belongs, or other relations of life as an opportunity in his own person to exalt certain gods to the exclusion of others, or to mention these particular exploits and results alone, or to emphasize exclusively the observations or maxims he has interpolated. From a further point of view, however, the lyric poet is absolutely free, inasmuch as it is not the external occasion as such, but rather the poet's *own* soul-life which is here the subject; and consequently it entirely depends on the particular views of the poet and the character of his general mood, what aspects of the subject-matter and in what threads of connection and sequence they shall be composed. In other words, we are unable to predict decisively and *a priori* the degree in which the objective occasion with its given content, or the purely personal factor of poet, shall be predominant, or whether both aspects shall on equal terms coalesce.

(γγ) Furthermore, it is not the incentive and its positive reality, but the ideal movement and conception of the individual soul which supplies the *focus of unity*. The particular mood or general review, which is aroused poetically by the occasion, these constitute the centre, radiating from which not merely the colour of the whole, but also the embrace of the particular features unfolded, the very mode of the execution and construction, and therewith the build and coalescence of the poem as a work of art are determined. In this way, to return to our previous example, Pindar possesses in the life-conditions of his victors a genuine core of reality for differentiation or amplification. In the particular poems, however, which he has written it is

269

invariably other points of view, another mood altogether, whether it be of warning, comfort, or exaltation, which he makes most pervasive, and which, although such exclusively belong to the poet in his creative capacity, do none the less give him precisely that grasp of all he wishes to touch upon, execute, and hand to posterity in those historical facts, while unfolding therewith the illuminating and constructive power of genius, without which he would fail to secure the lyric effect intended.

(γ) But, *thirdly*, it is not absolutely necessary for the genuine lyrical poet to start from the external occurrence, which he recounts in a medium rich with emotion, or, indeed, from any such objectively real stimulus of his efforts. He is, let us repeat, a truly exclusive world *in himself*. He may find there both the original incentive and content, and consequently go no further than this ideal world of condition, event, and passion discovered in his own heart and soul. This is that domain in which man becomes, in virtue of his private inner life, himself the work of art; while the epic poet avails himself exclusively of the hero and his exploits and experiences for this purpose.

(αα) And yet in this field, too, an element of narrative may enter, where, as in the case of the songs of Anacreon, bright little pictures of adventure with Eros and the like receive the finish of delightful miniatures. Such an event, however, must obviously rather resemble the unveiling of a condition of personal soul-life. In a somewhat different mode of the same thing Horace, in his *Integer vitæ* makes use of the fact of his meeting a wolf, not to the extent that we can, therefore, call his poem the verse *occasion*, but rather regarding this fact as the prompting force of his first sentence and the serenity of the feelings of affection with which he concludes.

(ββ) As a rule we may also observe that the situation under

which the poet depicts himself should not restrict itself merely to the *inner personal* life as such. It must rather attest itself as concrete, and thereby we may even say external totality. The poet, in short, reveals himself not merely in that inward personal life, but as one of the objects of the external world. In the example just cited of the Anacreon odes the poet depicts himself among roses, fair maidens, and youths in the merry enjoyment of wine and dance, without regret or yearning, without obligation, and yet without dislike of loftier aims, which, indeed, are not present at all; reveals himself rather as a hero, who freely and without reserve, and consequently without hesitation or loss, is just this unity, is what he is, a man of his own type, and figures as such in this intimate artistic presentment. In the love-songs of Hafis also we may observe the entire vital individuality of the poet in all its changes of content, pose, and an expression which approaches close to self-conscious humour. And yet his poetry is without any specific theme, any objective picture, any god, or mythology; or, rather, when we peruse these light-hearted ebullitions, one feels as though it would be impossible for the Oriental to possess any such definite picture and constructive art. He passes easily from one object to another; he takes his walks abroad, but it is a scene in which the entire man, with his wine, his damsels, his court-life, and all the rest of it, is placed before us with delightful unreserve, without passion or self-seeking in the simplicity of his enjoyment eye to eye and soul to soul. Improvisations of this type adapt themselves in the most various ways not merely to a reflection of the soul-life, but also to external condition. If, however, the poet is absorbed in his own individual experience, we are not so much concerned to hear his particular fancies, love affairs, domestic arrangements, and the history of his uncles and aunts. We are so invited, for instance, in Klopstock's Eidli and Fanny, as to nave some vision given us of what is of

271

universal human interest, in order that our sympathies may be roused. From this point of view, therefore, such lyrical poetry can readily degenerate into the spurious assumption that what is essentially private and particular must necessarily awaken interest. On the contrary, it would be no incorrect description of many songs of Goethe if we called them "Songs of *Comradeship*," although they are not exactly executed by the poet under such a category. In other words, it is not so much himself that a man offers in society; rather he places his particularity in the background, and converses with the help of something else, whether it be a story or an anecdote, seizing its specific features in some particular mood, and communicating them agreeably to such a temper. In a case like this it is not exactly the poet, and yet it is himself for all that. It is not himself he gives us, but something else as best he can. He is, in short, an actor, who runs through an infinite variety of parts. First he lingers on this, then on that; he reviews momentarily a scene, then maybe a group of people. But whatever he may endeavour to reproduce, it is throughout his individual artistic soul-life, his own experience, his own feeling, which is vitally interwoven with it.

(γγ) But, further, in so far as the individuality of self-conscious life is the true source of the Lyric, the poet is justified in limiting his expression to his own moods and reflections without any further combination of them in a concrete situation that includes a truly objective character. It is in this direction that examples of what is little more than an empty fluting for fluting's sake, the song and trill simply on its own account, will yet give us genuine lyrical satisfaction. In such the words are to a more or less extent merely the vehicle of cheerfulness or sorrow, whose effect, moreover, very readily serves as an invitation to musical accompaniment. Folk-songs especially very often amount to little more than this. In the songs of Goethe, too, though we may no doubt discover here a more defined and abundant mode of expression, it is not unfrequently simply a single and transitory bit of merriment that is vouchsafed, a passing mood that the poet does not attempt to throw aside, but on the tune of which he pipes for a moment in his tiny song. In others, of course, his treatment of similar moods is on a larger scale, even systematic, as, for instance, in the poem: "*Ich hab mein Sach' auf nichts gestellt,*" in which the poet passes before us as things that come and vanish, first, money and property, then women, travel, fame, honour, and, last of all, fight and war, retaining throughout as the ever-recurring refrain of stability his own free and careless cheerfulness. Conversely, however, the intimate individual life may from the same point of view grow in depth and expansion, in conditions of the soul of the most imposing proportions and ideas that embrace the world itself. A considerable number of Schiller's poems are of this type. What is great, what opens to intelligence, this is the incentive of his heart. But he will neither celebrate in hymn fashion a religious or otherwise profound subject; nor will he be the minstrel who looks for inspiration without him to the pertinent fact or occasion. He sings in the presence of, and inspired by, his own soul-life, the highest interest of which are the ideals of life, beauty, and the imperishable claims and thoughts of our humanity.

(*c*) There is a *third* consideration we have to deal with in connection with the general character of lyric poetry. It is the nature of the general stage of human development and culture from which the isolated poem originates.

In this respect, too, the Lyric occupies a position which is to be contrasted with Epic poetry. In other words, while we regarded as necessary for the full bloom of the true Epos a phase in the nation's growth which was, speaking generally,

273

undeveloped, at least in the sense that it had not ripened in the prosaic acceptance of its actual life, the times which favour most of all lyrical composition are those which already are in possession of a more or less fixed organization of social condition. It is in such a period that the individual seeks a reflection of his intimate personal life in contrast to this outer world, creating from it and within its limits an independent whole of emotion and idea. For in the Lyric it is not, we repeat, the objective solidarity and individual action, but the individual person as self-conscious life which supplies both content and form. This, however, must not be understood in such a way as though the individual, in order to express himself in lyrical form, must perforce disjoin himself from every connection with national interests and the opinions, and with rigid and exclusive severity remain as he stands.

On the contrary, with such an abstract self-subsistency we should only have left us for content the wholly contingent and particular passion, the mere caprice of concupiscence and affection, false idiosyncrasies and distorted originality would have unlimited opportunities. Genuine lyrical poetry, like all other poetry, has no doubt to express the content of the human heart in its truth. Yet none the less, regarded as the content of the Lyric, what is most a matter of fact and substantial must appear absorbed in personal feeling, vision, imagination, and thought. And, in the *second* place, the question here is not so much simply expression of the personal inner life, is not so much concerned with a primary and direct statement in the epic fashion, what the facts are, as with an expression of the poetical nature in a manner both artistically fruitful and wholly different from chance and ordinary modes. It follows that the Lyric requires, precisely on account of the fact that the concentrated life of the heart unfolds itself in manifold feelings and

274

comprehensive views, and the individual is conscious of the poetry of his most intimate life as nested in a world that is already more prosaically organized—an artistic culture already secured, which must assert itself as the flower and independent product of the individual's natural endowment thus trained to a perfect result. For these reasons the Lyric is not limited to particular epochs of the spiritual development of a people, but is the rich blossom of the most varied. To an exceptional degree is it favoured in more recent times, in which everybody is entitled to have and express his own views and emotions.

I will, however, draw attention, in the interest of really important distinction, to the following general considerations.

(a) In the *first* place, we have the type of lyrical expression peculiar to *folk-songs*.

(αα) In these above all we have witness to the varied and distinct qualities of national character. It is on account of this, and consonant with the widely-prevailing curiosity of our generation, that great efforts are made to collect folk-songs of every kind, in order to increase our acquaintance with the peculiarities of every national spirit, and therewith our sympathies and vital contact with such. Already Herder has done much in this direction. Goethe, too, with the help of his own more independent imitations, has materially assisted an approach to very different examples of this style of poetry. Complete sympathy is, however, only possible for the songs of one's own people; and however much we Germans are able to make ourselves at home in the work of foreign lands, the fact remains that the ultimate aroma in song[5] of the intimate life of another folk can only appear as alien, that we shall only catch the echo of the tone of feeling that truly belongs to it, with the assistance of a more native

275

reflection of its content.[6] This Goethe has imported into his songs of a foreign subject-matter, stamped as they are with the finest sympathy and beauty. We may take as an example the lament of the noble spouse of Asan Aga, imitated from the Icelandic—only so far as to retain throughout the unique spirit of such poems unimpaired.

($\beta\beta$) The general character of the lyrical folk-song is comparable to the primitive Epos in virtue of the fact that here too the poet does not make himself his subject-matter, but is absorbed in his selected material. Although, therefore, intensity of soul in its extreme concentration may express itself in the folk-song, it is nevertheless not a single person with the artistic expression of whose private experience we are made acquainted. It is rather a national state of feeling, which the author completely assimilates, in so far as it possesses, when taken by itself, no intimate form of idea or feeling wholly independent of the nation's existence and interests. And a condition is necessary, as the presupposition for such an inseparable union, in which independent personal reflection and culture is not yet awakened, so that the poet is simply in his creative capacity merely the vehicle in the background, by means of whom the national life is expressed in its lyrical emotion and general outlook. This directly primitive character no doubt communicates to the folk-song an unconscious freshness of downright grasp and striking veracity, which is often very effective; but it receives thereby along with it very readily a fragmentary appearance; it is defective in the continuity of its exposition, which may amount to actual obscurity. The feeling dives into depth, but cannot and will not attain to full utterance. Moreover, as before observed, what is absent from such a point of view throughout, however much the form in general is wholly lyric, in other words subjective, is just the lyrical individuality, which expresses this form and its content as the possession of its *own* heart and mind, and the creation of its *own* artistic resources.

(γγ) Peoples, therefore, which confine themselves to poetry of this type, and do not combine such composition with that of the further stages of lyrical, epic, or dramatic work, are as a rule in great measure barbarous nations, uncultured, characterized by transitory feud and catastrophes. If they themselves, in such heroic ages, really combined to form a truly pregnant whole, whose particular aspects were already fused together in an independent and withal harmonious objective union, which could supply the ground for essentially concrete and individually distinct exploits, we should find in them, along with such primitive poetry, epic poets as well. The condition, out of which such songs assert themselves as the single and ultimate mode of poetic expression, is therefore rather limited to the field of family life and the association of clans, without any further organization such as belongs already to the riper perfection of the heroic community. If we are reminded here and there of national exploits, such are for the most part conflicts waged against foreign aggressors, expeditions of pillage, reprisals of savagery with savagery, or deeds of one individual against another in the same people, in the narration of which lament and dejection or ecstatic jubilation over one conqueror after another, are the moods throughout prevailing. The national life as it actually is, as yet unfolded in its wholly free development, is relegated to the background in contrast with the world of more personal feeling, which also, on its own account, betrays an immaturity; and, however much thereby we gain in concentration of effect, the result only too frequently remains, so far as content is concerned, rude and barbarous. The question then, whether folk-songs should possess for us a poetic interest, or on the contrary repel us to some extent, depends on the kind of situation and emotion they portray. That which appears admirable to the imagination of one people, will readily strike another as wanting in taste, horrible, and offensive. There is, for example, a folk-song which tells us the story of a wife who was immured at the command of her husband, and all that her plea for mercy could effect was that apertures should be left open for her breasts, in order that she might suckle her child; we are told that she remained alive until her child was weaned. This is a barbarous and frightful situation. And in the same way tales of robbery, exploits of the bluster or sheer savagery of individuals, possess nothing in them in which alien peoples of a higher culture can sympathize. Folksongs, consequently, very often run into great detail as to the quality of which there is no fixed standard of comparison, because such is too far removed from our common humanity. When we consequently, in more recent times, are made acquainted with the songs of the Iroquois, the Esquimaux, and other wild nationalities, the circle of a true poetic enjoyment is in no wise thereby enlarged.

(β) Further, inasmuch as the Lyric is the entire expression of the inward life of Spirit, it can neither restrict itself to the mode of expression nor the content of the genuine folksong, or of later poems composed in a similar spirit.

(αα) In other words, on the one hand, it is of essential importance, as already remarked, that the wholly self-absorbed soul should detach itself from this absolute concentration and its direct introspection, and should pass on instead to the free grasp of itself which, in the conditions above described, is only incompletely the case. On the other, it is necessary that it should expand in a world abundant in ideas, passions, varied conditions, and conflicts, in order to endow with ideal expression everything that the human heart is essentially able to apprehend, and then communicate as the birth of its own spirit. For the collective wealth of lyrical poetry should express in poetic form all that the inner life comprises, so far as the same can pass into poetry, and therefore finds itself at home alike in all phases of spiritual culture.

($\beta\beta$) And, *secondly*, with the advent of a free self-consciousness is bound up the freedom of an assured *art* of its own. The folk-song sings forth, just as any natural song, straight from the heart. A free art, however, is aware of itself; it requires a knowledge and desire of that which it produces; and requires culture to promote this knowledge, as also an executive power, which is expert in the finest composition. When, consequently, genuine epic poetry has to conceal the individual creative power of the poet, or rather it lies with the entire character of the age of its origin that such should not yet be visible, this result is merely because of the fact that the Epos deals with the nation's positive existence rather than that which issues from the personal life of the poet himself, and that it is not present in poetry in such a close personal relation, but rather appears as a self-evolved product essentially independent. In lyrical poetry, on the contrary, the creative activity no less than the content are inseparable from the inner life, and are bound to declare themselves as such in actual fact.

($\gamma\gamma$) In this respect, later forms of lyric art are expressly distinguishable from the folk-song. There are, no doubt, folk-songs which originate contemporaneously with the works of a genuine lyrical *art*. These latter, however, belong to a range and type of individuals such as—far from participating in more modern stages of artistic culture—are, in the entire nature of their general outlook, not yet liberated from the immediate popular sense. We must, however, not regard this distinction between the Lyric of the folk-song and the artistic poem as though it was only when reflection and the artistic consciousness, in union with deliberate executive ability, appear with all the elegance of such a union, that the Lyric attains to its perfection. Such a notion would really amount to this—that a Horace, for instance, and the Roman lyric poets generally, were to be reckoned among the finest writers of this type, or even in their own range that the Master Singers were preferable to the preceding epoch of the genuine Minnesong. Such an extreme deduction from our previous statement is not justified. What we ought to conclude is this, that individual imagination and art directed to the service of this very self-consistent personal life, which in fact constitutes its principle, presupposes also, for the basis of their true perfection, a free and self-trained recognition of imaginative idea no less than artistic activity.

(γ) We have our *final* phase of composition to distinguish from those already discussed. The folk-song appears before the true elaboration of a prosaically organized condition of actual conscious life. Lyric poetry of the truly artistic type, on the other hand, wrests itself away from the prosaic coordination which surrounds it, and creates from the poet's imagination, in its acquired independence, a new poetic world of inward observation and emotion, by means of which, for the first time, the true content and type of expression truly adequate to the human soul, as seen from within, becomes the object of vital art. There is, however, over and above this, a form of intelligence which, from this point of view, stands in a more exalted position than the imagination of the emotional or conceptive life, inasmuch as it is able, with more penetrative universality and more necessary coalescence to bring its content before our free cognition than is ever possible to art. This is *philosophical thought*. Conversely, however, this form is attached to the abstract condition of being exclusively evolved in the medium of thought, posited as wholly ideal universality; and, in consequence, the concrete man may find himself also constrained to express the content and the results of his philosophical consciousness in a concrete way, that is, as permeated by his temperament and sensuous perception, his imagination and feeling, in order thereby to possess and exhaust the absolute expression of all that engages either soul or intellect.

From such a standpoint we may distinguish between two principal types of conceptive activity. It may, in short, either be the imagination which, straining beyond its own domain, struggles with the movement of pure thinking, without successfully attaining the clarity and secured exactness of philosophical exposition. In this case the Lyric is for the most part the ebullition of a soul engaged in strife and contention, which in its fermentation does violence both to art and abstract thought. It transgresses one province without the ability to make itself at home in another. Or we may find that it is rather the tranquil movement of philosophical thought in its essential medium, which may seek to animate its clearly grasped and systematically developed thoughts with emotion, to make them perceptible to sensuous apprehension, and to exchange the explicit scientific process and sequence in its causal necessity for that free play of particular aspects, beneath the apparently loose connection of which art is the more compelled to conceal their ideal bonds of association in proportion as it is disinclined to narrow itself to the jejune style of purely didactic exposition. As an illustration of this latter tendency, we may point to many of Schiller's poems.

2. PARTICULAR ASPECTS OF LYRICAL POETRY

Having thus considered the general character of the content of lyric poetry, and the mode of its expression, as also the varied grades of culture which are more or less consonant with its fundamental principle, it will be our further task to examine these general points of view more nearly in the *detail* of their more important features and relations.

Here, too, I ought at starting once again to emphasize the distinction which obtains between epic and lyrical poetry. In our consideration of the former we directed our attention above all to the primitive national Epos, and merely referred incidentally to the inadequate collateral branches, as also to the poet in his creative capacity. This we are unable to do in the case of the type under discussion. On the contrary, we shall find that subjects of the greatest importance invite our review as respects the individual creative power; and, on the other hand, in respect to the classification of the several types in which lyrical poetry, whose general principle it is to disintegrate and isolate the content and its configurations, is respectively differentiated. We may define the subsequent course of our investigation as follows:

First, our attention will be directed to the lyrical poet himself.

Secondly, we propose to examine the lyrical work of art as the creation of the individual poet's imagination.

282

Thirdly, we shall classify the types which are deducible from the general notion of lyrical composition.

(*a*) *The Lyric Poet*

(*α*) Now the content of the Lyric embraces, as we have seen, first, a type of contemplation, which connects the universal quality of determinate being with its conditions, and, secondly, the manifold character of its detailed aspects. Regarded, however, as pure generalizations and particular points of view of emotional condition these constituents, both of them, are nothing more than abstractions. In order that these may acquire a vital lyrical individuality, a principle of combination is necessary which can only be of an ideal, in other words really personal[7] character. Consequently the creatively concrete person, the *poet* himself, must be further presupposed as the focus and in fact realized content of lyrical poetry. He must be there, however, in a form which is not carried to the point of definitive act and deed, or to that of the evolved movement of dramatic conflicts. His exclusive expression and activity is on the contrary restricted to the fact that he endows his inner experience with an articulate speech such as portrays the spiritual significance of himself as subject in his self-expression, whatever the material selected may be, and endeavours to arouse in and keep the hearer alive to the like meaning and spirit, the same soul-state, the similar course of reflection.

(*β*) But, furthermore, the expression cannot rest alone in this result, however successful, in so far as it is for others a free overflooding of buoyant delight, or the resolution and reconciliation of grief in song and lyric, or the yet profounder impulse, which issues in the most serious emotions of heart and the most far-reaching views of intelligence. The man who sings and can write poetry has a necessary vocation thereto. He composes because he *cannot do otherwise.* At the same time the external incentive, the direct invitation and the like are by no means excluded. The great lyric poet, however, in such a case soon swerves aside from such an external stimulus. His supreme object is himself. To take the example once more to which we have constantly recurred, Pindar was frequently invited to celebrate this or that laurel-crowned victor, nay, he frequently accepted payment therefor; and yet, for all that, it is he himself, the minstrel, who changes places with his hero. He combines freely his own unfettered imagination with his praise of the exploits of ancestors, or it maybe his memory of myths; or, when he gives voice to his profound views of life, of wealth, of mastery, of all that is great and deserving, of the supremacy and loveliness of the Muses, and above all of the high vocation of the singer. It is not so much the hero in the renown that he spreads far and wide, that he honours in his poems. We are invited to listen to him, the poet. The honour is not to him in that he celebrates the victor, but rather to the victor that he is celebrated by Pindar. And it is this emphatic personal sense of greatness which constitutes the nobility of the lyric poet. Homer, as an individual person, is in his Epos so entirely sacrificed that people nowadays are loth to admit that he ever existed at all. His heroes live on for ever. Pindar's heroes are for us little better than empty names. He himself, however, the self-celebrated and self-honoured, remains before us immortal as the poet. The fame which his heroes claim is merely an appanage to that of the lyric singer. Even among the Romans the lyric poet to some extent aspires to such an independent position. Suetonius tells us, for instance, that Augustus wrote these works to Horace; *an vereris, ne apud posteros tibi infame sit, quod videaris familiaris nobis esse.* Horace, however, with the exception of those times, easily demonstrable, where he writes in an *ex officio* manner of Augustus, betrays for the most part a precisely similar proud self-consciousness. His fourteenth ode of the third book, for example, opens with a reference to the return of Augustus from Spain after his victory over the Cantabrians. But the poet goes on to celebrate the fact, that on account of the tranquillity, which the emperor has given the world, he himself as poet is able quietly to enjoy his easy-going leisure and his muse; he calls for garlands, unguents, and venerable wine to celebrate the occasion, and invites in all haste his mistress—in a word, he is simply preoccupied with the arrangements for his own banquet. We hear, however, at this time less of his love difficulties than in his youth, when Plaucus was consul, an occasion where he expressly says to the messenger he despatches:

> *Si per invisum mora janitorem*
> *Fiet, abito.*

We may regard it as an even more honourable trait of Klopstock, that he felt in his day the independent worth of the singer, and by his free expression of this and his regulation of his behaviour consonantly thereto, disengaged the poet from his subservience to a court and any or every patron,[8] as also from a tedious and useless toying with trifles, which is the ruin of a man. However, the fact remains that it was no other than this very Klopstock whom, in the first instance, the bookseller regarded as his poet. It was Klopstock's publisher in Halle who paid him one or two thaler, it appears, for the manuscript of his Messias, adding over and above this, however, an order for a waistcoat and breeches, and introduced him thus set up into society, letting it clearly be seen from the nature of such a get up that he was responsible therefor. In some contrast to this, so at least we are informed at a later date on evidence, however, that is not irreproachable,[9] the Athenians erected a statue to Pindar, because he had celebrated them in one of his poems, and sent him, moreover, twice the amount of the fine[10] the Thebans refused to exempt him from on account of the inordinate praise he had lavished on an alien city. Indeed we have the statement that Apollo himself declared through the mouth of the Pythian prophetess that Pindar was worthy of receiving half of all the gifts which the whole of Hellas, as in custom bound, brought to the Pythian games.

(γ) Throughout the entire compass of lyric poetry the synthetic unity of a single personality asserts its presence in virtue of its poetic soul-movement. The lyric poet is, in fact, moved to express everything that assumes a poetic form either in his emotional or intelligent life in the song. In this type of composition Goethe is pre-eminently noteworthy, who in all the variety of his full life was thus continuously creative. He was unquestionably in this respect a quite exceptional model. It is rarely that we find an artistic personality, who, while retaining as Goethe's did, an interest so active on all sides and is able to live a life, despite all such self-expansion, so entirely self-possessed, so ready to transmute everything it touches into the poetic vision. His life in its public relations, the peculiar nature of his heart, which rather impressed with its reserve than the ease of its approach, the indefatigable effort of his scientific pursuits and enquiry, the general conclusions of his trained and practical experience, his ethical maxims, the impressions, which the varied and conflicting facts of his times made upon him, the inferences he deduced from such, the effervescent joy of life and courage of his youth, the well-organized force and ideal beauty of his manhood, the comprehensive genial wisdom of his old age—all this passed into the magic crucible of his lyrics, where the most delicate play of emotion, no less than the most severe and painful conflicts of spirit, alike find their expression and by this means their deliverance.

(b) The Lyric Work of Art

Secondly, in respect to the lyric poem as a poetic work of art, we are no doubt in general not able to advance much. The fortuitous character of the abundance of its many modes of expression, and the forms of its equally varied and incalculable content make this inevitable. The peculiarly personal nature of this class of work, however much the same is imperatively subject to the general principles of beauty and art, none the less brings with it the necessary result, that the range of the formal and melodious possibilities of its exposition admit of no theoretic definition. For our purpose, therefore, the only question of importance is the nature of the distinction of artistic type that obtains between the lyric and the epic product.

Upon this I will briefly draw attention to the following points of importance:

First, the unity of the lyric composition.

Secondly, the nature of its progressive disclosure.

Thirdly, the external aspect of its verse-measure and general exhibition.

(α) The importance, which the Epos possesses for art lies, as already observed, and pre-eminently so, in the case of the primitive Epopaea, in the consummate elaboration of the perfected artistic form, which as from the repository of the full embrace of the national spirit, places before our vision one and the same composition in all the wealth of a completely evolved content.

(αα) The true lyric work of art will not undertake to present thus before us a synthesized whole of such extension. The principle of personality can no doubt proceed to a comprehension of subject-matter of universal pretensions.

287

To be able truly to enforce itself, however, in its individual independence, it necessarily implies the collateral principle of disintegration and isolation. At the same time a variety of truth, phenomenal or ideal, derived from natural environment, the memory of one's own or another's experience, from mythical and historical events, and the like, is not therefore excluded: but such an extension of view must not be permitted, as with the Epos, on the ground that it belongs to the unified *complexus* of a given sphere of reality, but is rather solely justifiable for the reason that it springs to renewed life in the memory of the poet, and in his impulse and gift of vivid association.

($\beta\beta$) We must consequently regard the intimate personal life as the true integrating principle of the lyric poem. This inward life, taken simply, is in part the wholly formal unity of the self-conscious self; in part also it is split up and dispersed in the most varied particularity, and the most diverse content of ideas, feelings, impressions, and perceptions, whose power of combination is solely due to the fact that it is one and the selfsame personal identity which serves essentially as their vehicle. In order therefore that this selfidentical subject may form the focal centre of the work of art, it must, on the one hand, have reached the point where the mood or situation is *defined* in its *concreteness*, and on the other it must *affiliate* itself with this isolation of its own possessions as with itself to the extent that it feels and pictures itself in the same. It is only by this means that it becomes an essentially defined whole of such a personal character, and exclusively expresses that which is emphasized by reason of such definition, and is yet coalescent with it.

($\gamma\gamma$) Lyrical in the most pertinent sense is in this connection the emotional mood or colour as concentrated in a concrete condition, inasmuch as the sensitive heart is that which is the most vital and personal factor of the subjective lips. Reflection and a contemplation which is mainly absorbed in generalization very readily tend to the didactic, or are likely to assert what is substantive and positive in the content under an epic mode.

(β) With respect to our *second* point, viz., the progressive disclosure of the lyric subject-matter, speaking generally, exact definition is here too out of the question. I shall, therefore, restrict myself to a few searching observations.

(αα) The progressive exposition of the Epos is of a dilatory description, and it expands throughout in the display of an actual world of diversified character. In the Epos the poet projects himself into the *objective* world, which is set before us in the independent form and movement of its own reality. In contrast thereto it is the emotions and reflection which in the lyric composition absorb the given world into themselves, animate the same within this ideal element, and, only after it is itself converted into a constituent of this personal life, give form and expression to it in language. In contrast to the epic principle of extension we have therefore in the Lyric that of *assimilation*,[11] and have above all to seek for our effect by means of the implied ideal depth of expression rather than the diffuseness of descriptive or explanatory detail. None the less, however, between the extremes of an almost speechless conciseness and the idea worked out into absolute lucidity of speech every conceivable sort of nuance and degree of clarity is still possible. To as little extent is it necessary that a ban be placed on all reflection of external objects. On the contrary genuinely concrete lyric compositions disclose the individual in his external conditions; they accept, therefore, as an essential feature of their content, natural and local environment. In fact there are poems entirely limited to such descriptions. In such cases, however, it is not so much the reality in its objective presence and its plastic presentment, as the accord with which such objects affect the soul, the mood excited by them, the feelings of the heart under such positive conditions, which are, in fact, the lyric result. It is in short not this or that object as presented to our eyes, in its several features, which ought mainly to impress our inward vision, but the emotional forces which are made vital in the same, and which have for their aim a similar state of feeling and contemplation in ourselves. Romances and ballads are perhaps the most obvious illustration of this, which, as I have previously maintained, approach the lyrical type in proportion as they exclusively emphasize those characteristics of a given event which are consistent with the state of the inner life, in which the poet writes, and disclose the course of his narrative in such a way, that we receive a distinct and life-like echo back again of this personal temper. For such reasons all out and out reproduction of material objects, even though stamped with considerable emotion, nay, even the diffuse characterization of emotional states, can only be of subordinate effect in lyrical effort, if compared with concise concentration of effect and the vivid and significant expression.

($\beta\beta$) We may add that *episodes* are permissible as well to the lyric poet; but he ought to employ them on other grounds than those which justify their epic use. In the latter case they are implied in the notion of the externally independent collocation of the different aspects contained; and, in respect to the advance of the epic action, they also are significant as points of retardation and hindrance. Their lyrical justification is rather subjective in its character. The living personality in short surveys his private world more rapidly; his memory recurs to the most varied subjects on equally various occasions; he combines material of the most divergent nature; and, without departing from his true and fundamental emotional state, or the object of his thought, gives free play on all sides to his imagination and contemplation. An animating spirit of the same kind pervades the inner poetical life, although for the most part it is impossible to say whether this or that feature in a lyric poem is to be understood as episodical or not. As a general rule, however, digressions, so long as they do not violate the unity, and above all unexpected changes, witty combinations and sudden, or even violent transitions are peculiarly appropriate to the Lyric.

(γγ) On account of this the nature of the forward movement and bond of connection in this domain of poetry may be various, and in some measure marked by excessive contrast. Generally no doubt the Lyric, quite as little as the Epos, adopts the caprices of ordinary conscious life, or the purely scientific consequences, or the speculative process of philosophical thought in its necessary development. It requires indeed a freedom and self-subsistency in its single features. But whereas, in the case of the Epos, this relative isolation is referable to the form of the phenomenal reality, in the type of which its realization is centered, the lyric poet, on the contrary, communicates to the particular emotions and ideas, in which he is himself expressed, the character of a free self-assertion. Each and all, although equally distrained from similar modes of feeling and observation, nevertheless, as viewed separately, absorb his spirit, which remains concentrated upon each severally, until it is diverted to other points of view or other emotional states. The movement of the whole may therefore have little to arrest its tranquil flow, but with equal right we may find it pass without any mediation, and in one bound to material of a totally different character. The poet, instead of following the logical current of his thought, becomes, it would seem, in this sudden flight of ecstatic intoxication mastered by a force, the pathos of which rules and carries him away in spite of himself. The impulse and conflict of such passionate intensity is so characteristic a feature of certain forms of lyric composition, that, for example, Horace in many of his poems is at pains to harmonize with deliberate artistic means such apparently dislocating breaks in the poem's connection. For the rest I must entirely pass over the various intermediate phases of treatment, which fall between the extremes of the most lucid connection and most even flow on the one side, and that of the unrestrained impetuosity of passion and enthusiasm on the other.

(γ) *Finally*, of our above three divisions of the immediate subject, we have left us to discuss the *external form* and actual presentment of the lyric composition. Above all we shall have to deal with *metre* and the *musical accompaniment.*

(αα) It is obvious enough that the hexameter in its even, sustained and none the less life-like forward movement is most exceptionally fitted as the measure of the Epic. The demand of the Lyric is rather for an extreme *variety* of metres with every kind of co-ordination in their form. The material of the lyric poem in short is not the object in the form wherein it unveils itself in Nature, but the movement of the poet's own soul, the regularity or change of which, its perturbation or repose, its peaceful flow or tumultuous wave and leap, must find expression in the time-movement of the word-length, in which such inward life is asserted. The nature of the prevailing mood and the mode of imaginative conception throughout ought to meet with an echo in the verse-measure itself. The lyric effusion indeed is placed in a far more intimate relation to time, regarded as the external medium of its communication, than the epic narrative, which consigns its phenomenal facts to the past, and associates or interweaves them under a mode of extension more analogous to that of spatial condition. The

Lyric, in contrast to this, displays the momentary emergence of emotion and idea in the temporal juxta-position of their origin and elaboration. It has therefore to clothe in artistic form the varied temporal movement itself. To this distinctive character belongs, in the *first* place, the more diverse sequence of long and short syllables in a more strongly emphasized inequality of rhythmical feet; and, *secondly*, the more varied use of the caesura verse—and *thirdly* the rounding off of the strophes, which not only admit of abundant alternation in respect to the comparative length of particular lines, but also relatively to the rhythmic configuration of these on their own account and in their immediate sequence to each other.

(*ββ*) Yet more lyrical in its effect—a second feature this—is the musical sound of words and syllables simply. The most important examples of this are alliteration, rhyme and assonance. In the system of versification under discussion what is predominant, as I have already explained in a previous passage, is, on the one hand, the ideal significance of syllables, the accent of the meaning, which disjoins itself from the purely natural element, as taken by itself, of their assured quantity, and then defines under the direction of the mind their duration, emphasis and subordination; which, from a further point of view, asserts itself in isolation as the expressly concentrated sound of definite letters, syllables, and words. The Lyric is pre-eminently associated with this spiritualizing process effected by ideal significance, no less than this emphatic insistence of sound. It in fact not merely restricts its acceptance and expression of all that positively is or appears to the meaning which such possesses for the inward life, but also lays hold of sound and musical tone as the significant medium of its communication. No doubt in this sphere, too, the element of rhythm may associate with rhyme; but even here this is effected in a manner which is closely related to the time-beat of music. Strictly speaking, therefore, the poetic use of assonance, alliteration and rhyme is limited to the province of the Lyric. For although the Epos of the Middle Ages is, in accordance with the nature of more modern languages, unable to keep itself aloof from these forms, this is mainly permitted for the reason that here, too, the lyrical element is throughout more insistently active within the domain of epic poetry itself, and effects a more forceful entrance where the subject-matter consists of heroic songs, romances, ballads, tales, and the like. And we find the same thing in dramatic poetry. What, however, is the peculiar possession of the Lyric, is the diversified configuration of rhyme, which is elaborated and perfected by means of the recurrence of similar or the alternation of different letters, syllables and verbal quantity in variously organized and alternated strophes of rhyme. Such differentiation is also of undoubted service both to epic and dramatic poetry, but only on the same ground that rhyme itself is not excluded altogether. The Spaniards, for instance, in the most cultured epoch of their dramatic development, gave the freest play to such craft in the expression of passion by no means appropriate to the genuine drama, interweaving octave rhymes, sonnets and the like with more usual verse-measures. By so doing they at least testify, in the continuity of such assonances and rhymes, their predilection for the musical element in language.

(γγ) *Finally*, lyric poetry, to a far more considerable extent than is possible with the unassisted aid of rhyme, avails itself of *music*, by means of which the uttered word becomes veritable melody and song. Such a leaning may, moreover, be completely justified. Or, in other words, the less lyric subject-matter and content possess on their own account independence and objective stability, but are rather, above all, of an ideal character, rooted exclusively in the personal life, while at the same time an external medium of articulate arrest is essential, to that extent is the demand for a decisive medium of communication more insistent. Precisely for the reason that it remains of ideal intention, the means it employs as a stimulus to others must be the more effective. Such an excitant of our emotional life can only be music.

We find consequently, even in respect to external execution, that lyric poetry is almost invariably associated with musical accompaniment. At the same time we should note an essential gradation in this power of combination. The romantic and above all the modern lyric, no doubt more exceptionally so in such songs, in which the temper, the emotional mood is predominant, and the function of music is to emphasize and expand this inner beat of soul-life in actual melody—are no doubt most readily adapted to such melodic fusion. The folk-song is an obvious example which both delights in and demands a musical accompaniment. We shall find in modern times more rarely a composer for the canzonet, elegy, epistle, or even the sonnet. The reason of this is that in cases where idea, reflection, nay, even emotion are made completely explicit in the poetry, and increasingly liberated from the bare point of spiritual selfconcentration, and, further, from the sensuous medium of the art, the Lyric already secures, in its deliverance as speech, a greater self-stability, and lends itself less simply to a free association with the vague definition of music. On the other hand in proportion as the inner life expressed is not made explicit to that extent the aid of melody is required. How it came about, however, that the ancients, despite the pellucid clarity of their diction, availed themselves of music in its actual delivery, and the measure in which they did thus make use of it, I shall have occasion to deal with subsequently.

(c) *Types of the Genuine Lyric*

With regard to specific types, in which we may classify lyrical composition, I have already referred with more detail to some which form the transition step from the narrative form of the Epos to the more subjective mode of exposition. From a contrary point of view it might seem desirable in the same way to demonstrate the beginnings of the dramatic. This inclination, however, of passage to the animation of the drama is exclusively and in essentials restricted to the circumstance that the lyric poem too as conversation, without, however, carrying the movement of action to the point of actual conflict, may itself accept the external form of dialogue. We shall nevertheless omit further allusion to these intermediate and hybrid stages, and restrict our cursory examination to those forms in which the real principle of the Lyric fully asserts itself. The main cause of this distinction is to be found in the attitude, which the artistic consciousness assumes relatively to its object.

(*a*) To be more definite the poet—this at least is one direction—annuls the particularity of his emotion and idea, and is absorbed in the general contemplation of God or gods, whose greatness and might permeates the whole of the personal life, and causes the poet as an individual person to vanish. Hymns, dithyrambs, paeans, psalms, all belong to this class, which are moreover quite differently treated by different peoples. I propose merely to draw general attention to the following characteristic of such poetry.

(*αα*) The poet, who is raised above the narrow limitation of his own purely personal life and external conditions, or the ideas which are therewith associated, replacing these with that which appears to him and his people as absolute and divine, may, in the *first* instance, completely depict the divine in an objective presentment, and set forth this, as thus projected and executed for the spiritual vision of others, to the honour and power of the glorified god. The hymns which are ascribed to Homer are of this character. They contain above all mythological situations and histories of the divine Being, in whose celebration they are composed, which are not merely conceived in the ideas of symbolism, but are clothed in the downright objectivity of the Epos.

($\beta\beta$) In contrast to this, *secondly*, the dithyrambic impulse, in its more *personal* aspect of an exalted divine service—overwhelmed, as it is, by the power of its object, shattered and stunned to its soul-foundations—cannot, by reason of the general diffusion of its emotional state, go so far as to present an objective image and form. It is more akin to the lyrical absorbtion. We have here simply ecstatic rapture of soul. The singer breaks out and forth from himself; he is so exalted directly into the Absolute, steeped in the being and might of whom he exultantly sings his praise of the Infinite, into the depth whereof he plunges, or that of the natural world, in whose splendour the profound wealth of the Godhead is declared.

The Greeks, in the solemnities of their worship, have not limited themselves for long to such mere outcries and appeals. They have sought to intermingle with such ecstasies the narrative of, definite mythical situations and actions. Such expositions interposed between the effusion of lyric poetry, became gradually of most importance, and created the drama, such narratives being asserted as action in its lifelike form, and independently on its own account, a drama, which again in its turn received as a constituent feature the lyrics of its choruses.

Even more searching in its utterance is this impulse of exultation, this adoration, jubel and outcry of soul to the One; wherein the individual discovers the end of conscious life and the true object of all might and truth, no less than glory and praise, as we meet it in many of the sublime psalms of the Old Testament. Take the words of the thirty-third psalm, for example:

"Rejoice in the Lord, O ye righteous, for praise is comely for the upright.

"Praise the Lord with harp: sing unto him with psaltery and an instrument of ten strings.

"Sing unto him a new song; play skilfully with a loud noise.

"For the word of the Lord is right; and all his works are done in truth.

"He loveth righteousness and judgment: the earth is full of the goodness of the Lord.

"By the word of the Lord were the heavens made; and all the host of them by the breath of his mouth."[12]

Or take the twenty-ninth psalm: "Give unto the Lord, O ye mighty, give unto the Lord glory and strength.

"Give unto the Lord the honour due unto his name: worship the Lord in the beauty of holiness.

"The voice of the Lord is upon the waters: the God of glory thundereth: the Lord is upon great waters.

"The voice of the Lord is powerful, the voice of the Lord is full of majesty.

"The voice of the Lord breaketh the cedars; yea, the Lord breaketh the cedars of Lebanon.

"He maketh them to skip like a calf; Lebanon and Sirion like a young unicorn.

"The voice of the Lord divideth the flames of fire.

"The voice of the Lord shaketh the wilderness; the Lord shaketh the wilderness of Kadesh," etc.

An exaltation and lyric sublimity such as the above contain a power of personal detachment,[13] and is consequently less adapted to self-absorbtion in the concrete content, wherein the imagination can lay hold of the fact in tranquil satisfaction. It is rather inclined to soar up in an indefinite enthusiasm, which strains to make present to feeling and perception what is unutterable for the intelligence. In this atmosphere of indeterminacy the individual soul is unable to envisage its unreachable object in quiescent beauty, or enjoy its self-expression in a work of art. Instead of a tranquil picture the imagination sets forth external phenomena without co-ordination and in fragments; and, inasmuch as it does not succeed with emotional effort in any consistent articulation of its separate ideas, in its positive artistic form, too, it employs a somewhat arbitrary and insurgent rhythm.

The *prophets*, who oppose the mass of the community, partly in the fundamental tones of grief and lamentation over the condition of their people, partly, too, in this feeling of alienation and decadence, carry to yet a further extreme this type of paranetic lyric in the sublime flame of their emotion and political indignation.

In a more modern age of imitation this sublime passion, however, is exchanged for a more artificial warmth, which easily cools and becomes abstract. Thus, for example, we have much hymn and psalm-writing of Klopstock, which possesses neither depth of thought, nor the tranquil development of any religious content whatever. What is expressed is, above all, an effort of this exaltation to the Infinite, which, agreeably with modern scientific ideas, merely discloses the empty incommeasurability and inconceivable might, greatness, and splendour of God, in its contrast to the very intelligible impotence and finitude of the poet.

299

(β) From a second point of view, we have those types of lyric poetry which may be described generally as odes, in the more modern meaning of the term. In these, as distinguished from the type above described, it is the *personal life* of the poet, in its independence, which asserts itself as a fundamental feature. It is, indeed, the culmination, which may be enforced in a twofold manner.

($\alpha\alpha$) From one point of view the poet may, within this new mode of expression, select, as he previously did, a subjective matter itself of essential importance, such as the glory and celebration of gods, heroes, princes, love, beauty, art, friendship, and the like, while he displays his inner life as so completely steeped and carried away by this content and its concreteness, that it appears as though, in this impulse of enthusiasm, the subject has wholly mastered his soul, and is present in it now, as the one predominant power. If this was entirely so the facts which master him might secure, in their independence, the plastic form, motion, and stability of an epic sculpturesque image.

Or, as a converse case, it is just the personal life of the poet himself and its greatness which he seeks to express and make real on its own account. As for the object itself, it is that whereof he makes himself master; he assimilates this in his own life, expresses himself in and through this. By so doing he freely and without reserve breaks up the more positive course of his subject with his own emotion or reflection; he illuminates it from within; he changes it; and the final result is that it is not so much the subject, but rather the *personal enthusiasm* in which it has steeped him, which is most effective. In this connection, however, we have two distinct aspects to consider. First, there is the compelling force of the subject-matter; secondly, we have that independent freedom of the poet which flashes into view in its conflict with that which would otherwise master it. It is above all the stress of this opposition, which renders inevitable the swing and the boldness of utterance and image, the apparent absence of order in the ideal construction and course of the poem, its digressions, *lacunae*, and sudden transitions, and which preserves the ideal elevation of the poet, by means of the mastery with which he is enabled, through the artistic perfection of his work, to overcome this disunion, and to produce an' essentially harmonious whole, which places him, as *his* work, in relief above the greatness of his subject.

It is to such a type of lyric enthusiasm that many of the Pindaric odes are referable, whose triumphant, albeit personal glory is disclosed in a mode of rhythm equally conspicuous for its varied movement, and yet for all that stringently regulated measure. Horace, on the contrary, more especially where he aims most at self-assertion, is rather lacking in warmth and insipid. We detect here an imitative artificiality, which vainly endeavours to conceal the purely technical preciosity of his composition. The enthusiasm of Klopstock in the same way is never entirely genuine. It too frequently gives the impression of laboured artifice, despite the fact that many of his odes are rich in true and genuine emotion, and stamped with an engaging masculine worth and force of expression.

(ββ) From another point of view, however, it is not at all necessary that the content itself should be substantial or important. The poet is himself, in his own personality, of such weight that he can attach to even the more trifling objects worth, nobility, or at least in a general way a more exalted interest owing to the fact that they are embodied in his poetic work. Many of the Odes of Horace are of this type. Klopstock, too, with many another, may be included in such a category. In such cases it is not the importance of the material itself, which engages the poet's effort, but on the contrary that of the process in virtue of which he exalts what is on its own account insignificant, either in external facts or petty occurrences, to the height of the emotion and idea they excite in himself.

(γ) In conclusion, the entire infinite multiplicity of lyrical mood and reflection reaches its fullest compass in the sphere of the *song*, in which consequently differences of national custom and creative individuality have their freest play. Characteristics of every extreme of diversity meet together here, and the task of adequate classification is beset with difficulty. We will restrict ourselves to pointing out a few of the most general character.

($\alpha\alpha$) We have, then, *first*, the *genuine song* intended for singing or purely musical practice,[14] whether in private or before others. Much intelligible content, ideal greatness and loftiness is not necessary. On the contrary, worth, nobility, weight of thought can only prove an obstacle to the desire of direct self-expression. Imposing ideas or reflections, or sublime emotions compel the artist to detach himself from his immediate personality and its interests. And yet it is precisely this immediacy of joy and sorrow, what we may call the unrestricted and momentary personal experience, which ought to find its expression in the song. And it is on this account that every folk is in a peculiar way at home and at ease in its songs. Despite the unlimited variety of content and of melodic exposition that offers itself here, every song is without exception distinct from types previously considered by virtue of the simplicity of its subject-matter, movement, metre, verbal expression, and images. The point of departure is direct from the soul; the movement of inspiration is not so much from one object to another, but is, generally speaking, centered exclusively in one and the same content, whether it be a single emotional state, or any definite expression of delight or sorrow, that mood, in short, the effect of which carries the heart with it. In this emotion or temper the song persists with no interruption in its flight and impression, quietly and simply abiding therein without any strikingly bold contrast or transitions of idea; and it creates thereby in the even flow of its images this one perfected whole, sometimes without any interruption or disunion, at others in a more expansive and consequential survey, employing therewith rhythms adapted to song or the recurrence of rhymes easily intelligible and without any considerable complexity. Inasmuch, however, as it possesses for the most part as its content what is essentially transitory we are not to suppose that a nation is likely to sing the same songs over and over again, for a hundred or a thousand years. A people which can at all claim progressive development is neither so poor nor so so barren as only to possess poets of the song at one period of its life. It is just the poetry of the song, which, in contrast to the Epopaea, does not so much die as it is forever being awakened anew. This field of blossom starts up afresh every spring; and it is only in the case of oppressed peoples, peoples precluded from every advance, which are unable to experience the ever requickened delight in poetic composition, that the old and the oldest songs are retained. The particular song, just like the particular mood, arises, and then passes; it animates, delights, and is forgotten. Whoever knows or sings, for example, the songs which fifty years ago were everywhere known and beloved? Every century strikes its own particular keynote; the previous one sounds out of tune, until it stops altogether. None the less, however, must every song possess not so much a revelation of the personality of the singer as a certain community of sentiment, which meets with response from all sides; which excites in others a like emotion and so, too, passes from mouth to mouth. Songs which are not generally current as such in their time are seldom of the genuine stamp. As an essential distinction in

303

the composition of song I will merely emphasize two main aspects which I have already referred to. On the one hand the poet may express his inner life in its emotions quite openly and without reserve, more especially the feelings and state of joyfulness, and so that he communicates completely all that he experiences. On the other hand, and in extreme contrast to this, he may only suffer us to surmise through his very speechlessness, what is brought to a focus in the unopened chamber of his heart. The first type belongs mainly to the East, and more especially to the careless hilarity and contented expansiveness of Mohammedan poetry, the splendid outlook of which loves to dilate itself hither and thither in all the breadth of sensuous perception and witty conceit. The second type, on the contrary, applies with more force to our Northern self-concentration and intimacy of soul-life, which in its compressed tranquillity is often only able to seize hold of objects which are wholly external and to put suggestions in *them*, while the essentially suppressed spirit is unable to express itself or find a bent, but rather, like the child with whom that father in the Erl King rides through the night and the wind, dies away with its glow on the wick. The distinction above noticed applies also in a broader sense to other forms of lyrical composition such as the folk-song and more elaborate poetry; it recurs again in the simple song with many shades and intermediate links in its variety. With regard to particular forms applicable to this class of composition I will restrict myself to the following examples.

We may mention, to start with, the *folk-song*, which, on account of its direct appeal, is mainly of the nature of the simple song, being also generally adapted to singing, or, rather, requiring the musical accompaniment. Its subject-matter is in part national exploit and event, in which the nation is emotionally made aware of and recalls again its most essential life; in part, too, feelings and situations are directly expressed which relate to particular classes. It associates, in short, civic life with its natural condition and its closest human relations, and it does so with every variety of note, whether of exultation or sorrow, which may duly harmonize with such. In contrast to the above, we have, secondly, songs of a more various and enriched culture, a culture which finds its entertainment in the companionable amusement of all kinds of pleasantry, graceful turns of phrase, casual occurrences, or polite modes of address, or, with more intensity of feeling, recurs to the pathos or necessities of less favoured conditions of life, describing therein both the facts and the consequent feelings they excite, the poet always making his appeal from his own breast and the facts of his own sympathetic experience. If such songs go no further than the bare narrative, more particularly of natural phenomena, the result is likely to be trivial and to betray the lack of imaginative resources. The bare description of emotional states, moreover, not unfrequently fares little better. The truth is that our poet in such descriptions, whether of objective facts or emotions, must not restrict his survey to the narrow outlook of direct wishes and desires, but must already in the freedom of his intelligence have raised himself into a more serene atmosphere wherein the main thing of importance to himself is the satisfaction which the exercise of his imagination has afforded. An undisturbed sense of freedom such as this, through expansion of heart and delight in conceptive idea on its own account, confers on many songs of Anacreon, as also certain poems of Hafis and the Westöstliche Divan of Goethe the rarest charm of an unfettered creative gift.

There is a yet further type of composition of this general class, to which we must concede a more exalted or, at least, a more widely embracing content. The large majority of Protestant hymns composed for spiritual edification are essentially songs. They express the yearning after God, the plea for His grace, repentance, hope, trust, doubts, faith, and the like of the religious heart; no doubt, in the first instance, to meet the importunity of the individual soul, but at the same time in a manner of general significance, wherein such feelings and states of soul may or ought to apply, to a greater or less extent, to every member of the Christian Church.

($\beta\beta$) We may further return to another division of this class, the *sonnet, sestine, elegy, epistle,* and a few other such modes. These latter assert themselves as distinct from the ordinary sphere of song previously discussed. The immediacy of feeling and expression is emphasized in this class as a mediating bond with reflection, and a contemplation which, while remaining alert to many features of its subject, conceives the particular detail of perception and soul-experience under more general points of view. Science, learning, and, in short, a wide culture may be here effective; and if also in all the relations thus established the personal life, which connects and mediates in itself the particular fact with the general concept, is and remains the insistent and predominant factor, yet the standpoint presupposed is of a wider and more universal import than that of the ordinary song. The Italians in particular have given us splendid examples of a highly sensitive type of feeling and reflection in their sonnets and sestines. Such not only directly expresses in a given situation states of yearning, grief, longing, and the like, or the counterfeit of external objects, with a peculiarly intimate concentration, but includes many a diversion, many a shrewd glance into mythology and history, whether past or present, while remaining throughout able to return upon itself, true to the fundamental demand of selfrestriction and concentration. The simplicity of the song is incompatible with a culture of this kind. The exalted character of the ode is equally disallowed. As a primary consequence of this the possibility of actual musical delivery vanishes; but, on the other hand, as some set-off to the absence of musical accompaniment, the verbal expression itself, in its sound and composed rhymes, becomes a melodic flow of speech. The Elegy, moreover, may, in the measure of its syllables, its meditation, its comments, and the descriptive display of emotional life, assume the form of the Epic.

($\gamma\gamma$) The *third* type of composition in this class is characterized by a mode of treatment which in recent times is most clearly represented among us Germans in the work of Schiller. The majority of his lyrical poems, such as those named by him Resignation, the Ideals, the realm of Shades, Artists, the Ideal and Life, are just as little songs in the true sense as they are odes or hymns, epistles, or elegies in the classic sense. Their position, on the contrary, is distinct from all these types. Their significance consists above all in the imposing fundamental thought of their content by the force of which, however, the poet neither appears to be carried away as a dithyrambic poet might be, nor in the press of his enthusiasm is there any appearance of conflict with the greatness of his subject. He remains rather throughout completely master of the same, and unfolds all that is therein implied from every point of view with his own poetic reflection. And he does this in the full impulse of genuine feeling, no less than with the comprehensive breadth of his intelligence, expressed with a compelling force in the most admirable and full-toned utterance and image, and yet, withal, for the most part in quite simple, if really arresting rhythms and rhymes. These great thoughts and fundamental interests, to which his entire life was dedicate, appear consequently as the most intimate possession of his spirit. But he does not sing so much as one tranquilly self-absorbed,[15] or to a circle of companions, as the rich-songed mouth of Goethe was wont to do, but as a singer who delivers himself of what is on its own account intrinsically of worth in a storehouse of all that is most excellent and distinguished. His songs ring out, in fact, much as he says of his bell:

> Hoch über'm niedern Erdenleben
> Soll sie im blauen Himmelszelt,
> Die Nachbarin des Donners, schweben
> Und grenzen an die Sternen weit,
> Soll eine Stimme seyn von oben,
> Wie der Gestirne helle Schaar,
> Die ihren Schöpfer wandelnd toben
> Und führen das bekränzte Jahr.
> Nur ewigen und ernsten Dingen
> Sei ihr metall'ner Mund geweiht,
> Und stündlich mit den schnellen Schwingen
> Berühr' im Fluge sie die Zeit.[16]

3. HISTORICAL EVOLUTION OF THE LYRIC.

It will already have sufficiently appeared from what I have pointed out in relation to the general character, as also the more detailed features discussed with reference to the poet, the lyrical composition and the several types of the art that to a singular degree in this province of poetry a concrete treatment is only possible which accepts the historical narrative as a constituent feature. The universal, which can be set forth in its independence, does not merely remain restricted in its compass, but is also abstract in its valid worth. And this is so because in no other art to the like extent does the particularity of the time, condition, and nationality, no less than the specific idiosyncracy of individual genius, supply the determining factor of the content and form of the artistic product. But in proportion as the strength of the demand forces itself on our attention that such an historical exposition should be avoided, I feel myself obliged, in the interests of the very variety of material comprised in the embrace of lyric composition, to limit myself exclusively to a very partial survey of all that I am acquainted of in this particular class of work, and in which my lively interest could have been extended.

As the basis of our general classification of the varied national and more personal lyric compositions, as in the case of epic poetry, we cannot do better than follow the order of those radical types under which artistic creation generally is unfolded, and which we now know as symbolic, classic, and romantic art. As the main division, therefore, of our present subject-matter, we may, in other words, adopt a similar sequence from Oriental compositions to the Lyric of the Greeks and Romans, and then from this to the Slavonic, Romance, and German peoples.

(a) Taking, then, the Oriental lyric first, we may observe that it differs essentially from the lyrical composition of the West through its inability to attach to it the independent personality and free spirit of the poet, or that unity which characterizes every content of romantic art, its essential infinity, reflecting, in fact, the potential depth of the romantic soul. Such a distinction is only in keeping with the universal principle of the East. The individual conscious life is here, referably to its content, directly absorbed in the detail of external fact, expressing itself under the condition and specific relations of this inseparable unity. And, from a further point of view, it asserts itself, without being able to secure a firm ground of stability in itself, as opposed to what it conceives to be of potency and substance in Nature and the conditions of human existence, which it wrestles to reach whether through emotion or imagination, at one time situated towards it rather in the relation of pure opposition, at another with more freedom, but in either case with ultimate failure. What we find here, therefore, if we confine our attention to *form*, is not so much the poetic expression of independent ideas over objects or their connections, as it is the bare mirror of this unreflecting absorption,[17] wherein the individual consciousness does not disclose itself in its own self-concentration as free personality,[18] but rather in its self-annulment[19] before the external object or condition. Thus regarded, the Oriental lyric frequently, particularly in its contrast to the romantic, assumes a more objective tone. Here we shall often enough find that the poet does not so much express facts and conditions as they affect him, but rather as they are in themselves, a disclosure which frequently bestows on them an independent soul of vitality of their own. For illustration we may take that exclamation of Hafis:

"Come, O come! The nightingale passeth from the soul of Hafis once again over the scent of the roses of delight."

Regarded in another light, the tendency of this lyrical poetry, by freeing the poet from the limitations of his private individuality, is to replace this with a kind of primitive expansion of soul, which, however, very easily loses itself in mere boundlessness, or is merged in a deliberate effort to express that which it accepts as object but cannot fully penetrate, because this content is itself the formless substance. For this reason, speaking generally, the lyric of the East, more especially among the Hebrews, Arabs, and Persians, possesses the character of hymns of exaltation. With spendthrift prodigality all greatness, might, and glory are lavished upon the creature, in order to make all such transitory splendour vanish before the unspeakable majesty of God; or, at least, it never is tired of stringing together in

310

some precious chain everything that is lovable or fair, in order to present the same as a thankoffering to the object, be it Sultan, the beloved, or the wine-shop, which the poet has set himself above all things to celebrate.

In conclusion, if we look more closely at form of expression in this type of poetry, we shall find that it is mainly the *metaphor*, the *image*, and the *simile* which are favoured. For, in the first place, on account of the fact that he is not himself wholly free to express his own personal life, the poet can only disclose himself in something else, something external to himself, with the aid of life that can compare with himself. And also we may observe that what is here universal and substantive remains abstract; that is to say, it is unable to merge itself in the definite form of a free individuality, so that now, even on its own account, it is only in comparisons with the varied phenomena of the world that it is able to envisage itself; and we may add that both these cases, in the last instance, only possess the worth of being able to assist some comparable approach to that One which alone possesses significance, and is worthy of honour and praise. These metaphors, images, and similes, however, in which the individual soul, as it asserts itself, is exclusively identified almost to the point of visibility, are not the actual feeling and spiritual state itself, but rather a mode of expression which is wholly personal and of the poet's composition. What, therefore, the lyrical artist here loses in the concreteness of his spiritual freedom, this we find is replaced by the freedom of his expression, which moves forward through all the most manifold phases; that is, from the naïve simplicity of its images and similes to every conceivable audacity and the acutest ingenuity of novel and surprising combinations. As regards particular nations in which we find this Oriental type of lyric represented, we may mention, first, the Chinese; secondly, the Hindoos;

thirdly, and to a pre-eminent degree, the Hebrews, Arabs, and Persians. I cannot, however, enter into any closer description of these.

(*b*) In the case of the second principal division of our present poetic type, that is in the Lyric of the Greeks and Romans, it is the principle of *classic* individuality which, above all, distinguishes its character. In accordance with this principle, the artistic consciousness, which seeks for lyrical expression, neither loses itself in the facts of the natural world, nor exalts itself over itself to the height of that Sublime outcry to all creation: "Let all that hath breath praise the Lord!" Nor is it absorbed, after divesting itself joyfully from all the bonds of finite existence, in that One Being in which all live and move. Rather the poet here is freely merged in the Universal, regarded as the very substance of his own spirit; and in this personal union within himself attains his self-conscious poetic activity.

And just as the Lyric of the Greeks and Romans is distinct from that of the *Orientals*, so too, from another point of view, it differs from the *romantic*. In other words, instead of unveiling its depths in the intimacy of particular moods and states of feeling, it rather elaborates, to the point of the most explicit definition, this inward life of its individual passion and meditation. And by doing so it even retains, even as the expression of this inward spirit, so far as this is permitted to the Lyric, the plastic type of classic art. All that it communicates, in short, of the views and maxims of life and wisdom, despite all the penetration of its general principle, nevertheless does not dispense with the free individuality of independent thought and conception. It expresses itself less in the wealth of image and metaphor, than directly and categorically. At the same time, also, the personal feeling, at one time in more general relations, at another in the form of vision itself, is on its own account objective. In the same mode of individuality the particular types may be classified as distinct from each other in conception, expression, phraseology, and verse-measure, until they reach the culminating point of their independent elaboration. And as we have found it true of the soul itself and its ideas, so, too, the external presentment is of more plastic type. In other words, from a musical point or view, it emphasizes less the ideal soul-melody of emotion than the sensuous verbal quantity in the rhythmical measure of its movement, to which it may further attach the complex mazes of the dance.

(α) With the richest originality this artistic form of Greek lyric poetry is perfected. In the first instance we may trace it in those *hymns* possessing a content as yet more akin to the epic mode, which do not so much express in their epic metre a personal enthusiasm as they set before us a plastic image of gods in deliberately objective outlines. The next step, so far as metre is concerned, we mark in the *elegiac* syllabic measure, which associates the pentameter with the hexameter, which, in the regular recurrence of its ending after the hexameter, and with its two equally divided sections, opens the way to the complete singularity of the verse strophe. The elegy is also throughout in its tone of the lyric type. This is so in the case of the political elegy no less than the erotic, although, particularly as gnomic elegy, it still closely approaches the epic insistence upon and expression of the substantive as such, and for this reason almost exclusively belongs to the Ionians, with whom the objective point of view was generally predominant. In respect also to its musical side, it is primarily the aspect of rhythm which is here successfully worked out. And, on parallel lines with it, we may observe, thirdly, the development of the *Iambic* poem in a novel verse-measure. This, however, is, by reason of the keenness of its invectives, from the first of a more subjective or personal tendency. The

313

genuine mode of lyrical reflection and passion, however, receives for the first time its full development in the so-called *Melisian*[20] lyric. The metres are more varied, more capable of change; the strophes are more rich; the suggestions of musical accompaniment are more complete in virtue of the nature of the accepted modulation. Each poet creates a syllabic measure which corresponds with his or her lyrical nature. Thus Sappho adapts one to a type of composition which is sensuous, inspired with the glow of passion and expressed with an effect which works up to a supreme crisis. Alcaeus moulds one in harmony with his masculine and bolder odes. To an exceptional degree, too, the Scoliasts supply many indications of the finer nuances of diction and metre by reason of the variety of their content and melodic utterance.

Last of all, the lyric of the *chorus* is richest of all in the wealth of what it unfolds, and not merely so in what concerns idea and thought, boldness of transition and connection or the like, but also relatively to its external presentment. The choral song may be interchanged for the single voice, and the ideal movement is not merely satisfied with the bare rhythm of speech and the modulations of music, but summons as its associate the plastic pose and movement of the dance. The ideal aspect of the Lyric is consequently balanced to perfection with the sensuous character of its delivery. The subject-matter of this type of inspired verse is the most substantive and weighty. Such poems celebrate the power and glory of the gods, or that of victors in the games. Greeks, who not unfrequently were divided in their political relations, found in them the positive vision of their national unity. And, partly for this reason, aspects of their ideal construction are not wanting which approach the objective standpoint of the Epic. Pindar, for example, who reaches the highest point of attainment in this type of composition, moves with ease, as I have already pointed out, from the external motives of his compositions to profound observations upon the general nature of ethical principle and divine matters, or it may be upon heroes, heroic exploit, the foundations of States, and the like. His creative gift possesses, in short, the plastic sense of realization quite as much as the individual sweep of imaginative energy. On this very account, however, it is not so much the facts which follow their independent course in the epic manner, as the personal enthusiasm, carried away by its object so completely that the latter appears to be the burden and product of the soul.

Later lyric verse of the Alexandrines is less an independent development and more a mere scholastic imitation and affectation of elegance and correctness of expression, until finally it dissipates itself in trifling graces and pleasantries, or seeks to bind up afresh flowers of art and life already to hand in a garland of tender feeling and conceit, and the witty experiment of eulogy or satire.

(β) Among the Romans lyric poetry finds a soil no doubt fashioned for it in various ways, but of less original productive qualities. The period of its splendour is limited mainly to the age of Augustus, in which it is cultivated as the elaborate expression and relaxation of cultured society; or indeed, to a considerable degree, it is rather an affair of the clever translator or copyist, and the fruit of taste and research, than that of spontaneous feeling and really original conception. At the same time it must be admitted that, despite the learning and an alien mythology, to say nothing of the preferred imitation of Alexandrine models, where the warmth of life is least apparent, yet as a rule the characteristics of Roman personality no less than the individual genius of particular poets, do assert an independent position, and, so long as we put entirely on

315

one side the most intimate soul and expression of the art of poetry, have accomplished sterling and consummate results, not merely in the province of the ode, but also in that of epistles, satires, and elegy. On the other hand, the later type of satire, which follows as a kind of supplement, in its bitterness toward the decadence of the times, its goaded indignation and virtuous declamation, fails to represent the genuine sphere of an unperturbed poetical vision just in the degree that it possesses nothing whatever to oppose to its picture of a demoralized present save this very indignation and abstract rhetoric of virtuous excitement.

(c) For this reason, consequently, it is only after more modern nationalities have appeared that a really original content and spirit are communicated to lyrical composition, as we have previously seen, was the case, too, with the Epic. This is due to the German, Romance, and Slavonic peoples, which already, in their previous pagan days, but principally after their conversion to Christianity, both in the Middle Ages and in more recent times, have brought into being, and continuously elaborated in various ways, a *third* fundamental revival of lyrical creation in what we may generally characterize as the *romantic* art-type.

In this third branch of its activity, lyric poetry is of so overwhelming an importance that its principle is enforced, more —especially in the first instance, relatively to the Epos, but consequently in its more modern development and relatively to the drama, with a far profounder significance than was possible with either Greek or Roman. Indeed, among certain nations, even genuine epic materials are treated exclusively under the type of the lyric narrative; in this way we have compositions as to which we may find real difficulty in deciding the class to which they more truly belong. The cause of this conspicuous tendency towards lyric composition is mainly due to the fact that the entire evolution of the life of these nations is based on this very principle of subjectivity, which is constrained to assert and clothe what is substantive and objective as its own from its own resources, and grows more and more self-conscious of this penetration into its own personal wealth. Such a principle declares its vigour in its least perturbed and most complete character among the German peoples. The Slavonic races have, on the contrary, first to wrestle forth from the Oriental absorption in the substantive One and Universal. Between the two we may place the Romance stock, which are confronted, in the conquered provinces of the Roman Empire, not merely with the residue of Roman science and culture, but a social system more elaborate from every point of view. In the process of self-fusion with such conditions, they inevitably lose a part of their original character. As for the subject-matter of this poetry, we may describe it as dealing with pretty nearly every phase of national or individual development, capable of expressing either the religious or secular life of these nations as it expands in ever widening range, and through the process of the centuries reflects in varied condition and emotional state the heart of its spiritual substance. And the fundamental type of it is either the expression of an emotional state, concentrated to the most intimate self-possession, whether the immediate object of attraction be national and other events, Nature and external environment, or simply and solely itself, or whether it be of the nature of reflection, both searching and self-introspective, upon all that is implied for itself in such an extension of culture. Regarded on its formal side, the plastic character of rhythmical versification is exchanged for the music of alliteration, assonance, and manifold alternations of rhyme. These novel elements it makes use of sometimes in a quite simple and unassuming manner; in other connections with much art and invention of modes of versification wholly distinct in character. At the same time the external delivery becomes increasingly more elaborate in its powers of adaptation to the accompaniment of vocal and instrumental music.

In our classification of the extensive compass of this group, we cannot do better than follow that we accepted in the case of epic poetry.

Firsts we have the lyric composition of these modern nations while still in the state of primitive paganism.

Secondly, there is the richer development of this type in the Christian Middle Ages.

Thirdly, there is that lyric art based in some measure on the reawakened study of ancient art, and in part on the fundamental principle of modern Protestantism, a principle essential to its final elaboration.

In the present work, however, I shall be unable to discuss with more detail the characteristics of the above development. I will, by way of conclusion, merely draw attention to one German poet, whose influence has given in modern times a quite extraordinary impetus to the lyric poetry of our own fatherland, and whose services in this respect are by no means appreciated by contemporary criticism as they deserve to be. I refer to the poet of the Messias. Klopstock is among the great Germans, who have inaugurated the new artistic epoch of their people. He is a great figure, who, by means of courageous enthusiasm and superb self-respect, wrested our poetry from the stupendous insignificance of the Gottsched[21] period, which with its blockish superficiality had completely destroyed the life of all that is noble and of worth in the genius of our race; who has, in short, given us poems fully awake to the highest demand of the poet's vocation, in a form of thorough artistic excellence, if also somewhat austere, the majority of which are stamped with the permanency of a classic. Some of the odes of his youth are dedicated to a generous *friendship*, which was to him at once symbolic of nobility, staunchness, honour, the pride of his soul, a temple of his spirit. Others

319

have reference to a *personal* attachment of real emotional depth, although it is precisely in this field that we meet with many compositions which a critical sense can only regard as so much prose. "Selmar and Selma" is a poem of this class, a gloomy and tedious altercation between lovers, which, not without many tears, woe, empty yearning, and useless feats of melancholy emotion, revolves round the one mouldy and musty question, which of the two, Selmar or Selma, is first to die. But in Klopstock we find at least a genuine impulse of patriotism alive in every pore. As a good Protestant the Christian mythology, with its sacred legends and so forth — we must except the angels, for whom he retained as a poet a profound respect, although they can only appear abstract and lifeless in a type of poetry such as his, which claimed the realism of life — neither satisfied his sense of the ethical seriousness of art, nor yet the vigour of life and an intelligence, which aspired to something more than blind wailing and self-abasement, was, in short, both self-respecting and actively religious. The need of some mythology, however, and one connected with Germany impressed him strongly as a poet, in order that he might have definite names and characters ready to hand as a stable basis of his imaginative creation. It is impossible to associate such patriotic sentiments with the gods of Greece. Consequently Klopstock attempted, we may justly say from genuine national pride, to give a renewed life to the old mythology of Wodan, Hertha and the rest. He was unfortunately as little able to carry his aim to the point of objective effect and sufficiency by this adoption of names of gods, which are no longer really Germanic, however much they may have been so, as, let us say, the imperial museum in Regensburg is qualified to stand for the ideal of our present political life. However strongly, then, he may have felt the need to be able to realize in poetry and as fact in a national form a general folk-mythology, the truth of Nature and conscious life, these twilight gods remain entirely devoid of essential truth; we may add there is a kind of childish self-flattery in the belief that either reasonable people or the national faith could take such an attempt seriously. Apart from this, as objects of interest to the imagination, the figures of Greek mythology are elaborated in ways with incomparably more variety, infinitely stronger appeal to our aesthetic taste, our sense of delight and freedom. In lyric poetry, however, it is the self-revelation of the poet that is all-important. We ought at least to honour in our patriotic poet this his solicitude and effort, an effort which was sufficiently effective to bear subsequent fruit, and, even in the field of poetry, to stimulate by its suggestion composition on similar subjects. We have, however, to conclude our review, no word to say against the purity, excellence, and admirable influence of this patriotic sentiment of Klopstock as expressed in his enthusiasm for the honour and value of our German speech, and certain characters of our former history, that of Herrmann, for example, and above all particular German Kaisers, who in some instances have even been self-celebrated in song. Vital in him throughout is his justifiable pride in the German muse, and his faith in her increasing courage to contend on equal terms and in high-spirited self-reliance with that of the Greek, the Roman, and the Englishman. And no less a genuine reflection of his patriotism is the nature of his survey of the royal princes of Germany, the expectations which their character have or had it in their power to arouse on all that generally concerns honour, art, and science, questions of public import and spiritual objects of essential value. On the one hand we find him expressing his contempt of our princes, who, as he tells us, remain on their comfortable chairs, surrounded with the tobacco smoke of courtiers, buried in present obscurity and yet deeper to be buried in the future.

321

Or he may express his feelings in the lament that even Frederick II

> Nicht sah, dass Deutschland's Dichtkunst sich schnell erhob,
> Aus fester Wurzel daurendem Stamm, und weit,
> Der Æste Schalten wurf![22]

With pain of a like quality those vain hopes, too, return back to him, in which he saw in Kaiser Joseph the uprise of a new world of spiritual effort and poetry. And, finally, it is an honour to the heart of the old veteran at least as great that he sympathizes with the present fact that a people had shattered its fetters of every kind, had trodden under foot the injustice of a thousand years, and for the first time sought to found its political life on reason and right.

He greets this new

> Labende, selbst nicht geträumte Sonne.
> Geseegnet sei mir du, das mein Haupt bedeckt,
> Mein graues Haar, die Kraft, die nach sechzigen
> Fortdauert; denn sie war's, so weithin
> Brachte sie mich, dass diess Erlebte![23]

Nay, he will even express his gratitude to France:[24]

> Verzeiht, O Franken (Namen der Bruder ist
> Der edle Name) dass ich den Deutschen einst
> Zurufte, das zu fliehen, warum ich
> Ihnen jetzt flehe, euch nachzuahmen.

And, naturally, the acerbation of the poet was all the more bitter, when this fair dawn of freedom changed to a day that was steeped in horror and blood, one that murdered liberty. Klopstock, however, was unable to give poetical expression to such painful feelings. What he did find the opportunity to say was all the more prosaic, without definite structure and logical consequence on account of the fact that he had no higher purpose,[25] veiled in such facts, to set off against his disappointed hope. His genius was in short entirely blind to any more profound demand of reason in the facts of such a revolution.

The greatness of Klopstock consists then essentially in his national sympathies, his keen sense of freedom, friendship, love, and his staunch Protestantism. We may justly honour him for his noble character and his noble art, for his effort and achievement. And if, too, in many directions he shares the limitations of his own times, and in truth is responsible for many odes that are solely of interest to the critic, the grammarian, the metrist, odes deficient in all poetic vitality, we may affirm, nevertheless, that with the single exception of Schiller, we shall find in our subsequent literature no more noble figure, no disposition of such serious and masculine independence.

We have, indeed, to compare with him Schiller and Goethe, who are not merely the poetic exponents of their own times in a spirit resembling his own, but in their experience as poets are of course far more comprehensive. And, above all, in the songs of Goethe we Germans unquestionably possess the most consummate, profound, and influential poetic compositions of modern times. If they are wholly an expression of the poet they are equally the treasure of his people; and, in fact, as the genuine growth of his native soil, are completely in accord with the fundamental tones of our national life and genius.

━━

[1] *Subjectivität.* Individual self-conscious life.

[2] *Das Subject,* here the individual consciousness which composes.

[3] *Ergusses,* the pouring out into a mould.

[4] Vol. iv, pp. 169-172.

[5] This appears to be the meaning of the words *die letzte Music eines nationalen Inneren.*

[6] I presume by *Nachhülfe* Hegel practically means imitation rather than translation. It may be very much doubted whether any composition, involving a change of language, can give anything but the faintest knowledge of the original folk-song. Goethe's genius could produce poetry out of strange materials, but he could not reproduce the music of another medium.

[7] *Subjektiver Art.*

[8] Or as the text runs, "and as everybody's poet."

[9] Pausanias, I, c. 8.

[10] Æschines, ep. 4.

[11] *Zusammengezogenheit.* The idea of concentration is also present.

[12] I have taken the revised translation.

[13] *Äussersichseyn.* The being beside or aloof from oneself, not so much in the sense of infatuation as ecstasy.

[14] I presume Hegel means this by the words *nur zum Trällern;* it might mean "merely to be hummed."

[15] *Still in sich.*

[16] High above the life of earth beneath it shall wave in the blue band of heaven, neighbour to the thunder, on the boundary of the starry world. It shall be a voice from above, ay, as the bright choir of the stars, who praise their Creator in their motion and conduct the garlanded year. Its voice of bronze is dedicate to eternal and earnest matters alone, and, hour by hour, as it swiftly swings backwards and forwards, it is one with Time in its flight.

[17] *Einlebung.* This vital fusion with the object.

[18] *In seiner in sich Zurückgenommenen Innerlichkeit.*

[19] *In seinem Aufgehohenseyn.*

[20] That is, of the isle of Melos, Sappho's birthplace.

[21] Readers of the Xenien of Goethe and Schiller will recall the unsparing attacks which were directed against this formalist and pedant.

[22] Even Frederick II "did not see that the art of German poesy was raising itself swift on high from the enduring stock of a stable root, and spread the shade of its branches far abroad."

[23] He greets this new "reawakened sun, no mere dream at least of mine. Verily I bless thee, who sweepest over my head, my grey hairs, the strength of me that still endures after its sixty years. Ay, for was it not this strength which has carried me so far to see this very vision!"

[24] "Forgive me, brother of France, and brotherhood is the noblest tie after all, that I once cried to my Germans to flee from that, which I now implore them to follow—imitation of you." The reference is of course to the French Revolution.

[25] Hegel may mean that Klopstock was unable to see the real benefits which would result from the French Revolution despite its apparent failure. The sentence which follows would, however, suggest an alternative interpretation that the poet was unable to see the higher demand which the facts of Revolution made upon the French people, and which from the first, that is, even when Klopstock admired them, they did not either frankly face or successfully respond to. I think, indeed, this latter is most probable.

C. DRAMATIC POETRY

The reason that dramatic poetry must be regarded as the highest phase of the art of poetry, and, indeed, of every kind of art, is due to the fact that it is elaborated, both in form and substance, in a whole—that is the most complete. For in contrast to every other sort of sensuous *materia*, whether it be stone, wood, colour, or tone, that of human speech is the only medium fully adequate to the presentation of spiritual life; and further, among the particular types of the art of articulate speech, dramatic poetry is the one, in which we find the objective character of the Epos essentially united to the subjective principle of the Lyric. In other words it presents directly before our vision an essentially independent action as a definite fact, which does not merely originate from the personal life of character under the process of self-realization, but receives its determinate form as the result of the substantive interaction in concrete life of ideal intention, many individuals and collisions. This mediated form of epic art by means of the intimate personal life of an individual viewed in the very presence of his activity does not, however, permit the drama to describe the external aspects of local condition and environment, nor yet the action and event itself in the way that they are so described in the epic. Consequently, in order that the entire art-product may receive the full animation of life, we require its complete scenic representation. And, finally, the action itself, regarded in the full complexus of its ideal and external reality, is adapted to two distinct types of composition of the most opposite character, the predominant principles of which, regarded severally as the tragic and comic type, create in their turn also a further fundamental and specific point of view in our attitude to the dramatic art.

Starting then from the vantage of these general observations we may indicate the course of our inquiry as follows:

Firsts we propose to consider the dramatic composition, both in its general and more detailed features, in the contrast it presents to epic and lyrical poetry.

Secondly, our attention will be directed to its scenic presentation and the conditions of this necessity.

Thirdly, we shall pass under review the different types of dramatic poetry as we find them realized in the concrete facts of past history.

1. THE DRAMA AS A POETICAL ART-PRODUCT

What we have, in the first instance, to define more emphatically is the poetic aspect of the dramatic composition as such, that is to say in its independence of the fact that the same is necessarily presented to our direct vision on the stage. Our investigation of this will do well to concentrate itself on the following points:

Firsts there is the general principle of dramatic poetry.

Secondly, we have the several specific types of dramatic composition.

Thirdly, there is the relation which obtains between these and the public audience.

(*a*) *The Principle of Dramatic Poetry*

The demand of the drama, in the widest sense, is the presentation of human actions and relations in their actually visible form to the imaginative consciousness, that is to say, in the uttered speech of living persons, who in this way give expression to their action. Dramatic action, however, is not confined to the simple and undisturbed execution of a definite purpose, but depends throughout on conditions of collision, human passion and characters, and leads therefore to actions and reactions, which in their turn call for some further resolution of conflict and disruption. What we have consequently before us are definite ends individualized in living personalities and situations pregnant with conflict; we see these as they are asserted and maintained, as they work in co-operation or opposition — all in a momentary and kaleidoscopic interchange of expression — and along with this, too, the final result presupposed and issuing from the entirety of this interthreading and conflicting skein of human life, movement, and accomplishment, which has none the less to work out its tranquil resolution. The mode of poetical composition adapted to this novel type of content can be, as already suggested, no other than a mediating union of the principles of epic and lyrical art respectively.

(α) The *first* point of importance we have to settle to our satisfaction is that of the *time* at which dramatic poetry is able to assert itself in all its predominance. Drama is the product of an already essentially cultured condition of national life. It already presupposes as essentially a feature of past history not only the primitive poetic period of the genuine Epos, but also the independent personal excogitation of lyrical rapture. The bare fact that, while combining these two points of view, it is satisfied with neither sphere in its separation proves that this is so. And in order that we may have this poetic combination the free self-consciousness of human aims, developments and destinies must be already fully alert and awake, must have attained, in short, a degree of culture such as is only possible in the intermediate and later epochs of a nation's development. For this reason, too, the greatest exploits and events of a nation's primitive history are rather of an epic than a dramatic type. Such are features of the national existence for the most part related to communities outside it, such as the Trojan war, or the wave of popular migration, as illustrated in the Crusades, or the national resistance to a common enemy, as was the case in the war of Greece against Persia. It is only at a later stage that we meet with the more stable independence of single heroes, who create for themselves and out of themselves in their isolation definite ends, and carry through the undertakings they imply.

(β) We may add the following remarks upon the nature of this *mediation* between the opposed principles of *epic* and *lyric poetry*.

The Epos already makes an action visible to our imaginative sense. It is, however, here presented as the substantive entirety of a national spirit under the form of definite events and exploits of external life, in which personal volition, the individual aim and the externality of vital conditions, together with the obstructions which such external facts present, are retained in an equal balance. In the Lyric, on the contrary, it is the individual person, which is emphasized in the independence of his subjective life and as such expressed.

(αα) In combining these two points of view drama has in the *first* place, following in this respect the Epos, to bring before our vision an event, action, or practical affair. But above all in everything that is thus presented the factor of bare externality must be obliterated, and in, its place the self-conscious and active personality is posited as the paramount ground and vital force. The drama, in short, does not take exclusive refuge in-the lyric presence of soul-life, as such stands in contrast to an external world, but propounds such a life in and through *its* external realization. And in virtue of this the event does not appear to proceed from external conditions, but rather from personal volition and character; it receives in fact its dramatic significance exclusively in its relation to subjective aims and passions. At the same time the individual is not left exclusively rooted in his self-exclusive independence; he comes to his own through the peculiar nature of the conditions in which he is placed, and subject to which his character and purpose become the content of his volitional faculty, quite as much so in fact as in virtue of the nature of the particular purpose itself in its opposition to and conflict with other ends. Consequently the dramatic action in question must submit to a process of development and collision with other forces, which themselves, on their own account, and even in a contrary direction to that willed and intended by the active personality, effect the ultimate course of the events through which the personal factor, in its essential, characteristics of human purpose, personality, and spiritual conflict, is asserted. This substantive or objective aspect, which is enforced along with the individual character, in other respects acting independently from its own ideal resources, is no other than the very point of view which we find effective and vital in the principle of dramatic poetry, when it coincides with that of the epic composition.

(ββ) However much, therefore, we may have as a centre of attraction the intimate soul-life of particular men and women, nevertheless dramatic composition cannot rest content with the purely lyrical conditions of the emotional life; nor can the poet of such merely limit his sympathy to the dusty record of exploits that are already complete, or, speaking generally, merely describe the experience of enjoyment or other states of emotional or contemplative life. The drama, on the contrary, has to exhibit situations and the spiritual atmosphere that belongs to them as definitely motived by the individual character, which is charged with specific aims, and which makes these an effective part of the practical content of its volitional self-identity. The definition of soul-life, therefore, in the drama passes into the sphere of impulse, the realization of personality by means of active volition, in a word, effective action; it passes out of the sphere of pure ideality, it makes itself an object of the outer world, and inclines itself to the concrete facts of the epic world. The external phenomenon, however, instead of attaining existence in the bare fact of an event, is here, in the view of the acting character himself, charged with the opinions and aims he forms on his own account. Action is here the executed will, which as such is at the same time *recognized*, recognized, that is, not merely in its origin and point of departure from the soul-life, but also in respect to its ultimate purpose. In other words, all that issues from the action, issues, so far as the personality in question is concerned, from himself, and reacts thereby on his personal character and its circumstances. This constant relation of the entire complexus of external condition to the soul-life itself of the self-realized and self-realizing individuality, who is at once the basis and assimilating force of the entire process, marks the point where dramatic poetry falls in line with the truly lyrical principle.

($\gamma\gamma$) It is only when thus regarded that human action asserts itself as *action* in the supreme sense, that is, as actual execution of ideal intentions and aims with the realization of which the individual agent associates himself as with himself, discovers himself and his satisfaction therein, and thereupon further takes his stand with his entire being in all that proceeds from it as a constituent of the objective world. A character which is dramatic plucks for himself the fruit of his own deeds.

Inasmuch, however, as the interest, in a dramatic sense, restricts itself to the personal aim, whose hero the active personality is, and it is only necessary in the artistic work to borrow from the external world so much as is bound in an essential relation to this purpose, which originates in self-conscious life, for this reason the drama is *primarily* of a more abstract nature than the epic poem. For on the one hand the action, in so far as it reposes in the self-determination of character, and is deducible from this vital source and centre, does not presuppose the epic background of an entire world through all the varied aspects and ramifications of its positive realization, but is concentrated in the simpler definition of circumstance subject to which the individual man is absorbed in his immediate purpose and carries the same to accomplishment. And from a further point of view we have not here the type of personality which asserts its development to our vision in the *entire complexity* of national qualities as such are displayed by the epic, but rather character viewed in *direct* relation to its action, character which possesses a *definite* end directed to spirit life in its universality. This end or purpose, this eventual fact on which it depends, is placed in a more exalted position than is possible to the extension of the purely individual life, which appears inclusively as living organ and animating vehicle of the same. A more widely extended unveiling of character under the most varied aspects which are present either in no connection at all or only in a more remote one to its action, as we find it concentrated on *one* single point of interest would be a superfluity; consequently in this respect, too, that is, in its relation to the active personality, dramatic poetry ought to be more simply concentrated than epic poetry. The same generalization is applicable to the number and variety of the characters represented. For in virtue of the fact, as previously insisted, that the movement of the drama is not thrown upon the background of a national existence essentially complete in its envisagement of every conceivable variety of class, age, sex, activity, and so forth, but on the contrary, rivets our attention throughout on *one* fundamental purpose and its achievement, a realization of objective fact so extended and intricate as this would not merely be ineffective, but would actually impair the result proposed. At the same time, however, and *secondly*, the end and content of an action is only dramatic by reason of the fact that on account of its defined character, in the distinctive qualities of which the particular personality itself can alone lay hold of it under equally definite conditions, it calls into being in other individuals other objects and passions opposed to it, This pathetic excitant[1] may, no doubt, in each separate active agent, assume the form of spiritual, ethical, and divine forces, such as duty, love to fatherland, parents, wife, relations, and the like. If, however, this essential content of human feeling and activity is to assert itself as dramatic it must in its specialization *confront* us as distinct ends, so that in every case the action will inevitably meet with obstruction in its relation to other active individuals, and fall into subjection to changing conditions and contradictions, which alternately prejudice the success of their own particular fulfilment. The genuine content, the essential operative energy throughout may therefore very well be the eternal forces, the essentially explicit ethical State, the gods of vital reality, in a word the divine and the true, but it is not these in the might of their tranquillity, in that condition, so to speak, wherein the unmoved gods abide, saved from all action, as some serene figures of sculpture self-absorbed in a state of blessedness. What we have here is the divine in its community, as content, that is, and object of human personality, as concrete existence in its realization,[2] invited to act and charged with movement.

If, however, as above described, the godlike presence constitutes the most vital objective truth in the external precipitate[3] of human action, then, *thirdly*, the deciding factor in the course and original departure of such an evolution and conflict cannot reside with particular individuals, which are placed in a relation of opposition to one another; it must be referred to the divine presence itself, regarded as essential totality: and for this reason, the drama, it matters not in what form it may be shaped, will have to propound to us the vital energy of a principle of Necessity which is essentially self-supporting, and capable of resolving every conflict and contradiction.

(γ) Consequently, we have before everything else the demand made on the dramatic *poet* in his creative capacity, that to the fullest extent his intelligence is awake to that ideal and universal substance which is at the root of human ends, conflicts, and destinies. He must fully acquaint himself with all the contradictions and developments which the particular action will, under the proposed conditions, necessarily involve and display. He must not merely be aware of them in so far as they originate in personal passion and the specific characterization of particular individuals, or as he finds such related to the actual content of human designs and resolves; but also in so far as they are simply referable to the external relations and circumstances of concrete life. And, along with this, it should be within his powers to recognize what the real nature of these paramount forces are, which apportion to man the just guerdon of his achievements. The rightful claim, no less than the wrongful misuse of the passions, which storm through the human heart, and excite to action, must lie disclosed to him with equal clarity, in order that precisely in those cases where the ordinary vision can only discover the ascendancy of obscurity, chance, and confusion, he, at least, will find revealed the actual selfaccomplishment of what is the essence of reason and truth itself. It follows, therefore, that the dramatic poet ought as little to confine his efforts to the indefinite exploration of the depths of emotional life, as the one-sided retention of any single exclusive mood of soul-life, or any limited partiality in the type of his sense-perception and spiritual outlook generally. He ought, rather, to exclude nothing from his vision that may be embraced by the widest expansion of Spirit conceivable. And this is so because the spiritual powers which are exclusively distinct in the mythological Epos, and which, by virtue of the many-sided aspects of *actual individualization*[4] tend to lose the *clear definition* of their significance, assert themselves in dramatic poetry in consonance with their simple substantive content as pathos altogether, and as apart from individual characters. The drama is, in fact, the resolution of the one-sided aspect of these powers, which discover their self-stability in the dramatic character. And this is so whether, as in tragedy, they are opposed to such in hostility, or, as in comedy, they are displayed within these characters themselves, without further mediation, in a condition of resolution.

(b) *Dramatic Composition*

In discussing the drama as a concrete work of art, I propose to emphasize, briefly, the following fundamental points:

First there is the unity of the same viewed in contrast to that of the Epos and the lyric poem.

Secondly, we have to consider the articulation of its parts, of its separate parts and their development.

Thirdly, there is the external aspect of diction, dialogue, and verse-measure.

(α) What we have in the first instance to observe and, from the broadest point of view, to establish with regard to the unity of the drama, is connected with a remark made in a previous passage to the effect that dramatic poetry, in contradistinction to the Epos, must be more strenuously self-concentrated. For, although the Epic makes a specific event its centre of unity, this is none the less expanded over a wide and manifold field of the national existence, and may break up into very various episodes and the independent presentation which belongs to each as parts of the entire panorama. An analogous appearance of merely general connection, on grounds which are converse to the above, is permissible to certain types of lyrical poetry. Inasmuch, however, as in dramatic poetry, from one point of view, that epic foundation, as we have seen, falls away—and as, otherwise regarded, the individual characters do not find their expression under the insulation proper to lyric

335

expression, but rather assert in such a way their mutual relations to one another, by means of the opposed features of their characterization and aims, that it is just this personal relation which constitutes the ground of their dramatic realization—it follows, as by a law of necessity, that the synthetic unity of the entire composition is of a more stringent character. Now this more restricted homogeneity is quite as much objective as it is ideal in its nature. It is objective relatively to the features of the practical content of the objects, which the different characters carry out in a condition of conflict. It is ideal or subjective in virtue of the fact that this essentially substantive content appears in dramatic work as the passion of particular characters, so that the ill-success or achievement, fortune or misfortune, victory or defeat, essentially affect the individuals, whom such concern, in their actual intention.[5]

The more obvious laws of dramatic composition may be summarized in the time-honoured prescription of the so-called unities of place, time, and action.

(αα) The inalterability of one exclusive *locale* of the action proposed belongs to the type of those rigid rules, which the French in particular have deduced from classic tragedy and the critique of Aristotle thereupon. As a matter of fact, Aristotle merely says[6] that the duration of the tragic action should not exceed at the most the length of a day. He does not mention the unity of place at all; moreover, the ancient tragedians have not followed such a principle in the strict sense adopted by the French. As examples of such a deviation, we have a change of scene both in the Eumenides of Æschylus and the Ajax of Sophocles. To a still less extent can our more modern dramatic writing, in its effort to portray a more extensive field of collision, *dramatis personae* of whatever kind and incidental event, and, in a word, an

336

action the ideal explication of which requires, too, an external environment of greater breadth, subject itself to the yoke of a rigid identity of scene. Modern poetry, in so far, that is, as its creations are in harmony with the romantic type, which as a rule displays more variety and caprice in its attitude to external condition, has consequently freed itself from any such demand. If, however, the action is in truth concentrated in a few great motives, so that it can avoid complexity of external exposition, there will be no necessity for considerable alternation of scene. Indeed, the reverse will be a real advantage. In other words, however false such a rule may be in its purely conventional application, it contains at least the just conception that the constant transition of scene, without any particular reason why we should have one more than another, is obviously quite inadmissible. The dramatic concentration of the action ought necessarily to assert itself also in this external aspect, and thus present a contrast to the Epos, which is permitted in the most varied way to adapt itself to the fresh expatiation in the form of the spatial condition and its changes. Moreover, from a further point of view, the drama is not, as the Epos, composed exclusively for the imaginative sense, but for the direct vision of our senses. In the sphere of the pure imagination we can readily pass from one scene to another. In a theatrical representation, however, we must not put too great a strain on the imaginative faculty beyond the point which contradicts the ordinary vision of life. Shakespeare, for example, in whose tragedies and comedies there is a very frequent change of scene, had posts put up with notices attached to them indicating the particular scene on view. A device of this kind is a poor sort of affair, and can only impair the dramatic effect. For this reason the unity of place is at least commendable to the extent that its intelligibility and convenience are *primâ facie* assured, in so far, that is, that all confusion is thus avoided. But after all, no doubt, much may still be trusted to the imagination, which would conflict with our ordinary perception and notion of probability. The most convenient course in this, as in other matters, is a happy mean; in other words, while not wholly excluding the claim of purely natural fact and perception, we may still permit ourselves considerable license in our attitude to both.

(ββ) The unity of *time* is a precisely similar case. In the pure realm of imaginative idea we may no doubt, with no difficulty, combine vast periods of time; in the direct vision of perception we cannot so readily pass over a few years. If the action is, therefore, of a simple character, viewed in its entire content and conflict, we shall do best to concentrate the time of such a conflict, from its origin to its resolution, in a restricted period. If, on the contrary, it demands character richly diversified, whose development necessitates many situations which, in the matter of time, lie widely apart from one another, then the formal unity of a purely relative and entirely conventional duration of time will be essentially impossible. To attempt to remove such a representation from the domain of dramatic poetry, on the *primâ facie* ground that it is inconsistent with the strict rule of time-unity would simply amount to making the prose of ordinary facts the final court of appeal, as against the truth of poetic creation. Least of all need we waste time in discussing the purely empirical probability that as audience we could, in the course of a few hours, witness also, directly through our sense, merely the passage of a short space of time. For it is precisely in the case where the poet is most at pains to illustrate this conclusion that, from other points of view, he wellnigh invariably perpetrates the most glaring improbabilities.

(γγ) In contrast to the above examples of unity, that of *action* is the one truly inviolable rule. The true nature, however, of this unity may be a matter of considerable dispute. I will therefore develop my own views of its significance at greater length.

Every action must without exception have a *distinct* object which it seeks to achieve. It is through his action that man enters actively into the concrete actual world, in which also the most universal subject-matter is in its turn accepted in the poetic work and defined under more specific manifestation. From this point of view, therefore, the unity will have to be sought for in the realization of an end itself essentially definite, and carried under the particular conditions and relations of concrete life to its consummation. The circumstances adapted to dramatic action are, however, as we have seen, of a kind that the individual end meets with obstructions at the hands of other personal agents, and this for the reason that a contradictory end stands in its path, which in its turn equally strives after fulfilment, so that it is invariably attached to the reciprocal relation of conflicts and their devolution. Dramatic action in consequence rests essentially upon an action that is involved with *resistance;*[7] and the genuine unity can only find its *rationale* in the entire movement which consists in the assertion of this collision relatively to the definition of the particular circumstances, characters, and ends proposed, not merely under a mode consonant to such ends and characters, but in such a way as to resolve the opposition implied. Such a resolution has, precisely as the action itself has, an external and an inside point of view. In other words, on the one side, the conflict of the opposed *ends* is finally composed; and on the other the particular *characters*, to a greater or less extent, have committed their entire volitional energy and being to the undertaking they strive to accomplish. Consequently the success or misadventure of the same, to complete or partial

339

execution, the inevitable disaster or the secure union effected with intentions that are apparently opposed to their extent, also determine the destiny of the character in question, that it is inextricably involved with that which it was impelled to commit to such activity. A true end is therefore only then consummated, where the object and interest of the action, around which all revolves, are identified with the individuals concerned, and absolutely united to them. And whether the difference and opposition of the dramatic character assumes a simple form or branches out in various accessory episodes and individuals, the unity in either case may be of a more severe or less stringent nature. Comedy, for instance, in the many-sided features of its worked-out intrigue does not require such deliberate self-concentration as tragedy does, which is as a rule motived on grandiose and simple lines. Romantic tragedy, however, is also in this respect more varied and less consistent in its unity than is classic tragedy. And even where there is more licence the relation of the episodes and supplementary characters must be throughout recognizable; and the entirety of the piece should also naturally and without strain fit in with and help to complete the conclusion. So, for example, in "Romeo and Juliet," the discord between the families, which lies outside the lovers and their object and destiny, is no doubt the base on which the action is shaped, though not the actual matter on which all actually depends. Shakespeare consequently devotes the necessary, if also wholly subordinate attention to the final issue of this conflict in his conclusion. In the same way in "Hamlet" the fortunes of Denmark remain a subsidiary interest, though with the entrance of Fortinbras they are apparently considered, and are settled at last satisfactorily.

No doubt in the particular end, which resolves the colliding factors, the possibility of fresh interests and conflicts may be presented; it is, however, the *one* collision with which the action is concerned, which has to discover its final adjustment in the essentially independent composition. Of this type are the three tragedies of Sophocles borrowed from the Theban cycle of myths. The first contains the discovery by Œdipus of the murderer of Laius; the second his peaceful death in the home of the Eumenides; the third the fate of Antigone. And, despite of this connection, every one of the three is equally an intrinsically complete whole independent of the other two.

(β) With regard to our *second* point, namely, that of the mode of denouement in a dramatic composition, we have three main features of distinction to consider between it and epic composition or the song, namely, the size of its extension, the nature of its progression and its division into scenes and acts.

(αα) We have already seen that the embrace of a drama—is not so extensive as the demand of the epos implies. I propose, therefore—over and above the two features already discussed of that world-condition, which is necessarily implied in the complete picture of the epic, and the more simple collision which is an equally essential constituent of the content of drama—merely to advert to the further ground, that in the drama the greater part of everything that the muse of the epic poet has to describe and linger over as servant of our imaginative vision, is omitted altogether from the scenic reproduction. And, further, in the case of drama it is not actual exploit, but the exposition of personal passions which is here the main thing. This personal life, however, in contrast to the expanse of the phenomenal world, is concentrated in simple emotions, sentences, decisions, and the like; and here, too, as distinct from the collateral display of epic narration and its historical part, it gives effect to the principle of lyric absorption and the origination and expression in present time of passion and idea. Dramatic poetry is, however, not satisfied with merely *one* situation;[8] it presents the ideal world of emotional life or intelligence in active self-assertion as a totality of circumstances and ends of very various character, which expresses taken together, all that, if viewed relatively to its activity, passes in such an inward world. In comparison with the lyrical poem, the drama reaches out to and is completed in a far more extensive embrace of subject-matter. To summarize this comparative relation we may say, perhaps, that dramatic poetry stands as a mean between the wide embrace of the Epopaea and the concentrated compression of the Lyric.

(ββ) Yet more important than this aspect of external extension is the nature of the *dramatic progression* as opposed to the mode of the epic's devolution The form of the epic objectivity demands throughout, as we have seen, a lingering style of description, which may along with this become more intense and pointed in its display of active obstruction. It is possible that we may at first blush incline to the view that, inasmuch as other ends and characters resist the main end and principal character in dramatic exposition, dramatic poetry is entitled to accept this sort of pause and obstacle as an essential feature of its principle. As a matter of fact just the reverse is the case. The true dramatic progression is a *continuous* movement *onwards* to the final catastrophe. This is clear from the simple fact that it is in *collision* that we find the emphatic turning point. In consequence of this we have the twofold view of, in the first place, a general strain towards the outbreak of this conflict, and, secondly, the necessity implied in this discord and contradiction of views, ends, and activities, that they should find some resolution to which they are driven forwards. By this we by no means assert that mere celerity of forward movement is simply in itself beautiful in the dramatic sense. On the contrary, the dramatic poet should have himself room to supply every situation on its own account with all the motives which it truly implies. Episodical scenes, however, which only impede the action are contrary to the nature of the drama.

(γγ) As a final point, we may divide the course of the dramatic work most naturally by simply following the stages implied in the notion of dramatic movement itself. In this connection Aristotle[9] long ago remarks that a whole is that which possesses a beginning, a middle, and a conclusion. He further defines a beginning 'as that which, of itself necessary, does not issue from something else, and out of which something other than itself issues and proceeds. The end is the reverse of this, namely, that which originates from something else, either of necessity, or mainly so at least, but which does not itself lead to further consequence. The middle is that which both issues from something else, and also is that from which something else proceeds.

Now no doubt in the reality of our experience every action includes many presuppositions which make it a difficult matter to decide the exact point where we may find the true commencement. In so far, however, as dramatic action rests essentially on a definite state of collision, the right point of departure will lie in the situation, out of which the future devolution of that conflict, despite the fact that it has not as yet broken out, will none the less in its further course issue. The end, on the contrary, will then be attained, when the resolution of the discord and its development is secured in every possible respect. In the midway condition between origination and end we have the conflict of ends, and the struggle of individual persons in collision. These different section's are in dramatic composition, so to speak, the phases or moments of the action of what are also actions, and the definition of this is admirably indicated by the *acts* of the piece. They are now of course more or less equivalent to pauses of time, and a prince on one occasion, who was either in a hurry, or wished the action to proceed without interruption, blamed his chamberlain openly that such a pause occurred. With regard to their *number three* such acts for every kind of drama is the number that will adapt itself most readily to intelligible theory. Of these the *first* discloses the appearance of the collision, which is thereupon emphasized in the *second* with all the animation of conflicting interests as the positive difference of such discord and its progression, until, *finally*, driven as it were upon the very apex of its contradiction, it is necessarily resolved. We may cite—as some kind of illustration of this division which the nature of such an action suggests—from ancient drama, in which no doubt the dramatic articulation is as a rule less distinct, the trilogies of Æschylus, in which each single play combines with the others to form a single and completely exclusive whole.[10] In modern poetry the Spaniards mainly follow such a division into three acts. The English, French, and Germans, on the contrary, for the most part divide the entire play into *five* acts, in which the initial exposition is assigned to the first, the three next are occupied with the various aggressions and reactionary effects, the complex intentions and conflicts of the opposed parties; and it is not until the fifth that we reach the entire resolution of such contending forces.

(γ) The third and final important aspect we have to investigate in our present connection is the nature of the *external means*, in so far as the employment of the same by dramatic art can be held distinct from and independent of the actual scenic representation that is otherwise essential to its complete display. An account of the specific nature of diction which is frequently dramatic generally, secondly, of the distinguishing features of the monologue, dialogue, and the like, and, lastly, of verse measure, will be all that is necessary here. As we have more than once insisted in the drama the fact of the action is not the external aspect to which we refer, but the exposition of the ideal spirit of the action, not merely in respect to the *dramatis personae* and their passion, pathos, resolve, interaction, and mediation, but also relatively to the universal essence of the action in its conflict and destiny. It is this ideally pregnant spirit, in so far as poetry gives embodiment to it in poetic form, which pre-eminently discovers an appropriate expression in the language of poetry, viewing this, as we should, as the most spiritual way of expressing emotions and ideas.

(αα) But, moreover, just as the drama combines the principles of the Epos and the Lyric, dramatic diction, too, is compelled both to carry and assert within itself elements that are lyrical and those that are epic. The *lyrical* approach is rather a special feature of modern drama, and as a rule in those cases where the personal life is or tends to be self-absorbed, and seeks in its decision and action throughout to retain the self-consciousness of its inward resources. But none the less this unveiling of the individual heart-life, if it is to remain dramatic, ought not merely to be the exploitation of a vague and variable cloud of emotions, memories, and visions; it should keep its relation to the action constant throughout, should make its result identical with that of the different phases of the same.

In contrast to this subjective pathos the epic character of the diction, which we may define as the *objective* pathos, is mainly concerned with the unfolding of what is substantive in dramatic relations, ends, and persons on lines rather directed to the vision of the audience. Such a point of view can also in part assume a lyrical tone, remaining when it

345

does so dramatic only in so far as it does not more entirely in its independent force form the progress of the action and its asserted relation to the same. And over and above this, as a second residue, so to speak, of epic poetry, we may have the records of narrative, descriptions of battles and the like thrown in. But these also, in genuine dramatic composition, ought to be marked with greater compression and animated movement, and, relatively to their presentment as narrative, a necessary connection with the progress of the action should be evident.

In conclusion, genuine dramatic art consists in the expression of individuals in the conflict of their interests and the discord roused between their characters and their transitory passions. It is here that the twofold aspect of lyric and epic poetry[11] will assert its power in true dramatic union: and we have then attached to this the aspect of positive external fact expressed likewise in the medium of language, as where we have, for instance, the departure and entrance of *dramatis personae* as a rule announced beforehand; not unfrequently also their external habit or demeanour is indicated by other persons.

A fundamental distinction over the entire field now under review is the so-called realistic mode of expression, as opposed to a conventional speech of the theatre and its rhetoric. Diderot, Lessing, Goethe, and Schiller also in their youth addressed themselves in modern times above all to this attitude of direct and natural expression. Lessing did so with the powers of a trained and sensitive observation Schiller and Goethe did so with their predilection for the direct animation of unembellished robustness and force. That men should converse with one another as in the Greek, or with more insistance—and in this latter respect the criticism has a reasonable basis—as in French comedy and tragedy was scouted as contrary to Nature. This type of naturalism, however, may very readily, with its superfluity of merely realistic traits, fall into the other extreme of dryness and prose, in so far, that is, as the characters are not developed in the essential qualities of their emotional life and action, but only as they happen to express themselves in the literal accuracy of their individual life, without indicating therein any more significant self-consciousness or any further sense of their essential position. The more natural the characterization is allowed to remain in this sense the more prosaic it becomes. In actual life men converse and strive with one another before everything else on the mere basis of their *distinct singularity*. If our object is to depict them simply as such it is impossible that they should also be represented in their truly substantive significance.[12] And, if we look at the essence of the matter, this question of crudeness and urbanity can only be in the last instance treated subject to the above considerations. In other words while, on the one hand, such crudeness or coarseness is made to issue from the particular personality, which is exclusively committed to the unmediated dictation of an imaginative type of outlook and feeling, in the converse treatment an urbanity is the outcome of a purely abstract and formal generalization of consideration for others, recognition of the claims of personality, love, honour, and the like, in which nothing that is suggestive of a rich and objective content can be expressed.[13] Between these two extremes of a purely formal generality and this natural expression of unpolished peculiarities we have the true universal, which is throughout neither formal nor destitute of individuality, but finds its concrete realization in a twofold way from the defined content of character and the objective presence of opinions and aims. Genuine poetry will therefore consist in the assertion of what belongs to immediate and actual life as characteristic and individual in the purifying medium of universality,[14] both aspects being permitted to mediate each other. In this case we are conscious, even in respect to diction, that without being wholly banished from the basis of reality and its actual traits of truth, we are nevertheless carried into another sphere, that is to say the ideal realm of art. Of this latter character is the diction of Greek dramatic poetry, the later diction of Goethe, and in part, too, that of Schiller, and in his own way Shakespeare's also, although the Englishman, owing to the peculiar conditions of the contemporary stage, is forced in part now and again to accommodate his verbal language to the actual ability of the actor.[15]

(ββ) We may *further* classify the mode of dramatic expression as that of choral interlude, monologue, and dialogue. It is the ancient drama which has pre-eminently elaborated the distinction between chorus and dialogue. In our modern drama this falls away. What, in the classical composition, was presented by the *chorus*, is now rather placed in the mouths of the leading characters. The choric song expresses, among the ancients, by way of contrast to the particular characters and their more personal or more reciprocal conflict, the general or more impersonal view of the situation, and the emotions it excites, in a manner which at one time inclines to the objective style of epic narrative, at another to the impulsive movement of the Lyric. In the *monologue*, on the other hand, it is the isolated individual who, in a given situation of the action, becomes objective on his own account. Monologues are, therefore, dramatically in their right place at those moments chiefly when the emotional life is entirely self-concentrated as the result of previous events; when it sums up, as it were, the nature of the cleft between itself and others, or its own spiritual division; or when it arrives at some sudden decision, or comes to the final point of resolve on matters already long debated.

The *third* and complete form of the drama, however, is the *dialogue*. For in this the *dramatis personae* are mutually able to express their character and aims, not merely relatively to their personal attitude to each other, but also to the substantive character of the pathos disclosed; they engage in conflict, and thereby actually advance the movement of the action. We may further distinguish in the dialogue between the expression of a pathos that is *subjective* and one that is *objective*. The first rather appertains to a given passion of more accidental a nature, whether it be the case in which it is retained essentially in suppression, and is only expressed aphoristically, or that in which it finds a vent in the most complete and exhaustive explosion. Poets, who endeavour to arouse the full movement of personal emotion by means of poignant scenes, are exceptionally partial to this type of pathos. Nevertheless, despite all their endeavour to depict personal suffering and unrestrained passion, or the unreconciled inward dissension of soul-life, it remains the fact that the human soul, in its depth, is less effected thereby than it is through a pathos, wherein at the same time a genuine objective content is evolved. For this reason the earlier plays of Goethe, despite all the real penetration of their subject-matter and the natural force of their dialogue, make on the whole a weaker impression. And, in the same way, outbreaks of unrelieved distraction and unrestrained fury, effect a truly healthy sense only in subordinate degree; and, above all, what is wholly frightful rather chills us than makes the blood flow. The poet may describe passion with all the overwhelming power possible. It is ineffective; the heart is merely rent in pieces,[16] and turns aside from it. What we fail to find here is that which art can least dispense with, the positive aspect of reconciliation. The ancient tragedians, therefore, mainly sought for their effect by

349

means of the objective type of pathos; nor is there wanting here genuine human individuality, so far as this was compatible with their art. The plays, also, of Schiller possess this pathos of a great spiritual force,[17] a pathos which is penetrative throughout, and is manifested and expressed everywhere as fundamental to the action. It is, above all, to this circumstance that we may ascribe the lasting effect which the tragedies of Schiller produce even in our own day; I refer in particular to their scenic reproduction. For that which produces a profound dramatic effect of universal and enduring appeal can be only the substantive in action — by which I mean, viewing it as definite content, the ethical substance therein, or, in its more formal aspect, the grandeur of ideal reach and character, in which respect, again, Shakespeare is supreme.

($\gamma\gamma$) I will, in conclusion, add merely a word or two on the point of *verse-measure*. Dramatic metre is best when it lies midway between the tranquil, uniform flow of the hexameter and the more interrupted and split-up syllabic metres congenial to the Lyric. In this respect the iambic metre is above all others commendable. For the iambus, with the rhythm of its onward movement, which may be either accelerated by anapaests, or be made more solemn and weighty with the spondee, forms a most fitting accompaniment to the march of the action; and in quite a peculiar way the senarius possesses a real tone of noble and restrained emotional force. Among modern authors the Spaniards, with an artistic purpose the reverse of this, adopt trochaeic tetrameters, the effect of which is one of tranquil retardation; a measure which, with its variety of interwoven rhymes and assonances, in part, too, with its alternative absence of rhyme, is admirably adapted to the imaginative exuberance of phantasy, and to the fine-drawn argumentative antitheses, which characterize this poetry and impede rather than advance the action. In a contrast of a similar kind, the French Alexandrine is harmonious with the formal carriage and the declamatory rhetoric of passions, sometimes held in restraint and at others expressed at full heat, the conventional expression of which the art of French drama has tasked itself to elaborate. The more realistic Englishman, whom we Germans too have followed in more recent times, has, on the contrary, retained the iambic metre, which Aristotle long ago defined as τὸ μάλιστα λεκτικὸν τῶν μέτρων[18] He has, however, not accepted the same in identical form with the Greek trimeter, but substituted a measure of less pathetic character, if capable of the greatest freedom of treatment.

(c) The Relation of the Dramatic Composition to the General Public.

Although the advantages or defects of diction and metre are important, also, in epic and lyrical poetry, we must nevertheless ascribe a more emphatic effect to them in dramatic compositions, in virtue of the circumstance that we are in this case dealing with opinions, characters, and actions which have to appear before us in all the reality of life itself. A comedy of Calderon, for example, with all the interplay of fantastic wit we may assume, embodied, however, in the kind of diction we associate with this poet, with its logical niceties and its bombast—subject, also, to all the variations of his lyrical metres—would not, we may presume, on the simple ground of this manner of expression, be likely to arouse any general sympathy. It is on account of this visual presence and nearness of approach that the other aspects of the content, apart from that of purely dramatic form, are brought into a far more direct relation to the public before whom they are reproduced. We should like shortly to explain the nature of this.

Scientific compositions and lyrical or epic poems either possess a distinct public, whose interest in such works is associated with their profession, or it is a matter of chance into what hands compositions of this character may fall. If a book does not please anyone it can be neglected, just as a man passes by the picture or statue that he does not like; such works may, in fact, be held to carry to some extent with them the author's admission that his book is not written for such. The case is somewhat otherwise with dramatic works. Here we have a distinct public for which the author has to cater, and he is under certain obligations towards it. Such a public possesses the right of applause no less than expressed displeasure; inasmuch as a work is represented before it in its entirety, and the appeal is made that it should be enjoyed, with sympathy in a given place and at a stated time. A public of this sort, as in the case of any—other public jury, is of a very varied character; it differs in its education, interests, accustomed tastes, and hobbies, so that to secure complete success in certain distinct respects a talent in the display of vulgar effect, or at least a relative shame-facedness in regard to the finest demand of genuine art, may be necessary. No doubt the dramatic poet has always the alternative left him to despise his public. But in that case he obviously fails to secure the very object for which dramatic writing exists. With us Germans, to an exceptional extent, it has become the fashion since the times of Tieck thus to scorn the public. Our German play-writer will express his own particular individuality, but takes no trouble to commend the result to his audience. The ideal of our German egotism is quite the reverse, namely, that every man must turn out something different to that of other people, in order that he may prove his originality. It was owing, in part, to this that Tieck and the brothers Schlegel, men who, from the very nature of their sentimental irony, were quite unable to master the emotional forces and intelligence of their nation and time, fell foul of Schiller, and tried to blacken his poetical reputation on the ground that he did among us Germans manage to strike the right key, and obtain a popularity unsurpassed. With our neighbours, the French, we find the opposite. Their authors write with the present effect on the public always in view, which further, on its own account, is capable of being a keener and less indulgent critic of the author, owing to the fact that a more definite artistic taste is already fixed in France: with us anarchy prevails, and everyone expresses his critical views, applauds or condemns just as he likes, or as his opinions, emotion, and mood may chance to dictate.

Inasmuch, however, as it is an essential part of the definition of the dramatic composition that it should possess the vitality able to command a favourable popular reception, the dramatic poet should submit to the conditions—quite apart, that is, from the accidental circumstances or tendencies of the time—which are likely to secure this result in an artistic form. What these are I will attempt to explain, at least in their more general features.

(*a*) Now, in the *first* place, the ends, which in a dramatic work come into conflict and are resolved out of such conflict, either possess a general human interest, or at least have at bottom a pathos, which is of a valid and substantive character for the people for whom the poet creates his work. In such a case, however, the universal human quality and what is more definitely national, in so far as either are connected with the substance of dramatic collisions, may lie very widely apart. Compositions, which stand in the national life, at the very summit of their dramatic art and development, may consequently quite fail to be appreciated by another age and nation. We find, for example, in Hindoo lyrical poetry, even in our own time, much that carries with it a real charm, tenderness, and fascinating sweetness. The particular collision, however, around which the action in the "Sakontala" revolves, in other words, the furious curse upon Sakontala of the Brahman, because she does not see him, and omits to make her obeisance, can only strike us as absurd, so much so in fact that, despite all other excellences in this quite exceptionally beautiful poem, we fail to discover any interest in the very culminating crisis of the action. We may affirm very much the same thing of the way in which the Spaniards treat the motive of personal honour with the abstract severity of a logic, the brutality of which outrages most deeply all our ideas and feelings. Let me recall, for example, the attempt made by our own theatrical management to bring upon the stage one of the less famous plays of Calderon entitled "Clandestine Revenge for Clandestine Insult," an attempt condemned to failure from the first on this ground. Another tragedy, which on similar lines portrays a more profound human conflict, "The Physician of his own Honour," under the changed title of "The Intrepid Prince," has after some revision secured more leeway; but this, too, is handicapped by its abstract and unyielding Catholic principle. Conversely, and in an opposite direction, the Shakespearian tragedies and comedies are appreciated by a public that is constantly increasing. We find here that, despite all their nationality, the universal human interest is incomparably greater. Shakespeare has only failed to secure an entrance where the national conventions of art are so narrow and specific that they either wholly exclude or materially weaken works of the Shakespearian type. A similar position of advantage, such as that we allow to Shakespeare, would be attributable to the tragedies of the ancients, if we did not, apart from our changed habits in respect to scenic reproduction and certain aspects of the national consciousness, make the further demand of a profounder psychological penetration and a greater breadth of particular characterization. So far, however, as the *subject-matter* of ancient tragedy is concerned, it could never at any time fail in its effect. We may, therefore, broadly affirm that, in proportion as a dramatic work accepts for its content wholly specific rather than typical characters and passions, conditioned, that is, exclusively by definite tendencies of a particular epoch of history, instead of mainly concerning itself with human interests substantive in all times, to that extent, despite of all its other advantages, it will be more transitory.

(β) And, *further*, it is necessary that universal human ends and actions of this kind should emphasize their poetic individualization to the point of animated life itself. Dramatic composition does not merely address itself to our sense of vitality, a sense which even the public certainly ought to possess, but it must itself, in all essentials, offer a living actual presence of situations, conditions, characters, and actions.

($\alpha\alpha$) I have already, in a previous passage of this work,[19] entered into some detail relatively to the aspect of local environment, customs, usages and other matters which affect the visual representation of action. In this respect dramatic individualization ought to be either so thoroughly poetical, vital, and rich with interest that we can discount what is alien to our sense, and feel ourselves attracted to the performance by this vital claim on our attention, or it should not pretend to do more than present such characteristics as external form, which is entirely outshone by the spiritual and ideal characteristics which underlie it.

($\beta\beta$) More important than this external aspect is the vitality of the *dramatis personae*. Such ought not to be merely specific interests personified, which is only too frequently the case at the hands of modern dramatists. Such abstract impersonations of particular passions and aims are wholly destitute of dramatic effect. A purely superficial individualization is equally insufficient. Content and form in such cases, as in the analogous type of allegorical figures, fail to coalesce. Profound emotions and reflections, imposing ideas and language offer no real compensation. Dramatic personality ought to be, on the contrary, vital and self-identical throughout, a complete whole in short, the opinions and characterization of which are consonant with its aims and action. It is not the breadth of particular traits which is here of first importance, but the permeating individuality, which synthetically binds all in the central unity, which it in truth is, and displays a given personality

356

in speech and action as issuing from one and the same living source, from which every characteristic, whether it be of idea, deed or manner of behaviour, comes into being. That which is merely an aggregate of different qualities and activities, even though such be strung together in one string, will not give us the vital character we require. This presupposes from the point of view of the poet himself a creative activity which is instinct with life and imagination. It is to the latter type, for instance, that the characters of the Sophoclean tragedies belong, despite the fact that they do not possess the variety of particular characteristics which distinguish the epic heroes of Homer. Among later writers Shakespeare and Goethe are pre-eminently famous for the vitality of their characterization. The French, on the contrary, particularly in their earlier dramatic compositions, appear to have been rather content to excogitate characters that are little more than the formal impersonations of general types and passions, than to have aimed at giving us true and living persons.

(γγ) But, *thirdly*, the task of dramatic creation is not completed with the presentment of vital characterization. Goethe's Iphigeneia and Tasso throughout are good enough examples of this poetic excellence—and yet they are not, if we look at them more strictly, by any means perfect examples of dramatic vitality and movement. It is for this reason that Schiller long ago remarked of the Iphigeneia, that in it is the ethical content, the heart experience, the personal opinion which is made the object of the action, and is as such visually reproduced. And unquestionably the display and expression of the personal experience of different characters in definite situations is not by itself sufficient; we must also have real emphasis laid on the collision of the *ultimate ends* involved, and the forward and conflicting movement which such imply. Schiller is consequently of the

357

view that the movement of the Iphigeneia is not sufficiently disturbed; we are permitted to linger within it too long and easily. He even maintains that it without question inclines to the sphere of epic composition, if we contrast it at least with any strict conception of tragedy. In other words, dramatic effect is action simply as action; it is not the exposition of personality alone, or practically independent of the express purpose and its final achievement. In the Epos play may be permitted to the breadth and variety of character, external conditions, occurrences and events; in the drama, on the contrary, the self-concentration of its principle is most asserted relatively to the particular collision and its conflict. It is thus that we recognize the truth of Aristotle's dictum,[20] that tragic action possesses two sources (αἴτια δύo), opinion and character (διάνοια καὶ ἦδoς), but what is most important is the end (τέλoς), and individuals do not act in order to display diverse characters, but these latter are united with a common bond of imaginative conception to the former in the interest of the action.

(γ) As a matter for our *final* consideration in this place there is the relation in which the *poet* is placed to the general public. Epic poetry in its truly primitive state requires that the poet place wholly on one side his distinctive personality in its contrast to his actually objective work. He offers us the content of that and only that. The lyric poet, on the contrary, deliberately expresses his own emotional life and his personal views of the world.

(αα) We might imagine that the poet must perforce withdraw himself in the drama by reason of the very fact that he brings action before us in its sensuous presence, and makes the characters speak and active in their own names, to a greater extent than in the Epos, in which he appears at any rate as narrator of the events. Such an impression is only, however, very partially valid. For, as I have already contended, the drama is exclusively referable in its origin to those epochs, in which the personal self-consciousness, both relatively to the general outlook on life and artistic culture, has already reached a high degree of development. A dramatic composition therefore should not, as an epic one does, present the appearance as though it originated from the popular consciousness simply, for the display of which content the poet is merely an instrument of expression which possesses no reference to the poet's personal life; rather what we seek to recognize in the complete work is quite as much the product of the self-aware and original creative force, and by reason of this the art and virtuosity of a genuine poetic personality. It is only thereby that dramatic productions attain to the genuine excellence of their artistic vitality and definition, as contrasted with the actions and events of natural life. It is on this account that where the authorship of dramatic works is a subject of controversy we find such to be nowhere more frequent than where it concerns the primitive Epopaea.

(ββ) From the opposite point of view the general public too, if it has itself preserved a true sense of meaning of art, will not submit to have placed before it in a drama the more accidental moods and opinions, the peculiar tendencies and the one-sided outlook of this or that individual, the expression of which is more appropriate to the lyric poet. It has a right to demand that in the course and final issue of the dramatic action, whether of tragedy or comedy, what is fundamentally reasonable and true should be vindicated. Being myself convinced of this I have in a previous passage given a place of first importance to the demand that the dramatic poet must in the profoundest sense make himself master of the essential significance of human action and the divine order of the world, and along with this of a power to unfold this eternal and essential foundation of all human characters, passions and destinies in its clarity as also in its vital truth. It is no doubt quite possible that a poet, in rising equal to this demand upon his powers of penetration and artistic achievement, may under particular circumstances find himself in conflict with the restricted and uncultured ideas of his age and nation. In such a case the responsibility for such a disunion does not rest with himself, but is a burden the public ought to carry. He has the single obligation to follow the lead of truth and his own compelling genius, the ultimate victory of which, provided it is of the right quality, is no less assured than that of ultimate truth itself universally. It is impossible to define closely the limits within which a dramatic poet is entitled to bring his actual personality before the public. I will therefore merely recall attention to the fact in a general way that in many periods of history dramatic poetry, no less than other kinds, is induced to disseminate with a vital impulse novel ideas upon politics, morals, poetry, religion, and the like. So early as Aristophanes we have polemics in those comedies of his youth against the domestic condition of Athens and the Peloponnesian war. Voltaire again frequently endeavours in his dramatic works to popularize his free thought principles. But above all worthy of notice is the effort of our Lessing in his "Nathan" to vindicate his ethical faith against the strait waistcoat of a blockish orthodoxy. In still more recent times too Goethe has in his earliest works challenged the prose of our German life and its defective views of art. Tieck has to some extent followed his lead in this respect. Where personal views of the above type are not only of superior worth, but are further not expressed in such deliberate separation from the action of the drama as to make the latter appear as a mere means for their exploitation, the claims of true art are not likely to suffer injury. If, however, the freedom of the composition is thereby impaired, though no doubt the poet may possibly produce no inconsiderable impression on the public by his introduction of his own predilections into his work; yet, however true they may be, if they are at the same time unable to coalesce with the work as an artistic whole the interest thereby aroused can only be limited to the matters thus handled; it is in fact no true artistic interest at all. The worst case of all is that, however, where a poet with similar deliberation seeks, out of pure flattery and in order to please, to give prominence to some popular prejudice which is entirely false. His sins of commission are in that case twofold, not merely against art, but truth no less.

(ββ) One further remark may be perhaps admitted in this connection to the effect that among the particular types of dramatic art a more limited measure of indulgence is permitted to tragedy than to comedy in this more free expatiation of the personality of the poet. In the latter type the contingency and caprice of individual self-expression is from the first agreeable to its main principle. Thus we find that Aristophanes frequently makes matters of immediate interest to his Athenian public the subject of his parabases. In portions of these he gives free utterance to his own views upon contemporary events and circumstances, and withal shrewd advice to his fellow citizens. He is at other times concerned to defend himself from the attacks of political opponents and his artistic rivals. Indeed there are passages in which he deliberately eulogizes himself and his peculiarities.

---

2. THE EXTERNAL TECHNIQUE OF A DRAMATIC COMPOSITION

Poetry, alone among the arts, completely dispenses with the sensuous medium of the objective world of phenomena.

Inasmuch moreover as the drama does not interpret to the imaginative vision the exploits of the past, or express an ideal personal experience to mind and soul, but rather is concerned to depict an action in all the reality of its actual presence, it would fall into contradiction with itself if it were forced to remain limited to the means, which poetry, simply as such, is in a position to offer. The present action no doubt belongs entirely to the personal self, and from this point of view complete expression is possible through the medium of language. From an opposite one, however, the movement of action is towards objective reality, and it requires the complete man to express its movement in his corporeal existence, deed and demeanour, as well as the physiognomical expression of emotions and passions, and not only these on their own account, but in their effect on other men, and the reactions which are thereby brought into being. Moreover, in the display of individuality in its actual presence, we require further an external environment, a specific *locale*, in which such movement and action is achieved. Consequently dramatic poetry, by virtue of the fact that no one of these aspects can be permitted to remain in their immediate condition of contingency, but have all to be reclothed in an artistic form as phases of fine art itself, is compelled to avail itself of the assistance of pretty well all the other arts. The surrounding scene is to some extent, just as the temple is, an architectonic environment, and in part also external Nature, both aspects being conceived and executed in pictorial fashion. In this *locale* the sculpturesque figures are presented with the animation of life, and their volition and emotional states are artistically elaborated, not merely by means of expressive recitation, but also through a picturesque display of gesture and of posture and movement, which, in its objective form, is inspired by the inward soul-life. In this respect we may have brought home to us a distinction which recalls a feature I have at an earlier stage indicated in the sphere of music as the opposition implied in the arts of declamation and melody. In other words, just as in declamatory music language in its spiritual signification is the aspect of most importance, to the characteristic expression of which the musical aspect is entirely subordinate, whereas the movement of melody is unfolded freely on its own account in its own specific medium, although it too is able to assimilate the content of language—so also dramatic poetry, on the one hand, avails itself of those sister arts merely as instrumental to a material basis and environment, out of which the language of poetry is in its free domination asserted as the commanding central focus, upon and around which all else really revolves. From the further point of view, however, that which in the first instance had merely the force of an assistant and accompaniment, becomes an object on its own account, and receives the appearance in its own domain of an essentially independent beauty. Declamation passes into song, action into the mimic of the dance, and scenery in its splendour and pictorial fascination itself puts forward a claim to artistic perfection.

In contrasting, then, a contrast frequently insisted upon, and more particularly in recent times, poetry in its simplicity with the external dramatic execution such as we have above described, we may continue the course of our review under the following heads of discussion.

Firsts there is the dramatic poetry, whose object is to restrict itself to the ordinary ground of poetry, and consequently does not contemplate the theatrical representation of its productions.

Secondly, we have the genuine art of the theatre, to the extent that is in which it is limited to recitation, play of pose and action, under the modes in which the language of the poet is able throughout to remain the definitive and decisive

363

factor.

Lastly, there is that type of reproduction, which admits the employment of every means of scenery, music and dance, and suffers the same to assert an independent position as against the dramatic language.

(*a*) *The Reading and Recitation of Dramatical Compositions.*

The true sensuous medium or instrument of dramatic poetry is, as we have seen, not only the human voice and the spoken word, but the entire man, who not merely expresses emotions, ideas, and thoughts, but, as vitally absorbed in a concrete action, in virtue of all that he is influences the ideas, designs, the action and behaviour of others, experiences similar effects on himself, or maintains his independent opposition to them.

(*a*) In contrast to such a definite view, which is based upon the essential character of dramatic poetry itself, it is a feature of modern notions on the subject, particularly so among ourselves, to regard the organization of drama with a view to its theatrical reproduction as unessential and subsidiary, although as a fact all dramatic authors, even when they adopt this attitude of indifference and contempt, entertain the wish and hope to see their compositions on the stage. The result is that the greater number of more recent dramas are unable ever to find a stage, and the simple reason of this is that they are undramatical. We are not of course, therefore, in a position to deny that a dramatic composition may satisfy the conditions of genuine poetry in virtue of its intrinsic worth. What we affirm is that it is only to an action, the dramatic course of which is admirably adapted to theatrical representation, that we are to attribute such intrinsic dramatic worth. The best authority for such a statement is supplied by the Greek tragedies. It is true that we no longer see these on the contemporary stage, but they do nevertheless, if we regard the facts more closely, completely satisfy us to a real extent precisely on this ground that they were written without reserve for the theatre of their day. What has banished them from the theatre of today is not so much the character of their dramatic organization, which differs mainly from that of to-day in its employment of the chorus, as in the nature of national predilections and conditions, upon which for the most part, if we consider their content, they are based, and in which owing to the distance in which they are placed relatively to our own contemporary life we are unable now to feel ourselves at home. The malady of Philoctetes, for instance, the loathsome ulcer on his foot, his ejaculations and outcries, are as little likely to awaken the genuine interest of a modern audience as the arrows of Hercules, about which the main course of that drama revolves. In a similar way, though we may admit the barbaric cruelty of the human sacrifice in the Iphigeneia in Aulis and Tauris in an opera, we find it absolutely necessary in tragedy at any rate that this aspect should be wholly revised as Goethe has in fact done.

(β) The difference, however, thus indicated between ancient and modern customs, which effects the mere perusal of such works, no less than the complete and vital reproduction of them as a whole, has had the further effect of pointing out to us another by-way, in which poets to some extent deliberately fashion their work exclusively for the reader's perusal, and in a manner by which the difficulty above indicated no longer affects the character of such compositions. There are no doubt in this connection isolated points of view, which merely refer to features of external form, which are implied in the so-called knowledge of the stage, and an indifference as to which does not lessen the poetical worth of a dramatical production. To these belong, for example, the careful regulation of the scenic arrangements, that one scene can follow without difficulty after another, though it requires great alterations in the scenery, or that the actor is given sufficient time to make the necessary change of costume, or to recover from his previous exertions. A knowledge and aptitude of this nature is neither indicative of any poetical superiority or the reverse; they rather depend upon the naturally varying and conventional arrangements of the theatre. There are, however, other features relatively to which the poet, in order to be truly dramatical, must have the animated reproduction visibly present in its substance, must make his *dramatis personae* speak and act conformably thereto, that is, in complete congruity with an actually present realization. Viewed in this light theatrical reproduction is a real test. For in the presence of the supreme court of appeal of a sound and artistic public the mere speeches and tirades of our so-called exquisite diction, if dramatic truth is not thereby asserted, will not hold water. There are periods, no doubt, in which the public also is corrupted by the culture it is the fashion so highly to praise, I mean by heads generally overstocked with the current opinions and fancies of the connoisseur and critic. Let it however only retain its own essentially sterling commonsense, and it will only be satisfied in those cases where characters express themselves and act precisely as the reality of life no less than art demands and necessitates. If the poet, on the contrary, writes exclusively for the single reader he very readily gets no further than making his characters speak and behave much as they might do in an epistolary correspondence. If any one thus gives us the reasons for his aims and what he does, or unbares his heart in any other respect, instead of that which we should at once remark thereupon we get between the receipt of the letter and our immediate reply time for all kinds of reflection and idea. The imagination opens in this case a wide field of possibilities. In the *actually present* speech and rejoinder we have to presuppose that as between man and man the volition and heart, the movement of feeling and decision are more direct, that in short the dialogue passes on without any such recourse to considerable reflection, but at once from soul to soul, as eye to eye, mouth to mouth, and ear to ear. Only in such a case the actions and speeches are expressed with life from the actual personality, who has no time left him to make a careful selection from one out of many possibilities. Under this view of the case it is not unimportant for the poet throughout his composition to keep his eye on the stage, which renders such a direct type of animation necessary. Nay, for myself I go to the length of maintaining that no dramatic work ought to be printed, but rather, as no doubt with the ancients, it should belong to the stage repertory in manuscript form,[21] and only receive quite an insignificant circulation. We should at least in that case limit very considerably the present superabundance of dramas, which it is possible possess the speech of culture, fine sentiments, excellent reflections, and profound thoughts, but which are defective in the very direction which makes a drama dramatical, that is, in the display of action, and the vital movement which belongs to it.

(γ) In the mere *perusal* and *reading aloud* of dramatic compositions we find a difficulty in deciding whether they are of a type which would produce the due effect from the stage. Even Goethe, whose experience of stage management in his later years was exceptional, was far from being dependable on this head, a result no doubt mainly due to the extraordinary confusion of our public taste, which is able to accept with approval almost anything and everything. If the character and object of the *dramatis personae* are on their own account great and substantive the manner of composition no doubt presents less difficulty. But as regards the motive force of interests, the various phases in the progress of the action, the suspended interest and development of situations, the just degree in which characters assert their effect on each other, the appropriate force and truth of their demeanour and speech—in all such respects the mere perusal unassisted by a theatrical performance can only in the rarest cases arrive at a reliable decision. Reading a work aloud is only under great qualification a further assistance. Speech in drama requires the presence of separate individuals. The delivery of *one voice*, however artistically it may adapt itself to different shades of tone in alternate or varying change is insufficient. Add to this the fact that in reading aloud we are throughout confronted with the difficulty whether on every occasion the persons speaking should be mentioned or not. Both alternations are equally open to objection. If the delivery is that of one voice the statement of the names of the characters speaking becomes an indispensable condition of intelligibility, but by doing so the expression of pathos throughout suffers violence. If, on the other hand, the delivery is vitally dramatic, and we are carried thereby into the actual situation, a further kind of contradiction can hardly fail to appear. For with the satisfaction of our sense of hearing that of sight puts forward a certain claim of its own. For when we listen to an action we desire to see the acting persons, their demeanour and surroundings; the eye craves for a completed vision, and finds instead before it merely a reciter, who sits or stands peacefully in a private house with company. Reading aloud or recitation is consequently always an unsatisfying compromise between the unambitious pretensions of private perusal, in which the aspect of realization is absent entirely and all is left to the imagination, and the complete theatrical presentation.

(b) *The Art of the Actor*

In conjunction with actual dramatic reproduction there is along with music a second practical art, namely, that of *acting*, the complete development of which belongs entirely to more recent times. Its principle consists in this, that while it summons to its assistance dramatic posture, action, declamation, music, dance, and scenery, it accepts as the predominant mark of its effort human speech and its poetical expression. And this is for poetry in its simplest significance the exclusively just relation. For if mere mimicry or song or dance once begin to assume an independent position of their own, poetry viewed as a fine and creative art is degraded to the position of an instrument, and loses its ascendancy over the in other respects accompanying arts. We will venture to point out a few characteristic distinctions in this connection.

(*a*) The primary phase of the art of acting is to be found among the Greeks. Here, as one aspect of the matter, the art of speech is affiliated with that of sculpture. The acting *dramatis personae* stands before us as an objective figure in his entire bodily realization. In so far as here this statuesque figure is animated, assimilates and expresses the content of the poetry, enters into every movement of personal passion and at the same time asserts it through word and voice, this presentation is more animated and more spiritually transparent than any statue or picture.

As to this quality of living animation we may draw a distinction between two distinct ways of regarding it.

(*αα*) *First*, there is declamation in the sense of artistic speech. Declamation was not carried far among the Greeks; intelligibility is here what is of most importance. We desire to recognize in the tone of the voice and in the quality of the recitations the characterization of soul-life in its finest shades and transitions, as also in its oppositions and contrasts, in short, in its entire concreteness. The ancients, on the contrary, added a musical accompaniment to declamation, partly to emphasize rhythm, and in part to increase the modulation of the verbal expression. At the same time it is probable that the dialogue was either not at all or only very lightly accompanied. To the reproduction of the choruses, however, the lyric association of music was essential. It is highly probable that singing, by means of its more definite accentuation of the meaning of the language used in the choice strophes and antistrophes, made the same more intelligible; only under such an assumption can I myself understand how it was possible for a Greek audience to follow the choruses of either Æschylus or Sophocles. I admit that such choruses might not necessarily present to a Greek all the difficulties *we* ourselves experience; at the same time I confess that, though I know the German language well and am not wholly destitute of imagination, German lyrics written in the same style, if declaimed from the stage, even with the full accompaniment of song, would still be far from wholly intelligible.

(ββ) A *further* means of interpretation is supplied by the pose and movement of the body. In this respect it is worth noticing that with the Greeks the play of facial expression is entirely absent, by reason of the fact that their actors wore masks. The facial contour returned an unalterable sculpturesque image, the plastic outlines of which were as unable to assimilate the varied expression of particular states of soul, as to reproduce the acting characters, which fought through a pathos securely fixed and universal in the nature of its dramatic conflict, and neither deepened the substance of this pathos to the ideal intensity of our modern emotional life, nor suffered it to expand into all the particularization of the world of dramatic individualities now in vogue. The action was equally simple, for which reason we do not possess any tradition of famous Greek mimes. Sometimes the poet himself was actor; both Sophocles and Aristophanes are examples. To some extent the mere citizen, who was not strictly a professional actor at all, took a part in tragedy. As a set-off to such difficulties the choric songs were accompanied with the dance, a procedure which can only appear frivolous to us Germans in the view we generally take of the dance. With the Greeks it belonged as an essential feature to their theatrical performances.

($\gamma\gamma$) To summarize, then, we find that among the ancients not only was the poetical claim of language, and the intelligible expression of general emotional states, freely admitted, but also the external realization received the most complete elaboration by means of musical accompaniment and the dance. A concrete unity of this kind gives to the entire presentation a plastic character. What is spiritual is not on its own account idealized as part of a personal soul-life, nor is it expressed under such a mode of particularization; the main effect is to bring about its complete affiliation and reconciliation with the external aspect of sensuous appearance whose correspondent claim is equally recognized.

(β) In rivalry with music and the dance speech suffers injury, in so far as it ought to remain the *spiritual* expression of spirit. Our modern art of the theatre has consequently succeeded in liberating itself from such features. The poet is by this means exclusively placed in a relation to the actor simply, who, by his declamation, play of facial expression, and posture, has to represent to vision the poetical work. This relation of the author to the external material is, however, in its contrast to other arts, quite unique. In painting and sculpture it is the artist himself, who executes his conceptions in colour, bronze, or marble; and although musical execution is dependent upon the hands and voices of others, yet the feature thus added, albeit, of course, the element of soul in the delivery ought not to be absent, is none the less, to a more or less degree, overwhelmingly mechanical technique and virtuosity.[22] The actor, on the contrary, appears before us in the entire personality which combines his bodily presence, physiognomy, voice, and so forth, and it is his function to coalesce absolutely with the character he portrays.

($\alpha\alpha$) In this respect the poet has the right to demand of the actor that he enters with all his faculties into the part he receives, without adding thereto anything peculiar to himself, that, in short, he acts in complete consonance with the creative conception and means of its display supplied by the poet. The actor ought, in fact, to be the instrument upon which the author plays, an artist's brush which absorbs all colours and returns the same unchanged. Among the ancients this was more easily achieved for the reason that declamation, as above stated, was mainly restricted to clarity of meaning, and music looked after the aspect of rhythm, while masks concealed the faces, and, moreover, not much scope was left to the action. Consequently, the actor could without real difficulty conform in his delivery to a universal tragic pathos; and although too, in comedy, portraits of living people such as Socrates, Nicias, Creon, and so forth, had to be represented, in a real measure the masks reproduced characteristic traits with sufficient force, and further we should note that a detailed individualization was less necessary, inasmuch as the comic poets, as a rule, merely introduced such characters in order to represent general tendencies of the time.

($\beta\beta$) The position is different in the modern theatre. Here, to start with, we have no masks or musical accompaniment, but have instead of these the play of facial expression, the variety of pose, and a richly modulated style of declamation. For, on the one hand, human passions, even when they are expressed by the poet in a more general and typical characterization, have none the less to be asserted as part of an inner and personal life; and for the rest our modern characters receive, for the most part, a far more extended compass of particularization, the distinctively appropriate expression of which has in the same way to be placed before us with all the animation of present life. The characters of Shakespeare are, above all, entire men, standing before us in distinctively unique personality, so that we require of our actors that they, for their part, give us back the entire impression of such complete creations. There is no specific rôle here that does not require a definite kind of expression fitted to it, and which covers in fact every feature of its display, whether we regard that which we cannot see or that which we do, whether it be in the tone of the voice, the mode of delivery, gesticulation, or facial expression. For this reason, apart from the nature of the dialogue, the varied character of the pose and gesture, through every possible shade, receives an entirely new significance. In fact, the modern poet leaves to the actor self-expression here much that the ancients would have expressed in words. Take the example of the final scene of Wallenstein. The old Octavio has assisted materially in the downfall of Wallenstein. He finds him treacherously murdered by the machinations of Buttler, and at the very moment when the Countess Terzky makes the announcement that she has taken poison, an imperial letter arrives. Gordon, after reading the same, hands it to Octavio with a glance of reproach, adding the words, "To the Lord Piccolomini." Octavio is confounded, and, pained to the heart, glances heavenwards. That which Octavio experiences in this reward for a service, for the bloody issue of which he himself is mainly responsible, is in this passage not expressed in so many words, but is left solely to the gesture of the actor.

(γγ) Owing to demands of this kind made by our modern art of acting, poetry may, relatively to the material of its presentation, not unfrequently opens up difficulties unknown to the ancients. In other words, the actor, being the man he is, possesses, in respect to voice, figure, physiognomical expression, as everybody else, his native peculiarities, which he is compelled to set on one side, either owing to their incompatibility with a pathos of universal import and a really typical characterization, or to bring them into harmony with the more complete personalities of a type of poetry rich in its power of individualization.

Actors claim the title of artists, and receive all the honours of an artistic profession. According to our modern ideas, no taint of any sort, whether ethical or social, is implied in the fact of being a dramatic actor. This view is the right one. The profession demands conspicuous talent, intelligence, perseverance, energy, practice, knowledge, and, indeed, its highest attainment is impossible without the rare qualities of genius. The actor has not only to assimilate profoundly the spirit of the poet and the part he accepts, and to make his own individuality conform entirely to the same, both inwardly and outwardly; he has, over and above this, in many respects to supplement the part with his own creative insight, to fill in gaps, to discover modes of transition, and generally, by his performance, to interpret the poet by making visibly and vitally present and intelligible meanings which lie beneath the surface, or the less obvious touches of a master's hand.

(c) *The Theatrical Art which is more Independent of Poetical Composition*

Finally, we shall have that further, or *third* aspect of the art in its actual employment, where it liberates itself from the exclusive precedency of articulate poetry, and accepts as an independent end what was previously, to a more or less extent, a mere accompaniment or instrument, and elaborates the same on its own account. To carry out this emancipation, music and the dance are quite as much essential features of the dramatic development as the art of the actor simply.

(a) In respect to this change in the art, there are broadly speaking two systems. The first, according to which the performer tends to be simply in spirit and body the living instrument of the poet, we have already referred to. The French, who make much of professional rôles[23] and schools, and are, as a rule, more typical in their theatrical representations, have shown an exceptional fidelity to this system in their tragedy and *haute comédie*. What we may define here as the position of the art of acting reversed consists in this, that the entire creation of the poet now tends to be purely an appendage or frame to and for the natural endowment, technical ability, and art of the actor. It is by no means uncommon to hear actors make the demand that poets should write expressly for them. The soul function of poetical composition is, in this view, to give the artist an opportunity to display and unfold in all its brilliance his emotional powers and art, to let us see the final outcome of his particular individuality. Among the Italians, the *commedia dell' arte* belongs to this type. Here, no doubt, we have certain definite types of character such as those of the *arlecchino*, *dottore*, and the like, with appropriate situations and series of scenes; the more detailed execution is, however, almost entirely left to the discretion of the actors. Among ourselves, the dramatic pieces of Iffland and Kotzebue, and many others besides, though in large measure regarded as poetry, unimportant or even bad compositions, nevertheless offer such an opportunity for the creative powers of the actor, who is compelled to initiate and shape something from such generally sketchy and artificial productions, which on account of a vital and independent performance of this kind receives a unique interest exclusively united to one and no other artist. It is here, more especially, that we find our much belauded realistic effects are displayed, a style carried to such lengths that a mere mumble and whisper of articulate speech, quite impossible to follow, will pass as an admirable performance. In protest to such a style, Goethe translated Voltaire's "Tancred" and "Mahomet" for the Weimar stage, in order to compel its actors to drop this vulgar naturalism, and accustom themselves to a more noble exposition. And this is invariably the case with the French, who, even in all the animation of the farce, always keep the audience in view, and throughout address themselves to it. As a matter of fact, mere realism and imitation of our everyday expression is as little exhaustive of the real problem as the mere intelligibility and clever use made of characterization. If an actor seeks to produce a really artistic effect in such cases, he will have to extend his powers to a genial virtuosity similar to that I have described already in a previous passage when referring to musical execution.[24]

(β) A *second* province belonging to the type under consideration is that of the modern *opera*, in the direction, at least, which it more and more is inclined to take. In other words, although in opera, generally speaking, the music is of most importance, which of course possesses a content in partnership with the poetry and the libretto, albeit it treats and executes the same freely as it thinks best, yet in more recent times, and particularly among ourselves, it has become increasingly an affair of luxurious display. It has carried its *accessoires*, in the splendour of its decorations, the pomp of its costumes, the completeness of its choruses and their grouping, to a degree of independence that throws all else into the shade. It was a magnificence of this kind, sufficiently criticized among ourselves, which Cicero long ago complains of when referring to Roman tragedy. In tragedy, where the poetry is always the most essential thing, such a lavish display of the sensuous side of things is no doubt not in its right place, although Schiller, in his "Maid of Orleans," shows a tendency here to run astray. In the opera, on the contrary, with its sensuous exuberance of song and the melodic, thundering chorus of voices and instruments, we may with more reason admit such an emphasized charm of external embellishment and display. If the decorations are splendid, then the groups and processions, to give point to them, must be equally gorgeous, and everything else must be adapted to the same scale. The subject most suited to a sensuous luxuriance of this kind, which, no doubt, is always some indication of the decline of genuine art, is that part of the entire performance which inclines to the wonderful, fantastic, or fairy tale. Mozart, in his "Magic Flute," has supplied us with an example which is not too extravagant, and is worked out on completely artistic lines. At the same time, we may entirely exhaust all the arts of scenic display, costume, instrumentation and the rest, but the fact remains that, if we are not really in earnest with that part of the content which concerns real dramatic action, the impression upon us can be at the strongest merely that of a perusal of the fairy-tale of "The Thousand and One Nights."

(γ) The same observations apply to the modern *Ballet*, which above all is most suited to fairy-land and miracle of all kinds. Here, too, we note as one supreme feature, quite apart from the picturesque beauty of the grouping and tableaux, the kaleidoscopic splendour and fascination of the decorations, costumes, and lighting, to an extent that ordinary persons find themselves transported into a world in which common sense and the laws and pressure of our daily life vanish altogether. As a further aspect of these performances, connoisseurs in such subjects will go into ecstacies over the elaborately trained dexterity and virtuosity of legs, which is nowadays an essential feature of the dance. If, however, any more spiritual significance is to flash athwart such mere physical agility, which we have reduced to the final ultimatum of senselessness and ideal poverty, we ought to have associated with the complete command over all the executive difficulties implied a real measure and euphony of movement, a freedom and grace such as finds a response in the soul; and it is only very rarely that we do so. As a further element in association with the dance here, which stands in the place of the choruses and solos of the opera, we find as real expression of action the Pantomime. This, however, in proportion as our modern dance has advanced in technical dexterity, has fallen from the rank which it once possessed, and, indeed, has so deteriorated that the very thing tends once more to drop out of the modern ballet altogether, which is alone able to lift the same into the free domain of art.

3. THE TYPES OF DRAMATIC POETRY AND THE PRINCIPAL PHASES OF THEIR HISTORICAL DEVELOPMENT.

Viewing for a moment the course of our present inquiry in retrospect, it will be seen that we have, *first,* established the principle of dramatic poetry in its widest and more specific characteristics, and, further, in its relation to the general public. *Secondly,* we deduced from the fact of the drama's presenting an action distinct and independent in its actually visible development the conclusion that a fully complete sensuous reproduction is also essential, such as is for the first time possible under artistic conditions in the theatrical performance. In order that the action, however, may adapt itself to an external realization of this kind, it is necessary that both in poetic conception and detailed execution it should be absolutely definite and complete. This is only effected, our *third* point, by resolving dramatic poetry into *particular types*, receiving their typical character, which is in part one of opposition and also one of mediatory relation to such opposition, from the distinction, in which not only the end but also the characters, as also the conflict and entire result of the action, are manifested. The most important aspects emphasized by such distinction and subject to an historical development are those peculiar to tragedy and comedy respectively, as also the comparative value of either mode of composition. This inquiry in dramatic poetry is for the first time so essentially important that it forms the basis of classification for the different types.

In considering more closely the nature of these distinctions we shall do well to discuss their subject-matter in the following order.

First, we must define the general principle of tragedy, comedy, and the so-called drama.

Secondly, we must indicate the character of ancient and modern dramatic poetry, to the contrast between which the distinctive relation of the above-named types is referable in their historical development.

Thirdly, we will attempt, in conclusion, to examine the concrete modes, which these types, though mainly comedy and tragedy, are able to exhibit within the boundary of this opposition.

(*a*) *The Principle of Tragedy, Comedy, and the Drama, or Social Play*

The essential basis of differentiation among the types of epic poetry is to be found in the distinction whether the essentially substantive displayed in the epic manner is expressed in its universality, or is communicated in the form of objective characters, exploits, and events. In contrast to this, the classification of lyric poetry, in its series of varied modes of expression, is dependent upon the degree and specific form in which the content is assimilated in more or less stable consistency with the soul experience, according as such content asserts this intimate life. And, finally, dramatic poetry, which accepts as its centre of significance the collision of aims and characters, as also the necessary resolution of such a conflict, cannot do otherwise than deduce the principle of its separate types from the relation in which *individual persons* are placed relatively to their purpose and its content. The definition of this relation is, in short, the decisive factor in the determination of the particular mode of dramatic schism and the issue therefrom, and consequently presents the essential type of the entire process in its animated and artistic display. The fundamental points we have to examine in this connection are, speaking broadly, those phases or features in the process, the mediation of which constitutes the essential purport of every true action. Such are from one point of view the substantively sound and great, the fundamental stratum of the realized divine nature in the world, regarded here as the genuine and essentially eternal content of individual character and end. And, on its other side, we have the *personal conscious life* simply as such in its unhampered power of self-determination and freedom. Without doubt, essential and explicit truth is asserted in dramatic poetry; it matters not in what form it may be manifested from time to time in human action. The specific type, however, within which this activity is made visible receives a distinct or, rather, actually opposed configuration, according as the aspect of substantive worth or in its opposition thereto, that of individual caprice, folly, and perversity is retained as the distinctive *modus* of operation either in individuals, actions, or conflicts.

We have therefore to consider the principle in its distinctive relation to the following types:

First, as associated with tragedy in its substantive and primitive form.

Secondly, in its relation to comedy, in which the life of the individual soul as such in volition and action, as well as the external factor of contingency, are predominant over all relations and ends.

Thirdly, in that to the drama, the theatrical piece in the more restricted use of the term, regarding such as the middle term between the two first-mentioned types.

(*a*) With respect to *tragedy*, I will here confine myself to a consideration of only the most general and essential characteristics, the more concrete differentiation of which can only be made clear by a review of the distinctive features implied in the stages of its historical process.

(*aa*) The genuine content of tragic action subject to the *aims* which arrest tragic characters is supplied by the world of those forces which carry in themselves their own justification, and are realized substantively in the volitional activity of mankind. Such are the love of husband and wife, of parents, children, and kinsfolk. Such are, further, the life of communities, the patriotism of citizens, the will of those in supreme power. Such are the life of churches, not, however, if regarded as a piety which submits to act with resignation, or as a divine judicial declaration in the heart of mankind over what is good or the reverse in action; but, on the contrary, conceived as the active engagement with and demand for veritable interests and relations. It is of a soundness and thoroughness consonant with these that the really tragical *characters* consist. They are throughout that which the essential notion of their character enables them and compels them to be. They are not merely a varied totality laid out in the series of views of it proper to the epic manner; they are, while no doubt remaining also essentially vital and individual, still only the one power of the particular character in question, the force in which such a character, in virtue of its essential personality, has made itself inseparably coalesce with some particular aspect of the capital and substantive life-content we have indicated above, and deliberately commits himself to that. It is at some such elevation, where the mere accidents of unmediated[25] individuality vanish altogether, that we find the tragic heroes of dramatic art, whether they be the living representatives of such spheres of concrete life or in any other way already so derive their greatness and stability from their own free self-reliance that they stand forth as works of sculpture, and as such interpret, too, under this aspect the essentially more abstract statues and figures of gods, as also the lofty tragic characters of the Greeks more completely than is possible for any other kind of elucidation or commentary.

Broadly speaking, we may, therefore, affirm that the true theme of primitive tragedy is the godlike.[26] But by godlike we do not mean the Divine, as implied in the content of the religious consciousness simply as such, but rather as it enters into the world, into individual action, and enters in such a way that it does not forfeit its substantive character under this mode of realization, nor find itself converted into the contradiction of its own substance.[27] In this form the spiritual substance of volition and accomplishment is ethical life.[28] For what is ethical, if we grasp it, in its direct consistency—that is to say, not exclusively from the

382

standpoint of personal reflection as formal morality—is the divine in its secular or world realization, the substantive as such, the particular no less than the essential features of which supply the changing content of truly human actions, and in such action itself render this their essence explicit and actual.

(ββ) These ethical forces, as also the characters of the action, are *distinctively defined* in respect to their content and their individual personality, in virtue of the principle of differentiation to which everything is subject, which forms part of the objective world of things. If, then, these particular forces, in the way presupposed by dramatic poetry, are attached to the external expression of human activity, and are realized as the determinate aim of a human pathos which passes into action, their concordancy is cancelled, and they are asserted *in contrast* to each other in interchangeable succession. Individual action will then, under given conditions, realize an object or character, which, under such a presupposed state, inevitably stimulates the presence of a pathos[29] opposed to itself, because it occupies a position of unique isolation in virtue of its independently fixed definition, and, by doing so, brings in its train unavoidable conflicts. Primitive tragedy, then, consists in this, that within a collision of this kind both sides of the contradiction, if taken by themselves, are *justified*; yet, from a further point of view, they tend to carry into effect the true and positive content of their end and specific characterization merely as the negation and *violation* of the other equally legitimate power, and consequently in their ethical purport and relatively to this so far fall under *condemnation*.

I have already adverted to the general ground of the necessity of this conflict. The substance of ethical condition is, when viewed as concrete unity, a totality of *different* relations and forces, which, however, only under the inactive condition of the gods in their blessedness achieve the works of the Spirit in enjoyment of an undisturbed life. In contrast to this, however, there is no less certainly implied in the notion of this totality itself an impulse to move from its, in the first instance, still abstract ideality, and transplant itself in the real actuality of the phenomenal world. On account of the nature of this primitive obsession, [30] it comes about that mere difference, if conceived on the basis of definite conditions of individual personalities, must inevitably associate with contradiction and collision. Only such a view can pretend to deal seriously with those gods which, though they endure in their tranquil repose and unity in the Olympus and heaven of imagination and religious conception, yet, in so far as they are actual,[31] viewed at least as the energic in the definite pathos of a human personality, participate in concrete life, all other claims notwithstanding, and, in virtue of their specific singularity and their mutual opposition, render both blame and wrong inevitable.

(γγ) As a result of this, however, an unmediated contradiction is posited, which no doubt may assert itself in the Real, but, for all that, is unable to maintain itself as that which is wholly substantive and verily real therein; which rather discovers, and only discovers, its essential justification in the fact that it is able to *annul* itself as such contradiction. In other words, whatever may be the claim of the tragic final purpose and personality, whatever may be the necessity of the tragic collision, it is, as a consequence of our present view, no less a claim that is asserted—this is our *third* and last point—by the tragic resolution of this division. It is through *this* latter result that Eternal Justice is operative in such aims and individuals under a mode whereby it restores the ethical substance and unity in and along with

384

the downfall of the individuality which disturbs its repose. For, despite the fact that individual characters propose that which is itself essentially valid, yet they are only able to carry it out under the tragic demand in a manner that implies contradiction and with a onesidedness which is injurious. What, however, is substantive in truth, and the function of which is to secure realization, is not the battle of particular unities, however much such a conflict is essentially involved in the notion of a real world and human action; rather it is the reconciliation in which definite ends and individuals unite in harmonious action without mutual violation and contradiction. That which is abrogated in the tragic issue is merely the *one-sided* particularity which was unable to accommodate itself to this harmony, and consequently in the tragic course of its action, through inability to disengage itself from itself and its designs, either is committed in its entire totality to destruction or at least finds itself compelled to fall back upon a state of resignation in the execution of its aim in so far as it can carry this out. We are reminded of the famous dictum of Aristotle that the true effect of tragedy is to excite and purify *fear* and *pity*. By this statement Aristotle did not mean merely the concordant or discordant feeling with anybody's private experience, a feeling simply of pleasure or the reverse, an attraction or a repulsion, that most superficial of all psychological states, which only in recent times theorists have sought to identify with the principle of assent or dissent as ordinarily expressed. For in a work of art the matter of exclusive importance should be the display of that which is conformable with the reason and truth of Spirit; and to discover the principle of this we have to direct our attention to wholly different points of view. And consequently we are not justified in restricting the application of this dictum of Aristotle merely to the emotion of fear and pity, but should relate it to the principle of the *content* the appropriately artistic display of which ought to purify such feelings. Man may, on the one hand, entertain fear when confronted with that which is outside him and finite; but he may likewise shrink before the power of that which is the essential and absolute subsistency of social phenomena.[32] That which mankind has therefore in truth to fear is not the external power and its oppression, but the ethical might which is self-defined in its own free rationality, and partakes further of the eternal and inviolable, the power a man summons against his own being when he turns his back upon it. And just as fear may have two objectives, so also too compassion. The first is just the ordinary sensibility —in other words, a sympathy with the misfortunes and sufferings of another, and one which is experienced as something finite and negative. Your countrified cousin is ready enough with compassion of this order. The man of nobility and greatness, however, has no wish to be smothered with this sort of pity. For just to the extent that it is merely the nugatory aspect, the negative of misfortune which is asserted, a real depreciation of misfortune is implied. True sympathy, on the contrary, is an accordant feeling with the ethical claim at the same time associated with the sufferer—that is, with what is necessarily implied in his condition as affirmative and substantive. Such a pity as this is not, of course, excited by ragamuffins and vagabonds. If the tragic character, therefore, just as he aroused our fear when contemplating the might of violated morality, is to awake a tragic sympathy in his misfortune, he must himself essentially possess real capacity and downright character. It is only that which has a genuine content which strikes the heart of a man of noble feeling, and rings through its depths. Consequently we ought by no means to identify our interest in the tragic *dénouement* with the simple satisfaction that a sad story, a misfortune merely as misfortune, should have a claim upon our sympathy.

Feelings of lament of this type may well enough assail men on occasions of wholly external contingency and related circumstance, to which the individual does not contribute, nor for which he is responsible, such cases as illness, loss of property, death, and the like. The only real and absorbing interest in such cases ought to be an eager desire to afford immediate assistance. If this is impossible, such pictures of lamentation and misery merely rack the feelings. A veritable tragic suffering, on the contrary, is suspended over active characters entirely as the consequence of their own act, which as such not only asserts its claim upon us, but becomes subject to blame through the collision it involves, and in which such individuals identify themselves heart and soul.

Over and above mere fear and tragic sympathy we have therefore the feeling of *reconciliation*, which tragedy is vouched for in virtue of its vision of eternal justice, a justice which exercises a paramount force of absolute constringency on account of the relative claim of all merely contracted aims and passions; and it can do this for the reason that it is unable to tolerate the victorious issue and continuance in the truth of the objective world of such a conflict with and opposition to those ethical powers which are fundamentally and essentially concordant.[33] Inasmuch as then, in conformity with this principle, all that pertains to tragedy pre-eminently rests upon the contemplation of such a conflict and its resolution, dramatic poetry is—and its entire mode of presentation offers a proof of the fact— alone able to make and completely adapt its form throughout its entire course and compass to the principle of the art product. And this is the reason why I have only now found occasion to discuss the tragic mode of presentation, although it extends an effective force, if no doubt one of subordinate degree, in many ways over the other arts.

(β) In tragedy then that which is eternally substantive is triumphantly vindicated under the mode of reconciliation. It simply removes from the contentions of personality the false one-sidedness, and exhibits instead that which is the object of its volition, namely, positive reality, no longer under an asserted mediation of opposed factors, but as the real support of consistency.[34] And in contrast to this in *comedy* it is the purely *personal experience*, which retains the mastery in its character of infinite self-assuredness.[35] And it is only these two fundamental aspects of human action which occupy a position of contrast in the classification of dramatic poetry into its several types. In tragedy individuals are thrown into confusion in virtue of the abstract nature of their sterling volition and character, or they are forced to accept that with resignation, to which they have been themselves essentially opposed. In comedy we have a vision of the victory of the intrinsically assured stability of the wholly personal soul-life, the laughter of which resolves everything through the medium and into the medium of such life.

($\alpha\alpha$) The general basis of comedy is therefore a world in which man has made himself, in his conscious activity, complete master of all that otherwise passes as the essential content of his knowledge and achievement; a world whose ends are consequently thrown awry on of their own lack of substance. A democratic folk, with egotistic citizens, litigious, frivolous, conceited, without faith or knowledge, always intent on gossip, boasting and vanity—such a folk is past praying for; it can only dissolve in its folly. But it would be a mistake to think that any action that is without genuine content is therefore comic because it is void of substance. People only too often in this respect confound the merely *ridimlous* with the true comic. Every contrast

388

between what is essential and its appearance, the object and its instrument, may be ridiculous, a contradiction in virtue of which the appearance is absolutely cancelled, and the end is stultified in its realization. A profounder significance is, however, implied in the comic. There is, for instance, nothing comic in human crime. The satire affords a proof of this, to the point of extreme aridity, no matter how emphatic may be the colours in which it depicts the condition of the actual world in its contrast to all that the man of virtue ought to be. There is nothing in mere folly, stupidity, or nonsense, which in itself necessarily partakes of the comic, though we all of us are ready enough to laugh at it. And as a rule it is extraordinary what a variety of wholly different things excite human laughter. Matters of the dullest description and in the worst possible taste will move men in this way; and their laughter may be excited quite as much by things of the profoundest importance, if only they happen to notice some entirely unimportant feature, which may conflict with habit and ordinary experience. Laughter is consequently little more than an expression of self-satisfied shrewdness; a sign that they have sufficient wit to recognize such a contrast and are aware of the fact. In the same way we have the laughter of the scoffer, the scornful and desperation itself. What on the other hand is inseparable from the comic is an infinite geniality and confidence[36] capable of rising superior to its own contradiction, and experiencing therein no taint of bitterness or sense of misfortune whatever. It is the happy frame of mind, a hale condition of soul, which, fully aware of itself, can suffer the dissolution of its aims and realization. The unexpansive type of intelligence is on the contrary least master of itself where it is in its behaviour most laughable to others.

(ββ) In considering with more detail the kind of content

389

which characterizes and educes the object of comic action, I propose to limit myself to the following points of general interest.

On the *one* hand there are human ends and characters essentially devoid of substantive content and contradictory. They are therefore unable to achieve the former or give effect to the latter. Avarice, for example, not only in reference to its aim, but also in respect to the petty means which it employs, is clearly from the first and fundamentally a vain shadow. It accepts what is the dead abstraction of wealth, money simply as such, as the *summum bonum*, the reality beyond which it refuses to budge; and it endeavours to master this frigid means of enjoyment by denying itself every other concrete satisfaction, despite the fact too that, in the impotency of its end no less than the means of its achievement, it is helpless when confronted with cunning and treachery, and the like. In such a case then, if anyone identifies *seriously* his personal life with a content so essentially false, to the extent of a man confining the embrace of his soul-life to that exclusively, and in the result, if the same is swept away as his foot-hold, the more he strives to retain that former foot-hold, the more the life collapses in unhappiness—in such a picture as this what is most vital to the comic situation fails, as it does in every case where the predominant factors are simply on the one side the painfulness of the actual conditions, and on the other scorn and pleasure in such misfortune. There is therefore more of the true comic in the case where, it is true, aims intrinsically mean and empty would like to be achieved with an appearance of earnest solemnity and every kind of preparation, but where the individual himself, when he falls short of this, does not experience any real loss because he is conscious that what he strove after was really of no great importance, and is therefore able to rise superior with spontaneous amusement above the failure.

A situation which is the reverse of this occurs where people vaguely grasp at aims and a personal impression of real substance, but in their own individuality, as instruments to achieve this, are in absolute conflict with such a result. In such a case what substance there is only exists in the individual's imagination, becomes a mere appearance to himself or others, which no doubt offers the show and virtue of what is thus of material import, but for this very reason involves end and personality, action and character in a contradiction, by reason of which the attainment of the imaged end or characterization is itself rendered impossible. An example of this is the "Ecclesiazusae" of Aristophanes, where the women who seek to advise and found a new political constitution, retain all the temperament and passions of women as before.

We may add to the above two divisions of classification, as a distinct basis for yet *another*, the use made of external accident, by means of the varied and extraordinary development of which situations are placed before us in which the objects desired and their achievement, the personal character and its external conditions are thrown into a comic contrast, and lead to an equally comic resolution.

($\gamma\gamma$) But inasmuch as the comic element wholly and from the first depends upon contradictory contrasts, not only of ends themselves on their own account, but also of their content as opposed to the contingency of the personal life and external condition, the action of comedy requires a *resolution* with even more stringency than the tragic drama. In other words, in the action of comedy the contradiction between that which is essentially true and its specific realization is more fundamentally asserted.

That which, however, is abrogated in this resolution is not

by any means either the *substantive* being or the *personal* life as such.

And the reason of this is that comedy too, viewed as genuine art, has not the task set before it to display through its presentation what is essentially rational as that which is intrinsically perverse and comes to naught, but on the contrary as that which neither bestows the victory, nor ultimately allows any standing ground to folly and absurdity, that is to say the false contradictions and oppositions which also form part of reality. The masculine art of Aristophanes, for instance, does not turn into ridicule what is truly of ethical significance in the social life of Athens, namely genuine philosophy, true religious faith, but rather the spurious growth of the democracy, in which the ancient faith and the former morality have disappeared, such as the sophistry, the whining and querulousness of tragedy, the inconstant gossip, the love of litigation and so forth; in other words, it is those elements directly opposed to a genuine condition of political life, religion and art, which he places before us in their suicidal folly. Only in more modern times do we find in such a writer as Kotzebue the baseness possible which throws over moral excellence, and spares and strives to maintain that which only exists under a condition of sufferance. To as little extent, however, ought the individual's private life suffer substantial injury in comedy. Or to put it otherwise, if it is merely the appearance and imagined presence of what is substantive, or if it is the essentially perverse and petty which is asserted, yet in the essential self stability of individual character the more exalted principle remains, which in its freedom reaches over and beyond the overthrow of all that such finite life comprises, and continues itself in its character of self-security and self-blessedness. This subjective life that we above all identify with comic personality has thus become master of all the phenomenal presence of the real. The mode of actual appearance adequate to what is, so to speak, substantive, has vanished out of it; and, if what is essentially without fundamental subsistence comes to naught with its mere pretence of being that which it is not, the individual asserts himself as master over such a dissolution, and remains at bottom unbroken and in good heart to the end.[37]

(γ) Midway between tragedy and comedy we have furthermore a *third* fundamental type of dramatic poetry, which is, however, of less distinctive importance, despite the fact that in it the essential difference between what is tragic and comic makes an effort to construct a bridge of mediation, or at least to effect some coalescence of both sides in a concrete whole without leaving either the one or the other in opposed isolation.

(αα) To this class we may, for example, refer the *Satyric* drama of the ancients, in which the principal action itself at least remains of a serious if not wholly tragic type, while the chorus of its Satyrs is in contrast to this treated in the comic manner. We may also include in such a class the tragic-comedy. Plautus gives an example of this in his "Amphitryo," and indeed in the prologue, through verses given to Mercury, asserts this fact; the declamation runs as follows:

> Quid contraxistis frontem? Quia Tragoediam
> Dini futuram hanc? Deus sum: commutavero
> Eamdem hanc, si voltis: faciam, ex Tragoedia
> Comoedia ut sit, omnibus eisdem versibus.
> Faciam ut conmista sit Tragicocomoedia.

He offers us as a reason for this intermixture the fact, that while gods and kings are represented among the *dramatis personae*, we have also in comic contrast to this the figure of the slave Sofia. With yet more frequency in modern dramatic poetry we have the interplay of tragic and comic situation; and this is naturally so, because in modern compositions the principle of an intimate personal life has its place too in tragedy, the principle which is asserted by comedy in all its freedom, and from the first has been predominant, forcing as it does into the background the substantive character of the content in which the ethical forces, I have referred to previously, are paramount.

(ββ) The profounder mediation, however, of tragic and comic composition in a new whole does not consist in the juxtaposition or alteration of these contradictory points of view, but in a mutual accommodation, which blunts the force of such opposition. The element of subjectivity, instead of being exercised with all the perversity of the comic drama, is steeped in the seriousness of genuine social conditions and substantial characters, while the tragic steadfastness of volition and the depth of collisions is so far weakened and reduced that it becomes compatible with a reconciliation of interests and a harmonious union of ends and individuals. It is under such a mode of conception that in particular the modern play and drama arise. The profound aspect of this principle, in this view of the playwright, consists in the fact that, despite the differences and conflicts of interests, passions and characters, an essentially harmonious reality none the less results from human action. Even the ancient world possesses tragedies, which accept an issue of this character. Individuals are not sacrificed, but maintained without serious catastrophe. In the "Eumenides" of Æschylus, for example, both parties there brought to judgment before the Areopagus, namely Apollo and the avenging Furies, have their claims to honorable consideration vindicated. Also in the "Philoctetes" the conflict between Neoptolemos and Philoctetes is disposed of through the divine interposition of Hercules and the advice he gives. They depart reconciled for Troy. In this case, however, the accommodation is due to a *deus ex machinâ* and the actual source of such is not traceable to the personal attitude of the parties themselves. In the modern play, however, it is the individual characters alone who find themselves induced by the course of their own action to such an abandonment of the strife, and to a reciprocal reconciliation of their aims and personalities. From this point of view the "Iphigeneia" of Goethe is a genuine model of a play of this kind, and it is more so than his "Tasso," in which in the first place the reconciliation with Antonio is rather an affair of temperament and personal acknowledgment that Antonio possesses the genuine knowledge of life, which is absent from the character of Tasso, and along with this that the claim of ideal life, which Tasso had rigidly adhered to in its conflict with actual conditions, adaptability and grace of manners, retains its force throughout with an audience merely in an ideal sense, and relatively to actual conditions at most asserts itself as an excuse for the poet and a general sympathy for his position.

($\gamma\gamma$) As a rule, however, the boundary lines of their intermediate type fluctuate more than is the case with tragedy or comedy. It is also exposed to a further danger of breaking away from the true dramatic type, or ceasing to be genuine poetry. In other words, owing to the fact that the opposing factors, which have to secure a peaceful conclusion from out of their own division, are from the start not antithetical to one another with the emphasis asserted by tragedy; the poet is for this reason compelled to devote the full strength of his presentation to the psychological analysis of character, and to make the course of the situations a mere instrument of such characterization. Or, as an alternative, he admits a too extensive field for the display of the material aspect of historical or ethical conditions; and, under the pressure of such material, he tends to restrict his effort to keep the attention alive to the interest of the series of events evolved alone. To this class of composition we may assign a host of our more recent theatrical pieces, which rather aim at theatrical effect than claim to be poetry. They do not so much seek to affect us as genuine poetical productions as to reach our emotions generally as men and women; or they aim on the one hand simply at recreation, and on the other at the moral education of public taste; but while doing so they are almost equally concerned to provide ample opportunity to the actor for the display of his trained art and virtuosity in the most brilliant manner.

(b) The Difference between Ancient and Modern Dramatic Poetry

The same principle which offered us a basis for the classification of dramatic art into tragedy and comedy also will give us the essential points of arrest in the history of their development. The progress we find in this course of evolution can only appear after we have placed such particular phases in the process side by side for comparison and analysis. They subsist, in short, in the notion of dramatic action, with the result that on the one hand the entire composition and its theatrical execution emphasizes what is *substantive* in the ends, conflicts, and characters, and on the other that the *personal* factor of conscious and individual life constitutes the focal centre throughout.

(a) With regard to such an inquiry we may at once in the present work, which does not attempt to include an exhaustive history of art, leave out altogether those origins of dramatic art which we find among Oriental peoples. Despite the considerable progress made by Eastern poetry in the epic and certain types of lyrical composition the entire world-outlook of such peoples nevertheless from the first excludes an artistic development favourable to dramatic art. And the reason is that to genuine *tragic* action it is essential that the principle of *individual* freedom and independence, or at least that of self-determination, the will to find in the self the free cause and source of the personal act and its consequences, should already have been aroused; and we may observe that to a still more emphatic degree is this free claim of the personal life and its self-recognized *imperium* a necessary condition to the appearance of comedy. In the East we find in neither case such a condition satisfied. In particular remoteness from any and every attempt at real dramatic self-expression is that imposing sublimity of Mohammedan poetry, although from a certain point of view it is capable with real power of vindicating the claim of individual independence. But it necessarily fails, because it is an equally essential assumption of it that the One substantive Power overrules every created being and determines his irreversible destiny, and with all the more irresistible fatality in proportion as such a spirit is asserted. The justification of a particular content of individual action and of a personal life which explores its own most intimate substance, in the sense that dramatic art presupposes, is here impossible; indeed it is precisely in Mohammedanism that the subjugation of the individual self to the will of God is the more abstract in proportion as the One predominant Power, who rules the universe, is more abstractly conceived in his universality, and in the last instance will not tolerate one shred of particularity to remain. We consequently only find origins of dramatic composition among the Chinese and Hindoos. But here, too, so far as our present scanty evidence carries us, these do not so much amount to the execution of any free and individual action; they merely reflect the animated life of events and emotions under the mode of definite situations, which are displayed in their course as they actually happen.

(β) The true beginning of dramatic poetry we have consequently to seek among the Hellenes, with whom for the first time and in every respect the principle of free individuality renders the perfect elaboration of the classic type of art possible. Compatibly with this type of art, however, and in its relation to human action, individuality is only so far asserted as it directly demands the free animation of the essential content of human aims. That which pre-eminently is of valid force in ancient drama, therefore, whether it be tragedy or comedy, is the universal and essential content of the end, which individuals seek to achieve. In tragedy this is the ethical claim of human consciousness in view of the particular action in question, the vindication of the act on its own account. And in the old comedy, too, it is in the same way at least the general public interests which are emphasized, whether it be in statesmen and the mode in which they direct the State, questions of peace or war, the general public and its moral conditions, or the condition of philosophy and its decline. And it is owing to this that here neither the varied exposition of personal soul-life and exceptional character, nor the equally exceptional plot and intrigue can obtain the fullest play, nor does the main interest revolve so much around the fate of individuals. In the place of this interest for such particular aspects of the drama above all else sympathy is evoked and claimed for the simple conflict and issue of the essential powers of life, and for the godlike manifestations of the human heart,[38] as distinctive representatives of which the heroes of tragedy are set before us in much the same way as that in which the figures of comedy make visible the general perversity of mankind, to the expression of which, in the reality of the actual present, even the fundamental institutions of public life have been corrupted.

399

(γ) In *modern* romantic poetry, on the contrary, it is the individual passion, the satisfaction of which can only be relative to a wholly personal end, generally speaking the destiny of some particular person or character placed under exceptional circumstances, which forms the subject-matter of all importance.

From such a point of view the poetic interest consists in that greatness of characters, which, in virtue of their imaginative power or their disposition and talents, display a spiritual[39] elevation over their situations and actions no less than over the entire wealth of their soul-life, and show it as the real substance of political forces, though often, too, these may be obstructed and, indeed, annihilated in the stress of particular circumstances and the current of events; and we may add that in the greatness of such natures it is not infrequent to find that a power of recovery[40] is further contained. With regard to the particular content of the action in this style of composition it is not therefore the ethical vindication and necessity, but rather the isolated individual and his conditions to which our interest is directed. From a standpoint such as this, therefore, a fundamental motive will arise in such qualities as love and ambition; indeed, crime itself is not excluded. But in the latter case we may easily find rocks ahead difficult indeed to clear. For an out and out criminal, and irrevocably so when he is weak and a thoroughly mean scamp, as is the hero in Milliner's drama, "Crime," is something more than a sorry sight. What we require therefore above all in such cases is at least the formal[41] greatness of character and power of the personal life which is able to ride out everything that negates it, and which, without denial of its acts or, indeed, without being materially discomposed by them, is capable of accepting their consequences. And on the other side we find that those substantive ends, such as patriotism, family devotion, loyalty, and the rest, are by no means to be excluded, although for the individual persons concerned the main question of importance is not so much the substantive force as their own individuality. But in such cases as a rule they rather form the particular ground upon which such persons, viewed in the light of their private character, take their stand and engage in conflict, rather than have supplied what we may regard as the real and ultimate content of their volition and action.

And further, in conjunction with a personal self-assertion of this type we may have presented the full extension of individual idiosyncrasy, not merely in respect to the soul-life simply, but also in relation to external circumstances and conditions, within which the action proceeds. And it is owing to this that in distinctive form the simple conflicts which characterize more classical dramatic composition, we now meet with the variety and exuberance of the characters dramatized, the unforeseen surprises of the ever new and complicated developments of plot, the maze of intrigue, the contingency of events, and, in a word, all those aspects of the modern drama which claim our attention, and the unfettered appearance of which, as opposed to the overwhelming emphasis attached to what is essentially most fundamental in the content, accentuates the type of romantic art in its distinction from the classic type.

But again, even in the cases above indicated, and despite all this apparently untrammelled particularity, the whole ought to continue to be both dramatic and poetical. In other words, on the one hand, the harshness of the collision, which has to be fought through, ought to be visibly obliterated, and on the other, pre-eminently in tragedy, the predominant presence of a more exalted order of the world, whether we adopt the conception of Providence or Fatality, ought to plainly discover itself in and through the course and issue of the action.

(c) The Concrete Development of Dramatic Poetry and its Types

Within the essential distinctions of conception and poetical achievement which we have just considered the different types of dramatic art assert themselves, and, for the first time in such association, and in so far as their development follows either one or the other direction, attain a really genuine completeness. We have, therefore, in concluding the present work, still to concentrate our inquiry upon the concrete mode under which they receive such a configuration.

(*α*) Excluding as we shall do for the reasons already given from our subject-matter the origins of such poetry in Oriental literature, the material of first and fundamental importance which engages our attention, as the most valuable phase of genuine tragedy no less than comedy, is the dramatic poetry of the *Greeks*. In other words, in it for the first time we find the human consciousness is illuminated with that which in its general terms the tragic and comic situation essentially is; and after that these opposed types of dramatic outlook upon human action have been securely and beyond all confusion separated from each other, we mark first in order tragedy, and after that comedy, rise in organic development to the height of their achievement. Of such a successful result the dramatic art of Rome merely returns a considerably attenuated reflection, which does not indeed reach the point secured by the similar effort of Roman literature in epic and lyrical composition. In my examination of the material thus offered my object will be merely to accentuate what is most important, and I shall therefore limit my survey to the tragic point of view of Æschylus and Sophocles, and to Aristophanes so far as comedy is concerned.

402

($\alpha\alpha$) Taking, then, tragedy first, I have already stated that the fundamental type which determines its entire organization and structure is to be sought for in the emphasis attached to the substantive constitution of final ends and their content, as also of the individuals dramatized and their conflict and destiny.

In the tragic drama we are now considering, the general basis or background for tragic action is supplied, as was also the case in the Epos, by that world-condition which I have already indicated as the *heroic*. For only in heroic times, when the universal ethical forces have neither acquired the independent stability of definite political legislation or moral commands and obligations, can they be presented in their primitive jucundity as gods, who are either opposed to each other in their personal activities, or themselves appear as the animated content of a free and human individuality. If, however, what is intrinsically ethical is to appear throughout as the substantive foundation, the universal ground, shall we say, from which the growth of personal action arrests our attention with equal force in its disunion, and is no less brought back again from such divided movement into unity, we shall find that there are two distinct modes under which the ethical content of human action is asserted.

First we have the simple consciousness, which, in so far as it wills its substantive content[42] wholly as the unbroken identity of its particular aspects, remains in undisturbed, uncriticized, and neutral tranquillity on its own account and as related to others. This undivided and, we may add, purely formal[43] state of mind in its veneration, its faith, and its happiness, however, is incapable of attaching itself to any definite action; it has a sort of dread before the disunion which is implied in such, although it does, while remaining itself incapable of action, esteem at the same time that

403

spiritual courage which asserts itself resolutely and actively in a self-proposed object, as of nobler worth, yet is aware of its inability to undertake such enterprize, and consequently considers that it can do nothing further for such active personalities, whom it respects so highly, than contrast with the energy of their decision and conflict the object of its own wisdom, in other words, the substantive ideality of the ethical Powers.

The *second* mode under which this ethical content is asserted is that of the individual pathos,[44] which urges the active characters to their moral self-vindication into the opposition they occupy relatively to others, and brings them thereby into conflict. The individuals subject to this pathos are neither what, in the modern use of the term, we describe as characters, nor are they mere abstractions. They are rather placed in the vital midway sphere between both, standing there as figures of real stability, which are simply that which they are, without aught of collision in themselves, without any fluctuating recognition of some other pathos, and in so far—in this respect a contrast to our modern irony— elevated, absolutely determinate characters, whose definition, however, discovers its content and basis in a particular ethical power. Forasmuch as, then, the tragic situation first appears in the *antagonism* of individuals who are thus empowered to act, the same can only assert itself in the field of actual human life. It results from the specific character of this alone that a particular quality so affects the substantive content of a given individual, that the latter identifies himself with his entire interest and being in such a content, and penetrates it throughout with the glow of passion. In the blessed gods, however, it is the divine Nature, in its indifference, which is what is essential; in contrast to which we have the contradiction, which in the last instance is not treated seriously, rather is one which, as

I have already noticed when discussing the Homeric Epos, becomes eventually a self-resolving irony. These two modes or aspects—of which the one is as important for the whole as the other—namely, the unsevered consciousness of the godlike, and the combating human action, asserted, however, in godlike power and deed, which determines and executes the ethical purpose—supply the two fundamental elements, the mediation of which is displayed by Greek tragedy in its artistic compositions under the form of *chorus* and *heroic figures* respectively.

In modern times, considerable discussion has been raised over the significance of the Greek chorus, and the question has been raised incidentally whether it can or ought to be introduced into modern tragedy. In fact, the need of some such substantial foundation has been experienced; but critics have found it difficult to prescribe the precise manner in which effect should be given to such a change, because they failed to grasp with sufficient penetration the nature of that in which true tragedy consists and the necessity of the chorus as an essential constituent of all that Greek tragedy implies. Critics have, no doubt, recognized the nature of the chorus to the extent of maintaining that in it we find an attitude of tranquil meditation over the whole, whereas the characters of the action remain within the limits of their particular objects and situations, and, in short, receive in the chorus and its observations a standard of valuation of their characters and actions in much the same way as the public discovers in it, and within the drama itself, an objective representative of its own judgment upon all that is thus represented. In this view we have to this extent the fact rightly conceived, that the chorus is, in truth, there as a substantive and more enlightened intelligence, which warns us from irrelevant oppositions, and reflects upon the genuine issue. But, granting this to be so, it is by no means a wholly disinterested person, at leisure to entertain such thoughts and ethical judgments as it likes as are the spectators, which, uninteresting and tedious on its own account, could only be attached for the sake of such reflections. The chorus is the actual substance of the heroic life and action itself: it is, as contrasted with the particular heroes, the common folk regarded as the fruitful heritage, out of which individuals, much as flowers and towering trees from their native soil, grow and whereby they are conditioned in this life. Consequently, the chorus is peculiarly fitted to a view of life in which the obligations of State legislation and settled religious dogmas do not, as yet, act as a restrictive force in ethical and social development, but where morality only exists in its primitive form of directly animated human life, and it is merely the equilibrium of unmoved life which remains assured in its stability against the fearful collisions which the antagonistic energies of individual action produces. We are made aware of the fact that an assured asylum of this kind is also a part of our actual existence by the presence of the chorus. It does not, therefore, practically co-operate with the action; it executes by its action no right as against the contending heroes; it merely expresses its judgment as a matter of opinion; it warns, commiserates, or appeals to the divine law, and the ideal forces imminent in the soul, which the imagination grasps in external guise as the sphere of the gods that rule. In this self-expression it is, as we have already seen, lyrical; for it does not act and there are no events for it to narrate in epical form. The content, however, retains at the same time the epic character of substantive universality; and its lyric movement is of such a nature that it can, and in this respect in contrast to the form of the genuine ode, approach at times that of the paean and the dithyramb. We must lay emphatic stress upon this position of the chorus in Greek tragedy. Just as the theatre itself possesses its external ground, its scene and environment, so, too, the chorus, that is the general community, is the spiritual scene; and we may compare it to the architectural temple which surrounds the image of the god, which resembles the heroes in the action. Among ourselves, statues are placed under the open sky without such a background, which also modern tragedy does not require, for the reason that its actions do not depend on this substantive basis, but on the personal volition and personality, no less than the apparently external contingency of events and circumstances.

In this respect it is an entirely false view which regards the chorus as an accidental piece of residuary baggage, a mere remnant from the origins of Greek drama. Of course, it is incontestable that its source is to be traced to the circumstance that, in the festivals of Bacchus, so far as the artistic aspect is concerned, the choral song was of most importance until the introduction and interruption of its course by one reciter, whose relation finally was transformed into and exalted by the real figures of dramatic action. In the blossoming season of tragedy, however, the chorus was not by any means merely retained in honour of this particular phase of the festival and ritual of the god Bacchus; rather it became continuously more elaborate in its beauty and harmonious measures by reason of the fact that its association with the dramatic action is essential and, indeed, so indispensable to it that the decline of tragedy is intimately connected with the degeneration of the choruses, which no longer remain an integral member of the whole, but are degraded to a mere embellishment. In contrast to this, in romantic tragedy, the chorus is neither intrinsically appropriate nor does it appear to have originated from choric songs. On the contrary, the content is here of a type which defeats from the first any attempt to introduce choruses as understood by Greek dramatists. For, even if we go back to the most primitive of those so-called mysteries, morality plays and farces of a similar character, from which the romantic drama issued, we find that these present no action in that original Greek sense of the term, no outbreak, that is, of opposing forces from the undivided consciousness of life and the god-like. To as little extent is the chorus adapted to the conditions of chivalry and the dominion of kings, in so far as, in such cases, the attitude of the folk is one of mere obedience, or it is itself a party, involved together with the interest of its fortune or misfortune in the course of the action. And in general the chorus entirely fails to secure its true position where the main subject-matter consists of particular passions, ends, and characters, or any considerable opportunity is admitted to intrigue.

In contrast to the chorus, the *second* fundamental feature of dramatic composition is that of the *individuals* who act in *conflict* with each other. In Greek tragedy it is not at all the bad will, crime, worthlessness, or mere misfortune, stupidity, and the like, which act as an incentive to such collisions, but rather, as I have frequently urged, the ethical right to a definite course of action.[45] Abstract evil neither possesses truth in itself, nor does it arouse interest. At the same time, when we attribute ethical traits of characterization to the individuals of the action, these ought not to appear merely as a matter of opinion. It is rather implied in their right or claim that they are actually there as essential on their own account. The hazards of crime, such as are present in modern drama—the useless, or quite as much the so-called noble criminal, with his empty talk about fate, we meet with in the tragedy of ancient literature, rarely, if at all, and for the good reason that the decision and deed depends on the wholly personal aspect of interest and character, upon lust for power, love, honour, or other similar passions, whose justification has its roots exclusively in the particular inclination and individuality. A resolve of this character, whose claim is based upon the content of its object, which it carries into execution in one restricted direction of particularization, violates, under certain circumstances, which are already essentially implied in the actual possibility of conflicts, a further and equally ethical sphere of human volition, which the character thus confronted adheres to, and, by his thus stimulated action, enforces, so that in this way the collision of powers and individuals equally entitled to the ethical claim is completely set up in its movement.

The sphere of this content,[46] although capable of great variety of detail, is not in its essential features very extensive. The principal source of opposition, which Sophocles in particular, in this respect following the lead of Æschylus, has accepted and worked out in the finest way, is that of the *body politic*, the opposition, that is, between ethical life in its social universality and the family as the natural ground of moral relations. These are the purest forces of tragic representation. It is, in short, the harmony of these spheres and the concordant action within the bounds of their realized content, which constitute the perfected reality of the moral life. In this respect I need only recall to recollection the "Seven before Thebes" of Æschylus and, as a yet stronger illustration, the "Antigone" of Sophocles. Antigone reverences the ties of blood-relationship, the gods of the nether world. Creon alone recognizes Zeus, the paramount Power of public life and the commonwealth. We come across a similar conflict in the "Iphigeneia in Aulis," as also in the "Agamemnon," the "Choephorae," and "Eumenides" of Æschylus, and in the "Electra" of Sophocles. Agamemnon, as king and leader of his army, sacrifices his daughter in the interest of the Greek

409

folk and the Trojan expedition. He shatters thereby the bond of love as between himself and his daughter and wife, which Clytemnestra retains in the depths of a mother's heart, and in revenge prepares an ignominious death for her husband on his return. Orestes, their son, respects his mother, but is bound to represent the right of his father, the king, and strikes dead the mother who bore him.

A content of this type retains its force through all times, and its presentation, despite all difference of nationality, vitally arrests our human and artistic sympathies.

Of a more formal type is that second kind of essential collision, an illustration of which in the tragic story of Œdipus the Greek tragedians especially favoured. Of this Sophocles has left us the most complete example in his "Œdipus Rex," and "Œdipus in Colonos." The problem here is concerned with the claim of alertness in our intelligence, with the nature of the obligation[47] implied in that which a man carries out with a volition fully aware of its acts as contrasted with that which he has done in fact, but unconscious of and with no intention of doing what he has done under the directing providence of the gods. Œdipus slays his father, marries his mother, begets children in this incestuous alliance, and nevertheless is involved in these most terrible of crimes without active participation either in will or knowledge. The point of view of our profounder modern consciousness of right and wrong would be to recognize that crimes of this description, inasmuch as they were neither referable to a personal knowledge or volition, were not deeds for which the true personality of the perpetrator was responsible. The plastic nature of the Greek on the contrary adheres to the bare fact which an individual has achieved, and refuses to face the division implied by the purely ideal attitude of the soul in the self-conscious life on the one hand and the objective significance of the fact accomplished on the other.

For ourselves, to conclude this survey, other collisions, which either in general are related to the universally accepted association of personal action to the Greek conception of Destiny, or in some measure to more exceptional conditions, are comparatively speaking less important.

In all these tragic conflicts, however, we must above all place on one side the false notion of *guilt* or *innocence*. The heroes of tragedy are quite as much under one category as the other. If we accept the idea as valid that a man is guilty only in the case that a choice lay open to him, and he deliberately decided on the course of action which he carried out, then these plastic figures of ancient drama are guiltless. They act in accordance with a specific character, a specific pathos, for the simple reason that they are this character, this pathos. In such a case there is no lack of decision and no choice. The strength of great characters consists precisely in this that they do not choose, but are entirely and absolutely just that which they will and achieve. They are simply themselves, and never anything else, and their greatness consists in that fact. Weakness in action, in other words, wholly consists in the division of the personal self as such from its content, so that character, volition and final purpose do not appear as absolutely one unified growth; and inasmuch as no assured end lives in the soul as the very substance of the particular personality, as the pathos and might of the individual's entire will, he is still able to turn with indecision from this course to that, and his final decision is that of caprice. A wavering attitude of this description is alien to these plastic creations. The bond between the psychological state of mind and the content of the will is for them indissoluble. That which stirs them to action is just in this very pathos which implies an ethical justification and which, even in the pathetic aspects of the dialogue, is not enforced in and through the merely personal rhetoric of the heart and the sophistry of passion, but in the equally masculine and cultivated objective presence, in the profound possibilities, the harmony and vitally plastic beauty of which Sophocles was to a superlative degree master. At the same time, however, such a pathos, with its potential resources of collision, brings in its train deeds that are both injurious and wrongful. They have no desire to avoid the blame that results therefrom. On the contrary, it is their fame to have done what they have done. One can in fact urge nothing more intolerable against a hero of this type than by saying that he has acted innocently. It is a point of honour with such great characters that they are guilty. They have no desire to excite pity or our sensibilities. For it is not the substantive, but rather the wholly personal deepening[48] of the individual character, which stirs our individual pain. These securely strong characters, however, coalesce entirely with their essential pathos, and this indivisible accord inspires wonder, but does not excite heart emotions. The drama of Euripides marks the transition to that.

The final result, then, of the development of tragedy conducts us to this issue and only this, namely, that the twofold vindication of the mutually conflicting aspects are no doubt retained, but the *onesided* mode under which they were maintained is cancelled, and the undisturbed ideal harmony brings back again that condition of the chorus, which attributes without reserve equal honour to all the gods. The true course of dramatic development consists in the annulment of *contradictions* viewed as such, in the reconciliation of the forces of human action, which alternately strive to negate each other in their conflict. Only so far is misfortune and suffering not the final issue, but rather the satisfaction of spirit, as for the first time, in virtue of such a conclusion, the necessity of all that particular individuals experience, is able to appear in complete accord with reason, and our emotional attitude is tranquillized on a true ethical basis, rudely shaken by the calamitous result to the heroes, but reconciled in the substantial facts. And it is only in so far as we retain such a view securely that we shall be in a position to understand ancient tragedy. We have to guard ourselves therefore from concluding that a *dénouement* of this type is merely a moral issue conformably to which evil is punished and virtue rewarded, as indicated by the proverb that "when crime turns to vomit, virtue sits down at table." We have nothing to do here with this wholly personal aspect of a self-reflecting personality and its conception of good and evil, but are concerned with the appearance of the affirmative reconciliation and with the equal validity of both the powers engaged in actual conflict, when the collision actually took place. To as little extent is the necessity of the issue a blind destiny, or in other words a purely irrational, unintelligible fate, identified with the classical world by many; rather it is the rationality of destiny, albeit it does not as yet appear as self-conscious Providence, the divine final end of which in conjunction with the world and individuals appears on its own account and for others, depending as it does on just this fact that the highest Power paramount over particular gods and mankind cannot suffer this, namely, that the forces, which affirm their selfsubsistence in modes that are abstract or incomplete, and thereby overstep the boundary of their warrant, no less than the conflicts which result from them, should retain their self-stability. Fate drives personality back upon its limits, and shatters it, when it has grown overweening. An irrational compulsion, however, an innocence of suffering would rather only excite indignation in the soul of the spectator than ethical tranquillity. From a further point of view, therefore, the reconciliation of *tragedy*

413

is equally distinct from that of the *Epos*. If we look at either Achilles or Odysseus in this respect we observe that both attain their object, and it is right that they do so; but it is not a continuous happiness with which they are favoured; they have on the contrary to taste in its bitterness the feeling of finite condition, and are forced to fight wearily through difficulties, losses and sacrifices. It is in fact a universal demand of truth that in the course of life and all that takes place in the objective world the nugatory character of finite conditions should compel attention. So no doubt the anger of Achilles is reconciled; he obtains from Agamemnon that in respect of which he had suffered the sense of insult; he is revenged upon Hector; the funeral rites of Patroclus are consummated, and the character of Achilles is acknowledged in all its glory. But his wrath and its reconciliation have for all that cost him his dearest friend, the noble Patroclus; and, in order to avenge himself upon Hector for this loss, he finds himself compelled to disengage himself from his anger, to enter once more the battle against the Trojans, and in the very moment when his glory is acknowledged receives the prevision of his early death. In a similar way Odysseus reaches Ithaca at last, the goal of his desire; but he does so alone and in his sleep, having lost all his companions, all the war-booty from Ilium, after long years of endurance and fatigue. In this way both heroes have paid their toll to finite conditions and the claim of nemesis is evidenced in the destruction of Troy and the misfortunes of the Greek heroes. But this nemesis is simply justice as conceived of old, which merely humiliates what is everywhere too exalted, in order to establish once more the abstract balance of fortune by the instrumentality of misfortune, and which merely touches and affects finite existence without further ethical signification. And this is the justice of the Epic in the field of objective fact, the universal reconciliation of what is simply accommodation.

[49] The higher conception of reconciliation in tragedy is on the contrary related to the resolution of specific ethical and substantive facts from their contradiction into their true harmony. The way in which such an accord is established is asserted under very different modes; I propose therefore merely to direct attention to the fundamental features of the actual process herein involved.

Firsts we have particularly to emphasize the fact, that if it is the onesidedness of the pathos which constitutes the real basis of collisions this merely amounts to the statement that it is asserted in the action of life, and therewith has become the unique pathos of a particular individual. If this one-sidedness is to be abrogated then it is this individual which, to the extent that his action is exclusively identified with this isolated pathos, must perforce be stripped and sacrificed. For the individual here is merely this single life, and, if this unity is not secured in its stability on its own account, the individual is shattered.

The most complete form of this development is possible when the individuals engaged in conflict relatively to their concrete or objective life appear in each case essentially involved in one whole, so that they stand fundamentally under the power of that against which they battle, and consequently infringe that, which, conformably to their own essential life, they ought to respect. Antigone, for example, lives under the political authority of Creon; she is herself the daughter of a king and the affianced of Haemon, so that her obedience to the royal prerogative is an obligation. But Creon also, who is on his part father and husband, is under obligation to respect the sacred ties of relationship, and only by breach of this can give an order that is in conflict with such a sense. In consequence of this we find immanent in the life of both that which each respectively combats, and they are seized and broken by that very bond which is rooted in the compass of their own social existence. Antigone is put to death before she can enjoy what she looks forward to as bride, and Creon too is punished in the fatal end of his son and wife, who commit suicide, the former on account of Antigone's death, and the latter owing to Haemon's. Among all the fine creations of the ancient and the modern world—and I am acquainted with pretty nearly everything in such a class, and one ought to know it, and it is quite possible—the "Antigone" of Sophocles is from this point of view in my judgment the most excellent and satisfying work of art.

The tragic issue does not, however, require in every case as a means of removing both over-emphasized aspects and the equal honour which they respectively claim the downfall of the contestant parties. The "Eumenides" does not end, as we all know, with the death of Orestes, or the destruction of the Eumenides, these avenging spirits of matricide and filial affection, these opponents of Apollo, who seeks to protect unimpaired the worth of and reverence for the family chief and king, the god who had prompted Orestes to slay Clytaemnestra, but will have Orestes released from the punishment and honour bestowed on both himself and the Furies. At the same time we cannot fail to see in this adjusted conclusion the nature of the authority which the Greeks attached to their gods when they presented them as mere individuals contending with each other. They appear, in short, to the Athenian of everyday life merely as definite aspects of ethical experience which the principles of morality viewed in their complete and harmonious coherence bind together. The votes of the Areopagus are equal on either side. It is Athene, the goddess, the life of Athens, that is, imagined in its essential unity, who adds the white pebble, who frees Orestes, and at the same time promises altars and a cult to the Eumenides no less than Apollo. As a contrast to this type of objective reconciliation the settlement may be, *secondly*, of a more personal character. In other words, the individual concerned in the action may in the last instance surrender his onesided point of view. In this betrayal by personality of its essential pathos, however, it cannot fail to appear destitute of character; and this contradicts the masculine integrity of such plastic figures. The individual, therefore, can only submit to a higher Power and its counsel or command, to the effect that while on his own account he adheres to such a pathos, the will is nevertheless broken in its bare obstinacy by a god's authority. In such a case the knot is not loosened, but, as in the case of Philoctetes, it is severed by a *deus ex machinâ*.

But as a *further* and final class, and one more beautiful than the above rather external mode of resolution we have the reconciliation more properly of the soul itself, in which respect there is, in virtue of the personal significance, a real approach to our modern point of view. The most perfect example of this in ancient drama is to be found in the ever admirable "Œdipus Coloneus" of Sophocles. The protagonist here has unwittingly slain his father, secured the sceptre of Thebes, and the bridal bed of his own mother. He is not rendered unhappy by these unwitting crimes; but the power of divination he has of old possessed makes him realize, despite himself, the darkness of the experience that confronts him, and he becomes fearfully, if indistinctly, aware of what his position is.[50] In this resolution of the riddle in himself he resembles Adam, losing his happiness when he obtains the knowledge of good and evil. What he then does, the seer, is to blind himself, then abdicate the throne and depart from Thebes, very much as Adam and Eve are driven from Paradise. From henceforward he wanders about a helpless old man. Finally a god calls the terribly afflicted man to himself,[51] the man, that is, who refusing the request of his

417

sons that he should return to Thebes, prefers to associate with the Erinnys; the man, in short, who extinguishes all the disruption in himself and who purifies himself in his own soul. His blind eyes are made clear and bright, his limbs are healed, and become a treasure of the city which received him as a free guest. And this illumination in death is for ourselves no less than for him the more truly visible reconciliation which is worked out both in and for himself as individual man, in and through, that is, his essential character. Critics have endeavoured to discover here the temper of the Christian life; we are told we have here the picture of a sinner, whom God receives into His grace; and the fateful misfortunes which expire in their finite condition, are made good with the seal of blessedness in death. The reconciliation of the Christian religion, however, is an illumination of the soul, which, bathed in the everlasting waters of salvation, is raised above mortal life and its deeds. Here it is the heart itself, for in such a view the spiritual life can effect this, which buries that life and its deed in the grave of the heart itself, counting the recriminations of earthly guilt as part and parcel of its own earthly individuality; and which, in the full assuredness of the eternally pure and spiritual condition of blessedness, holds itself in itself calm and steadfast against such impeachment. The illumination of Œdipus, on the contrary, remains throughout, in consonance with ancient ideas, the restoration of conscious life from the strife of ethical powers and violations to the renewed and harmonious unity of this *ethical content itself.*[52]

There is a further feature in this type of reconciliation, however, and that is the *personal* or ideal nature of the satisfaction. We may take this as a point of transition to the otherwise to be contrasted province of *comedy*.

(*ββ*) That which is comic is, as we have already seen, in

general terms the subjective or personal state, which forces and then dissolves the action which issues from it by its own effect into and in contradiction, remaining throughout and in virtue of this process tranquil in its own self-assurance. Comedy possesses, therefore, for its basis and point of departure that with which it is possible for tragedy to terminate, that is, a soul to the fullest extent and eventually reconciled, a joyous state, which, however much it is instrumental in the marring of its volitional power, and, indeed, in itself comes to grief, by reason of its asserting voluntarily what is in conflict with its aim, does not therefore lose its general equanimity. A personal self-assurance of this character, however is, from a further point of view, only possible in so far as the ends proposed, and withal the characters include nothing that is on its own account essentially substantive; or, if they do possess such an intrinsic worth, it is adopted and carried out intentionally under a mode which is totally opposed to the genuine truth contained, in a form, therefore, that is destitute of such truth, so that in this respect, as in the previous case, it is merely that which is itself essentially of no intrinsic importance, but a matter of indifference which is marred, and the individual remains just as he was and unaffected.

Such a view is, too, in its general lines the conception of the old classic comedy, in so far as tradition reflects it in the plays of Aristophanes. We should, however, be careful to notice the distinction whether the individuals in the play are aware that they are comic, or are so merely from the spectator's point of view. It is only the first class that we can reckon as part of the genuine comedy in which Aristophanes was a master. Conformably to such a type a character is only placed in a ridiculous situation, when we perceive that he himself is not serious in what is actually of such a quality in his purpose and voluntary effort, so that this constituent of either is throughout the means of his own undoing, inasmuch as throughout such a character is unable to enter into any more noble and universally valid interest, which necessarily involves it in a situation of conflict;[53] and, even assuming that he does actually partake of it, merely does so in a way that shows a nature, which, in virtue of its practical existence, has already annihilated that which it appears to strive to bring into operation, so that after all one sees such a coalescence has never been really effected. The comic comes, therefore, rather into play among classes of a lower social order in actual conditions of life, among men who remain much as they are, and neither are able or desire to be anything else; who, while incapable of any genuine pathos, have no doubt whatever as to what they are and do. At the same time the higher nature that is in them is asserted in this that they are not with any seriousness attached to the finite conditions which hem them in, but remain superior to the same and in themselves essentially steadfast and self-reliant against mishap and loss. This absolute freedom of spirit, which brings its own essential comfort from the first in all that a man undertakes, this world of the blitheness of human soul-life is that to which Aristophanes conducts us. Without a reading of him it is hardly possible to imagine what a wealth of exuberance there is in the human heart.

The interests among which this type of comedy moves are not necessarily taken from the opposed spheres of religion, morality, and art. On the contrary the old Greek comedy remains no doubt within the limits of this positive and substantive content of human life; but it is the individual caprice, the vulgar folly and perversity, by reason of which the characters concerned bring to nought activities which in their aim have a finer significance. And in this respect an

420

ample and very pertinent material is supplied Aristophanes partly by Greek gods, and partly by the life of the Athenian people. In other words, the configuration of the divine in human impersonation itself possesses, in its mode of presentation and its particularization, to the extent at least that it is further enforced in opposition to that which is merely one-sided and human, the contradiction that is opposed to the nobility of its significance; it is thus permitted to appear as a purely empty extension of this personal life which is inadequate wholly to express it. More particularly, however, Aristophanes revels in the follies of the common folk, the stupidities of its orators and statesmen, the blockheadedness of war, and is eager, above all, and with all the politeness of his satire and the full weight of his ridicule, but also not without the profoundest meaning, to hand over the new tendencies of the tragedies of Euripides to the laughter of his fellow-citizens. The characters he has imported into the substance of his amazing artistic creations he runs into the mould of fool from the start with a sportive fancy that seems inexhaustible, so that the very idea of a rational result is impossible. He treats all alike, whether it be a Strepsiades, who will join the ranks of philosophers in order to be rid of his debts, or a Socrates, who offers to instruct the aforesaid Strepsiades and his son, or Bacchus, whom he makes descend into the lower world, in order to bring up a genuine tragic poet, and in just the same way Cleon, the women and the Greeks, who would like to pump up the goddess of Peace from the well. The key-note that we find in all these various creations is the imperturbable self-assurance of such characters one and all, which becomes all the more emphatic in proportion as they prove themselves incapable of carrying into effect that which they project. Our fools here are so entirely unembarrassed in their folly, and also the more sensible among them possess such a tincture of that which runs contrary to the very course upon which they are set, that they all, the more sensible with the rest, remain fixed to this personal attitude of prodigious imperturbility, no matter what comes next or where it carries them. It is in fact the blessed laughter of the Olympian gods, with their untroubled equanimity, now at home in the human breast, and prepared for all contingences. And withal we never find Aristophanes merely a cold or evil-disposed mocker. He was a man of the finest education, a most exemplary citizen, to whom the weal of Athens was of really deep importance, and who through thick and thin shows himself to be a true patriot. What therefore is in the fullest sense resolved in his comedies is, as already stated, not the divine and what is of ethical import, but the thoroughgoing upside-down-ness which inflates itself into the semblance of these substantive forces, the particular form and distinctive mode of its manifestation, in which the essential thing or matter is already from the first no longer present, so that it can without restriction be simply handed over to the unconcerned play of unqualified personal caprice. But for the very reason that Aristophanes makes explicit the absolute contradiction between the essential nature of the gods, or that of political and social life, and the personal activities of individual persons or citizens, who ought to endow such substantive form with reality, we find in this very triumph of purely personal self-assertion, despite all the profounder insight which the poet displays, one of the greatest symptoms of the degeneracy of Greece. And it is on account of this that these pictures of a wholly unperturbed sense of "everything coming out right in the end" [54] are as a matter of fact the last important harvest which we have from the poetry created by the exuberant genius, culture, and wit of the Greek nation.

(β) I shall now direct attention to the dramatic art of the modern world, and here, too, I only propose to emphasize the more general and fundamental features which we find of importance, whether dealing with tragedy or the ordinary drama and comedy.

($\alpha\alpha$) Tragedy, in the nobility which distinguishes it in its ancient plastic form, is limited to the partial point of view that for its exclusive and essential basis it only enforces as effective the ethically substantive content and its necessary laws; and, on the other hand, leaves the individual and subjective self-penetration of the dramatic characters essentially unevolved; while comedy on its part, to complete what we may regard as the reversed side of such plastic construction, exhibits to us the personal caprice of soul-life in the unfettered abandonment of its topsy-turvydom and ultimate dissolution.

Modern tragedy accepts in its own province from the first the principle of subjectivity or self-assertion. It makes, therefore, the personal intimacy of character—the character, that is, which is no purely individual and vital embodiment of ethical forces in the classic sense—its peculiar object and content. It, moreover, makes, in a type of concurrence that is adapted to this end, human actions come into collision through the instrumentality of the external accident of circumstances in the way that a contingency of a similar character is also decisive in its effect on the consequence, or appears to be so decisive.

In this connection we would subject to examination the following fundamental points:

Firsts the nature of the varied *ends* which ought to come into the executive process of the action as the content of the characters therein.

Secondly, the nature of the tragic *characters* themselves, as

423

also of the collisions they are compelled to face.

Thirdly, the nature of the final *issue* and tragic reconciliation, as these differ from those of ancient tragedy.

To start with, we may observe that, however much in romantic tragedy the personal aspect of suffering and passions, in the true meaning of such an attitude, is the focal centre, yet, for all that, it is impossible in human activity that the ground basis of definite ends borrowed from the concrete worlds of the family, the State, the Church, and others should be dispensed with. In so far, however, as in the drama under discussion, it is not the substantive content as such in these spheres of life which constitutes the main interest of individuals. Such ends are from a certain point of view particularized in a breadth of extension and variety, as also in exceptional modes of presentment, in which it often happens that what is truly essential is only able to force itself on our attention with attenuated strength. And over and above this fact, these ends receive an entirely altered form. In the province of religion, for example, the content which pre-eminently is asserted is no longer the particular ethical powers exhibited imaginatively under the mode of divine individuals, either in their own person or in the pathos of human heroes. It is the history of Christ, or of saints and the like, which is now set before us. In the political community it is mainly the position of kingship, the power of vassal chiefs, the strife of dynasties, or the particular members of one and the same ruling family which forms the content of the varied picture. Nay, if we take a step further we find as the principal subject-matter questions of civic or private right and other relations of a similar character; and, further, we shall find a similar attention paid to features in the family life which were not yet within the reach of ancient drama. And the reason of this is that, inasmuch as in the spheres of life

424

above-mentioned the principle of the personal life in its independence has asserted its claim, novel phases of existence make their inevitable appearance in each one of them, which the modern man claims to set up as the end and directory of his action.

And, from a further point of view in this drama, it is the right of subjectivity, as above defined, absolutely unqualified, which is retained as the dominating content; and for this reason personal love, honour, and the rest make such an exclusive appeal as ends of human action that, while in one direction other relations cannot fail to appear as the purely external background on which these interests of our modern life are set in motion, in another such relations on their own account actively conflict with the requirements of the more individual state of emotion. Of more profound significance still is wrong and crime, even assuming that a particular character does not deliberately and to start with place himself in either, yet does not avoid in order to attain his original purpose.

And, furthermore, in contrast to this particularization and individual standpoint, the ends proposed may likewise either in one direction expand to cover the universality and all-inclusive embrace of the content, or they are in another apprehended and carried into execution as themselves intrinsically substantive. In the first respect, I will merely recall to memory that typically philosophical tragedy, the "Faust" of Goethe, in which, on the one hand, a spirit of disillusion in the pursuit of science, and, on the other, the vital resources of a worldly life and earthly enjoyment—in a word, the attempted mediation in the tragic manner of an individual's wisdom and strife with the Absolute in its essential significance and phenomenal manifestation, offers a breadth of content such as no other dramatic poet has hitherto ventured to include in one and the same composition. The "Carl Moor" of Schiller is something of the same fashion. He rebels against the entire order of civic society and the collective condition of the world and the humanity of his time, and fortifies himself as such against the same. Wallenstein in the same way conceives a great and far-reaching purpose, the unity and peace of Germany, an object he fails to carry into effect by the means which, in virtue of the fact that they are wielded together in an artificial manner, and one that lacks essential coherence, break in pieces and come to nought precisely in the direction where he is most anxious of their success; and he fails in the same way by reason of his opposition to the imperial authority, upon which he himself and his enterprise are inevitably shattered. Such objects of a world-wide policy, such as a Carl Moor or a Wallenstein pursue, are as a rule not accomplished at the hands of a single individual by the simple means that other men are induced to obey and co-operate; they are carried into effect by the commanding personality, partly acting in conjunction with the wills of many others, and in part in opposition to, or at least on lines of which they have no knowledge. As an illustration of a conception of objects viewed in their essential significance, I will merely instance certain tragedies of Calderon, in which love, honour, and similar virtues are respectively to the rights and obligations in which they involve the characters of the action, treated as so many unyielding laws of independent force with all the stringency of a code. We find also frequently much the same thing assumed in Schiller's tragic characters, though the point of view is no doubt wholly different, at least to the extent that such individuals conceive and combat for their ends with the assumption they are universal and absolutely valid human rights. So in the early play of "Kabale und Liebe" Major Ferdinand seeks to defend the rights of Nature against the conveniences of fashionable society, and, above all, claims of the Marquis Posa freedom of thought as an inalienable possession of humanity.

Generally speaking, however, in modern tragedy it is not the substantive content of its object in the interest of which men act, and which is maintained as the stimulus of their passion; rather it is the inner experience of their heart and individual emotion, or the particular qualities of their personality, which insist on satisfaction. For even in the examples already referred to we find that to a real extent in those heroes of Spanish honour and love the content of their ultimate ends is so essentially of a personal character that the rights and obligations deducible from the same are able to fuse in direct concurrence with the individual desires of the heart, and to a large extent, too, in the youthful works of Schiller this continual insistence upon Nature, rights of man, and a converted world somewhat savours of the excess of a wholly personal enthusiasm. And if it came about that Schiller in later years endeavoured to enforce a more mature type of pathos, this was simply due to the fact that it was his main idea to restore once again in modern dramatic art the principle of ancient tragedy.

In order to emphasize still more distinctly the difference which in this respect obtains between ancient and modern tragedy, I will merely refer the reader to Shakespeare's "Hamlet." Here we find fundamentally a collision similar to that which is introduced by Æschylus into his "Choeporae" and that by Sophocles into his "Electra." For Hamlet's father, too, and the King, as in these Greek plays, has been murdered, and his mother has wedded the murderer. That which, however, in the conception of the Greek dramatists possesses a certain ethical justification—I mean the death of Agamemnon—relatively to his sacrifice of Iphigeneia in the contrasted case of Shakespeare's play, can only be viewed as an atrocious crime, of which Hamlet's mother is innocent;

427

so that the son is merely concerned in his vengeance to direct his attention to the fratricidal king, and there is nothing in the latter's character that possesses any real claim to his respect. The real collision, therefore, does not turn on the fact that the son, in giving effect to a rightful sense of vengeance, is himself forced to violate morality, but rather on the particular personality, the inner life of Hamlet, whose noble soul is not steeled to this kind of energetic activity, but, while full of contempt for the world and life, what between making up his mind and attempting to carry into effect or preparing to carry into effect its resolves, is bandied from pillar to post, and finally through his own procrastination and the external course of events meets his own doom.

If we now turn, in close connection with the above conclusions, to our *second* point of fundamental importance in modern tragedy—that is to say, the nature of the characters and their collisions—we may summarily take a point of departure from the following general observations.

The heroes of ancient classic tragedy discover circumstances under which they, so long as they irrefragably adhere to the *one* ethical state of pathos which alone corresponds to their own already formed personality, must infallibly come into conflict with an ethical Power which opposes them and possesses an equal ethical claim to recognition. Romantic characters, on the contrary, are from the first placed within a wide expanse of contingent relations and conditions, within which every sort of action is possible; so that the conflict, to which no doubt the external conditions presupposed supply the occasion, essentially abides within the *character* itself, to which the individuals concerned in their passion give effect, not, however, in the interests of the ethical vindication of the truly substantive claims, but for the simple reason that they are the kind of men they are.

Greek heroes also no doubt act in accordance with their particular individuality; but this individuality, as before noted, if we take for our examples the supreme results of ancient tragedy, is itself necessarily identical with an ethical pathos which is substantive. In modern tragedy the peculiar character in its real significance, and to which it as a matter of accident remains constant, whether it happens to grasp after that which on its own account is on moral grounds justifiable, or is carried into wrong and crime, forms its resolves under the dictate of personal wishes and necessities, or among other things purely external considerations. In such a case, therefore, though we may have a coalescence between the moral aspect of the object and the character, yet, for all that, such a concurrence does not constitute, and cannot constitute—owing to the divided character of ends, passions, and the life wholly personal to the individual, the *essential* basis and objective condition of the depth and beauty of the tragic drama.

In view of the great variety of difference which further separates particular characters in this type of poetry, it is impossible to do much in the way of generalization. I will, therefore, restrict myself to a reference to the following fundamental points of view. A primary opposition which at once invites notice is that of an *abstract*, and consequently formal, characterization in its contrast with the actual individuals whom we are accustomed to meet in the concrete living world. As example of this type, we may with exceptional pertinency cite the tragic characters of the French and Italians, which, originating in the imitation of ancient drama, to a greater or less degree merely amount to pure personifications of specific passions, such as love, honour, fame, ambition, tyranny, and so forth, and which, while they present the motives of their actions, as also the gradation and quality of their emotions to the best advantage with a lavish display of declamation, and all the arts of rhetoric, none the less by doing so rather resemble the dramatic failures of Seneca than the dramatic masterpieces of the Greeks. Spanish tragedy also receives the stamp of this abstract style of character-drawing. In this case, however, the pathos of love, in its conflict with honour, friendship, royal prerogative, and the rest is itself of so abstract a subjective character that in the case where the intention is to make this equally ideal[55] substantiality stand out as the genuine object of interest, a more complete particularization of characters is hardly feasible. The characters of Spanish drama, however, often possess a certain kind of solidity, and, if I may use the expression, inflexible personality, however wanting in content it may be, a feature that is absent from French work; and at the same time Spanish writers, here also in contrast to the cold simplicity which the movement of French tragedies exhibits even in their tragic composition, know how to make up with the cleverly invented abundance of interesting situations and developments the deficiency referred to in the matter of characterization.

In contrast to both these schools, and in their mastery of the exposition of fully developed human characters and personality, the English are exceptionally distinguished; and among them, and soaring above the rest at an almost unapproachable height, stands Shakespeare. For even in the cases where a purely formal passion, as for instance ambition in Macbeth, or jealousy in Othello, claims as its field the entire pathos[56] of his tragic hero, such an abstraction impairs by no fraction the full breadth of the personality. Despite of this restriction of analysis[57] the characters remain throughout entire men. In fact, the more Shakespeare on the infinite embrace of his world-stage, proceeds to develop the extreme limits of evil and folly, to that extent, as I have already observed, on these very boundaries—of course, not without real wealth of poetic embellishment—he concentrates these characters in their limitations. While doing so, however, he confers on them intelligence and imagination; and, by means of the image in which they, by virtue of that intelligence, contemplate themselves objectively as a work of art, he makes them free artists of themselves, and is fully able, through the complete virility and truth of his characterization, to awaken our interest in criminals, no less than in the most vulgar and weak-witted lubbers and fools. Of a similar nature is the style of expression he makes his tragic characters adopt. It is at once individual, realistic, emphatically vital, extraordinarily various, and, moreover, where it seems advisable, it can rise to sublimity and is marked by an overwhelming force of utterance. Its ideal intensity and its qualities of invention are displayed in images and simile that flash from each other with lightning rapidity. Its very rhetoric, here the barren child of no school, but the growth of genuine emotion and penetration into human personality, is such that, if we take into account this extraordinary union of the directness of life itself and ideal greatness of soul, we shall find it hard indeed to point to a single other dramatic poet among the moderns whom we are entitled to rank in his company. No doubt Goethe in his youth made a real effort to achieve some approach to a like natural truth and detailed characterization; but in the ideal force and exaltation of passion his rivalry collapses. The style of Schiller, again, has shown an increasing tendency to violent methods, the tempestuous expatiation of which lack the true core of reality for their basis.

Modern characters also differ in the nature of their *constancy* or their spiritual *vacillation* and distraction. We find, no doubt, the weakness of indecision, the fluctuations of reflection, the weighing of reasons, conformably to which a resolve should be directed, here and there in classic drama, and more particularly in the tragedies of Euripides. But Euripides is a writer whose tendency is already to forsake the wholly plastic completeness of characterization and action and to develop exceptional aspects of personal sensibility. In modern tragedy we meet yet more frequently such vacillating characters, more particularly on the ground that they are essentially under the sway of two opposed passions, which make them fluctuate from one resolve or one kind of deed to another. I have already made some observations on this attitude of vacillation in another context, and will now merely supplement this by stating that, although the tragic action must depend on colliding factors, yet where we find such a division in *one* and the same individual such a concurrence is always attended with precarious consequences. And the reason is that this disruption into interests, which are opposed to each other,

432

is due in part to an obscurity and obtuseness of the intelligence, and in some measure, too, to weakness and immaturity. We come across characters of this type in the creations of Goethe's younger days, notably Weisungen, Fernando in "Stella," and above all Clavigo. They are, as we may say, double men, who are unable to secure a ready, and so stable, individuality. It is wholly another matter when two opposed spheres of life or moral obligation are equally sacred to a character which, on its own account, is not deficient in stability, and such a person is under the necessity of ranking himself on *one* side to the exclusion of the other. In a case of that kind, the vacillation is merely a moment of passage, and does not itself constitute, as it were, the nervous system of the character. Again, of a somewhat similar kind, is the tragic case where the spiritual life is seduced, despite its nobler purpose, into objects of passion which are contradictory[58] to the same, as in the case of Schiller's "Holy Maid," and are then forced to seek a recovery from this division of the soul in their own intimate or objective life, or pay the penalty. At the same time, this personal tragedy of the distraction of soul-life, when it is made the pivot on which the tragic action revolves,[59] contains, as a rule, what is merely pitiful and painful, or, from another standpoint, exasperating;[60] and the poet will rather do better to avoid it than go out of his way to find it and develop it. The worst case is that, however, where such a vacillation and veering round of character and the entire personality is—the very dialectic of art being thrown awry for this purpose—made the principle of the entire presentation, as though the truth of all importance was to demonstrate that no character is in itself firmly rooted and self-assured. The one-sided ends of specific passions, it is true, ought not to bring about a realization which is secured without a battle; and also, in everyday life, they

433

cannot fail to experience, through the reactionary power of conditions and individuals which oppose them, their finite character and lack of stability. An issue of this kind, however, before the appearance of which we are unable to get the pertinent conclusion, ought not to be introduced as a dialectical piece of wheel adjustment[61] in the personality itself; if it is, the person concerned, viewed as *this* personal state of the soul, is a wholly empty and undefined form, whose collective living growth is found, no less in respect to its objects than in its character, to be wholly wanting in definition. In much the same way the case, also, is otherwise, where the change in the spiritual condition of the entire man itself appears as a direct consequent of just this, its own kind of self-detachment, so that only that is developed and emphasized which essentially and from the first lay secured in the character. As an example, we find in Shakespeare's Lear that the original folly of the old man is intensified to the point of madness much in the same way that Gloster's spiritual blindness is converted into actual physical blindness, in which for the first time his eyes are opened to the true distinction in the love he entertains for his two sons respectively. It is precisely Shakespeare who, as a contrast to that exposition of vacillating and essentially self-divided characters, supplies us with the finest examples of essentially stable and consequential characters, who go to their doom precisely in virtue of this tenacious hold upon themselves and their ends. Unsupported by the sanction of the moral law, but rather carried onward by the formal necessity of their personality, they suffer themselves to be involved in their acts by the coil of external circumstances, or they plunge blindly therein and maintain themselves there by sheer force of will, even where all that they do is merely done because they are impelled to assert themselves against others, or because they have simply come to the particular point they have reached. The rise of insurgent passion, one essentially consonant with a certain type of character, one which has not as yet fully emerged, but now secures its utmost expansion, this onward movement and process of a great soul, with all the intimate traits of its evolution, this picture of its selfdestructive conflict with circumstances, human and objective conditions and results, is the main content of some of Shakespeare's most interesting tragedies.

The last of the subjects which we have still to discuss as proposed is the nature of the *tragic issue* which characters in our present drama have to confront, as also the type of tragic *reconciliation* compatible with such a standpoint. In ancient tragedy it is the eternal justice which, as the absolute might of destiny, delivers and restores the harmony of substantive being in its ethical character by its opposition to the particular forces which, in their strain to assert an independent subsistence, come into collision, and which, in virtue of the rational ideality implied in its operations, satisfies us even where we see the downfall of particular men. In so far as a justice of the same kind is present in modern tragedy, it is necessarily, in part, more abstract on account of the closer differentiation of ends and characters, and, in part, of a colder nature and one that is more akin to that of a criminal court, in virtue of the fact that the wrong and crime into which individuals are necessarily carried, in so far as they are intent upon executing their designs, are of a profounder significance. Macbeth, for instance, the elder daughters of Lear and their husbands, the president in "Kabale und Liebe," Richard III, and many similar examples, on account of their atrocious conduct, only deserve the fate they get. This type of *dénouement* usually is presented under the guise that individuals are crushed by an actual force which they have defied in order to carry out their personal aims. Wallenstein, for example, is shattered on the adamantine wall of the imperial power; but the old Piccolomini, who, in order to maintain the lawful régime, betrays a friend and misuses the rights of friendship, is punished through the death and sacrifice of his son. Götz von Berlichingen, too, attacks a dominant and securely founded political order, and goes to ground, as also Weislingen and Adelheid, who range themselves, no doubt, on the side of this organized power, but, through wrongful deed and disloyalty, prepare the way to disaster. And along with this we have the demand emphasized, in virtue of the personal point of view of such characters, that these should of necessity appear themselves to acknowledge the justice of their fate. Such a state of acceptance may either be of a religious nature, in which case the soul becomes conscious of a more exalted and indestructible condition of blessedness with which to confront the collapse of its mundane personality; or it may be of a more formal, albeit more worldly, type, in so far, that is, as the strength and equanimity of the character persists in its course up to the point of overthrow without breaking asunder; and in this way, despite all circumstances and mischances, preserves with unimpaired energy its personal freedom. Or, as a final alternative, where the substance of such acceptance is of more real value, by the recognition that the lot which the individual receives is the one, however bitter it may be, which his action merits.

From another point of view, however, we may see the tragic issue also merely in the light of the effect of unhappy circumstances and external accidents, which might have brought about, quite as readily, a different result and a happy conclusion. From such a point of view we have merely left us the conception that the modern idea of individuality, with its searching definition of character, circumstances, and developments, is handed over essentially to the contingency of the earthly state, and must carry the fateful issues of such finitude. Pure commiseration of this sort is, however, destitute of meaning; and it is nothing less than a frightful kind of external necessity in the particular case where we see the downfall of essentially noble natures in their conflict thus assumed with the mischance of purely external accidents. Such a course of events can insistently arrest our attention; but in the result it can only be horrible, and the demand is direct and irresistible that the external accidents ought to accord with that which is identical with the spiritual nature of such noble characters. Only as thus regarded can we feel ourselves reconciled with the grievous end of Hamlet and Juliet. From a purely external point of view, the death of Hamlet appears as an accident occasioned by his duel with Laertes and the interchange of the daggers. But in the background of Hamlet's soul, death is already present from the first. The sandbank of finite condition will not content his spirit. As the focus of such mourning and weakness, such melancholy, such a loathing of all the conditions of life, we feel from the first that, hemmed within such an environment of horror, he is a lost man, whom the surfeit of the soul has wellnigh already done to death before death itself approaches him from without. The same thing may be observed in the case of Romeo and Juliet. The ground on which these tender blossoms have been planted is alien to their nature; we have no alternative left us but to lament the pathetic transiency of such a beautiful love, which, as some tender rose in the vale of this world of accident, is broken by rude storms and tempests, and the frangible reckonings of noble and well-meaning devices. This pitiful state of our emotions is, however, simply a feeling of reconciliation that is painful, a kind of *unhappy blessedness* in misfortune.

(ββ) Much as poets present to us the bare downfall of

particular people they are also able to treat the similar contingency of the development of events in such a way, that, despite of the fact the circumstances in all other respects would appear to give them little enough support, a happy issue of such conditions and characters is secured, in which they elicit our interest. No doubt the favour of such a destiny of events has at least an equal claim upon us as the disfavour. And so far as the question merely concerns the nature of this difference, I must admit that I prefer a happy conclusion. How could it be otherwise? I can myself discover no better ground for the preference of misfortune, simply on its own account as such, to a happy resolution than that of a certain condition of fine sensibility, which is devoted to pain and suffering, and experiences more interest in their presence than in painless situations such as it meets with every day. If therefore the interests are of such a nature, that it is really not worth the trouble to sacrifice the men or women concerned on their altar, it being possible for them either to surrender their objects, without making such surrender as is equivalent to a surrender of their individuality, or to mutually come to an agreement in respect thereof, there is no reason why the conclusion should be tragic. The tragic aspect of the conflicts and their resolution ought in principle merely to be enforced in the cases where it is actually necessary in order to satisfy the claim of a superior point of view. If this necessity is absent there is no sufficient ground for mere suffering and unhappiness. And it is simply due to this fact that social *plays* and *dramas* originate which form, as it were, an intermediate link between tragedies and comedies. I have already in a previous passage explained the poetical standpoint of this class of composition. Among us Germans we find it to some extent appropriating what readily moves us in the world of the citizen and family life; in another direction it is preoccupied with chivalry, a movement to which the Götz of Goethe has given a decided stimulus; mainly, however, we may call it the triumph of *ordinary morality*, which in the large majority of cases is the main thing celebrated. The subject-matter of such plays most in vogue are questions of finance or property, differences of status, unfortunate love affairs, examples of spiritual baseness in the more restricted conditions and affairs of life and so on. In one word, what we have here is that which otherwise is already before our eyes, only with this difference, that in such moral dramas, virtue and duty obtain the victory, and crime is shamed and punished, or betakes itself to repentance, so that in a moral conclusion of this kind the reconciliation ought to centre in this, namely, that whatever happens good is the result. Thereby the fundamental interest is concentrated in the personal or spiritual quality of views held and a good or evil heart. The more, however, the abstractly moral state of mind or heart supplies the pivot on which all turns, so much the less can it be the pathos of a particular matter, or an intrinsically essential object, to which the personality in question is attached. And add to this, from a further point of view, so much the less ultimately is the definite character able to maintain itself and persist in such self-assertion. If all is to be finally focussed in the purely moral aspects of the psychological state, or the condition of the heart, from a subjective point of view such as this, with its dominating emphasis on ethical reflection, no standing ground remains for any other definite characteristics, or at least specific ends to be proposed. Let the heart break and change its views. Such seems to be the idea. Pathetic dramas of this type, notably Kotzebue's "Menschenhass und Reue," and also too many moral offences in the dramas of Iffland, strictly speaking, have therefore an issue which we can neither call good or bad. I mean by this that the main thing is as a rule the question of pardon and the promise of moral improvement, and we are therefore confronted with that possibility of spiritual conversion and surrender of the self. No doubt in this fact we discover the exalted nature and greatness of Spirit. When, however, the jolly dog,[62] as the heroes of Kotzebue are for the most part, and not unfrequently Iffland's too, after being a scamp and a rascal, suddenly promises to turn over a new leaf, it is frankly impossible with a good-for-nothing chap of this sort that his conversion can be otherwise than mere pretence, or of so superficial a character that it merely affects his skin, and merely supplies a momentary conclusion to the course of events that has no substantial basis, but rather, by all ordinary reckoning, will take the knave to disreputable quarters, if we will only acquaint ourselves with his subsequent history.

(γγ) As regards our *modern comedy* I must draw particular attention to one point of difference, to which I have already alluded when discussing the old Attic comedy. The point is this—whether the folly and restricted outlook of the characters of the drama merely appears ridiculous to others, or is equally perceived as such by those persons themselves; whether in short the comic characters are an object of laughter only to the audience, or also to such characters. Aristophanes, that creator of genuine comedy, exclusively accepted as the main principle of his plays the latter alternative. Already, however, in Greek comedy of a later date, and subsequently in the hands of Plautus and Terence, the opposite principle came into vogue; and in our modern examples of comedy it has been carried to such a length that we find a large number of comic compositions the inclination of which is more or less the subject-matter which is ridiculous in a purely prosaic sense, or rather we might say matters that leave a sour taste in the mouth of and are repugnant to the comic characters. This is the

440

standpoint of Molière in particular in his best comedies, which have no right to be regarded as farces. The prosaic quality here is justified on the ground that the objects aimed at by such characters are a matter of bitter earnest. They are deadly serious in the pursuit of it; they are therefore quite unable to join with satisfaction in the laughter, when they are finally deceived, or themselves are responsible for its failure. They are in short merely the disillusioned objects of a laughter foreign to themselves and generally damaging to themselves. As an example: Molière's Tartuffe *le faux dévot*, viewed as the unmasking of a really damned rascal has nothing funny in it, but is a very earnest business, and the deception of the deluded Orgon amounts to a sheer intensity of misfortune, which can only be resolved by the *Deus ex machina*, in reference to whom the official of the court of justice utters the following exhortation:

Remettez-vous, monsieur, d'une alarme si chaude.
Nous vivons sous un prince, ennemi de la fraude,
Un prince dont les yeux se font jour dans les coeurs,
Et que ne peut tromper tout l'art des imposteurs.

We may add, too, that the odious abstract[63] excess of characters so stable as, for example, Molière's "Miser," the absolutely stolid and serious subjection of whom to his idiotic passion renders any emancipation from such fetters impossible, contains in it nothing that is genuinely comic.

It is pre-eminently in this field that for compensation of such defects a fine artistic power in the accurate and exhaustive delineation of character is manifested, or a true mastery of the craft discovers its best opportunity for an admirably thought-out intrigue. As a rule the occasion for such an intrigue is supplied by the circumstance that some character or other endeavours to secure his objects by deluding some one else, such a course appearing to

441

harmonize with these interests and advance them. As a matter of fact, however, it only results in the contradictory situation that it is through this pernicious demand they are self-destructive. In opposition to such a plot we find as a rule a similar plot of dissembled appearances put in motion, which has for its object the like confusion of the original plotter. Such a general scheme admits of an infinite number and degree of ups and downs in the interweaving of its situations which are adapted to every conceivable subtlety. The Spaniards are, in particular, the most consummate masters in the invention of such intrigues and developments, and have composed much that is delightful and excellent in this class of work. The subject-matter generally consists of the attractive incidents of love or affairs of honour and the like. In tragedy these bring about the profoundest collisions; in comedy, however, where such qualities as pride and love that has been long experienced do not assert themselves as such, but rather by doing the reverse and in the result give the lie to themselves, such interests can merely appear to us as entirely superficial and comic.[64] A word in conclusion as to the characters who hatch and carry out such intrigues. Such are usually, following the example of the slaves in the Roman comedy, servants or menials, who have no respect for the objects of their superiors, but rather make them subordinate to their own advantage or bring them to nought, and merely present us with the amusing position, that the real masters are the servants and the masters the slaves, or at least give rise to all kinds of comic situation, which come about accidentally, or are directly the result of intention. We of course, as audience, are in the know of such mysteries, and can fortify ourselves against every sort of cunning and deceit, which often carries the most serious consequences to fathers, uncles, aunts, and the rest, all of the most respectable antecedents; and we may laugh as we please over

442

the contradictory situations that appear before us, or are involved in such ingenious deceptions.

In this kind of way our modern comedy, generally speaking, gives play on the stage to private interests and personalities of the social life I have mentioned in their accidental vagaries, laughable features, abnormal habits and follies, partly by means of character delineation, and partly with the help of comic developments of situations and circumstances. A joviality so frank and genial as that which persists in the Aristophanic comedy as the mediating element of its resolution, does not animate this kind of comedy; or rather cases occur where it can be actually repulsive, that is to say, where that which is essentially evil, the tricks of menials, the treachery of sons and wards towards worthy men, fathers and guardians is triumphant, always assuming that the persons deluded have in no way themselves been influenced by false prejudices or eccentricities of such a kind that there is some reason why they should be made to appear ridiculous in their helpless stupidity and handed over as the sport of the aims of others.

In a converse way, however, and in contrast as such to the above generally prosaic type of treatment, the modern world, too, has elaborated a world of comedy which is both truly comic and poetical in its nature. The fundamental note here again is the cheeriness of disposition, the inexhaustible resources of fun, no matter what may be the nature of miscarriage or bad luck, the exuberance and dash of what is at bottom nothing better than pure tomfoolery, and, in a word, exploited self-assurance. We have here as a result, in yet profounder expatiation, and yet more intense display of humour, whether the sphere of it be more restricted or capacious, and whether the mode of it be more or less important, what runs on parallel lines with that which Aristophanes in the ancient world and in his own field

443

created beyond all rivalry. As the master, who in a similar way outshines all others in his field, or rather the particular portion to which I now refer, I will, though without now further entering into detail, once again emphasize the name of William Shakespeare.

*

Having completed our review of the types under which comedy is elaborated we have at last reached the absolute conclusion of our scientific inquiry. We started with symbolical art, in which the ideality of the human soul struggles to discover itself as content and configuration, and, in a word, to become an object to itself. We passed on to the plastic of classical art, which displays to human vision that which has become unveiled to itself as substantive being in man's vital personality. We reached our conclusion in the romantic art of the individual soul-life, that inward world united to the absolute medium of its self-conscious energy, which expatiates unfettered within its own ideal life of Spirit; and which, content with that realm, no longer unites itself with what is objective and particularized, and finally makes itself aware of the negative significance of such a resolution in the humour of the comic Spirit. Nevertheless we find that in this very consummation it is Comedy which opens the way to a dissolution of all that human art implies. For the aim of all art is nothing else than that identity asserted and displayed by the human Spirit, in which the eternal, the Divine, the essential and explicated truth is unfolded in the forms and phenomenal presence of the objective world to the apprehension of our external senses and our emotional life and imagination. If, however, as is the fact, comedy merely enforces this unity under a mode that annihilates it, inasmuch as the absolute substance,[65] which strives here to enforce its realized manifestation, perceives that this realization is,—through

444

the instrumentality of those interests which have now secured an independent freedom within the embrace of the objective world of Nature,[66] and are as such exclusively directed to what is contingent and personal to the soul, — itself shattered, it follows that the presence and activity of the Absolute is no longer truly asserted in positive coalescence with the individual characters and ends of existing objective reality, but rather solely gives effect to itself in the negative form that everything which does not correspond with itself is thereby cancelled, and all that remains is the presence of this free personal activity of soul-life which is displayed in and along with this dissolution as aware of itself and self-assured.

By such a path, then, as this we have arrived at our goal; and with the aid of our philosophical method have gathered every essential type and determinant of the beauty and conformation of art into a garland, the task of arranging which in its associate completeness belongs to the most worthy of any within the range of human science to undertake. For in human Art we are not merely dealing with playthings, however pleasant or useful they may be, but with the liberation of the human Spirit from the substance and forms of finite condition. We are occupied with the presence and reconciliation of the Absolute in sense and the phenomenal, with a revelation of truth, which is not exhausted of its wealth in natural-history, but is unfolded in the history of the world, as a constituent part of which Art supplies us with the most beautiful point of view, the most generous reward for the severe labours of our contact with objective reality and the grievous pains of knowledge. And for this reason it was impossible that our inquiry should wholly restrict itself to the criticism of individual works of art, or any mere recipe or inducement to their production. Rather it could have but the one object, namely, that of following up, of seizing and retaining in and through the instrumentality of thought the fundamental notion of beauty and art through all the stages which it passes in its process of realization.

If I may be permitted to assume that from the above explained point of view my exposition has not been wholly inadequate to general expectation, and that the bonds of obligation with which I have throughout been united to my reader in the pursuit of an object which we hold in common are now released, I will merely add the wish, it is my last word, that a bond yet more exalted and indestructible with the idea of beauty and truth may rivet itself between us in place of that released, and establish an union which shall now and for good remain secure.

[1] *Diess treibende Pathos.* Pathos is here used to signify the emotional state. This "motive force" would give the sense.

[2] *Als konkretes Daseyn zur Existence gebracht.*

[3] *In der äusseren Objektivität.*

[4] The reference is of course to lyric composition. By *reale Individualisirung* Hegel seems to refer to the apprehension by the lyric poet of the individual subjective experience in its independent reality.

[5] What Hegel means apparently by this statement is that the results of the action are in the view of the persons concerned primarily referred to their own act of volition and sense of responsibility, and as such they modify their future intention or conduct.

[6] Poet. c. 5.

[7] *Einem colliderenden Handeln.*

[8] As lyric poetry is.

[9] Poet., c. 7.

[10] The fact should be noted, however, that in the illustration each division is a complete whole in itself.

[11] Hegel apparently means this by his reference to *die beiden ersten Elemente*, but the passage is not very clear.

[12] *Gehalt*. That is, an imaginative personality, which seizes the type and our general humanity.

[13] In this obscure passage I have rather sought to emphasize what appears to me the general sense than adhere to literal accuracy. What is contrasted is clearly the naturalism of such a diction as Schiller's "Robbers" and the French classic diction.

[14] *Der Allgemeinheit*. We should say of "a more ideal or creative atmosphere." The creative poet imports his own universality into the final result both of diction and imaginative conception. Hegel adheres to the philosophical term, which, apart from explanation, is certainly very bald, and even, as it stands, unintelligible.

[15] It is not very clear to what Hegel here refers unless to the fact that female parts were played by youths.

[16] We should say rather "stunned as by a blow," *zerschmettert*, rather than *zerschnitten*.

[17] *Eines grossen Gemüths*. It is not clear how far the reference is to the poet or the characters. It applies to both.

[18] Poet., c. 4.

[19] Vol. i, pp. 355-379.

[20] Poet., c. 6.

[21] Apart from the practical impossibility of enforcing such a condition in modern times, Hegel appears here rather to overlook the fact that the printing of a work is of great convenience, and may even involve less expense where its repetition in several theatres is possible, and, after all, important drama is literature. Where the art is bad it is no more possible to prevent its appearance, if the artist is able to afford the expense of publication, than in any other art. In the one case as in the other public taste and the law of supply and demand are here the sole and ultimate tests. Sophocles may have written his dramas, no doubt, with a particular stage in view, but we are not therefore entitled to conclude that either he or Aristophanes would have refused assent to the publication of any or all of their works had there been a publisher willing to accept responsibility. Most certainly we

may suppose that Shakespeare would not have done so, at least after due representation and revision. I have, however, met with students of Shakespeare who maintain that no complete autograph manuscript of any single drama of this poet ever existed.

[22] I think it is obvious that if we take the case of the finest musical reproduction by individual artists of the first rank this distinction is not so emphatic as Hegel would make it out to be. A really great musical performance is something much more than a reproduction of musical sound. The effect of personality plays here a part of real and essential importance.

[23] *Rollenfächer.* Hegel may possibly mean "the professional adjustment of harmonious castes."

[24] See vol. iii, pp. 427-430.

[25] *Unmittelbaren Individualität.* Hegel means the individuality that is abstract, not soldered into the substance of concrete human life.

[26] *Das Göttliche.*

[27] *In Gegentheil seiner.* Hegel means, apparently, that the principle asserts itself positively rather than as the mere negation of the finite, as in exclusive asceticism.

[28] *Das Sittliche, i.e.,* concrete ethical condition.

[29] Hegel appears to understand by pathos here little more than a psychological state.

[30] *Element, i.e.,* apparently, "this primitive impulse of realization."

[31] Hegel's language, *wenn sie itzt aber wirklich,* seems to go as far as my translation. The difficulty of the entire passage, and it is no doubt considerable, is primarily due to the fact that Hegel is here importing into the notion of classic divinities the profounder significance of what he calls *sittlichen Mächte.* By doing this he can more readily shelve the problem how we are to regard the nature of their existence as potential forces of the Divine Being; that is, apart from their operative energy in human life, as also the *modus operandi* of such Divine energy in its original participation with a real world. He avoids, no doubt, one of the most disputed aspects of his philosophy. But if it is urged in criticism that at least in part his

448

present exposition tends rather to vagueness, or at least to accept a certain measure of symbolism rather than remain severely on the ground of genuine philosophical method and thought, to associate itself rather with Plato than Aristotle, in the present context, at any rate, I am inclined to agree with it.

[32] *Der Gewalt des Anundfürsichseyenden.* Lit., of that which is or becomes explicit on its own account, i.e., essentially. Hegel refers, of course, to the ethical forces in the process of life.

[33] Hegel here uses the word *einig* rather in its secondary sense than in its primary one of *unique.*

[34] *Als das zu Erhaltende,* viz., the consistency of concrete life.

[35] By *ihrer unendlichen Sicherheit* Hegel refers to the stability of the principle of self-conscious, and self-assured character, which in its weakness may be merely equivalent to cocksuredness.

[36] *Wohlgemuthkeit und Zuversicht.*

[37] Hegel seems to have in his mind characters in comedy of which Falstaff may be taken as a supreme example, and Shakespeare above all the creator of many such. Roy Richmond and Sancho Panza are of the same type.

[38] *Der in der Menschenbrust waltenden Götter.*

[39] In no religious or even strictly ethical sense of course.

[40] I am not quite sure what Hegel means by his use here of the word *Versühnung,* lit., reconciliation. I presume he means a power of harmonious recovery, whether in a good sense is not quite clear.

[41] Formal as contrasted with really ethical content.

[42] *Die Substanz.* I presume this is the meaning, *i.e.,* the substantive ideality of the ethical forces inherent in man. The entire passage is sufficiently difficult to translate, or indeed wholly to follow, or at least apart from its subsequent application to the chorus of Tragedy.

[43] *Allgemeine.* Formal in the sense that such a state is not concretely realized in action, but restricts itself to the ideal homogeneity of its form.

[44] It is perhaps best to repeat Hegel's own phrase.

[45] *Die sittliche Berechtigung zu einer bestimmten That.* The context shows that Hegel does not merely mean the justification in the individual conscience, which is demanded by and perfected in such activity, but the actual ethical claim

which is vindicated in such action.

[46] That is, the content of the dramatic action in Greek drama.

[47] By *Rechtfertigung* Hegel here seems to mean not so much the vindicated right as the degree of responsibility which a certain attitude of mind involves. It is the nature of the subjection to the vindicated right, or its absence.

[48] By *die subjektive Vertiefung der Persönlichkeit* Hegel would seem to mean the psychological analysis of character on its own account.

[49] *Blosser Ausgleichung.* The metaphor seems to be that of a final settlement of accounts, a general settlement would be perhaps a better translation.

[50] Hegel's statement is hardly supported by the facts as they are narrated in the "Œdipus Rex." It is the force of facts rather than a power of prevision, which arouse the knowledge of the terrible truth. But Hegel is here evidently most absorbed in the ideal and universal significance of the drama.

[51] That is, of course, in death. Sophocles himself of course only very indefinitely, through the evidence of an eye-witness, refers to such a possible apotheosis.

[52] The statement of the general contrast is no doubt true enough. It may be doubted, however, whether Hegel's own interpretation of the reconciliation of Œdipus as one consummated in death can be wholly brought under the ancient conception. It would seem truer to admit that in the spirit at least of the "Œdipus Coloneus" we have, at least in so far as that reconciliation is objective, and not merely a reconciling influence on our minds, the spectators, as in the case of the deaths of King Lear or Cornelia, in the sense that "death makes all things sweet," a mysterious approach to problems which Christianity first attempted seriously to solve, and which are usually regarded as insoluble without the assumption of a future state, or at least a divine absorption. Even admitting that Œdipus in his death became a real constituent of the harmonious unity of the civic life that received him, we cannot with truth say that such a reconciliation was one in which he shared personally, and whereof he was conscious, except in so far as he was aware of this by prevision; and to that extent the reconciliation was not

451

in his death, but rather, as in the Christian view, a condition of the soul, a conviction that by his death he would live again,— almost identical in fact with some modern interpretations of immortality.

[53] Hegel means the conflict between the universal social interest and the private interest, between the concrete social life and the wholly private life.

[54] I think this gives the nearest approach I can make to the self-coined word *Grundwohlseyns*, lit., "the at bottom well being."

[55] *Subjektiven Substantialität*. Ideal, that is, as opposed to a substantive content based on the facts of living people. Impersonations of qualities imagined rather than portraits of living men, ideal therefore in a theoretic and bad sense.

[56] As previously stated I adopt Hegel's expression, being unable to express it otherwise better. The whole emotional condition is more or less the meaning, but it is rooted in Greek literature.

[57] *In dieser Bestimmtheit*, lit., in this particular definition of their content.

[58] Hegel may mean that the passions are opposed to each other. The nett result is the same.

[59] Lit., "Is made the tragic lever."

[60] The epithet might mean also "suggestive of personal irritation," but the other epithets rather negative this rendering.

[61] *Räderwerk*. The whole of this passage, in its theoretical analysis, is extremely difficult not merely to translate, but to follow clearly.

[62] I presume this is the meaning of *Pursche* or *Bursche*, and not merely "youngster."

[63] Abstract in the sense that the vices are detached in their extreme from concrete human nature.

[64] I have made the best I can of a very badly expressed sentence, and, as I should add, a very meagre description of the aim of modern comic drama. I am, however, not quite satisfied that it is an adequate translation, or that I have grasped what Hegel means by the words *nicht gestehen zu wollen*. It

would apply very aptly to such a character as Sir Willoughby Patterne, but the pertinency of such an epithet as *lang empfunden* I fail to see. I doubt myself if we have here anything more than a chance note of Hegel tacked in by editors. The whole of the present paragraph is a very jejune description of the treatment of the love passion or affairs of honour by modern drama. A pity we cannot supplement it with the substance of Meredith's "Essay on Comedy." The passage, however, must be read as qualified by the further note lower down on the exuberance of one aspect of modern comedy. But the reference to "Comedy" in the modern sense is a mere fragment.

[65] That is, self-conscious life. The Absolute here seems to be identified with man's self-conscious activity.

[66] I think this is what Hegel must mean here by *im Elemente der Wirklichkeit*, in the element, that is, of material reality.

INDEX

reference to his "Iphigeneia," i, 262, 304-306, 373; iv, 307;
to "Faust," iv, 333; to his Tasso, iv, 307;
to "Hermann and Dorothea," i, 256, 353;
to "Werther," i, 271, 321;
to the "Bride of Corinth," ii, 270;
to the "Westöstlicher Divan," i, 372; ii, 96, 400; iv, 233;
to "Dichtung und Wahrheit," iii, 289;
to the "King of Thule," ii, 363; his "Mignon," iii, 298;
his theory of colour, i, 117 n.;
on the innate reason of nature, i, 179;
Goethe on Hamlet, i, 307; ii, 364;
his pathos contrasted with that of Schiller, i, 313;
rivalry of with Shakespeare, iv, 338;
quotation from Goetz von Berlichengen, i, 366;
the ripeness of his maturity, i, 384;
on Gothic architecture, iii, 76;
Xenien of, ii, 145; on harmonious colouring, iii, 283;
supreme quality of folk-songs of, 386;
songs of comradeship, iv, 205;
prose in his dramas, iv, 71;
imitation of Icelandic, iv, 208;
as a Lyric poet generally, iv, 217.

Greek art, origin of in freedom, ii, 183;
content of, ii, 184-186;
Gods of, ii, 224-228; iii, 183-186, 188;
absence of the sublime in, ii, 237;
incapable of repetition, iii, 396;
Greek epigrams, ii, 398;
character of dramatis personae in Greek art, iv, 317-320.

Greek chorus. See under Chorus.
Greek mysteries. See under Mysteries.
Greek oracles. See under Oracles,
Hafis, Lyrics of, iv, 237; quotation from, ii, 94, 95, 147.
Helmholtz, researches of in music, iii, 390 n.
Herder, his conception of Folkslied, i, 364.

to the universal concept or notion, i, 27, 28, 197;
    his relation to art generally, i, 141;
    citation from, i, 210; his use of simile, ii. 143.
Portraiture, in painting, iii, 307-311.
Praxiteles, iii, 190.
Prometheus, ii, 209-215.
Psalms, Hebrew, general character of, i, 378;
    illustrate the sublime, ii, 102-104;
    iv, 226-228.
Pyramids, the, iii, 55.

Racine, the "Esther" of, i, 361; his Phèdre, i, 321.
Ramajana, the, episodes from, ii, 51-53, 61.
    See also iv, 110, 112, 165, 175.
Raphael, general references to, i, 37, 212, 380, 385;
    possesses "great" manner with Homer and Shakespeare, i,
405;
    his Madonna pictures, iii, 227; cartoons of, iii, 242;
    mythological subjects, iii, 245;
    his "Sistine Madonna," iii, 255, 262, 304;
    his "School of Athens," iii, 254;
    vitality of drawings of, iii, 275;
    perfection of technique, iii, 328;
    translator's criticism on extreme praise
    of Raphael and Correggio, iii, 329 n.
Reni, Guido, sentimental mannerisms of, iii, 264.
Richter, J. P., Kaleidoscopic effects of, i, 402;
    sentimentalism of, ii, 365;
    humour of compared with Sterne's, ii, 387.
Rösel, Author of "Diversions of Insect life," i, 59.
Rumohr, von, Author on Aesthetic Philosophy, i, 148, 232;
    on style, i, 399; on Italian painters and in particular,
    Duccio, Cimabue, Giotto, Masaccio, Fra Angelico,
    Perugino, Raphael and Correggio, iii, 316-330.
Ruskin, J., i, 62 n., 72 n., 230 n.

Sachs, Hans, religious familiarity of, i, 359.

Satire, in Plautus and Terence, ii, 277; iv, 305;
in Sallust and Tacitus, ii, 278;
not successful in modern times, ii, 279;
belongs to third type after tragic
and comic drama, iv, 305.

Schelling, Art Philosophy of, iii, 23 n.

Schiller, rawness of early work, iii, 38;
his "Letters on Aesthetic," i, 84-86;
quotation from, i, 214;
reference to "Braut von Messina," i, 258;
to "Kabale und Liebe," i, 261; iv, 333;
to Wallenstein," iv, 288;
to the "Maid of Orleans," i, 261; iv, 291, 339;
extreme scenic effect of the latter drama, iv, 291;
narrative too epical in same drama, iv, 161;
reference to "Wilhelm Tell," i, 379;
pathos of Schiller, i, 394;
his use of metaphor, ii, 144;
attitude to Christianity, ii, 268;
profundity of, iii, 414;
character of his songs, iv, 207, 239;
his criticism of Goethe's Iphigeneia, iv, 275;
leaves much to actor, iv, 288.

Schlegel, F. von, Aesthetic theory of, i, 87-89;
art as allegory, ii, 134; statement of,
that architecture is frozen music, iii, 65.

Sculpture, drapery of, iii, 165-171;
materials of, iii, 195-201; Egyptian, iii, 203-210;
Etruscan, iii, 211; Christian, iii, 213;
the Laocoon group, iii, 178-191; soul-suffering of, iii, 256.

Shakespeare, William, materials of his dramas, i, 255, 324;
reference to drama "Macbeth," i, 277; to Lady Macbeth, i, 324;
to witches of "Macbeth," i, 307; ii, 366;

461

educated style of Roman poetry, iii, 11.

Tasso, his "Jerusalem Liberated," iv, <u>141</u>.
   See also iv, <u>132</u>, <u>149</u>, <u>159</u>, <u>189</u>,
   and for Goethe's play under head of Goethe.
Thorwaldsen, the "Mercury" of, i, 270.
Tieck, novels of, ii, 167; and for both Tieck
   and Solger under "Irony."

Van-Dyck, the portraiture of described, iii, 292.
Velasquez, reference to Turner and Velasquez, i, 336 n.
   See also iii, 337 n.
Vergil, artifice of V. and Horace, iv, <u>69</u>;
   eclogues of compared with idylls of Theocritus, iv, <u>170</u>.
   The "Æneid" as a national Epos, iv, <u>179</u>.
Versification, rhythmical of ancients discussed, iv, <u>81</u>-<u>84</u>.
   That of rhyme compared, iv, <u>84</u>-<u>98</u>.
Vishnu, the Conserver of Life in Hindoo theosophy, iii, 52;
   second Deity in triune Trimûrtis with Brahman and Sivas,
ii, 59.
Voltaire, contrasted with Shakespeare, i, 313;
   his "Henriad," iv, <u>132</u>; his "Tancred" and "Mahomet," iv,
<u>290</u>.
Watts, George, R.A., flesh colour of, i, 337 n.;
   relation to symbolism, ii, 27 n.
Weber, his "Oberon" and "Freischütz," i, 216.
Winckelmann, on Greek sculpture,
   iii, 138, 150-155, 172-176, 182, 184;
   on Greek coins, iii, 181.
Zend-Avesta, light-doctrine of, ii, 37-44; cultus of, ii, 44.

www.ingramcontent.com/pod-product-compliance
Lightning Source LLC
Chambersburg PA
CBHW031047110726
47900CB00003B/843